CRYSTAL VISIONS

R. E. SCHICCHI

For my family.

THIS IS AN ALTERNATE HISTORY. DATES AND EVENTS MAY VARY FROM REAL WORLD EVENTS.

PART I

1

Anne Sutton sat at her workbench gazing intently at her newest creation. There were ground glass prisms intertwined with metal parts that fit nicely together. When Anne placed it in the sun, the light danced around the room; it was mesmerizing. The item might seem odd and out of place to the average eye— but working on these odd contraptions, in her private space, gave Anne a freedom she did not enjoy in the main house.

She loved to take things apart; she loved to explore and see what new things she could create — anything to keep her mind occupied. Anne felt she had to keep her mind occupied for she feared that if she did not, she would become like her mother trapped within a mental prison of her own.

Her mother; one day she just stopped talking.

Her mother; no longer seemed to need Anne nor anyone in the family. Anne had given up trying to talk to her mother years ago; even when she had been taken away to the sanitarium Anne had refused to look at her or say goodbye.

Not that it mattered to her mother; she didn't even seem to notice they were taking her away.

With her hand, dusty from working on her creation, Anne wiped away a small tear from beneath her left eye. She reached for a tool and worked it into the corner of the device. Anne refused to feel sorry for herself. She would lose herself in this, her newest piece of art. She would proudly put it on her shelf then show it to her father when he came home from the sea, in this wooden shed he had built just for her. This was her special spot— a place she could come and remove herself from everything.

No one was allowed in here, not even her brother.

But, not everyone abided by her father's rules.

"Anne Sutton!" a voice bellowed loudly from outside the door. There was no knock, just a rough push and loud slam as the door hit the inside.

Anne cringed.

She refused to turn around and acknowledge the angry voice.

"You were to come inside over an hour ago!"

"I'm working on something Miss Barton," Anne answered in a low tone. She wasn't trying to be disrespectful but that didn't matter. Anne might compliment the woman, telling her she had on the most gorgeous dress Anne had ever seen; Miss Barton would still perceive Anne as being insubordinate. "My father said—"

"I don't care what your father said you insipid little brat. You are in my care and you will do as you are told."

Anne spun around in her chair and glared at Miss Barton, her governess. The woman was in her late thirties, her long blond hair, arranged in what was supposed to be a fashionable hairstyle but sadly failing, showed more than a few gray hairs. Her dress was ordinary and plain. The bottom was dirty from walking though the garden to come fetch her. Anne was sure this only added to Miss Barton's nasty mood.

Anne pointed towards the only window in the shed. There was still late afternoon light barely shooting through the thick grey clouds. "My father said I was allowed to stay in my workroom until dusk. Those are the rules you and he agreed upon when you were hired Miss Barton."

Miss Barton walked up to her. Anne did not move as her governess stood above her. She knew this woman would not dare hit her. Her father would never stand for it.

"You know your father and brother are coming home from sea tomorrow," Miss Barton snapped. "Your mother is coming home this evening and you WILL be presentable to her— and I will lock this silly playroom until then."

"You will not!" Anne stood up as she protested. "And this is not a playroom, this is a—"

"I know," Miss Barton tilted her head and mocked her. "It's your workshop."

Miss Barton was much taller than Anne. Her lanky body leaned over her charge and snarled. "You are turning eighteen years old in two months young lady. Two months more for you to be allowed your *transgressions,* as your parents agreed." The older woman waved her hand around at Anne's shelf and mocked her once again. "And your mother has insisted that you become the lady you are supposed to—"

"My mother might as well be DEAD!" Anne yelled. "She hasn't said anything in years! How is she to tell you what I am SUPPOSED TO BE?"

Miss Barton stood up straight and glared at Anne. She slapped Anne's new piece of art right out of her hands. The green crystal fell to the floor and smashed, pieces flying in all directions.

"Don't EVER speak about your mother like that again!" Miss Barton snapped.

Anne ignored her and knelt down. She was quiet as she slowly picked up a few pieces of glass and held them in her hand. Anne refused to cry. She refused to give Miss Barton the satisfaction.

"Get in the house now!" the older woman ordered.

Anne stood up slowly. She had no expression on her face as she walked out the door. Despite not wanting to react, the loud slamming of the door jolted Anne.

Anne had hoped to show the lights created by her crystal art piece to her mother. The piece that she had lovingly worked on for over three weeks. She had hoped maybe they could communicate once again, if only through a smile.

Now that hope was literally left dashed on her workroom floor.

THE EARLY EVENING was almost too much to bear. The rain was steady and depressing. Anne lay on her bed as the droplets pinged against her window glass, a soft rhythm that was beginning to put her to sleep. Were she to do that, Miss Barton would surely come in her room and yell at her once again.

She decided the best thing to do was to sit up. Her legs slid over the side but her head dipped low.

Her mother was to arrive any minute.

How would they greet each other?

Would her mother even notice her?

Anne sighed.

Her mother did little these days. In the first year the illness took shape, her mother started to slowly decline, first beginning to slow down in pace and paying little attention to anyone. Anne's father was not around when this was starting to take place. Only her brother, Michael, was there to assist.

He immediately sought help for their mother. The family was never wanting for money; theirs was an old and strong lineage. No one would turn away a chance to intervene in the business of the Suttons, especially if a large sum of money were added to the mix.

Since Anne was of marrying age now, helping her mother was not the only thing influential 'helpers' would seek.

Everyone was trying to marry off Anne Sutton.

Just thinking of this scared her. The last thing she wanted was to get married. She did not want to have children. Anne wanted to be like her brother, run away to sea and live her life— not have toddlers holding onto her legs and newborn babes suckling at her breasts.

Her friends tried to reassure her that women of her status did not raise children without help. Anne herself had nannies and governesses all her life, including the insipid Miss Barton. This did little to reassure Anne.

If other women helped raise the children, then what happened to her mother? Not wanting to have children herself, Anne assumed children, namely she and her brother, might have caused her mother's 'illness'.

The whole situation didn't make sense.

A shrill voice from downstairs demanded her attention.

Anne slowly got to her feet, squared her shoulders and took a deep breath.

Her mother had arrived.

Anne slowly walked down the stairs, careful to hold onto the railing and keep her nervousness in check. Her long skirt gracefully swished against her legs.

Anne took in another deep breath. Her fine skin was the color of porcelain. Long blond hair covered her shoulders as she apprehensively brushed it back with her right hand. She was not tall, barely a few inches over five feet with broad shoulders and wide hips.

Anne sighed as she looked down at her chest. She felt as if her breasts would never stop growing.

A small commotion fluttered in the breezeway. Anne did not want to step forward. She wanted to be as far away as possible.

As she reached the bottom, she stared at the front doorway... open, yet empty of life. There her mother stood. She was helped by a small woman who held her mother in a firm grip.

Anne's mother was small and frail, her blond hair carefully arranged in a bun; she wore a dress nicely fitted to her body. Her face was gaunt and devoid of emotion, her brown eyes... sad.

Still, she was beautiful beneath her illness.

Miss Barton stepped forward and took Lara's hand.

"Mrs. Sutton, it is so nice to have you home. Your daughter is excited to see you." Miss Barton seemed to mock as she eyed Anne. When the young woman did not step forward, her governess glared more harshly. "Are you not young lady?"

Anne forced a smile.

Deep inside she was indeed happy to see her mother but it was still painful. Her mother seemed to be falling deeper and deeper into an abyss, one Anne could not reach into and one the other could not seem to come out of.

"Mother," Anne stepped foreword and embraced her. There was no reaction. Lara Sutton did not hug her daughter back. She did not look at her in any way.

As Anne pulled back, she held herself high for she no longer wanted to cry. She had spent too much time doing that already.

"Perhaps we should bring Mrs. Sutton to her bedroom to rest?" The nurse suggested.

"Nonsense," Miss Barton said as she began to lead them towards the parlor. "Mrs. Sutton has been away too long to want to while away in her room. Let us have some tea and talk."

"Yes ma'am."

Miss Barton turned towards her young charge. "Young Miss Sutton here needs to spend some time with her mother before she tries to flee to her—sanctuary."

The mocking tone dug deep but Anne was not going to play that game. Again she forced a smile, took her mother's arm, gently but firmly, from her governess and led her mother into the parlor.

"Nonsense Miss Barton... I am very happy to spend time with my mother," she turned and could not resist. "Why don't you see to some tea and scones?"

Anne smiled when she saw she had insulted her governess with just the right amount of finesse.

2

The carriage traveled steadily through the masses of people in the port. Anne peeked her head out and surveyed the crowd. People of all classes, shapes and sizes were busy with their tasks. Some sailors mulled around and joyously beamed at being freed from their ships, at least for a while. Some of those who had been released from their assignments were oblivious to the fact that press gangs were more than happy to snatch them up; possibly lurking around the next corner. Many sailors never even got to see their families or make it home before being taken and thrown onto another ship.

These were some of the facts that Anne's brother, Michael, had told her. She loved hearing his wild stories about the sea. She was all too eager to hear more from him.

The carriage stopped and she stepped outside. Anne was always entranced by the ships in port, the sounds and smells; some not so pleasant. In front of her lay her father's ship, the HMS Journey.

She waited patiently as sailors dashed off the gangway. None paid much attention to her. There were so many women and families crowded around, that she didn't stand out.

There was many a happy reunion.

Anne smiled when she saw her brother wave. He was slightly taller than she, but only by three inches, and his blond hair and blue eyes matched hers as well.

Michael rushed down the gangway and scooped her up in his arms.

"My dear, how I have missed you," he said, then teased, "And how are the little ones at home? Missing their daddy are they?"

Anne released herself from his grip and smacked his arm.

"Stop that!" she playfully snarled. "Or your men will think me your wife!"

"I know... all the better to tease you I say."

She smacked him again then hugged him hard. Her embrace was tight as if she never wanted to let go.

Michael held her for a long time. When they parted Anne forced a smile. He touched her face gently and said nothing. Anne suspected Michael knew that beneath her smiling exterior she was still very upset.

Michael looked up into the ship's rigging for a long moment before speaking once again. "Mother is home already I take it?"

"Yes," Anne shook her head. "It is unbearable to watch... sometimes I wish I could just run away with you and father."

Michael reached in and hugged her once again. His embrace was fierce, compliments of a stocky body. When they released, Anne finally took in his appearance. Michael was handsome. He was so much the mirror image of a younger version of their father but so much older than when he left a year ago. His boyish face was starting to morph into the man he would become.

"My darling girl," said a familiar deep voice from behind.

Anne beamed as she turned around and hugged her father.

"Father!" she cried. "I have missed you so!"

"And I have missed you my dear!"

Michael smiled as he watched the reunion.

Anne's father stroked a loose hair out of his daughter's eye.

"Miss Barton is not treating you right?" he asked.

Anne choked up slightly. She did not need to bother him with such trivial things right now. "Can we talk of that later father?"

"Of course my child..."

Anne instinctively reached for her brother's hands. Michael grasped her warm touch. They had always been close. Anne missed him more than she could ever express. Anne needed him more than ever.

"Mother is home," she said softly to them both.

Captain Sutton glanced at his daughter then looked towards his ship. The deck was bustling with activity. "Michael— "

"Yes, captain?" her brother straightened up and was at once the attentive midshipman, not the son.

"See that Lieutenant Spencer is aware I will be leaving now and will send a courier with the time when I will return to relieve."

"Yes captain." Michael turned to his sister and touched her shoulder. "I will see you later."

"You are not coming home?"

"Tonight," her father said. "In time for dinner."

"Far be it from me to miss a real meal!" Michael joked as he darted back up the gangway.

Captain Sutton put his arm around his daughter's waist and walked her towards the carriage. "Please tell me how your mother is."

"She is..." Anne was hesitant to speak while her father opened the door. She entered and sat down in the seat facing the ship.

"The same?" he asked.

Anne did not want to lie to him. He seemed older, his blue eyes tired with wrinkles on his skin that had not been there before. She did not want to burden him with more troubles. All Anne could do was nod.

He inhaled deeply and closed the door.

As he dipped his head low, Anne put her head out the carriage window as her eyes wandered. She wanted to lose herself in the rigging and sails. The wind blew through them as they snapped in a rhythmic tune.

Anne looked up and saw her brother on what was called the main-deck. She laughed to herself. At least she knew a little about the ship. She admired how regal he looked in his uniform. Michael was proud. As he snapped to attention in front of a lieutenant, Anne smirked. He had been practicing that since he was six years old.

When the lieutenant turned around, Anne gasped.

Anne swore that the person in question was a woman.

"Father?" Anne tapped his shoulder and pointed. "Who is that?"

Captain Sutton peeked out the window and smirked, perhaps knowing that his daughter might notice the little idiosyncrasy.

"That my dear is Lieutenant Elizabeth Spencer."

"She's a she!" Anne was dumbfounded.

"Yes, and my first in command."

"How?" Anne eagerly asked.

He rubbed her shoulders and put his head near her ear as they both looked out the carriage door.

"Lots of hard work... but unfortunately she is no longer going to be a lieutenant after this cruise. I hate to see her go."

"Why? Is she being released?"

"Oh no," Captain Sutton seemed to beam with pride. "She is finally being promoted to captain once she visits the Admiralty. Hopefully they will give her a fine ship."

Anne stared in wonder. She watched the lieutenant, soon to be captain, talk to her brother. From what Anne could see Elizabeth Spencer had coal black hair tied up in a tight bun. Her face was long with high cheekbones. She was very tall with a thin build. She fit her uniform easily and had little extra weight on her.

"I want to meet her," Anne insisted.

"Perhaps we can invite her to dinner one night," her father said. "She will be in port for a while... but for right now, we must really be heading home. I must see your mother and how she is."

Anne did not want to tell him how much her mother had declined since he was last in port.

Instead, as their carriage went on its way, Anne could not help but stare in the direction of the female officer.

Anne desperately wanted to talk to Elizabeth Spencer. Anne wanted to run up the gangway and ask the woman how she had freed herself from the shackles of female oppression!

Oh how I wish I could be like her, Anne thought wildly.

≈

CAPTAIN TREVOR SUTTON was unsure exactly what he would find when he opened the door. He stood behind the intricately carved walnut barrier and waited for a long moment. He knew his wife would not be in the same condition as he left her. In fact, he was sure she would be in a far worse condition than when he had seen her sixteen months ago.

The door creaked slightly as he entered. The woman whom he loved dearly was sitting alone, in a chair looking out the window. Even though her face was gaunt and pale, she was dressed nicely with her hair up and perfectly done. What was going through her mind as she stared ahead, he wondered?

Did she remember how she would rush into his arms?

Oh how he wished she would turn and greet him as she had so many times in the past. She was always sad to see him go but so happy when he returned. His arms would wrap around her and sometimes lift her off the ground.

Oh how she loved when he would come home from sea.

Surely his dear wife must know some of what was going on. The streets were bustling with activity this morning. Noises were loud from the commotion of everyday life. Horses neighed, street vendors shouted their wares.

Trevor knelt by his wife's side and touched her hand.

She had no reaction.

"I would ask you how you are doing my dear wife," Trevor said softly. "But I know the answer all too well."

He slowly got up and let his arms wrap around her. Beneath his grip, he could feel a slight movement. Trevor wanted to believe she reacted to his touch out of love, but the doctors had told him this was simple muscle reaction. Still, he didn't care. He held her tightly as tears escaped, unaware that his daughter stood outside the door shedding her own.

≈

AFTER SPENDING the rest of the afternoon in her workroom, Anne quietly sneaked into the house. She did not want Miss Barton to know she was around simply because she did not have the energy to deal with the wicked woman. Anne had spent much of her time this afternoon avoiding both her mother and her governess.

Her father's tears still lay heavily on her mind. She had never seen him cry, never had heard him weep. Anne wanted to forget what she had heard. A terrible thought entered her mind. She could not even imagine she had even entertained such a feeling. *Would it be better if mother just died?*

As she turned the corner from the hallway, Anne was careful to walk silently up the stairs. A shrill laugh caught her attention. She turned back and headed that way.

Near the kitchen door, Anne stopped and observed the scene.

Miss Barton was close to her father, giggling, of all things, at something he said. She reached down and picked up a biscuit she had baked.

"Would you like to try one?" Miss Barton touched his hand gently, turned it over and placed the biscuit. "It is mighty sweet and... delicious."

Trevor smiled back as he tasted the delight.

"Very good... I've always enjoyed your cooking. I hope my daughter appreciates the care you give to her."

"Your daughter is a..." Miss Barton could not help herself as she touched his shoulder, pretending to brush away a piece of lint. "She is a precious and special girl. I am happy to be in your lives."

Miss Barton turned on her heel and slinked to the dry sink. She turned and leaned against the wood like a cat. "I'm here for... anything the family... or you... might need," her voice was low, almost a whisper, her intent clear.

Anne cleared her throat and made her presence known.

They both looked at her as if they were guilty of something. Her father dropped the rest of the uneaten biscuit and stepped forward but Anne walked away.

"Did you want to speak to me?" he followed his daughter down the hall and into the parlor.

Anne sat down on the couch, placed a book in her hands and pretended to start reading. "No father— I am fine."

"No, I believe you are not," he said as he sat down next to his daughter. "You have been under a lot of stress lately... too much for a young girl to be asked to do."

"I do not like Miss Barton."

"I know... she is very..."

"Phony?"

"That is one word for it."

Anne closed the book and looked at her father. "She seems to be trying to get close to you."

"I just flatter her dear. She seems to have so little in her own life that she consumes herself with ours."

Anne knew her father loved her mother deeply. The way he cried in the room when he saw her, oh how her illness affected him. The soft words he whispered to her when he thought no one was around. Miss Barton would never get that sort of attention from her father, nor any man for that matter. Her abrasive, phony personality had undoubtedly kept her a spinster for her many years.

Anne put down her book on the coffee table and turned back to her father.

"Tell me more about Captain Spencer?" Anne asked.

"Why does she interest you so?"

"I have never known of a woman in the Royal Navy. Why have you never told me such things. Why hasn't Michael?"

"Michael would not have known of Captain Spencer for she has been in the East Indies for a while. Michael and... Elizabeth only became my crew this last cruise."

He could see how intently his daughter was listening to the tale.

"Have you known her long?" Anne asked.

"We were young midshipmen together; before that I knew her growing up."

"Did you want to marry her?"

Her father was slightly amused at the comment as he chuckled. "Why would you ask that?"

"A female captain seems so, adventurous... daring... different."

"She and I are not... we were never compatible."

"Oh..." Anne did not know what that meant. She pushed her hands on her skirt, slightly nervous in what she was about to say. "Will I get to meet her soon?"

"You seem very eager. Why the sudden interest?"

"Because—" Anne didn't know how to phrase her answer. *Because I want to be like her? Because I see a chance to escape my fate? Because I can be a Sutton on the high seas, even though I am a girl?*

"Anne..." her father could read her, he knew what she wanted. "Ladies like you do not take on careers. They do not take up situations with bawdy men. Life on ships, no matter how glamorous your brother makes it, is not for a young girl."

"But Captain Spencer?— "

"Captain Spencer is not bred from the same stock as us, she is— "

"Low class?" Anne always hated that term.

"No... that is not it at all. Her situation in life did not give her the advantages and financial means that we have. The Royal Navy is all she has."

"So, she is just poor."

"Well, not anymore. She has made a significant amount of prize money over the years. In fact, her new assignment as I am told is to hunt down pirates in the West Indies... and, she is very good at that."

Anne smiled. "I still would like to meet her."

"Then I will arrange that for you... after the ball."

"Must I go?

"Yes. I know your mother would be proud to see you in your gown."

3

———

Anne again tried to lose herself in other thoughts. Her hand touched the crystal pyramid once again. Her father was always bringing her back intricate trinkets from his travels. This object was left on her desk; father must have been sure that she would find the crystal. The piece was beautiful. Clear through with a strong bluish hue, rainbow colors burst from one side when she held the crystal up to the light on the other. Anne had no idea how or why this happened but she knew she could use this in a manner she had been planning.

The workroom door suddenly slammed open.

Anne nearly jumped out of her skin as she grabbed at her chest and touched the leather work apron she wore. She turned to chastise the interrupter.

"Sarah!" Anne panted. "You gave me a fright! I might have been holding something sharp!"

Sarah, her best friend since childhood, only giggled as she jumped in the workshop and started to spin, her dress wildly twirling around her. Sarah was shorter than Anne but thin in the waist with barely a chest. Her long strawberry blond hair bounced with each movement.

"The only thing sharp around here is your tongue!" Sarah teased. "I heard you gave Miss Barton a lashing— according to my mother, you deserved a real one."

Anne folded her arms. "I have never been lashed in my life."

"I know dear friend." Sarah twirled purposely again in her dress.

Anne suspected what Sarah was trying to do. Sarah was trying to get Anne to notice the new garment her overbearing mother had made for her.

"I think that was the point Miss Barton was trying to make," Sarah giggled.

"Miss Barton is a cow."

"I overheard them gossiping again about you. I really hate when they do that."

"Your mother is a—"

"— Don't," Sarah cut her off sharply.

"I was going to say," Anne lied with a huge grin she knew would make her friend laugh. "An exquisite woman with impeccable taste."

"Not when you see the dress she had made for Diane," Sarah laughed. "It really is very ugly. But I could not tell her that. My sisters fawned all over the thing. I knew Diane was lying the most, you could tell by the hesitation in her voice. I just sat in the corner and wondered which blind seamstress she had hired to create that yellow monstrosity."

Anne laughed.

Sarah Winters and her family had always been neighbors with the Suttons. They were nearly the same age; Sarah would turn eighteen in three months.

"So?" Sarah said with excitement as she pushed up a section of the long skirt. "What do you think?"

"It is beautiful," Anne said. "I'm guessing the blind seamstress did not make this dress."

"Heavens no," Sarah giggled. "My sisters' and my dress were made by her apprentice."

"Who is obviously not blind."

"Slightly cross-eyed— see, by the stitching you can tell."

Anne leaned in close as Sarah showed her a section of fabric. Anne was confused. The stitching looked fine. Before she could say anything, Sarah pointed at her. "Ha— I made you look!"

Sarah stopped and studied her friend's attire. Anne had her arms folded across the long, leather apron she wore. Her dress underneath was disheveled and her leather boots were dusty.

"Anne? What have you been doing in here? You look a fright."

"Avoiding Miss Barton," Anne said as she took off the apron and secured it on a hook.

"Are you sure?" Sarah said with compassion in her voice. "Or are you avoiding your mother?"

Anne's eyes suddenly changed, filling with tears she tried to hold back. She turned and sat down on her stool. Her hands grabbed the crystal pyramid and started to nervously play with it.

"What is that?" Sarah asked.

Anne held the triangular prism in her hand.

"My father left this for me..."

"It is beautiful. What are you going to do with it?"

"I am working on... something."

Sarah stepped forward, knowing her friend was secretive for a reason. She decided to change the subject. "Have you shown your dress to your mother?"

"What's the point?" Anne said softly.

Sarah stepped up from behind and put her arms around Anne. Suddenly, that all too familiar feeling crept up as soon as her friend touched her. The rush almost took her breath away every time. She touched Sarah's hand as the sensation got stronger.

"Your mother will get better Anne you have got to believe in that."

"The only thing I believe anymore," said Anne. "Is that my mother is gone."

As Sarah held her tightly, Anne lost herself in the embrace. She did not understand why these last few years she felt so different around her friend. They had known each other for so long. They had played many games, done many foolish things as children— even kissed on the lips like mommies and daddies did— but something was changing lately. Anne tried so hard to bury these feelings for a long time now but was sadly losing. Anne wanted to turn around and really kiss Sarah. But she knew she couldn't. Girls only kissed boys and then only after they had been properly courted.

But now with everything going on, talk of marriages and losing my best friend to— life's obligations? Anne sighed as she exhaled deep.

She tried to tell herself she was feeling this way because of all the pressure that had been building within the household. She could not tell Sarah that she was feeling so lost. Anne was convinced Sarah would only laugh at her and tell her she was being silly.

"I can't wait for the ball on Saturday night. Your brother will look so handsome in his uniform."

"My brother may not have his new uniform yet."

"It doesn't matter. Your brother is handsome in anything he wears."

Sarah had been fawning over Anne's brother Michael since she had turned twelve. Anne found the whole topic of anything involving her brother repulsive. The girl might think Michael was handsome, but she hadn't seen him running around naked, caked in mud when he was eight, chasing pigs on their country estate.

"There will be other midshipmen there my mother has told me, many a young man for you to show off your new dress."

"I'd rather hammer a nail in my hand than attend the ball, let alone put myself on display for boys who think they are men just because they wear a uniform and sword."

"Anne?" Sarah said as she released her grip. Anne felt the sensation again as her friend pulled back. "Why do you never talk about wanting to get married?"

"Because I do not want to."

"Anne?" Sarah said confused. "We are to be eighteen soon. That is what we are expected to do. My mother has already been seeking beaus for me for over a year—"

"And my mother cannot!" Anne snapped. She was shaking slightly as she stared at the tools on her workbench. To give her hands something to do, Anne nervously started rearranging tools. "It doesn't matter anyway— I have no one—"

Anne could not finish her statement. She grabbed a dirty cloth and wrung it in her hands nervously.

Sarah touched Anne's shoulder and made her turn around. She waited until Anne looked her in the eye. "You have me."

Anne closed her eyes as Sarah touched her face gently. Anne reached up her own hand and touched Sarah's skin. When Sarah slowly pulled away, Anne finally opened her eyes.

"I'm afraid," Anne said with tears that finally began to seep out. "Of becoming a wife and mother. Of becoming the doting housewife who has too many children she cannot take care of and who will eventually drive her mad."

"You are not going to turn into your mother, Anne." Sarah knelt down at her side.

"You're going to get your dress dirty," Anne laughed slightly despite her sadness.

Sarah hugged her friend. Anne cried in her arms for a long moment. When they finally let go, Sarah took the dirty cloth from Anne's hand and wiped away the tears. The motion left a small streak across Anne's left cheek.

"There," Sarah giggled. "Now you look like the Anne I know."

"I have dirt on my face don't I?"

"All over."

Sarah got to her knees as Anne chuckled.

"You are going to my mother's inane ball Saturday night," Sarah said. "You are going to have fun and you will dance— even if it is only with me."

"Promise?"

"Yes."

Anne genuinely smiled. She would give anything to dance with Sarah Winters.

~

AFTER DINNER, Anne strolled into the parlor to see her mother sitting quietly in a chair. She had joined them for the meal, but she did not eat and Miss Barton was not going to feed her like a child in front of the family.

Sarah had cheered Anne up, if only for a little while. Besides Anne's brother Michael, Sarah was the only person she could confide in. Anne tried to tell herself she could be understanding of her friend being 'silly' over him.

Sarah had always been a 'silly' girl.

Anne loved her for that.

Still, the idea that Sarah loved her brother more… hurt.

The dinner had been quiet. Only Michael, her father and mother sat around the large table. The maid, hired to help with the extra family, served the meal prepared by a cook borrowed from Sarah's mother. The Suttons were well off, but since most of the family did not reside at home full time anymore, a large staff was not needed.

Now that Michael was at sea, Anne had no one to talk to except her friend Sarah. She refused to converse with Miss Barton, and as Sarah's mom would say, a lady must not become too familiar with the staff. Anne always thought that ridiculous. She had loved her nannies and most of her governesses. They were the ones who had dressed her, fed her, taken her to the park. She loved her mother, as best as one could to someone so cold and distant these last few years.

Still, she was her mother.

Anne tried to push her earlier thoughts out of her mind. She knelt down next to her mother and tried to look into her eyes. Lara did not respond, only stared straight ahead as she had always done these last few months.

"Anne?" A voice said.

She turned around and saw Michael standing, proud in his new uniform. Anne stood up and walked over to him. She took his right hand and held it close to her.

"I can't stand seeing her this way anymore Michael," Anne quietly whispered, afraid she might be overheard by her father in the other room.

Michael put his arm around her shoulder, holding her tight.

A rustle near the door interrupted them. Anne wiped her eyes quickly and sat next to her mother as Miss Barton walked in.

"Shall Mrs. Sutton retire for the night, or would you like her to stay?" The woman asked. Anne could not help but notice the unkind woman glare her way while the words were spoken. Anne opened her mouth to respond but her brother cut her off.

"My mother should stay with us for a while," he eyed his sister, sure she might say harsh words to the other woman. "We see so little of her that any time spent is a blessing."

"Of course young master," Miss Barton walked towards the door. "I shall take my leave."

Anne glared at the older woman as she slowly exited.

"I loath that woman," Anne said to him.

"Oh come now, she cannot be that bad."

"She would do better on your ship. Perhaps you can use her as cannon fodder?" Anne giggled.

Michael laughed. As he did, their father entered.

"What is so funny you two?"

"Nothing of interest... just Michael being crude as usual," Anne lied.

Before her father could chastise him, Michael sat down and crossed his legs. "I think Anne has something to show us," Michael blurted out.

Anne could have strangled him. She didn't know if she was ready to show the family what she had created. Her father was always tolerant of her endeavors, especially these last few years. She knew he felt the practice was an escape for her. That is why he had built the workroom for her.

Anne loved her father for that.

"I... I do not know if it is ready," Anne said, being as truthful as she could. Her device was ready, she was just hesitant that what she had worked so hard on would not make a difference.

"Oh come now Anne," her father insisted. "Anything you make is interesting to us. You are quite the inquisitive girl."

"I am almost eighteen father," Anne said. "Am I not a woman yet?"

"Not until you are married my sweet child."

And there it was again, the suggestion that she would only have worth when she became a wife and mother.

"I do not think Anne wants to marry..." Michael winked at her without her father seeing. "I think she wants to be a pirate on the high seas."

Anne ignored him. She left the room for a few minutes, only to return with a cylindrical metal device that had a hand crank on the side. Anne opened the back revealing a set of mirrors and fixture for a candle. She reached into her pocket and placed her recently acquired crystal on another fixture closer to the lens. Anne then lit the candle and replaced the housing.

"So, what does it do my dear?" her father asked.

"As I crank the handle, air will enter and feed the candle. It should produce a shimmer of light on to the wall through the crystal."

She pushed a small corner table into the center of the room as Michael blew out a few candles.

Anne slowly began to crank the lever. "Normally, one would hold up the crystal to the sunlight to get a rainbow affect. But since it is dark now, I am obviously using a candle."

"I'm not seeing anything," Michael joked.

"Don't tease her," their father softly chastised him. "Let her have a moment."

"Thank you father," Anne chuckled to herself. Her brother could be so annoying at times but how she had missed him always being around.

Quickly she cranked the lever as the candle light finally penetrated the prism. Soft patterns of colored light lit up the wall. The more she cranked, the more the light pattern danced.

The show was dazzling. Her brother started clapping.

Suddenly, her mother got up and walked towards the wall.

They were stunned.

Anne stopped cranking, for she did not know what to do. Her father got up and knelt by his daughter.

"Keep doing what you were doing dear," he instructed.

Anne quickly restarted her motions as her father jumped up and rushed to his wife's side. "Dear... oh dear," he said with tears in his eyes.

Anne had tears of her own, as she turned to her brother. He also was entranced by the lights. She realized he did not even notice their mother.

Anne turned back to the light show and no longer saw different colors on the wall. Instead, only one color of blue washed over the room... horizontal patterns slowly waving like the ocean on the wall.

"What the?" Anne said to herself, confused.

If I am seeing this, what is my brother seeing?

What is my mother seeing?

Anne no longer could imagine, for her mother crumpled in her father's arms as she passed out.

4

———————

The Winters' ballroom glistened with candles and gilded decorations everywhere. The women looked like so many flowers in their colorful dresses; the men like elegant garden statues, many in uniform.

Anne was completely bored.

She unhappily stood in the corner drinking punch from a crystal glass.

If only I could go home!

Mrs. Winters had forced Anne to dance with two young men so far; now she was happily approaching Anne with a third. Anne turned to see if she could escape but she wasn't quick enough. The annoying woman had the pace of a thoroughbred.

"Miss Sutton..." she cooed. "This is Mr. Bonlin."

Anne put out her hand, as was custom. He bent at the waist and kissed the gloved surface.

"Glad to make your acquaintance Miss Sutton," he said as he stood up.

Anne took him in for a moment. He was handsome. Broad shouldered with a trim body. His eyes were brown and his black hair was tied neatly behind in the traditional Royal Navy bow.

Too bad she felt nothing for him.

"Glad to make your acquaintance Mr. Bonlin."

"Would you care to dance?"

She looked out of the corner of her eye at the older woman glaring at her. There was no way Anne could turn down his offer as long as Mrs. Winters was standing over her like a vulture.

"Of course Mr. Bonlin."

He led her happily to the center of the room, joining the fun along with his fellow officers. She allowed him to place one of his hands around her waist as he led her in a waltz.

"So Miss Sutton, are you enjoying yourself this evening?" he asked.

"Not particularly."

"That is because you have surrounded yourself with bores this night. I noticed you danced with Mr. Tyler and Mr. Reynolds. I can assure you that they are not nearly as skilled... in the romance department."

Anne ignored him. She scanned the scene for Sarah. The blasted girl must have skipped out. Her friend had been having a wonderful time. She had danced with Michael for most of the evening.

Watching Sarah so happy, so bubbly was infuriating. She knew Mrs. Winters was beyond ecstatic. Anne cursed silently to herself. The last thing she wanted was that blasted woman spending too much time with the family. Then again, the love she felt for Sarah would make seeing the girl impossible if her mother were not invited to be around.

"What are you thinking my dear? About me I hope?" Mr. Bonlin asked.

"I was thinking how exquisitely bored I am."

"I could take you into the garden, if you prefer... we could... spice things up," his tone was condescending and not appreciated. She knew exactly what he meant. There was no way she was going into the garden with him. Surely he expected they would— *get to know one another better?*

Even if Anne was interested, what kind of girl did he think she was?

"Sir, you forget yourself."

The song ended and so did their dance. Anne spun on her heels and left him. She swore she could hear him laughing.

Anne ignored Mrs. Winters' look and walked over to where she had been standing before. She crossed her arms and leaned against the wall, in as unladylike a manner as she could manage. Maybe that infernal woman would send her home. She would rather spend time with her mother than dance with another man-boy.

A young sailor began to walk her way. He was short and his curly hair seemed out of place. He was not handsome by any means but he had a bubbly smile.

"Would you care to dance?" he asked sheepishly.

She silently laughed under her breath. Was Mrs. Winters sending her the bottom of the barrel now? The woman must have been desperate for Anne's father to see Anne show interest in someone, anyone.

"No thank you... I am feeling a little dizzy," Anne lied. She would have said the same thing to a handsome sailor.

"Then perhaps a walk Miss..." he asked as he looked for a name.

"Sutton."

"Then perhaps you would like to take a walk with me Miss Sutton?"

"Yes. Please get me out of here." Anne took his hand as they walked out towards the veranda. She had a feeling that Mrs. Winters was watching them. The woman probably told the young man to try to corral that filly.

MISS BARTON LAUGHED out loud as she gently knocked on the door. After all, Lara Sutton was a shell, never responding to anyone anymore. Not that Miss Barton really cared. She was the only one in the house this evening and the duty to check on the invalid fell to her.

God how she despised this family. If it weren't for her true love, she never would have come to this wretched place. And, she would have never agreed to the deeds she was required to do.

She closed the door behind her.

No eyes looked upon Miss Barton.

Lara Sutton was staring into the distance.

Is she studying the family portraits in front of her?

Who can tell? Miss Barton thought cruelly. *No one knows what is going on in that empty head.*

Small and large silver rectangular picture frames held painted portraits of family. Miss Barton picked up a picture of Anne and brought the frame over to Lara.

"This poor child," Miss Barton mocked in a condescending tone. "To be stuck with you for the rest of her life?" She sat on the bed, then giggled slightly. "Your daughter is at another ball right now, another one that you could not attend because of your... idiocy some might say. What poor fellow would want to marry such a girl who is burdened with you?"

Lara Sutton lay quietly on the bed, in her own world.

Miss Barton got up and placed the picture in a different spot. She went over to the dresser and opened a canvas bag. She brought out the crystal prism device that Anne had created in hopes of communicating with her mother. Miss Barton placed the device on the small table near Lara and opened the back housing. She placed Anne's crystal in its spot then snapped her fingers lighting the candle. She then closed it up and waved her hand over the metal housing. The crank began to work on its own. The dance of lights began to bounce off the wall creating a light show of many colors.

Miss Barton walked back over, gently lifted Lara up slightly, then began to fluff the pillow.

"Maybe you might be able to see beyond your own selfishness," Miss Barton whispered. "And end it."

With a wicked smile on her face, she left the subject of her distaste and made her way to the full length mirror in the corner of the room. She began to primp her hair, careful not to let a strand get out of place.

"Now it is up to you my dear," Miss Barton touched the mirror as she softly spoke to it. She spent a long moment looking at herself.

Finally, with a large smile Miss Barton turned and looked at her patient. Suddenly Lara broke out of her stupor and blinked her eyes. Lara stared intently at the light show in front of her, just as she had done in the parlor.

Miss Barton left the room with a large grin on her face.

~

"I AM SORRY, I forgot to tell you my name..."

When she said nothing as a polite female would do, he continued. "Mr. Finlay Travers."

"And I am Anne."

"What a beautiful name, Anne."

She snorted slightly to herself. She had been told by many sailors tonight that her name was... beautiful.

How many women swooned at the line? Anne wondered.

Anne walked slowly with Finlay by her side. She wasn't thinking much, in fact she really wasn't thinking anything important at all. The ball was a bore. Most of the guests appeared to be having a wonderful time. All Anne could think about was going home. But, if she disappeared so early, Mrs. Winters would certainly notice and alert her father to the insult. So instead, Anne allowed Finlay to walk her outside so she could enjoy the fresh air and rid herself of the pompous attitudes that had flooded the room.

She had made sure that Mrs. Winters saw they were walking into the garden together. Perhaps she could amuse herself with witty banter, if Finlay could keep up. She would then rid herself of his company and go to the sanctity of her workshop. She would rather have her hands coiled around metal and glass not the shoulders of young men she had been forced to dance with particularly if they had intentions of becoming her suitor.

Anne lost her balance on the uneven gravel walkway and fell forward towards the stone wall. Finlay stepped in and kept her upright. She put out her hand as she realized she had almost hit the stone with her face. He had unintentionally touched her lower backside in the process. He quickly pulled away and apologized.

"I'm sorry—" he said nervously as he stepped back. "I didn't mean—"

Anne shook her head for she did not care in the slightest bit over what just happened, though she did appreciate the save.

"No harm done Mr. Travers. I thank you for saving me from a fall. My silly mind was elsewhere." Anne was most embarrassed for showing this potential suitor a perceived feminine— *weakness*. She in fact did not have a silly mind. Her mind was quite fine and very aware that this whole courting ritual was in fact most— *idiotic.*

"I would not like to have seen you do harm to your lovely face," he said.

Anne looked at him oddly.

"And why is that Mr. Travers?" she questioned with a rigid tone.

"Please call me Finlay."

"All right, Finlay," she said, then preceded to give him a curt smile. "My face? Is that important to you?"

"Well," he stammered, unsure why she was asking these questions. "You are very beautiful and if you had fallen very hard into that stone you—"

She cut him off. "Might have done damage to my pretty face or damaged my eye?"

"Why, yes," he said as he forced a smile, unsure about the line of questions being asked of him.

Anne started walking again as he slowly followed. "It's funny how young men like yourself, dressed in your fancy uniforms with gilded swords, and flintlocks attached to your waists seek out ways to achieve bodily harm— or scars to prove your value in society."

Finlay tried to keep up with her fast pace.

"And if you come home from battle with a scar across your face, or a patch across your eye," she stopped and turned towards him, fire in her own eyes. "You would be celebrated as a hero who had done his duty to his country. And if I had suffered the same fate on this walkway tonight I would be perceived as less than the low status I already endure as a woman — and be something to talk about or hide, becoming even less than marriageable."

"But you did not hurt yourself."

"Thank heavens for that," she said sarcastically. "For I am still marriage material."

"And you are not yet a woman."

"Perhaps," she said. "Not like young men such as you, sailors who, even at your age, have most likely already partaken in the act of carnal love."

Finlay was somewhat shocked at what she just said as he slightly gasped. She laughed inside. His facial expression gave hint that he had no idea young women knew of these things, or what sailors did.

"Are you trying to drive me away from you, Anne?" he sharply asked but with a grin. "Mrs. Winters told me you were a little bit headstrong but—"

"This is a charade!" Anne turned around once again. Now she was really upset. "This whole idea that I should just find someone like you to marry me! Then what? A wedding night where I most likely will become pregnant, and off to sea you will go. And when you come back every season, leave me with another child that I do not want to take care of? Until my body or mind is worn out— or both!"

Finlay just looked at her. He wasn't upset at what she had said to him. He just saw pain in her eyes.

"Anne?" he said as he took her hands in his. "I'm not asking you for your hand in marriage. I just asked you to come take a walk with me for you looked as unhappy in there as I was."

"I'm sorry." Anne realized she was projecting anger that she knew he was not the cause of. "I didn't mean to be so... abrasive. I thought I was supposed to... I thought part of the purpose tonight was putting me on display."

"It's okay Anne." Finlay squeezed her hand tight. "I've met many a lady like you in my travels in the West Indies... headstrong and fearless, not afraid to tell a man what she thinks." Anne looked at him oddly as he continued. "It is a shame that our society looks down upon these virtues."

Anne was about to speak up but the sound of laughter caught her attention. She recognized the voice as she walked towards it.

Finlay followed her.

He saw the blood in Anne's face drain. Her eyes were fixed as they stared at something ahead.

There were Sarah and her brother Michael in the side atrium— kissing. They were somewhat concealed under the thick leaves and growth that snaked around the wooden poles. Anne felt the wind knocked out as she slowly watched her brother take his mouth and caress the inside of Sarah's with his tongue. The kiss was long and penetrating. His left hand reached inside of Sarah's top and caressed her in places it should not. When Sarah pulled back her lips and slightly gasped, Anne's shock turned to anger.

Sarah must have felt her gaze, for she turned and met eyes that said everything in one glance.

Hate.

Before Sarah could say anything, Anne spun on her heels and stormed away.

5

"Anne wait!"

The voice was close behind. Anne picked up her pace, lifted her skirt higher and tried to move more quickly. She caught the bottom of a bush and yanked the fabric. There was a ripping sound but Anne did not care.

She tried to run faster.

The only thing on her mind was to escape to her bedroom and drown her tears in her pillow. She could already feel her eyes welling up. She didn't want to cry.

She just wanted to go home.

When Anne finally arrived at the gate, a hand grabbed at her shoulder and tried to stop her. Anne spun around and confronted the voice that wanted attention.

"Leave ME BE!" Anne's voice was ragged, her whole body shook as the tears began to flow freely.

Sarah said nothing as she stared at her broken friend, shocked at the violent outburst. When Anne tried to open the gate once again, Sarah leapt forward and slammed the metal shut.

"I don't— I don't understand why you are so upset!"

"He had his HANDS all over YOU!" Anne was enraged, knowing that her best friend was oblivious to the real reason why. What could she tell her? That she wanted to be Michael's lips, his tongue? Anne had never seen a kiss like that before, and the moment she saw it she wanted so badly to be the one kissing Sarah, not her brother!

"You let him touch you!" Anne snapped.

"Just on my backside."

"Liar, I saw you!"

Sarah crossed her arms and lowered her head. "I'm sorry."

"No you're not," Anne spat. "You looked like a trollop!"

Sarah had enough.

"You're afraid!" she yelled back.

"What? No I am not."

"You are afraid I will get married and leave you alone!"

Anne could not look at her best friend. She stared at the rusted metal gate. She did not want to admit that fact, that her own little life was slipping away. Sarah was growing up. Her brother was almost a man. In fact, according to the Royal Navy he was.

And here she was, stuck and unsure of her own life and the reality she faced.

Anne opened her mouth, ready to apologize when a sudden scream from the distance startled them.

Her heart dropped.

"Mother?" she whispered as she pulled up her skirt and ran towards her house.

THE SCREAMS GOT LOUDER; Anne ran faster. She knew Sarah and Finlay were right behind her. When they got to her house, everyone could see Miss Barton yelling for help. When the woman saw Anne, she quickly ran up to the young woman.

"Your mother!" Miss Barton was almost incoherent.

"What has happened?" Anne yelled.

"The roof... she is on the roof!"

Anne pushed her governess aside and moved as fast as she could. She pulled up short at the north side of the house.

Her heart dropped.

Anne's mother was standing on the roof. The wind was fierce up high and the tiles wet. Her feet were bare and she had on only a shift and thin robe to cover her body.

Anne's heart dropped once again. Her mother was holding the prism device she had created. The woman seemed to be entranced by the crystal.

"It is so wonderful!" her mother said to the growing crowd.

What is my mother seeing?

"MOTHER! What are you doing?" Anne screamed, knowing her yells were fruitless— her mother would never truly hear her. She had been trapped in her own mind. How would she hear a daughter's cry for help?

Finlay and Sarah ran to her side.

"I will try to get her down," the young man said.

"Please hurry!" Sarah cried. She put her hand out to try and console but Anne ignored her and bolted away.

Anne tried desperately to understand what was going on; this didn't make sense! How could her mother have gotten to the roof on her own? Why was she holding the crystal creation? One wrong move and her mother would fall to her death!

More screaming and yelling came from behind. She turned and saw her father and brother. Michael quickly bolted after Finlay.

Her father pushed her to the side. "Go in the house Anne! Quickly!"

"No."

"Listen to me for once you infernal CHILD!" He demanded.

He was not angry, but scared. Miss Barton pulled her back as her father started yelling to his wife to go back into the window.

"You need to go into the parlor girl," Miss Barton said.

Anne tried to release herself from Miss Barton's grip. She needed to help her mother.

"Get off me you cow!" Anne bit as she shoved the governess. The woman lost her grip then her balance and fell into the mud.

Anne ran closer towards the scene and yelled. "Please mother! Whatever you think you are seeing! It is not real! Only a fantasy!"

"Don't you understand?" Anne's mother said. "I can see it now!"

"What are you seeing Lara?" Trevor pleaded.

"Paradise."

"No!" Trevor shook his head. "Don't listen to it. Listen to your child! To me! Go back inside." He could see Finlay and Michael hanging out the window, yelling to her to come back in.

"Whatever you are hearing is a lie mother!" Michael pleaded as he carefully maneuvered his way onto the roof. He almost slipped. A collective gasp came from the growing crowd. "Please give me your hand," he pleaded.

"Mother!" Anne yelled with a cry. "PLEASE! Take his HAND!"

"I must be going now," her mother whispered. "You are better off—"

As her mother stepped off, Anne ran forward.

She would catch her!

She would not allow her to die!

6

———————

nne sat on the sofa and stared into the distance. She heard nothing even though the house was bustling with activity. Voices had quieted in her head, the door no longer held the sound of opening and closing. Only the changes in air pressure alerted her to the presence of guests coming and going.

It had been three hours since the funeral. Three hours since they buried her mother in the family grave. Many mourners had attended, including the woman she had wanted to speak to. The female captain had tears in her eyes during the service.

Anne was too consumed by her own grief to even care. Anne had sat quietly with head tilted down while the vicar spoke. She hardly understood what he was saying, her mind ignoring him.

His words would have given her little comfort anyway.

At home, another mourner gave her his condolences then walked away towards the kitchen. She shifted in her seat and wrapped her arms around her chest. Nowhere was she safe from her grief.

Anne watched as her father walked a few guests to the door. As he turned, Captain Elizabeth Spencer hugged him. Anne had not seen her in the house until this very moment. Captain Spencer must have come in when Anne had fled upstairs for a brief moment before that blasted Miss Barton brought her back down.

When she realized the woman was beginning to leave, Anne bolted upright. She pushed her way through the crowd, only to be stopped by Mrs. Winters.

"Anne, I have not gotten a chance to tell you how sorry I am for your loss," the crotchety older woman said.

"Thank you," Anne faked gratitude. She tried to push forward but was blocked. "I need to go," Anne insisted as politely as she could.

"Nonsense girl... I would like to talk to you about your mother... she was such a kind soul..."

Anne tried unsuccessfully to get by once again. Her heart raced as she could see out of the corner of her eye the front door close. "Not now—"

Mrs. Winters ignored her. "I remember when your mother first moved into this house...she was so young then... I—"

"— You what?" Anne snapped. A few heads turned at the outburst. "Thought she was so beautiful and proper? Then how come you never came to visit her when she was sick? When her face was gaunt and her hair a mess... When she—"

Miss Barton stepped forward and yanked Anne's arm. She looked at the offended woman and smiled. "I'm sure she does not mean that Mrs. Winters. She is beside herself with grief and not thinking properly. Her feelings are— "

"— Do NOT presume to tell me how I am feeling!" Anne cut Miss Barton off and stepped back.

Gasps ensued as Anne rushed to the door. She opened the wood barrier and bolted down the steps, only to find that the carriage that held Captain Spencer was gone.

ANNE WALKED into the garden desperate to get away from the multitude of guests in the house. So many people who had never come to visit when her mother was sick... people who had once called her friend.

Anne sat down near the fountain. Softly, she put her hand in the water and slowly made ripples. Spring was almost over. Soon it would be summer. She was so tired of people bothering her.

Footsteps approached her from behind.

She didn't want to turn around. She didn't want to talk anymore to the vultures. Here it was peaceful.

Couldn't they just leave her alone?

"Anne?" Michael's voice was soft.

She turned her head, happy to hear him. "Remember when father put this fountain in?" Anne asked.

Michael sat down next to her. "How could I forget? We had a devil of a time trying to fish Jonathan out."

"After father fell in trying to fetch the little bugger."

They laughed as they reminisced about the neighbor child who was now also at sea as a midshipman.

"You are leaving, aren't you?" Anne wasn't really asking. She knew the answer already.

"Yes... I must get going. I am already a day late for my post."

"No chance they might sail without you?"

"No... we are scheduled to sail tomorrow morning," he sighed. "I was lucky that father was able to delay my report."

"But how could they have even thought about keeping you from mother's—" Anne could not say the word.

"Naval schedules must be kept."

She rubbed her hands on her dress. Anne was not ready to say goodbye to him. She needed to broach another subject. "I never asked you..." Anne looked into his eyes. "What you saw when we were in the parlor?"

He pursed his lips as he looked at her strangely.

"On the wall Michael..." she pressed. "What did you see?"

"I saw the color of the rainbow just as we all had."

"No you didn't. I did not see multiple colors... I saw blues... ocean blues that moved like the sea."

Michael looked at her as if she were insane. Anne took offense.

"Do not lie to me brother... you were entranced by it. Just like mother."

"She fell off the roof trying to find whatever stupid thing you were trying to show her!" he snapped.

Anne stood up quickly but he grabbed her by the arm and forced her to sit down.

"I'm sorry Anne..." he wept silently. "I am so sorry... I did not mean..."

"That it was my fault?"

"No. Mother was unwell. Who knows what was going on in her head. The doctors said she had an episode, that is all."

"She kept saying it is so pretty, don't you understand?" Anne looked at him with sadness in her eyes. "What was she trying to understand Michael?"

Michael sighed. "She loved us Anne. That is all that matters. Please don't dwell on something we are never meant to understand." He got up and straightened his jacket. Anne stood up and placed her hands on his shoulders. He gently took them in his own then hugged her tight.

Anne held back tears. She did not want to see him leave.

"I must be going now. Cannot be late for my new assignment." He stepped back and straightened his jacket once again as he forced a smile.

Before the funeral, Michael had been thrilled to be assigned to a frigate as a senior midshipman; since then he had just been sad.

Anne was happy he had finally found some cheer once again.

"Be safe brother."

"Be well sister."

As Michael began to walk away, Anne chased after him. "You never answered my question."

He stopped and turned to her. Michael could see she was determined that he answer the question. His sister was always an insistent one.

"Fire," Michael said softly. "I saw reds dancing like flames."

He slowly walked away.

Anne crossed her arms. She started to play with her necklace nervously.

What does that mean? Fire?

Is Michael's ship to catch fire?

She ran to the gate and looked both ways down the street.

Michael was gone.

ANNE HAD WAITED until the last of the guests left. As the carriages had made their way down the street, Anne had stood at the outside gate and watched the horses pull the carriages away. When Mrs. Winters had left with Sarah, Anne crouched low and hid near a bush when they walked by.

She had not talked to Sarah since that night. The girl had offered her condolences but Anne would not say anything to her other than to offer the customary thank you.

Slowly, Anne opened the back door and sneaked into the house. A rustle of noise from the kitchen alerted her. The staff that was hired by Mrs. Winters was probably busy cleaning up from the large crowd of mourners that had invaded the house. Anne knew no one that was in the kitchen cared where she had been.

She entered. They stopped for a moment then continued about the business they were hired to do. Anne walked over to a tray and picked up a biscuit. She had not eaten anything today for she'd had no appetite, until now.

Anne walked out and headed towards her room. Muffled voices from the parlor drew her attention. She crept forward so the voices would become more clear.

Miss Barton was talking to her father.

"What is the best welfare for young Anne? That is the question Mrs. Winters had spoken to me about," Miss Barton said.

"I know, she has told me of her intentions," Trevor said.

"Well what do you think sir?"

"Leaving Anne here would most likely be the best solution."

Anne was now angry. They were talking about her welfare without her?

"Mrs. Winters only wants what is best for the young woman," Miss Barton said. "As do I."

"She should have female influence. Something that would be a more stable solution. Would you be willing to carry on with your duties Miss Barton?"

"Of course sir. Miss Anne is a little bit of a spitfire but I am confident I can work with her. She is growing older now and should be coming out of her young rebelliousness but if she proves difficult— well, I am confident Mrs. Winters and I will be able to bring her to hand and eventually find her a match."

Anne gasped. They meant to take her like a filly and sell her to the highest bidder. She wanted to go in there and smack Miss Barton. How dare that woman think she had any right to her!

"Anne must find a husband," Trevor insisted. "I cannot worry about her while I am at sea. She has no one left."

"She has me," Miss Barton cooed, her intentions obvious. "I will always be here for your family and yourself... for as long as you need."

Anne did not want to hear another word.

She stormed away.

ANNE WAS FURIOUS. She whipped open her workroom door like a whirling dervish and ran inside. She did not even bother to close the door. Her hands scratched against the surface of her workbench as she breathed heavily.

How dare that wretched cow suggest she stay in London with her! And Sarah's mother of all people would find her a match! The mother of a traitorous friend who mocked her.

Anne tried to hold back her tears. How could she even think such a thing about Sarah? The girl had not even known how she felt about her. All Anne had done was concoct a story in her head that she loved her best friend.

Of course it was love.

They had a friendship that was deep.

They had known each other since childhood.

Knew each other's deepest secrets.

Knew each other's ideas of what they wanted to be when they were women.

Only, Anne had never had the courage to tell Sarah what she really wanted.

"Anne?" A soft voice said.

Anne turned around and saw the object of her desire.

"I figured you might be out here," Sarah whispered.

Anne quickly tried to wipe away her tears with her sleeve. There were only a few but still she did not want to show her weakness in front of Sarah.

Her friend walked into the workroom.

"How have you been?" Sarah asked as she crossed her arms behind her back.

"Fine," Anne lied.

"No you haven't."

Anne knew that normally Sarah would hug her about now, try to get her to come out of her depression... but it was most likely that their friendship had changed... forever.

"We never talked about what happened... in the garden?" Sarah said as she watched as Anne turned away.

"Yes we did... right before my mother killed herself!" Anne bit.

There was a moment of silence. Anne placed her hands on the rough, wood worktable and closed her eyes once again.

Sarah walked over to Anne and forced her to turn around and face her. She reached out her arms and touched Anne on the shoulders.

Anne inhaled at the touch. She closed her eyes and imagined a life so very different than the one the girl's mother and her own governess had planned out.

"Please do not be upset with me," Sarah pleaded. "I could never live with myself if you stayed mad at me."

"You have no idea why I am upset with you, do you?" The question was rhetorical.

"You were upset because I was indecent with your brother. I should have been more respectful to you— "

"No! You really do not understand," Anne cut her off. "You do not know what it is like to be me! You do not understand what it is like to be near you... to want to..."

Sarah stroked Anne's cheek. Anne's heart fluttered as she felt the warmth of the touch.

"I have..." Anne could barely get out the words. "...feelings for you."

Sarah did not have any reaction. She did not remove her gesture of friendship. Her arms stayed where they lay.

"What do you mean by feelings?" Sarah asked, softly.

"I think I love you."

"Of course you love me. I love you too, silly girl."

"That is not what I mean. I wish it had been me in the garden!" Anne finally confessed. "I wish you had been... kissing me!"

Sarah pulled back her arms and stood still with eyebrow cocked. Her expression had changed to one of confusion.

Anne felt she had been rejected.

"I wish I could kiss you." Anne turned around quickly and closed her eyes. "I am such a stupid girl!" She slammed her hand on the counter. Her many trinkets jumped at the violent motion.

"Then why don't you?" Sarah said as she placed a hand on Anne's shoulder and turned her around with the other. "Kiss me?"

Anne stared into her friend's beautiful blue eyes.

Had she really said those words?

"Are you saying?"

"Kiss me Anne Su— "

Anne did not wait. She took her hands and gently pulled Sarah's head forward and kissed her. Her months of waiting poured out as she felt her friend's lips caress her own. As Anne's mouth opened slightly, Sarah pushed herself deeper... her tongue finding the tip of the other one. They felt around each other only to find breath was needed. Anne pulled back but did not release her fingertips, which were entwined in Sarah's strawberry golden locks. They panted deeply as they stared into each other's eyes.

The whole world had stopped for Anne with one kiss.

Suddenly, Sarah's eyes opened wide as a look of horror crept onto her face.

Anne felt her own heart drop.

Had Sarah suddenly changed her mind?

"Go home Sarah," said the deep voice of Anne's father.

"Mr. Sutton... we were only playing around."

"Go HOME!" he snapped at her.

Sarah did not even look at Anne as she ran out of the workroom.

Anne turned around slowly. She was scared. Her father stood in front of her, his coat wet from the drizzle outside, his face red with anger. He looked as though he had been drinking.

Before Anne could say anything, he slapped her across the face— hard!

She did not have time to weep. He pushed her aside and grabbed a pipe Anne had on the table. He slammed the steel rod on the workbench then swung the weapon to the side and knocked some of her pieces off.

"Father!" Anne pleaded with him. "Please don't!"

Again he swung hard, this time knocking over a shelf to the ground. The device she had created for her mother fell in front of him. For a short moment he stared at the piece. He yelled as he swung the pipe and broke it. Pieces flew everywhere.

Anne lost her composure and started to cry.

Her father had lost his temper and his mind.

His last swing hit another shelf.

Anne turned and begged him. "Please! Don't!"

This time a candle fell down into a pile of rags and caught fire. Anne went to try and put the flames out but her father pushed her toward the door. Anne stumbled and managed to retrieve the crystal that had separated from the device as it was struck.

"Get OUT!" Anne's father yelled. His voice could not be any clearer. He was going to let her workroom burn down.

And that is exactly what happened.

7

Flinging her small bag over her slender shoulders, Anne moved amongst the hordes of people walking the seaport this night. Nobody paid mind to the lost, little girl even if she were almost a grown woman. In fact, she had blossomed so much over the last summer the neighboring girls teased she was the most womanly of them all. Anne hugged herself to ease her nervousness. If she could not gain passage on a ship as a young woman heading to the Americas, she would take bandages to her breasts and men's clothes to her body.

She was adamant about no longer staying in London.

Anne stopped in front of the dock of a schooner. She knew little about ships except what her brother and father would speak of over dinner. They would talk about sturdy sails and masts that held tall, none of which made enough sense to her to be useful in picking up sound passage.

A noise rustled behind her.

"What ya doing 'ere miss?" The burly old man said. His beard was long, his face gaunt and pocked. "Come to see old Ryam?"

Anne backed away from him. She was not as worldly as she would like, but she knew what some men could be— and she knew those pockmarks as being from one unclean.

As he reached out to grab her arm, she pulled back. Her body flung back into another body, which spun her around.

Anne, terrified, wiggled out and fled.

She bolted down the street, trying to keep the hem of her dress up. Anne cursed to herself. She wasn't brave, she didn't have a real plan. How would she ever run away and start a new life if she was so afraid?

Out of breath, Anne stopped and rested against a brick wall.

This was a really bad idea.

Maybe she should just go home and accept her fate.

Brave she was not.

"Get moving you git!" A foul mouthed, tawdry red headed woman snapped at her in a thick cockney accent. "Bugger off and find another post!"

Anne pushed herself upright.

"I'm sorry, I meant no offense ma'am. I just needed a moment."

The woman sauntered closer and held out a hand, fingers reaching for Anne's face. "You're a ri'ght lady you are."

Anne pulled away.

"Pretty," the redhead snarled.

"Goodnight," Anne tried to walk away, but the woman's arm pulled her back.

"Not so fast li'tle lady— Pretty lady," the redhead cooed. "You look sad. Did your sailor leave, or... did 'e not come back?"

Anne swallowed hard, afraid of speaking anything that might cause her added time with this person.

"Troubling times these are," the redhead said. "So many sailors going off to the West Indies, never coming back... the Spanish devils see to that."

As the woman continued to try to lull her, Anne felt a hand near her waist. She jumped back into another set of arms. This time a man laughed in her ear.

"What we got 'ere?" His breath poured down her neck. "You made a friend Eliza?"

"More of a— sport," Eliza giggled. "Best check to see if our li'tle piggy 'as a bank. I'm thirsty."

Anne tried to run, but the rugged hands of her accomplice pulled her back. He took his right hand and grasped her around the waist, his left began to feel around her stomach. When Anne tried to scream, he roughly covered her mouth with his filthy hand.

"No, no li'tle girl. You need to be quiet while old Liam makes you lighter."

Anne's eyes teared up as Liam pawed at her. He chuckled as he seemed to be enjoying the fact his hands had groped her breasts while searching. Her eyes pleaded with Eliza but the woman just sneered while twirling her own hair. Eliza actually seemed to be annoyed the whole process was taking so long.

"Oh puff guts!" Eliza reached down and pulled up his walking stick. "Just knock 'er out!"

Liam reached for the wood. Before he could grab the stick, Eliza dropped the stick and yelled in pain.

"What the bloody 'ell?" she cried as she looked down at her hand and could see blood dripping.

"Release the girl," a stern voice said. "Or I will do much worse."

Three pairs of eyes stared at a woman, dressed in the uniform of a captain of the Queen's Navy. Her right hand held a saber, her body posture set in attack stance.

Anne recognized Captain Elizabeth Spencer immediately. She wanted to run into her arms and wish away the madness surrounding them.

"Must be a theater wench," Liam teased as he held Anne tight. "Missing your 'ittle actress here?

He raised his head and nuzzled his paw close to Anne's head. His nose rubbed against her neck as he inhaled. "Smells fresh— 'ow much do you want for 'er? Surely she is worth less on the circuit."

Captain Spencer stepped forward and slashed at Liam's head. He pulled back and screamed. As he held his hand up, searching for the wound Anne ran towards her savior.

"Stand behind me," Captain Spencer instructed.

Liam felt blood on his neck. He touched the smooth surface then examined the wetness in his hand.

"You Goddamn wench!" Liam snarled as he stepped forward. As he did, the pointy end of the sword ended his march. The sharp pain in the center of his neck prevented him from moving.

If he stepped any further, the metal would sink in.

"We will be leaving now. Do not attempt to follow us," Captain Spencer ordered.

Anne felt Captain Spencer's hand pull her to the side. Anne followed without question as they started to back up, the sword never bending from its ready position. Liam jumped back and bent down. He then grabbed the wooden stick and leapt forward. As he swung, Captain Spencer pushed Anne down out of the way.

The captain then sank low. When she saw his momentum was off, she spun her body weight around and snapped his kneecap with a kick. Liam screamed in pain and fell.

He could not move, the saber tip at his throat once again.

"As I said— we will be leaving now and you will not attempt to follow us. I am indeed a member of Her Majesty's Royal Navy. And... if I see you again I will press you into service aboard my ship." The tramp's eyes were filled with terror. "I would tell you to run along, but seeing the predicament you now find yourself in— you really should limp away before I go and find a press gang."

Liam scrambled up the best he could. As he looked around, he realized Eliza had abandoned him.

Captain Spencer shook her head in disgust as she watched the man hobble away. She turned and eyed Anne, not happy at all with the situation she was forced into. She reached down and offered her hand. "Come with me young lady— You should not be wandering the streets so late at night."

Anne placed her own hand into Captain Spencer's and she was lifted to her feet.

"What is your name?" The older woman asked.

"Sarah," Anne lied.

"All right... Sarah," Captain Spencer said softly, most likely aware the girl was lying. "Where do you belong so late at night?"

"Umm..." Anne didn't know if she wanted to confess where she really belonged. What if this woman brought her home to her father? What would he say if he found out what had happened?

"Well then…" The older woman knew stalling when she saw it. "In the meantime, while you are figuring that out perhaps you would like to join me for a meal? I was on my way to the tavern when I… stumbled upon your misfortune."

"Yes… I would like that."

"Good then." She reached down and picked up Anne's small bag. "If you would fol—" The crystal fell out of the bag and hit the floor. Captain Spencer automatically bent down to pick it up.

"No, wait!" Anne reached forward, but it was too late.

The older woman held the triangular crystal in her hand and studied it. She seemed almost entranced by the thing as she turned the prism in her hand to look at the other side as light from the street lights bounced wildly.

"What is this?" she asked. "It's beautiful."

Anne reached out, begging to take the crystal back. "Something I do not want anymore… but something that is my responsibility."

"It is very unusual. Why do you not want this anymore?"

"Because," Anne waited until she had the device firmly back in her grip. "I fear it is evil. Its only place is at the bottom of the ocean where it cannot hurt anyone else."

"Is that why you are looking for passage?"

Anne opened her eyes wide, startled at the sudden question. She did not remember telling Captain Spencer why she was in the port tonight.

"Sarah, you would be down here for only two other reasons. Seeking a sailor that has forsaken you or looking for new employment." Captain Spencer reached out her hand. "You may give that to me dear girl. I will throw it overboard if it will keep you off the streets."

"I would appreciate that very much."

"Good then… let us eat something for this night has left me famished."

"I AM Captain Elizabeth Spencer by the way," the older woman said as she led Anne towards the back of the establishment. "But you may call me Elizabeth." She reached out her hand and directed the younger one to sit.

"Thank you Miss Elizabeth." Anne graciously accepted as she sat down on the wooden bench and folded in her skirt. She didn't bother to check if any grease were on the seat, for she was sure her dress was already done for after falling at the port earlier.

"Stay here," Elizabeth said softly. "I need a moment."

Anne watched her rescuer walk over to a young midshipman and begin to talk to him. Anne turned her head and looked around. She had never been in an establishment like this before. It was poorly lit, smelled of stale beer and staler bodies. The noise was loud, coming from the patrons both standing at the bar and sitting at tables. Most everyone had a stein in their hand and were happily drinking. In her previous experience Anne had only seen people drinking spirits out of crystal glasses and in small amounts at dinner and in the parlor. These people were mostly roughly dressed, except for those in uniform, and drank from mugs and, in some cases, directly from bottles.

Anne looked up when Elizabeth sat down. The older woman signaled towards the bar that there were two new customers. When Elizabeth turned back she noticed Anne pull out her change purse.

"No need for that. I am paying," Elizabeth said.

"But miss? I feel I should buy for you tonight. Without your assistance, I may have nothing left in this," Anne said, indicating her purse.

"Or worse dear girl— You need to learn how to defend yourself. Didn't your father ever teach you anything?"

"My father?"

"Yes— Captain Sutton."

Anne shifted uneasily in her seat. "You know who I am then?"

"Yes. You are Anne Sutton."

Anne lowered her head for a moment ashamed with her actions this night. She had no idea what she was doing thinking she would escape to the high seas. When she looked up Elizabeth stared back with kind eyes.

Now that Anne was close she could finally take in Captain Spencer's appearance. Elizabeth was close to her mother's age and very pretty. Her coal black hair was tied up in a neat bun with a few gray hairs beginning to sprout. Her face was long with a broad tipped nose. Elizabeth's eyes were brown and small. When she smiled through her thin lips they gave off a feeling of tenderness.

The tavern owner delivered two meat pies and two steins with ale. Elizabeth paid the owner. When she reached for the forks, she noticed Anne staring at the ground. "I'm sorry about your mother dear girl. She was a good woman."

"You knew her?"

"I did."

"I had seen you on my father's ship when we collected him. I thought it odd—"

"—To see a female in uniform?" Elizabeth broke the top crust and ate a small bite. "Do not worry... I'm used to it."

Elizabeth did not speak further. She waited patiently as she motioned for Anne to start eating. Anne took a fork and forced herself to eat a little bit of meat pie. She could sense the older woman watching her intently, most likely concerned with what brought Anne down here to the port so late at night.

"Why then would you run away and break your father's heart?" Elizabeth finally continued.

"I fear my father doesn't love me anymore."

"Why would you think that?"

"Because he hit me—" Anne had tears in her eyes. As she put down her fork, Elizabeth did the same. "He has never struck me before."

Elizabeth inhaled deeply and sighed. This seemed to truly bother her.

"Why would he do that if I may ask?"

"He caught me... kissing my friend."

"What?" Elizabeth laughed as she took a sip of ale. "I should slap him back for you. Your father was quite a charmer at the age of sixteen. The handsome midshipman he was. Of course his daughter would be just as beautiful. How could he not expect you to be fawned over by young men?"

Anne glanced away. Elizabeth tilted her head and studied the young woman in front of her. Anne looked as if she were guilty of something worse, but what the captain could not guess.

"You are sixteen, right?"

"Seventeen."

"Even so. You should not be ashamed of kissing a boy at your age. I kissed many a boy at your age. I'm sure your father overreacted. It's hard to see a daughter grow up into a young woman."

Anne nodded. She took a small sip and picked at her pie. She was not going to tell this woman it had been a female friend she had been caught kissing.

"You are not hungry I take it," Elizabeth asked, concerned.

"No."

"I am truly sorry about your mother dear."

"Thank you," Anne brushed her hair back with her left hand. Suddenly she felt very awkward.

Elizabeth watched her carefully. When Anne did not lift her head to continue speaking, the captain interjected. "Your mother was a kind woman."

Anne picked her head back up. "Did you know her well?"

"Yes. I considered her a friend."

"I saw you at the funeral... I have been wanting to talk to you... but I could not after what had happened."

"You cannot be expected to be in your right mind after what has happened to you," Elizabeth pushed forward and touched the young girl's hand. "We make bad choices when we are upset or scared— Why else would you rush from your father's safety over a disagreement?"

"It was more than that," Anne could not believe she was revealing herself to a woman she barely knew. "They want me to stay in London!— Alone, with that blasted governess of mine!" Elizabeth leaned back, slightly shocked at the girl's outburst. Anne surmised that the captain expected tears next to fall, but none came... only anger.

"All they want is to marry me off!" Anne bit.

"Families do not always have our best interest at heart," Elizabeth softly said.

"My governess is not my family... nor is Mrs. Winters. They are annoying hens that interfere wherever they can for their own benefit. My father is truly foolish if he believes Mrs. Winters has his interest— she wants to marry me off to her annoying nephew so she can be attached to our family lineage! She is already happy that Sarah— " Anne stopped before she let herself tell too much.

Elizabeth smiled as she reached for her ale. Anne noticed the change in demeanor. She had expected the older one to mock her but instead heard the exact opposite.

"You are very wise dear girl... much wiser than I was at your age," Elizabeth drank then put the mug down. "People do not normally do anything out of the goodness of their heart. Christian morality is fickle. Best that you have learned that lesson now."

"Then does that mean you want something from me too?"

"No Anne. Some of us still have morals. I am indebted to your father and as such, will see you home safely."

"Must I go?"

"I think you know the answer to that question," Elizabeth said. "But first, you must finish dinner and we may talk some more if you would like."

"Yes miss, I would like that very much."

8

———————

nne felt anxiety in the pit of her stomach. Only when Elizabeth touched her on the back, did she feel her fear lift slightly. Anne turned and smiled, thankful Elizabeth had been the one to find her and bring her home.

Anne had been so angry, so upset... she had not even thought about what could have happened to her. So many terrible evils might have befallen her in the port.

"Everything will work out," Elizabeth told her. "It might seem like the end of the world right now, but time heals... and you must hope for the best."

Anne nodded and closed her eyes; she had a sudden sensation to cry. The older woman must have sensed this for she rubbed Anne's back once again.

"My father said you were midshipmen together," Anne asked after a bit.

"Yes, when we were younger."

"How old were the both of you?"

"Your father was already at sea from the time he was twelve. I did not become a midshipman until I was fifteen."

"Why so late?"

"Circumstances…"

Anne realized by the way the word trailed off, that perhaps the older woman did not want to share what those circumstances were.

"You must have had many adventures together," Anne said.

"We had our fair share of— adventures. The West Indies can be a very rough place when you are looking for trouble."

"You both looked for trouble?" Anne giggled. "That seems so uncharacteristic of my father. He gets angry if we even step out of line at home."

"Being a father is different…" Elizabeth quietly looked down at her lap and forgot her train of thought. She turned to Anne and redirected her musing. "What I mean by trouble is… that was our duty. The purpose of our service is to protect the crown, the colonies and our citizens. Anyone or anything that disrupts that is our duty. So, we went after trouble because that trouble needed to be stopped."

"Have you ever been shot at?"

"More than once."

The carriage abruptly turned a corner. Dread hit Anne once again. She closed her eyes and listened to the horse's steps. The hooves clip clopped on the stone pavement, making sounds that were familiar to her.

Anne knew she was home.

She peered out the carriage window. Her father stood at the curb of the house… waiting. She could not tell what mood he was in.

Anne suddenly became uncomfortable in her seat. "He is going to thrash me."

"No he is not," Elizabeth leaned in. "Or he will have to deal with me."

Anne forced a smile. She truly hoped the older woman was right.

The carriage had hardly come to a stop when Anne's father stepped up and whipped open the door. Anne braced herself. Her father leaned in, grabbed her by the waist and hoisted her out.

"My dear girl!" he said as he embraced her.

Anne hugged him back.

Elizabeth slowly walked down the carriage steps and waited. When father and daughter finally released, Elizabeth crossed her arms and smiled. She looked away when she saw he had tears in his eyes. This was not her place to judge.

Trevor Sutton turned to his friend and whispered. "Thank you for bringing her home Elizabeth."

Trevor pulled Anne close and shook her arms. "Why did you run off girl? Captain Spencer said you went to see her! How did you even know where to find her?"

Elizabeth interrupted before Anne could even try to answer. "She must have overheard me at the wake. She took a cab down to the inn."

"I would have taken you Anne... why would you have worried me so?"

"I am sorry father."

"Never mind that now, my dear, please go in the house. Have Miss Barton make you some tea."

"Yes father."

Anne ran up the stairs, but stopped. She turned and watched Elizabeth talk to her father. She was beyond grateful that the woman had covered for her lie. Anne opened the door slightly to pretend she was going inside, but instead she eavesdropped the best she could.

"Well, I see you got my message," Elizabeth said to Trevor.

He pulled her close and hugged her tight. Elizabeth seemed awkward as she uneasily patted him on the back.

"Umm— is this appropriate?" she asked as Trevor released.

"I do not care, besides you are no longer a subordinate, but an equal."

"Well thank you Captain Sutton... it is nice to hear someone say that," Elizabeth laughed. "So, have you thought about my other suggestion?"

"Yes... I think that is a wonderful idea, though I am surprised considering you cannot stand the woman."

"This is not about me Trevor, this is about what is best for your daughter," Elizabeth said. "And perhaps this will get the sea-faring adventure out of the girl. Once she sees how rough a sailor's life is."

"Just like it did for you?" he chuckled.

Elizabeth raised an eyebrow and scowled at him. "You know I had little other choice."

"I kid my dear. You know I would never belittle you."

"I fear, once I enter the lioness' den I will get enough of that. I am sure your sister has not changed in the slightest."

ANNE SAT QUIETLY on the sofa, her legs perfectly still and her body in the correct posture. She had changed into her evening shift and had a silk robe on. Miss Barton had chastised her when she entered the house but Anne ignored her. Her father was not mad, so why should her blasted governess have any say? When he eventually left for the West Indies, Anne was sure she was going to have more than one fight with the woman.

But something had seemed to change inside Anne.

Elizabeth had given her the strength to realize a woman could have a mind of her own.

Anne smiled to herself. *Miss Barton is in for a rude awakening.*

The door opened and closed.

Her father sat next to her.

"I am sorry father," Anne apologized softly as she put the teacup down on the side table. "I let my emotions get the best of me. I never should have left without telling you or Miss Barton. I apologize."

"Anne you did something that could have ended tragically. You do understand that?"

"Yes father... if it is any consolation, Miss Elizabeth told me in so many words I was being a fool."

"Yes, you were. But you are no fool my daughter. You are like your mother..." he stopped mid-sentence. Instead of continuing, he fumbled as he reached inside his jacket and pulled out a ring. The band was silver engraved with celtic symbols and embedded with four stones; amethyst, emerald, red garnet and pink diamond.

He handed the ring to his daughter.

"This is yours now."

"Mother's ring?" Anne said as she held the item with reverence.

Her mother had always worn this ring around her neck on a chain. Anne had always thought it odd that her mother never wore the thing.

Anne had asked her once, only to find out her mother had no particular reason for it.

"Thank you," Anne said to him.

He watched as his daughter played with the ring. She moved her fingers over the surface, touching each stone with the tips of her fingers.

Anne did not know if she wanted to put the ring on her finger or wear the jewelry like her mother used to. She reached behind her neck and took off her pendant. Carefully, she replaced the silver trinket with her mother's beloved ring. When she went to put the necklace back on her neck, her father motioned to help her. Only when the chain was secure did she touch the surface once again.

The ring felt warm, odd for a cold piece of jewelry.

"I am also sorry father— about what you saw. Sarah and I? In no way had I meant to offend you."

"I overreacted... I know that young girls are very close and that I might have misjudged the situation."

Anne quickly blinked, surprised.

"Sarah came by... and explained," he added.

"She did?"

"She said you were practicing... so you both would not feel like fools when the time came to kiss your husbands at your wedding."

"Is that what she said?" Anne chuckled under her breath. *Had he actually believed that?*

"Silly games that girls play."

"Yes father— just a silly game," Anne played into the lie. "I am sorry you thought it was anything else."

Anne wondered if Sarah had really thought that was what they had been doing. But no. Anne could feel in her heart what they had shared in that brief moment was not a silly game.

"You are not to do that again!" he said sternly. "With any girl... or boy for that matter! Until you are married, do you understand?"

"Yes father."

Anne was perplexed. Two women had covered for her lies in such a short span. Had she been so bad that she needed to be protected?

"Elizabeth made a suggestion that I think you might like... of course you do not have to do it if you do not want."

"What is it?" Anne had anticipated this moment. She had overheard some of the conversation and prayed what was said would come true.

"You may live with your Aunt Miranda in Barbados if you like."

"Yes!" Anne exclaimed as she hugged him. "Yes... I would like that very much. I have been dreaming of the day I could visit her."

Trevor calmed his daughter down and made her sit back.

"You only met your aunt when you were three, I doubt you remember her."

"Is she a fright?"

"No, but she is very stern and strict. I am afraid, a little like Miss Barton."

"But she is family!" Anne was so happy. "I would be so very happy to meet her." She rubbed her hands on her robe, nervous. "Do you think she will like me?"

"Of course she will dearest! She is my sister, and your aunt. How can anyone not adore you Anne?"

Anne beamed. She jumped up once again, hugged her father and then quickly walked to the door. "I have much to do father. I must start to pack."

"I will tell Miss Barton... she will be, unhappy."

"That makes me even happier!" Anne smiled as she ran out the door.

No matter what she told herself, Anne was still sorry to leave. London would no longer be called her home and she would have to say goodbye to her friends too. She had dutifully made the rounds with her father as the polite daughter, thanking each and every one for their friendship and love. Each promised to write one another and tell stories about how their lives were going. Some were secretly jealous, others were concerned for her safety. The West Indies had a reputation for danger and sickness. Anne brushed their individual worries aside.

She knew she would be fine.

Even Sarah's mother, Mrs. Winters, got a civil goodbye. The woman seemed perplexed that Anne's father would choose such a rough, difficult life over staying in their own country. Anne knew the other woman's concern was mostly for her own sake. How would Mrs. Winters be able to fuss over Anne to prove loyalty to their family?

Anne brushed off such nonsense. Mrs. Winter's daughter Sarah was most likely going to marry her brother—

Sarah?

Anne stood at the dock and watched her friend who had tears in her eyes. The girl had come all the way out here just to say goodbye.

"Anne..." Sarah said. "I know this is what you have always wanted but I am sorry to see you go."

Before Anne could respond, Sarah hugged her tight.

Anne inhaled deeply and lost herself in the embrace.

Sarah, her lifelong friend and impossible object of her longing, was the hardest goodbye of all.

As they released, Sarah tucked a loose strand of Anne's hair back. "I hope to see you again soon my friend."

"Perhaps at your wedding?"

"Perhaps—"

"I know Michael will be the one."

"I hope so— that way we may be sisters forever!"

Sarah held Anne's hands in hers.

"I would like that," Anne smiled, grateful to have known such a kind and caring friend.

When Anne finally got on board the ship, she let herself shed a small tear. No matter what she told herself, it was still hard to leave Sarah behind. Anne had wished she could stay with her friend if only to love her for a little while. But Anne knew better. Even though they shared a mutual kiss, her father would never allow such a relationship to take place... and Miss Barton would have been constantly taking away that happiness.

Anne laughed. Speaking of Miss Barton, the woman looked furious. She had been required to help Anne's belongings get to the dock safely.

Now that Anne was going to the West Indies, she was no longer in need of her governess.

She watched as her father talked to the nasty woman. He handed her a small purse, most likely her last pay, and she went on her way.

Happily, Anne reached out her hand and was helped on board by feminine hands. As she looked up, a pleasant surprise was there to greet her.

Captain Elizabeth Spencer was also to make the journey.

PART II

9

Captain Spencer found Anne had been ecstatic to see her on board. Elizabeth explained to the younger woman she was also to go to Barbados, to receive a ship of her own. What type of ship Anne eagerly asked? Elizabeth only knew that the ship would be a frigate, with a small crew and a single gun deck with no more than twenty four guns.

Elizabeth was lucky to even get that.

An admiral or two remarked that there were other lieutenants waiting to receive commissions but the decision makers who ruled in her favor could not discount Elizabeth's superior mathematical and navigation skills. One had joked he would rather come safely home with a woman in charge, than a man who bluffed his way to promotion and delivered them straight to Davy Jones' Locker.

Elizabeth admired the ship they were now sailing on, the HMS Latitude. It was a monster, a second rate ship of the line, with 90 guns and over 800 men, including dozens of officers.

Anne's father had received a well-deserved promotion.

The wind in the upper sails snapped back and forth as the hands on top lowered them. A small jolt bucked the ship forward. Elizabeth rode the movement without incident, her legs slightly open, a well timed balancing act she had learned over the years.

She watched from the quarterdeck as men scurried about. There were those few, lost and unsure what to do, yelled at by officers and others to snap to. Elizabeth shook her head as a man leaned over and emptied the contents of his stomach onto a midshipman's shoes. The twelve year old looked terrified. He himself was green in the gills, and would surely spend his first nights at sea slung over his hammock and puking his guts out into a bucket.

This was the first time she was to be on a ship with absolutely nothing to do. Elizabeth did not know if she would be able to handle the four thousand mile journey simply as a passenger. If she asked Trevor for a work assignment, he would probably tell her that his crew might take offense.

Thinking about it, she would not allow it either. Perhaps he would allow her to help with correspondences? Trevor hated paperwork. In fact, she had done a lot for him when she was a lieutenant under his command.

Elizabeth watched as Anne sprinted up the stairs to the quarterdeck. The young woman bounced on her feet, excited. Anne seemed comfortable in her skin, a beauty at seventeen. Elizabeth remembered her own first time on a ship-of-the-line, angry and afraid, still reeling over the circumstances that had brought her there. A fifteen year old girl who knew she would have to prove herself to be better, faster and stronger in mind if she were to succeed.

Elizabeth smiled as the young woman hurried over. "How are you my dear? Have you gotten settled?"

"Yes ma'am!" Anne said. Her eyes darted around the deck, trying to take in the flurry of activity all at once. "I can't believe how small my father's cabin is on a ship this size!"

"We have to accommodate over 800 men."

"I don't see how."

"We pile them next to each other like a cord of wood. And of course they rotate watch periods."

"How uncomfortable."

"There is no comfort on a ship-of-the-line," Elizabeth said as she rubbed her own hands together. The weather was slightly chilly. "And you do not have to call me ma'am, Elizabeth will do fine."

"Yes... Miss Elizabeth."

Elizabeth knew that Anne was proper and would not find herself calling an adult by her Christian first name. *Miss Elizabeth will be fine for now.*

A lieutenant called out to a seaman who was not moving fast enough. He quickly barked orders and was obviously trying to impress Elizabeth, even though she was not in charge. She cupped her hands to her mouth and breathed on them, watching the lieutenant threaten to have the cat-o-nines take a whack at the hand's back.

Elizabeth smirked and walked towards the side railing.

Anne quickly followed.

"Why is he yelling at that man like that?" Anne asked, curious. "Is he not moving fast enough?"

"One can never move fast enough on a Queen's ship my dear, though I am sure the reaction is due more to the fact I was watching than what the young man may or may not have done."

"Will they really whip him with the cat?"

"I doubt that." Elizabeth took a quick look at her. "You know what a cat-o-nines is?"

"I've heard my brother tell his friends."

"Yes, young Sutton. He is a good officer, like his father."

"I heard it is a most dreadful sight... that it can make a person retch just by watching." Anne rubbed her shoulders as if she were chilled just by the thought. "I asked father, but he said Michael was exaggerating."

Elizabeth remembered the first time she had seen a flogging, the brutality of punishment that was a necessity, since a few could undermine the safety of the many and cause a ship's disaster. She herself did not enjoy the task, but had recommended that a few sailors over the years receive the cat. One had died as a result. His death haunted her to this day.

"To flog a sailor is a terrible, yet necessary punishment that must occasionally be dealt," Elizabeth confessed.

"Is it as violent as Michael described?"

Elizabeth did not know if she should tell the young woman the truth, or follow the father's wishes and simply say no? She knew Trevor would never admit to his daughter that he simply abhorred the practice, and that he had passed out the first time he had seen the act at the age of twelve— that they both had argued over the years at the need for such a punishment— that he had told her that her crew would lose faith in her if her dealings with them were too heavy handed.

"Yes it is— but that is not something you will ever witness my dear... at least I hope not."

"Anne?" Captain Trevor Sutton said from behind. He joined them at the side rail. "Are you enjoying the sights?"

"Yes," Anne said. "Although London looks... dirtier from this view."

Elizabeth let out a low chuckle. She put her hands to her face and blew on them again. "Are you not cold Anne?"

"Not really..."

"We are rounding Wapping point soon," Trevor said to Elizabeth.

She took her cue. "Anne. You should go settle yourself in the cabin for a bit... your father has lots to do..."

"I understand... I will see you later Miss Elizabeth... father."

Anne quickly darted toward the steps and disappeared out of sight.

"Miss Elizabeth?" Trevor snickered.

"Don't you start."

A loud call from the coxswain gathered their attention for a moment. They were having a hard time unfurling another sail.

"How long 'till I break in this crew?" Trevor asked Elizabeth.

"How many pressed?"

"Over two hundred..."

"...goodness!" Elizabeth watched as another newbie scurried on the lower deck. He hauled a bunch of ropes, most hanging over his shoulder and obscuring his view. Quickly, he caught his balance before he tripped.

Another loud call, this time pointing at Wapping Point.

Anne had not gone down into the cabin. She stood in-between the shadows of the stairs and looked out. Her eyes widened at the display. There were iron cages, suspended by a ring of chain, enclosed inside each was a body, tarred and hung on public display. Crows sat on top and pecked at the corpses that were left to rot. The practice was intended to warn sailors of the consequences of taking up the act of piracy.

"She didn't need to see this," Trevor said.

"No one really needs to see this captain." Elizabeth shook her head and walked to the stairs. As she descended, she saw Anne, eyes still wide at the sight and horrified. The young woman quickly darted away into the cabin.

It did not take long for Anne to feel the effects of the ocean waves. They were only at sea for less than an hour when she began to feel unwell. First, her head started to hurt, followed by dizziness. She had lain down on the cot in her father's cabin, hoping to allow herself time to recover.

Now she was bent over, throwing up into a wooden bucket.

Anne felt as if she were going to die.

She pulled herself back onto the cot and shivered under her blanket. Her skin was now pale and clammy. She pulled the covering over her head. If only the motions of the ship would stop! — up and down, side to side — all around!

Anne felt like a cracker in a bowl of soup.

The door opened. She lowered the blanket and looked up.

Elizabeth sat next to her and held out her hand. "Here... eat this," she instructed.

Just the thought of food made Anne queasy.

"I can't—" Anne could not finish her sentence. She bent over and retched into the bucket once again. When she finished, her hands pulled the blanket up as she started to shake.

Elizabeth offered the item up once again. "You need to at least suck on it," she instructed.

"What is it?" Anne timidly asked.

"Ginger root."

"Oh..." Anne remembered her mother making ginger tea when she was sick. She took the piece and popped the root into her mouth. The taste was not at all unpleasant.

Anne closed her eyes. She then heard the sound of water in a bowl, hands wringing out a rag. A wet cloth was put on her forehead. The soft touch was a welcome feeling.

"Miss Elizabeth?" Anne asked.

"Hmm..."

"Have you ever put any men in those cages?"

"They are called gibbets... and no, I have not."

"My father?"

There was a slight pause. Anne didn't know if that was a bad idea to ask. *Do I really want to know?*

"Not directly," Elizabeth finally answered. "But, yes he has."

Anne gasped.

The older woman dipped the rag in the water once again and continued. "Your father apprehended a few men last year. He simply arrested them for piracy. It is the Admiralty that hanged them."

Elizabeth told her the history of the gibbet, and why the men were put on public display. "Please tell me your father has never taken you to a public execution?"

"No. And it is something I do not want to ever see!"

"Smart girl."

"I heard people dress up and cheer... acting like it's a carnival with animals on display for them?"

"The animals are the crowds themselves."

Anne did not press further on the subject. She knew her new friend seemed to abhor the practice.

"It is late Anne," Elizabeth said. "You should try to get some sleep."

"I doubt I will. But I will try." Anne rolled over on to her side and bent into the fetal position. The ginger root had begun to make her stomach feel a little better.

Anne did not know how long she had slept, but when she turned Elizabeth was sleeping in the lone chair, head bent against the wall, her hands holding a book. The candle in the room was almost spent. Anne sniffed the air. There was a faint smell of some other substance. On the small desk was a pipe, still smoldering slightly. Anne found it odd that the smell was not one of tobacco, but a sweet floral scent.

Anne turned her body back and went to sleep.

10

———————

On the third night, Anne finally felt well enough to eat. She was happy to put on one of her finer dresses and stop wearing shifts all day long. Taking a bath was somewhat of a challenge since fresh water was not available. Her hair felt coarse after washing it in salt water; she had a hard time trying to pull the comb through it. Anne shrugged her shoulders and was determined to make the best of the situation.

As Anne entered the dining cabin, she was surprised to see the room was a favorable size. The table was large, fancily decorated with plates for a seating of eight. She thought it odd that two large cannons were in the room, seated at opposite sides with the muzzle of the guns positioned near two open ports.

The room was slightly stuffy. There was a small breeze coming in from the openings offering some relief. Anne wiped her brow with her handkerchief. She smiled at the officers around the table, including her father and Elizabeth.

"Anne." Trevor got up, as did the rest of the table. He walked over to her and led her to her chair. She sat down and allowed him to push her in. All around her the table's occupants bowed and introduced themselves.

There were two lieutenants, a dark haired, skinny man with sunken eyes and a full face and a plump man with red hair, short arms and a large belly. His uniform did not even fit properly. The captain of the marine guards sat to his right, followed by two midshipmen, ages fourteen and twelve. Anne nodded to each and every one and thanked them for their introductions.

Anne was famished.

Not eating for almost three days had made her act like she had been starved. She chuckled to herself what the youngest midshipman might think, devouring her food so quickly but always in a lady-like manner. As she drank some wine, he finally got the courage to speak up.

"Have you ever been on a ship before Miss Sutton?" His name was Higgins, a Mr. Higgins at his young age.

"No... this is the first time." Anne put down her crystal glass. "I did not expect such fine dining though."

"Beats millers, that is for sure!" The dark haired lieutenant barked. He immediately regretted his remarks when Captain Sutton glared at him. "I mean..."

"Millers?" Anne asked, her curious eyes suddenly aware this seemed to be a topic she should not be part of. "What are they?"

"Rats," Elizabeth spoke up.

"Rats?— you eat them?"

"Only when desperate."

There was uncomfortable laughter around the table. She caught her father giving Elizabeth a quick glance then laugh under his breath. Anne stared at her new friend, who had returned to her dessert.

"You are joking with me," Anne chuckled.

None of the men would answer her. Elizabeth simply smiled for a brief second, confirming Anne's suspicions that it might be a joke.

Captain Sutton broke the tension. He patiently asked each of the officers some questions pertinent to the crew's needs. Anne listened intently. She found out that a good majority of the crew needed to be trained on the guns, and that tomorrow there would be a drill at first light.

As the conversations became more technical, Anne found herself tired.

Her body was still weak from her ordeal. She took a large gulp of water, afraid she might be dehydrated. When the conversation turned to Elizabeth's promotion, Anne perked up.

"How many female officers are in the Royal Navy?" Anne asked. She was surprised she had never thought of asking the question before.

"I know of one midshipman on the HMS Unity," Trevor said to his daughter. "I am not sure about any lieutenants."

"Barkley..." The red haired officer piped up, "HMS Barkley has a lieutenant... well, had a lieutenant. I think she left to get married."

"I think it would be fun to serve with a girl... err... I mean lady..." The older midshipman squeaked. His voice was changing at a slower pace than perhaps he hoped.

"And why is that Mr. Canty?" Elizabeth asked furrowing her brows.

"I..." The boy hesitated, slightly nervous. "Well, I know that my mother runs our household, dealing with many different things every day. She joked that my father would never be able to juggle tasks like she!"

Elizabeth smirked at him. "You sir— are a smart young man."

Mr. Canty puffed out his chest and reached for the port decanter happy to pour himself another drink. He offered some to Anne but she politely declined. When he smiled back at Elizabeth, Anne had a feeling the young man might be smitten.

"Not everyone wants that life." Elizabeth caught Trevor's eye. He turned his head and drank from his wine goblet. "Some of us are destined for other things."

"Great things I hope!" Mr. Canty blurted out then quickly patted his napkin to his lips. He had been having a go at the wine a little too enthusiastically this night.

"Yes," Trevor chuckled and lifted his goblet. "To great things!"

All got to their feet and toasted to the new female captain.

"Sir?" The captain of the marines said in a low tone. "Before we depart for the evening I need to ask you some questions about... the Bruja del Fuego?"

"That means fire witch, right?" Mr. Higgins interjected. "I've been learning Spanish."

Trevor nodded his head. He walked over to his daughter and held out his hand. "Best you be going to bed now Anne."

"Of course." Anne got up and politely thanked them all for a wonderful evening. As she exited, the door was swiftly closed behind. She suspected that something serious was being discussed behind those wooden panels, something not for her ears.

ANOTHER BALMY NIGHT AT SEA; there were no clouds in the sky. The full moon shone brightly on the wooden deck. Anne knelt down and touched the smoothed surface. The wood had been holystoned earlier that morning. She had watched as men, on their hands and knees, moved the stones back and forth, tired, with arms sore and necks bent as if they were praying for forgiveness from torture.

The wood had to be constantly maintained, for on a ship everything was alive with salt water. Ship sides had to be scrubbed of barnacles and freed of ship worm. Always there was a constant battle against the sea and the creatures in it. It was a never ending struggle against the elements.

Anne stood up.

When she turned, something strange caught her eye. Anne walked forward slightly then gasped loudly and stopped dead.

Something or someone was standing, hidden in the shadows.

The silhouette looked like a woman, with ample bosom and wearing what appeared to be a long dress. The outline of hair was unlike anything Anne had ever seen before. The shape looked like draping ropes instead of strands of hair.

Anne could see nothing but this lone silhouette in the darkness.

Frightened, Anne backed away. A pair of hands touched her from behind. Startled, Anne yelped and fell into them.

"Anne?" Elizabeth held the girl's weight. "What is wrong?"

Anne whipped her head around, focused on her rescuer, then snapped back towards the shadows.

Nothing was there!

Did I really see anything?

"Sorry," Anne let out a small gulp as she faced Elizabeth. She quickly straightened out her dress. "I thought I saw something."

"What?"

"A figure of a woman?"

Elizabeth shook her head, confused. Eyebrows raised, Elizabeth crossed her arms and leaned inward. "There are no other women on this ship... besides us."

Anne was sure she had seen something but if she pressed the point?

Miss Elizabeth will think me mad!

Instead of pushing further, Anne chose to let the matter drop. Her father might send her back to England and she could take up residence in the madhouse where her mother had mostly lived these last few years.

Anne dipped her head low. *My mother...*

Just the thought of her mother made Anne's eyes well up with tears.

"Are you all right?" Elizabeth asked, concerned. She gently put her hand on Anne's shoulder.

Anne looked up. "I'll be fine."

Elizabeth rubbed the younger one's shoulder, trying to give some comfort. She looked Anne in the eyes and smiled.

Anne returned the gesture. She felt comfortable around her new friend. She was thankful to have her close tonight.

Elizabeth pulled a small, velvet pouch out of her own coat pocket. She opened the drawstring and dipped the pouch over Anne's right hand. Out fell the triangular blueish tinted crystal that had caused so much pain. "Do you still want to dispose of this?"

Anne inhaled sharply. She was desperate to get her tears under control. She nodded her head and held her breath for a long moment. Finally, she found her voice.

"Yes. I do," Anne nodded.

Anne touched the surface of the crystal. She rolled it around in her hand and began to remember that night.

The night my mother saw something in this.

Anne closed her palm and put it in front of her heart. *Mother seemed mesmerized. Kept saying that she could see it?*

What did she see? Anne desperately wanted to know.

Anne still did not understand how her mother had gotten hold of the prism device in the first place. *I left it in my room, under the bed. Mother could barely walk, let alone be lucid enough to search for it.*

Unless, it called to her in some way?

"May I ask why you are so adamant about getting rid of this crystal?" Elizabeth asked. "It is very pretty."

Anne did not want to explain why she was doing this. She did not want to relive the pain anymore. But somehow, Anne knew that she should tell Elizabeth something.

"It killed my mother." Anne quickly realized her explanation was blunt, but it was the truth. She had no idea what Elizabeth might be thinking.

She too might think me crazy.

I wonder what my father has told her?

Elizabeth walked to the rail and watched as the ship tore through the water. "What has your father told you of the sea?"

"What do you mean?" Anne slightly shrugged, confused. She did not understand the question.

Elizabeth motioned for younger woman to join her. Anne walked over and peered over the railing. She was entranced by the motion of the water racing away as the ship cut through it. The foam that spat out was faintly luminous.

"That's odd." Elizabeth creased her brow and forgot her questions.

"It's glowing!" Anne exclaimed.

"Yes…"

"But why is that odd?"

"The moon is so bright. You cannot normally see phosphorescence this clearly on moonlit nights."

"So it is glowing?"

"That is an observation one might say."

"Maybe it is alive?"

"Who knows." Elizabeth turned back and smiled. She did not want to tell Anne that sailors were superstitious of so many things, even something as innocent as water that seemed alive could be perceived as danger ahead. Elizabeth had never believed such notions. She put her hands on Anne's shoulders and turned her away from the water. "Your father told me what happened that night on the roof."

"My mother?" Anne felt suddenly mortified. She looked down and stared at the crystal. "I think this did kill my mother."

"Anne— your mother was ill. You did not know what was in her mind any more than the doctors did."

"—But?"

"Listen to me," Elizabeth was forceful, but gentle. She folded Anne's fingertips over the crystal. "This did not kill your mother. This is nothing more than an object. When we go to sea we leave the past behind. We take the wind in our sails and we move forward." Elizabeth paused for a moment. "Do you understand what I am saying Anne?"

Anne stared at her hand.

What lay in her palm was nothing more than a symbol.

A symbol of the past.

"Yes... I do," Anne nodded. She leaned on the railing and tossed the crystal into the sea. The object made a small splash, but the noise could not be heard for the wind that whipped the sails drowned the sound out.

The wind that was now her future.

"I love you mother," Anne whispered as she began to cry.

Elizabeth took her in her arms and held her while she sobbed. "You will always have her in your heart dear girl."

ANNE AWOKE to a loud roar of thunder that rattled her head and shook her cot. She grabbed her chest and felt her heart pound. Just as she exhaled from fright, the thunder happened again— a continuous pounding of noise that could not have come from a storm alone!

There was a quick knock, then the door suddenly swung open.

Elizabeth swiftly entered. "Sorry to burst in..." She closed her eyes for a brief moment as another roar shook their surroundings. "I had not realized they would be running the guns with live ammunition today. Are you all right?"

"Running the guns? Do you mean?" Anne jumped when the thunder shook the room again. "Cannons?"

"Yes— cannons."

"I want to see!" Anne exclaimed. She jumped up and quickly began to dress. Elizabeth laughed as she closed the door to allow the young woman some privacy.

When she bolted on deck, Anne could barely contain her excitement. Her father glanced at her, gave her a quick nod, then turned back to his duties. Elizabeth slowly made her way up the stairs and stood behind them both.

A small boy stood near her father, his drum almost as big as he. He tapped out small rat-a-tat-tats on the drum head. There was slight confusion as some men, unsure of where or what they were doing, were being yelled at or physically pushed into position.

There were five men per cannon.

Anne watched as they took turns carrying out the necessary duties. All around the men's feet, sand had been laid out onto the deck to prevent slipping. Water from the head pumps spat out a constant stream with the intention of preventing loose gunpowder from exploding. A large tampion was dipped in an adjacent bucket of water and rammed into the bore of the gun. Once removed, another sailor placed a cartridge into the muzzle. Next a round shot was placed, followed by a wad used as a bed for the cannonball.

More instructions were yelled out.

Point the gun!—

Prime the gun!—

Make ready!—

When a linstock with a slow match was lowered, it 'touched off'.

Fire!

And then the cannons let loose and expelled their contents with such force that the whole body recoiled. Anyone caught in that wild movement would surely be killed.

Over and over they practiced, each time getting a little faster.

The running of the guns proved to be the only highlight of Anne's days. Every morning the crew would drill, most of the time without live ammunition. The ship could not afford to spend powder and shot. Anne watched as the crews would wet the deck every morning, lay sand over it to prevent slipping, run the guns and then clean up everything by late morning.

The constant, never ending work seemed— *boring.*

As the weeks went by, Anne did the best she could to keep her mind occupied. She had spent many hours playing cards with Elizabeth. Her friend was well skilled, and taught her a thing or two to up the game. When Elizabeth told her not to share this information with her father, Anne had to chuckle. His daughter was learning to be *creative* with cards.

Anne had asked Elizabeth and her father about this Bruja del Fuego, but neither would tell her much. All Anne knew was that this Fire Witch had been harassing English ships for the last year. Her father would not tell her if he was to find this woman and stop her. Anne had an uneasy feeling that the Fire Witch was more dangerous than her father or Elizabeth made her out to be.

Finally, a few days out from Barbados, Anne had been leaning on the ship's rail and watched as the water crested up and down. Floating on top of the surface, long, thick masses of what appeared to be weeds caught her attention. They were unlike anything she had ever seen before.

"What is that?" Anne asked.

Elizabeth had been busy talking to the boatswain. The woman turned her attention. "Hmm?"

"That!" Anne pointed towards the long stretch of dark green fronds afloat. "What is that?"

"Gulfweed."

A weed? Anne thought the idea hilarious. *A weed of the sea?*

"How does a weed grow without soil?"

"Easily. The ocean is its soil."

Anne watched as Elizabeth instructed the boatswain to fetch a length of rope and bucket. He quickly found the items and tied the rope around the bucket's handle. Elizabeth then took the container and tossed it down the side of the ship. She skimmed the surface as not to overfill with water. When she was able to catch a good piece of weed, her arms swiftly pulled the prize up.

The weed smacked on the deck, its body intertwined in and around the rope and transport. Elizabeth picked up the flotsam. Her fingers rolled around what Anne thought might be berries.

"How odd." Anne observed the small bladders. "Must be how it floats?"

"I believe so."

Anne touched the sticky and rough surface. She felt the stem, the leaves what could be called a shrub where she came from.

"How does it eat?"

"I imagine the same way all plants do— the sun." Elizabeth pulled something off the weed with her fingers. "Ha... look..."

Anne took a moment to focus her eyes. She thought she was staring at another piece of the gulf weed. She widened her eyes, amazed when she realized what it was. "It's a fish?"

"Yes... they live in the gulf weed."

Anne was entranced by the creature. The body was perfectly camou-flaged to its environment. All over the fish, the skin resembled the weed it lived on. She gasped when the fish began to change colors, as it tried to camouflage to Elizabeth's hands.

"We should put this back in the water." Elizabeth put the fish back on the weed. She walked over to the railing and tossed the gulfweed back into the sea.

Anne scanned the horizon.

Maybe the ocean is not as barren as I thought?

Then what of the islands? Are they just as interesting?

Anne smiled happily. Soon she would be seeing the West Indies for the first time.

11

The rest of the time on the ship proved to be most forgettable. Her cabin was stuffy and unappealing. Anne chose to sit or walk the deck as much as she could. She would saunter around the quarterdeck, sometimes with Elizabeth, sometimes with her father. She quickly came to the realization that life on ship was boring unless you had a job to do.

Being a passenger was most uneventful.

The sailors were the ones who worked constantly. They were always busy reefing and stowing sails. When they weren't attending to mundane duties like swabbing the deck or grinding a holystone onto the wood, they spent their time drilling with canons. She wished she could light one. Unfortunately, attending to canons was very dangerous and she did not even bother to ask her father.

Many weeks after leaving London, the ship finally arrived in the port of Bridgetown on the island of Barbados. Her excitement quickly evaporated once she got a good look at the island.

There were no mountains as she had come to believe from books she had read, but on this island the terrain was covered with vast fields of bright green sugar cane. The buildings and houses were almost mirror-like as they reflected the sun off their white, coral surfaces. Dispersed between the structures were tall, sturdy trees with vast amounts of fruit hanging down.

As they sailed between other ships of the line, Anne's father pointed to a frigate careened at the end of the docks, resting on the sand. The keel was slightly tilted to the side and held up by large poles. The other side was held in place by heavy ropes and cables attached to palm trees and other braces.

"That is Captain Spencer's ship, the HMS Defiant," Trevor said. "Let us hope this Defiant is seaworthy."

Elizabeth walked in front of them and stared ahead at the monstrosity she had been given. "You have got to be kidding me—?"

"Well... it does not look that bad."

Elizabeth turned and scolded him. "The main mast is missing."

"Yes..."

"And there are multiple holes just on the side we can see; who knows what's on the other."

"They are patching them up," he tried not to laugh.

Anne enjoyed the friendly banter between them. She was happy to see her father smile again. So much tragedy had befallen them these past few weeks.

Elizabeth seemed to bring out the best in him.

As mother.

"Why did they give her such a bad ship father?" Anne asked.

"Because I am a woman," Elizabeth interjected. "And I am expected to fail."

"That does not seem fair. You are probably more capable than most men in the Royal Navy."

"You are a smart girl Anne... but a little naive."

"I am only saying..."

"I understand what you are saying. That is why we women have to prove them wrong." Elizabeth winked at her.

Anne smiled. Elizabeth was the only woman in her life that had told her, in so many words, you can strive for more than is expected of you.

The ship set anchor in the island's roadstead. Her father told her that the ship anchored here because there was not a space large enough near the docks to hold such a beast as his. The bay was also calm enough to avoid ocean rip currents.

"I am sorry to make you face Miranda without me," he said to Elizabeth.

"I've faced worse Trevor." Elizabeth put her arm on Anne's shoulder and guided her to the side rail. "I can handle your sister." This was the first time Anne had heard Elizabeth call her father by his first name. "I'll try not to strangle her 'till you get there."

"Is she that bad?" Anne interrupted with a look of worry on her face.

"No... Captain Spencer... she's..." Trevor sputtered trying not to express his true feelings. "...exaggerating."

Through the corner of her eye Anne saw Elizabeth smirk at him.

The coxswain had the pinnace prepared. Men then hoisted Anne's luggage and carefully placed the bags and trunks into the craft. When Anne saw how she was to be 'placed' into the pinnace, she widened her eyes, mortified.

Anne quickly looked at her friend, then at her father.

"Do I really have to get in that?" Anne whined.

When they both confirmed her fear, Anne sighed, then did as she was told.

She had been ready to dart over the side and crawl down like a seaman. Instead, she was mortified when they stuck her in a basket, large enough to hold her weight and maneuvered by strong hands.

Well, it wasn't exactly a basket— more like a large canvas bag with a wooden frame. She laughed when her feet hit the inside of the bouncing boat.

The coxswain carefully helped her out.

Anne sat down and watched as Elizabeth crawled down the side of the ship. Her friend would probably not be caught dead *taking a ride*, especially in front of the crew.

When they were safely in the pinnace, the coxswain gave orders to his men to row. As they did, Anne looked out at the many small fishing boats nearby. She was fascinated by the island men tossing nets in the water. This was the first time she had seen anyone with a darker skin tone.

"Are they... slaves?" Anne hesitantly asked.

"I am not sure," Elizabeth said with a frown. "Slavery does exist on this island."

Appalled at the thought, Anne turned quickly. "Surely not my aunt?"

Elizabeth shrugged. "I fear she may have started to replace her indentures since I was last here."

Anne sighed. "I didn't even think to ask my father about who tends to the plantation. I am not as worldly as I might try to pretend to be."

"He probably didn't even think to tell you." Elizabeth gently touched Anne's shoulder. "The world can be a cruel place Anne. But knowledge is key to traversing it."

Anne looked at her solemnly. "Why slaves then?"

"Indentures tend to fall into drunkenness and debauchery. Slaves are supposedly more easy to handle. But..." Elizabeth said, repulsed. "Beating people will make anyone submissive. It is a horrible thing."

Anne suddenly gasped when the closest boat pulled up a net. One of the fishermen opened the mesh and released the fish onto his deck and began to try and corral them. As she watched him carefully she thought about the little she knew regarding the slave practice. Words were written about the enslavement of men and women, and even children, but Anne had never paid much attention. When she caught the fisherman's eye, Anne quickly turned her head, sheepishly, wondering if her aunt indeed kept men like this.

When they arrived at the pier, Anne had a hard time maneuvering. Elizabeth climbed out and helped her. Anne looked around at the sights. The wharf was bustling with activity. Men were busy loading dray carts with large and small crates. Barrels marked sugar were being hoisted down into other boats.

Anne and Elizabeth walked towards a carriage that was waiting for them. As men loaded the back with her things, Anne took in a deep breath with more apprehension then she had expected.

Her new life had begun.

~

THE AIR FELT THICKER HERE. Anne could no longer feel a breeze. Her dress stuck to her skin with sweat. She had never felt heat such as this before.

Perhaps the heat is because of the stuffiness of this carriage?

"Why is it so hot?" Anne asked.

Elizabeth turned. She opened up the window next to her wider. "Come, sit here."

Anne quickly changed seats. There was now a slight breeze through the opening.

"We are in the tropics now," Elizabeth continued. "Suffused with an ungodly heat even Hades would detest."

"My father told me that it would be... warm is how he described it."

"Don't worry Anne, you will get used to the weather, after a time."

"Is there any relief?"

"Hot summer days give way to torrential downpours. There is a brief moment of... relief."

"Brief moment?"

"The rain adds to the weight of the air. That is why you are perspiring so much. The air is heavier here."

"Perhaps this is Dante's Inferno?" Anne teased.

"Some have compared the weather to Hell. I have never been myself so I cannot compare," Elizabeth chuckled, trying to give Anne a little boost. "But yes, the weather here can be wicked. But at least here you can breath better air, not like that stale air in London."

"Then I will count that as a blessing."

"As you should."

Anne looked out the windows at the sights. Her initial view of this island changed once they entered the town of Bridgeport. Women with skin the color of chocolate dressed all in white carried large baskets on their heads. Shacks built only of wood and palm fronds lined the sides of the streets. Other buildings with solid foundations of coral rocks were surrounded by a vast array of bright green flowering shrubs with the most vivid of colors.

Anne had never seen such beauty in nature before.

When they finally arrived at the plantation, the carriage passed under a great curved arch built of more coral rock. On the top was a large bell; on the sides of the bell was the name Rosewood carved into the surface.

Anne marveled at the rows of sugarcane being tended to by men. They chopped away with machetes and pulled large stalks. They then threw them to the side were a few women picked them up and carried them away. Then she realized... they were most likely slaves.

Anne swallowed hard, quick to realize she was to live on a plantation were people were owned like cattle. She turned to Elizabeth with questions in her eyes. The older woman just sighed, confirming Anne's suspicions.

The carriage pulled into a large, circular courtyard and stopped. Slowly, Anne got out of the coach and was truly impressed by the grand building.

This was nothing like she had ever seen in London.

The house had two stories, built of coral rock and wood painted white. Large shutters as wide as an entrance way were open on both floors.

A woman stepped out of the doorway. She fanned herself with a hand fan intricately painted with a scarlet bird. She had a polite smile on her round face but the edges of her mouth were tight. She descended only the first step of the stairs. The sun barely touched her shoulders, the overhang of the entry casting a deep shadow onto her face.

Anne stepped forward with Elizabeth by her side. They were not shielded from the harsh rays as was the proprietor of the plantation.

The woman sauntered down and stopped on the last step.

"My dear Anne. It is a pleasure to see you again as nearly a woman." She leaned downward and embraced her niece. "I am Miranda, your Aunt Miranda."

"Thank you Aunt Miranda," Anne said as they released. "And I you."

Anne took a moment to study her aunt. Miranda was tall, with barely any weight on her body. She had blue eyes with auburn hair. The strands had slight curls, though Anne did not know if that was natural or because of hairstyling. Miranda's nose was small and turned-up slightly, with a slight dent in the middle bridge.

Anne was pleasantly surprised how much her aunt resembled her father.

"I am sorry we had to meet under such dire circumstances," Miranda continued. She turned to Elizabeth then narrowed her eyes, staring down at the woman. She did not look happy to see her other guest.

"Ah... Elizabeth..." Miranda pursed her lips. "It has been a long time."

"Yes it has," Elizabeth said with a forced smile.

"Where is my brother?"

"Still with his ship... he will be here shortly."

Anne found the exchange— odd. She looked up at her aunt then at her friend. She realized her aunt had not stepped down from the last step. She loomed over Elizabeth like a parent to a child. Anne wondered if this show was to prove dominance in some way?

The awkward moment was interrupted as a young girl, no older than fourteen, stepped down with a tray of drinks.

Anne widened her eyes and marveled at the sight.

The girl had beautiful features. Her skin was the color of rich caramel, her cheekbones prominent with large brown eyes. Her hair was braided in the most intricate of patterns. She smiled at them and reached out the platter.

"A drink then?" Miranda waved her hand over the crystal glasses.

"Yes, please," Anne happily accepted. She was parched.

Quickly she drank the soft, orange liquid.

"Thank you," Elizabeth said as she accepted her own.

Anne drank so fast, she did not care if she looked unlady like.

"What is this?" She had never tasted something so sweet before. "This is delicious."

"It is a mango cocktail ma'am," The girl answered softly.

"Mango? What is a mango?"

"A fruit native to the island," Elizabeth said. "The drink is fermented with rum and sugar."

Anne pulled out a rind and examined it. The color was similar to a carrot. "Why is this in here?"

"For added taste ma'am," The girl answered.

"Am I supposed to eat this?"

"No," Miranda said. "It is a garnish."

"In a drink? How fascinating."

"What is your name?" Elizabeth asked the girl as she took another sip.

The girl hesitated then said softly, "My name is Zara."

"Did you make this Zara?"

"Yes madam."

"This is very good."

"Thank you madam," Zara answered. "It is a recipe I learned from my mother."

"Then I thank your mother for such a delectable experience."

Zara nodded as she backed up and handed the tray to another girl.

The sound of Anne's trunks being unloaded signaled Miranda.

"Zara will show you to your rooms," Miranda said. "The heat of the day is most intense in the afternoon. Perhaps you would like to rest for a spell and another drink?"

"Yes," Elizabeth said. "We need to remove ourselves from the sun."

"We should go inside. This heat is deadly... makes people..." Miranda glared at Elizabeth for a hard, cold moment, "...sick."

12

____

Anne's room was spacious. There was a large, four poster bed lined with mosquito netting. A heavy breeze blew through the tall, open shutters. Anne walked out onto the veranda and looked around. She could see her father's ship over the line of trees in the distance. The seamen on the decks looked so small from her vantage point. To the left, Elizabeth's new ship was on its side, careened and waiting for repairs.

"Would you like to freshen up ma'am?" Zara softly asked.

Anne turned and walked back into the room.

"Yes, I would like that."

In the corner, a fresh wash basin and station were laid out for her. Anne walked over, dipped her hands in and washed her face. The water was cool and a welcome relief to her skin. She then washed her hands, as Zara handed her a towel to dry them.

"Thank you ma'am," Zara said.

"Please..." Anne wanted to start off right, afraid to ask the question she really wanted to know. She did not know how slaves were to be treated, but she refused to treat this girl as any less than herself. "You do not have to call me ma'am."

"But I must. It is what you are. It is what I must do."

"Even if I ask you not to?"

"Mrs. Sutton-Langdon is the master of this house. I must do as she says."

"What if you only call me ma'am in her presence?"

"If that is what you want, I will do that."

"Please," Anne said. She found it odd that Zara never changed her expression. She seemed so serious.

Anne walked over to the full length screen. Zara had made a motion to help, but Anne had politely declined. She did not want to unclothe herself in front of the younger girl.

After Anne had dressed in a simple shift, fabric and design made with coolness in mind, she pushed the opening of the mosquito netting. Something brushed against her feet. She quickly looked down, then jumped backwards as she yelped.

The blue land crab ran across the floor and hid in the corner of the wash stand. The creature raised a claw in defense, ready to strike as beady eyes stared straight ahead.

"What is it doing in here?" Anne stammered, trying not to sound nervous.

"The crab goes where the crab goes." Zara picked up a small broom and shoed the crustacean outside. "Best to look where your feet land before stepping out of your bed."

"How strange?" Anne knelt on her knees and looked under the bed. There was nothing left to scare her. As she got up, she brushed her shift and laughed. "What other creatures shall I expect to visit me?"

"There are iguanas that roam the island."

"I've seen drawings... when may I see one?"

Zara raised an eyebrow. "You want to see one? On purpose?"

"Why would I not? I heard they are the most fascinating of creatures. Scaly skin like a snake, with rigid horns down their backs. It is like the return of dinosaurs I might imagine!"

Zara cracked a smile, the first time Anne had seen her do such a thing.

"The Englishwomen here are afraid of them. They shriek and yell to their servants to rid the house of those vile creatures."

Anne smiled. She was sure she had just succumbed to the *shrieking* many Englishwomen on the island suffered from. The crab was not something she feared, it just startled her. She would love to pick one up and study the creature.

"Many have explained to them that iguanas only eat vegetation and bugs," Zara continued. "Hence having one in your room is a good thing; they eat anything that crawls, including cockroaches."

Anne shivered for a moment.

Cockroaches I can do without!

She had seen one of those nasty creatures in the ship recently, and she thought she would die of fright. Her father laughed at her as he smashed his shoe on the bug, sending the gelatinous substance of innards all over the sole. Thinking about the scene made Anne shiver once again.

"Then I think I would like to find an iguana to take up residence with me," Anne suggested. "Perhaps as a pet?"

"Perhaps." Zara nodded her head as she headed for the door. "I will leave you to rest now."

As Zara exited, Anne checked near her feet once again before crawling into the cool sheets and disappearing into the lullaby of sleep.

ANNE WOKE up a few hours later. She was still tired. Despite the breeze in her room, the heat was intense. She felt drained of energy. Her muscles ached and she was once again parched.

Anne wondered if the heat had anything to do with this?

I've never felt so warm before.

She pulled back the netting and was about to put her feet on the floor when she quickly pulled them up. She had forgotten about the little guest that had visited earlier. Anne laid on her stomach and looked under the bed. When all was clear, her feet touched the floor.

Zara had laid out a dress on the settee. The style was what she was accustomed to, but the cloth was thinner. She picked the item up and felt the material. It was made of soft, breathable linen.

After she dressed, Anne made her way downstairs and was happy to see her father and Elizabeth talking. She greeted them then gave her father a hug.

"How are you getting along?" he asked.

Anne told him all about the crab in her room. She then spoke about the wondrous colors she had seen but that she could do without the heat.

Miranda walked by them and announced dinner was ready. The grand door opened, revealing a long, elegant table dressed as if royalty might be attending. Two candelabras lit up the room. They were of matching French design rich in swirls and curves.

"It's so pretty." Anne touched the linen table cloth. The center was lined with odd looking fruit. They consisted of tough leaves sprouted out on the top of a round, conifer shaped body.

"What are those?" Anne asked.

"Pineapple," her father said as he helped her into her chair. He turned and did the same for Elizabeth. When he turned to help his sister, she brushed him off and sat.

A portly man joined them. He sat himself at the other head of the table, facing his wife. Miranda scowled at him as he reached for his glass and almost knocked the crystal over. When he reached for a bottle of port, Miranda snapped to a servant to pour the liquid for him instead.

Anne watched the interaction closely.

Aunt Miranda seems to despise this man.

As Randal swallowed the contents of his glass in one large gulp, Anne stared at him.

Randal was large, at least six feet tall with a bulky frame. His face was long and plump, like his stomach. Randal's hair was unkempt and completely grey. Anne wondered if he had been handsome at one time, or always as unsightly as this?

"How long has it been Trevor?" Randal slurred as he lifted his glass for more port.

Anne cocked an eyebrow. *He's already drunk? Even before dinner?*

"Three years," Trevor answered.

"Three years?"

"We have been off in the East Indies."

"Yes, you and... Elizabeth." Randal gulped his port as quickly as an already intoxicated man could. "How cozy for you two."

"Randal— " Miranda interrupted.

Her husband scowled then turned his eye towards Anne. When he smiled at her, Anne recoiled. Something about the way he looked at her made Anne feel uneasy. She flinched slightly as her hands touched each other and pressed hard.

"And you must be Anne?" Randal asked. His lip turned upwards in a slight smirk.

"Yes sir," Anne answered.

"You look just like your mother."

Anne said nothing. She quickly diverted her eyes. She didn't mind the comparison but the thought made her sad. Her hand reached for the ring on her necklace. The jewelry offered her some comfort.

She really did miss her mother.

The arrival of plates of food broke the tension. Randal forgot his wandering and reached towards a plate before it was even put on the table. As he sucked on the piece of meat, Miranda rolled her eyes and drank.

Anne was amazed at the dishes. There were varied meats, fish and lobster. The baskets held sweet breads and other rolls. Various puddings and fruit were also offered. She was excited to try everything.

"This is more than enough food Miranda," Trevor said. "While I am thankful, why did you make so much?"

"Me?" she laughed.

"You know what I mean."

"Hard be it that I starve my brother and guests when I have not seen you in so long." Miranda put down her crystal glass. "Besides, they starve you on those ships... look at Elizabeth. Poor thing needs to put on a few pounds."

"I do just fine Miranda." Elizabeth raised her head then forced a smile.

Anne could sense her friend did not look happy to be called out. "But I thank you for inviting me to your table."

"Like I had a choice," Miranda sneered as she picked up her glass and started to drink again.

This confused Anne even more. She quickly glanced at her aunt then at her father. Anne wondered why the blatant display of animosity?

Do I dare even ask Miss Elizabeth what this is all about?

"I don't know how others on this island can eat only salt pork imported from home." Miranda took a quick sip. "I mean, I do have it made when I entertain, but I have converted a number of friends to try the bounty of this grand island."

"She acts like the island is hers," Randal laughed.

Miranda glared at him, shutting him up with one look.

The rest of the dinner continued with awkward conversation. Anne realized her aunt was a braggart and loved to talk about herself. Uncle Randal was a drunk, and both her father and Elizabeth were uncomfortably silent.

"So, Elizabeth?" Miranda said to the other woman. She dipped her spoon in the pudding. "You have a ship now?"

Elizabeth took a moment to finish her bite then wiped her mouth. "Yes. A frigate."

"The navy trusts you with that?"

"Of course they trust her Miranda," Trevor interjected. "She is a very good officer and seaman. It was about time they gave her a command."

"So how much did that cost you dear?" Miranda asked.

Elizabeth fidgeted in her seat for a second, uncomfortable. She put down her napkin and softly answered. "A considerable sum."

Anne glanced at her father then her friend. She did not understand why money was suddenly brought up.

Miranda continued to pry. "You could not afford a bigger ship?"

"They do not base promotions on ships." Elizabeth pursed her lips. "Just commissions."

"So, what you are telling me is you took space away from a more deserving officer?"

"Miranda?" Trevor scowled at his sister. "You have no right to—"

"No, Trevor..." Elizabeth put her hand up and cut him off. Now on the defensive, she put down her fork and leaned forward. "There are many officers in the Royal Navy who have received their rank based on family names or whom they know. I am no less qualified simply because I had to purchase my command. I had no other means of patronism. You should be grateful that there are people like me willing to risk their lives so that you may prosper at your plantations and gorge yourself on grand meals."

Miranda glared at her. She lifted her glass and sipped her port softly.

Elizabeth put her dinner napkin back onto her lap. When she reached for her own glass of port, she suddenly stopped. She looked down and saw a large black snake crawling across her dinner napkin. She jumped up quickly and pushed back her chair. Her abrupt movement startled the table.

As they all stared at her in bewilderment, Elizabeth glanced down for the snake.

The beast was gone.

"What's the matter dear?" Miranda said in a cool tone. "My food not to your liking?"

Trevor looked at his fellow officer. "Elizabeth? What is wrong?"

"Nothing," Elizabeth lied. "I'm just tired. I will excuse myself now."

"Pity," Miranda smirked.

Elizabeth put down her napkin and glared at Miranda before walking out. Trevor also excused himself for a moment and went to see if she was all right.

"Commoners," Miranda said as she took another sip of port. "They may pretend to have class, but really... it's not in their blood."

Anne looked at her aunt. She did not know what to say. Anne focused on her desert and silently began to eat.

❧

Elizabeth had a hard time trying to convince Trevor she was all right. He finally accepted her explanations and returned to the dinner with his daughter and sister.

But the truth was, Elizabeth was not all right. Her head was spinning from the heat and her stomach was in knots. She insisted to Anne that the girl drink as much water as she could stand. Of course, Elizabeth had made the mistake of drinking too much mango punch herself.

Now she was paying the price.

As she stood in the hall, trying to shake off her sudden bout of dizziness, she tried to contemplate if she had actually seen a snake on her lap.

Is Miranda dabbling in dark magic now?

Elizabeth always knew the other woman had… gifts. Elizabeth had seen things in that house when she was a servant to her. There were many times Elizabeth had witnessed events out of the ordinary— events that most normal people would run from!

But, Miranda had fascinated her.

Elizabeth was only eight when she and her mother came to work for the Suttons. A turn of misfortune had turned Elizabeth's status in life from wealth to destitution with one storm.

Elizabeth inhaled deeply then sighed loudly.

Soft sounds of whispering peaked her attention. She followed the noise into a large room. Covered on the walls were many portraits of men and women throughout the ages. Elizabeth recognized some of them immediately. These were some of the same portraits that lined another room back at the Sutton mansion. These were the same paintings she swore would sometimes whisper to her when she was not looking.

They are doing it again.

Elizabeth walked over to a familiar painting. The woman in the portrait was alive over 200 years ago. There was no smile as was the custom when sitting for a portrait. On her neck a thin, silver chain hung. At the end was a pendant with a purple, amethyst stone. Elizabeth remembered the older matriarch of the family, Trevor and Miranda's mother. *She also wore that same stone on her neck.*

Miranda wears the gemstone now. She finally inherited her mother's stone.

Elizabeth looked around. *As she inherited all these paintings.*

Elizabeth felt for her own chain. Her fingers found a small pendant, round with circular carvings. In the center, a small turquoise stone that her mother had given her.

This was the last thing my mother gave to me when my father was alive, and we still had money, Elizabeth remembered fondly.

The gold chain had been replaced with cheap silver years ago, sold when Elizabeth was at her lowest point. But no matter how desperate she had become in the past, Elizabeth refused to ever sell the pendant.

And still that woman mocks me.

To hell with Miranda, Elizabeth thought. She pushed a strand of hair out of her eye. *Miranda has no idea what it was like to have everything as a child and then lose all!*

If I had to buy my commission then so be it!

Something caught her attention through the corner of her eye. A full length mirror stood near the corner. Elizabeth walked over and looked at herself. She was proud to finally have her own ship. Her uniform looked good on her. She spent extra on having the tailor fit her form. The tailor was not used to fitting a woman for a Royal Navy uniform.

As Elizabeth stared into the mirror, she started to feel mesmerized, not by her appearance, but by a feeling of dread.

Something felt off.

The mirror was making her feel strange, as if her inner feelings of doubt wanted to creep to the surface and make her fall to her knees. She knew this was not a normal feeling for her. Elizabeth had felt doubt before but she felt as if the mirror were drawing it to the surface so as to pull it from her and draw her feeling into itself.

Elizabeth stepped away from the mirror and exited the room quickly.

Something is wrong with this place.

UNDER A FULL MOON, Anne stood on the patio in her bare feet. The night was beautiful here. The island air was still humid but there was a slight breeze that blew through her hair. Never once could she imagine walking barefoot outside like this in London. The weather was always cold and damp and even on a summer night the air was stale.

Not here.

Not in *paradise* as she had come to believe this place to be.

There were so many intriguing smells that permeated the air as she took in a deep breath. The trees were alive with blossoms and fruit. Tomorrow she would walk in the gardens and taste some. Zara had reluctantly agreed to take her around the grounds.

Anne had a feeling the girl resented her.

Of course she resents you. Anne sighed. *You are free and she is not.*

A light from the distance caught her attention. Anne scooted into a corner as she held her nightdress tightly around her. Perhaps being out here alone wasn't the smartest of ideas. Her anxiety subsided when she saw Elizabeth come out of the shadows dressed in her own nightdress and robe. Her friend held a candle close as she looked around.

Anne didn't know if she should announce herself. She did not know if Elizabeth would chastise her for being out by herself. *But this is supposed to be my home now.*

I should be allowed to wander and explore.

Anne watched as Elizabeth stepped into her father's bedroom from a side door. Anne was not sure what she was seeing. A bad feeling hit her stomach as she rushed to their room and peered through the shutter, careful not to be discovered. She watched as Elizabeth bent over and touched her father's shoulder. He had not been asleep. He sat up and moved to the side so that Elizabeth could sit next to him.

The room was very dark. Anne could barely see, only hear.

"Are you feeling better?" Trevor asked as he rubbed Elizabeth's shoulder.

"Slightly," Elizabeth answered. "I think the heat made me sick."

"You haven't been in the West Indies in a while."

"Yes," Elizabeth agreed. She was quiet for a moment.

"What is the matter? Something is bothering you."

"I... I do not think leaving Anne here is wise," Elizabeth finally confessed.

"Why not?"

"I'm not sure... something is wrong with this place... with your sister."

"You've never gotten along with my sister and you've been going at it since you were children."

"No, there's something different about her. I do not think Anne is safe here."

When he brushed her shoulder again, Elizabeth stood up.

"I'm telling you there is something— off. I feel as if someone were watching us since we got here... watching me..."

Elizabeth turned and glanced at the window. Anne quickly stepped to the side. Anne took in a deep breath, frightened she had been caught.

"The mirrors..." Elizabeth said as she turned and looked back at him.

"The mirrors?" Trevor snickered. "You are being paranoid."

"Trevor? You haven't seen your sister in three years!" Elizabeth crossed her arms, annoyed. "Can't you feel something is wrong?"

She walked to the corner mirror. Her hand touched the glass. Her fingertips lingered for a moment before leaving her print on the surface. Anne felt guilty watching such a strong woman in her own moment of doubt.

Miss Elizabeth seems scared.

"You know your sister has always been *special*," Elizabeth continued.

"Nonsense."

"Your sister would take over this damn island if she could!"

"My sister doesn't have that kind of power. Besides, she's unhappy. That's what's wrong. You would be too if you were married to that drunkard." Trevor patted the bed for her to come sit again. "She's trying to hide her sadness under a mask, nothing more."

"So, it's okay then if I'm unhappy?" Elizabeth sat next to him as Trevor leaned in and softly kissed her on the lips.

Anne felt a sudden pain hit her deep in the stomach. She wanted to scream, wanted them to know she was there!

Anne could not believe what she was seeing!

Elizabeth pulled back from him. "Is it possible that Anne has inherited your family's— affliction?"

Affliction? Anne gasped quietly.

What is she talking about?

Anne was already having a hard time breathing! *What on earth is this woman implying?* Anne leaned in closer to hear.

"I have never seen it in her." Trevor stroked a stray hair from Elizabeth's eyes. "It sometimes will skip a generation. At least that is what I was told. We may never have passed it down. Maybe that is why Lara went mad so soon?"

Anne lost her breath.

She could not even feel her legs as she tried to comprehend what was just said.

About me?

About my mother?

She watched in added horror as Elizabeth took off her nightdress and slipped in bed with her father.

13

———

Traitor!

Whore!

That was all Anne could think about after what she just witnessed!

Anne willed her legs to move but they would not budge. She closed her eyes for a brief moment and wanted to forget what she had just seen.

When her legs finally decided to cooperate, she turned and ran. As she bolted around the corner towards her room, her body slammed into a larger mass. A small candle was lifted up, revealing her Uncle Randal.

"What are you doing out here so late Anne?" Randal asked.

His eyes focused in on her. She turned her head quickly to avoid his gaze. "I just wanted to see the port under the moonlight," Anne said nervously. "I'm going to turn in now."

As Anne tried to walk by, he blocked her way and grabbed her arm. "Nonsense girl. I'd like to see the port myself. Come join me."

Anne did not want to go anywhere with him, especially in the direction he was dragging her. "No— I do not want to go that way."

"Hmm..." Randal stood in front of her and smirked. "You do not want your father to know you are out so late at night by yourself?"

"Yes sir."

"Well, you are with me but I will oblige your wishes." He led her to the edge of the veranda. "Let us stand over here."

Anne followed him. She looked towards the beauty of her father's ship under the moonlight.

"It is very beautiful out here," Randal said.

"Yes." Anne did not want to add to their conversation. She just wanted to go to bed.

"You are very beautiful. You look just like your mother."

"Yes, you told me that at dinner." Anne folded her arms and tried to cover herself. She knew he was trying to look down her nightdress. Under the moonlight, the fabric was slightly transparent. She silently cursed herself for being caught in this situation.

Randal touched her face. She pulled back and stared straight ahead at the ship. *Maybe if I ignore him he will leave me and go? If I scream, my father will come out and save me but father will also have to face the fact I know of his betrayal!*

Miss Elizabeth too!

Would they be able to face her knowing what they had done?

"How old are you now?" her uncle asked as he touched her face again and forced it towards him.

"Eighteen," Anne answered nervously. "I mean... almost eighteen." She turned her head away and silently willed her father to hear her thoughts. She wanted to run in there, regardless of what sins they would all have to face later.

"You don't want to disturb him now," Randal chuckled. "He is busy."

"How do you know that?" Anne snapped at him.

"Do you know what is going on in there right now?"

"Yes."

"Are you now curious?"

"I know what my father and Captain Spencer are doing," Anne bit. "I am no longer a child."

"That I can see," he said as he tried to touch her face again, but she pulled away. "Are you still... a child my dear?"

Anne said nothing.

"They have been having an affair for as long as I can remember."

"What?" Anne needed to get away, from both situations— now! "I will have to excuse myself for the night uncle. I must see my father off early in the morning."

As she tried to walk off, he grabbed her arm one last time. "If you need me for anything. I'm always here."

Anne pulled away from him and stormed off, unaware that he was heading towards the window to observe for himself this night's transgressions.

ANNE SPOKE LITTLE DURING BREAKFAST. She lied and said she was tired from all the excitement the day before but the truth was she was still angry about what she had seen last night. She had not been able to fall asleep. All she could think about was how Elizabeth and her father betrayed her mother's memory.

How long have they been having an affair?

My drunken uncle had said forever!

The carriage waited for the departing parties. They stood in the courtyard of the grand plantation that was now Anne's home. Both her father and Elizabeth were to attend to their ships. She knew Elizabeth did not want to stay in Miranda's house, preferring to take up residence in a hotel while her ship was being fixed. She had to be there to watch the repairs and make sure everything was taken care of. According to Anne's father, there were too many people eager to cut corners and make a few extra shillings by cheating the Royal Navy.

Anne thought it was hypocritical of them to talk about cheating so nonchalantly, when they were both guilty of their own crime.

"I love you my dear," her father said as he held her tightly in his arms as the time had come to say goodbye.

"I love you too father," Anne said, something she really meant even if she was angry at him. The sad fact was, she needed to tell him that. His job was dangerous and there was always a chance he would not come back. She swallowed her tears as they separated.

Trevor reached to his daughter. He wrapped his hand around her shoulder as they walked to the carriage. Elizabeth stood there and waited.

Anne had already said a short goodbye to the woman but she could no longer hold her tongue.

I have to know!

These were dangerous jobs that her father and Elizabeth undertook. As horrible as the thought was— *they might never come back from them.*

"Father? May I speak to Miss Elizabeth... alone."

"Of course dear," her father answered. He looked towards his fellow officer, eyebrow cocked, most likely wondering what the conversation could be about. The other woman only smiled.

"I will only be a moment," Elizabeth said to him.

Elizabeth followed Anne to the corner of the courtyard. Elizabeth could not help but notice prying eyes that stared their way. The young servant girl Zara stood uncomfortably close to Miranda. They eyed Elizabeth as if they knew what was about to be spoken. Elizabeth unconsciously touched the side of her head, as if old wounds were beginning to creep up. She brushed aside the thoughts. She truly had become paranoid in this house and could not wait to leave. She hoped Anne would be all right.

When they were finally out of sight, Anne whipped around. She crossed her arms and took on a whole new posture.

"Are you my father's mistress?" Anne accused.

Elizabeth widened her eyes, shocked at the comment. "Beg pardon?"

"Are you my father's mistress?" Anne accused once again.

"Anne? Why are you asking me this?"

"Because I saw you last night."

Elizabeth leaned back on her left leg and folded her arms. She held herself tight as she tried not to show weakness. Her young friend had accused her of something serious. "What exactly did you think you saw dear girl?"

"You sneaked into his room, stripped off your nightdress and crawled into bed with him."

Elizabeth turned her head and glanced at the bushes. The blooms caught her attention. She did not want to be having this conversation with a seventeen year old girl. "I really don't like that word."

"What are you then?"

Elizabeth looked directly at her. "A companion?"

"Who just happens to have carnal relations with my father?" When her friend did not respond, Anne got angrier. "I thought my mother was your friend!"

"She is—" Elizabeth said defensively, then softened her tone. "She was... but I never fell out of love with your father, nor him with me." Elizabeth felt she needed to explain. "You have to understand, the sea can be a very lonely place and when you are gone for years it can..."

Elizabeth realized the words were falling on deaf ears. "Perhaps this is not the best time to talk about this." She put on her hat. "As you know your father is leaving today but I will still be in port for a few weeks retrofitting my ship. If you want to come talk to me, about— well, I will still be here."

Anne said nothing.

"It was nice to make your acquaintance Miss Sutton," Elizabeth said with a smile. "You are a very bright, vibrant young lady who deserves the very best. Never let anyone take that from you."

Anne still said nothing. Elizabeth noticed the girl chose the icy demeanor she had learned from Miss Barton.

"I will be off then— good day," Elizabeth finally said.

When they walked back into the center courtyard, Anne ran up the steps and stood next to her aunt. Elizabeth turned away once she saw Miranda's hand on Anne's shoulder.

Elizabeth felt a brush of fear creep up her spine as Miranda smiled at her. Elizabeth nodded to her young friend once more then got into the carriage.

TREVOR WATCHED Elizabeth as she stared out the window. Her eyes were focused on the buildings and sugar cane fields that sailed by. She seemed lost in thought. He knew that leaving Anne would affect them all. Elizabeth and Anne had bonded over the long trip and now the separation was taking a toll.

"Are you all right?" Trevor asked as he touched her hand.

Elizabeth turned her head and smiled.

"I'm fine," she lied.

"Anne is better off here," he rubbed her hand gently. "She needs to be with family."

"Yes, I guess you are right."

"She's strong... like her mother."

"She is a remarkable young woman. She reminds me of—"

"You?"

Elizabeth smiled. "Yes."

"She likes you."

"And I her. I'm glad I got to know her— at least a little."

"You'll see her again. Perhaps she will join you at the hotel for lunch one day if you invite her?"

"Perhaps," Elizabeth lied once again. She did not know if she should tell him what Anne had accused. *If he knew, would he be ashamed?*

How can I burden him with this knowledge before he leaves?

Instead, Elizabeth chose to remain quiet.

They rode in silence for a while. Elizabeth watched him carefully as he rubbed his other hand twice on his pant leg. *He's been doing that since he was a child.* It was a nervous mannerism he had developed around her. Always, it meant he was being indecisive about something 'personal' to be asked.

Does he know?

Has he found out his daughter knows of our affair?

"Is there something you want to ask me?" Elizabeth asked with a smirk on her face. She could not help but smile. A confident man unsure of himself in her presence.

I'm not that captivating.

Trevor turned and took her other hand. Surprised, Elizabeth looked at him with eyebrow cocked.

"Will you marry me?" Trevor asked.

Elizabeth widened her eyes and had to blink several times before she realized he was being serious. She swallowed hard, not knowing how to respond to the question without destroying their relationship.

"No," Elizabeth stammered. She shook her head and pulled back her hands. His face creased in disappointment as he turned quickly, staring out the window instead. Elizabeth put her hand on his shoulder. "Trevor?"

He did not respond, only shook his head. She could see tears starting to form in his eyes.

"Trevor?" Elizabeth said forcefully, but kindly. "Please look at me?"

Finally, he turned around. Through wet eyes, he looked straight into hers.

"Why are you asking me this?" Elizabeth said. "Now?"

"I thought you would want to, since Lara is..." he said softly. "And Anne..." his voice trailed off.

"I can't." Elizabeth's own eyes began to tear. She thought about what Anne saw and the girl's reaction. She thought about Lara and her untimely death.

Lara was a good woman.

And I betrayed her trust.

"Besides, it's too soon..." Elizabeth looked at him. "Too soon to even be considered."

Trevor blinked, eyes sad but hopeful. "Will you... consider it then?"

Elizabeth quickly turned away and stared at the torn leather door instead. She did not want to lie to him. She had still loved him despite being married to another woman.

An adulterous love affair.

But despite this, they could not keep themselves from being together. Was he trying to make an honest woman of her? What did he expect in return? A wife back home in London, a mother to his motherless daughter?

She turned back just as the carriage stopped. Instead of giving him an answer, Elizabeth opened the door and swiftly got out. Trevor slowly followed.

Elizabeth looked at the sadness in his eyes. He was disappointed. Most of all, he was still grieving.

Still, she refused to give him a solid answer.

They said nothing as the coachman took her bags and brought them to the inn door. Elizabeth turned her head towards the seawall and looked out at her ship careened and being repaired.

She shook her head, befuddled at the sight of her ship.

Trevor finally laughed.

"It's not funny," Elizabeth chuckled, glad that the subject had changed.

A group of sailors walked by and saluted.

"Would it be inappropriate to kiss the captain?" Trevor asked her.

"Very."

Trevor leaned in and gave her a quick hug. "Then we will have to settle for this— until next time."

He saluted her as she did the same.

"Good luck." Trevor got back in the carriage.

Elizabeth watched the vehicle leave.

"Anne knows," Elizabeth whispered to herself, having wanted to tell him but not having the courage. She sighed as she walked to the inn door.

14

———————

It wasn't until close to dusk that Miranda took her niece out for a tour of the sugar plantation. Anne noticed that Zara was never far from her aunt's side. The servant girl was walking behind them, quietly, always staring ahead with a look of irritation on her face. Anne tried to have a conversation with her but Zara was aloof. She seemed to be detached.

Anne gave up and maintained her pace next to her aunt.

They walked down a long, dirt path that led from the main house to the fields. As they passed a few small huts Anne studied the faces of a few women and men tending to their small gardens. Some were busy hoeing the dirt or digging, others were taking care of the small plot of crops such as yams and potatoes.

Many of the people were white.

"Are they also slaves?" Anne quietly asked.

"No." Miranda walked by the gardens, ignoring the fact that many eyes were staring at her. "These people are indentured servants— criminals and prostitutes— traitors from Ireland and Scotland. It was either this or the gallows," Miranda huffed. "I prefer slaves... these people don't work as hard. I will be happy when I rid myself of them."

"How long do they have to stay?" Anne watched a young girl, no older than she, catch her eye line, then turn in embarrassment.

"Seven to ten years depending on how well they serve me."

"Seems like slavery to me."

Miranda stopped and glared at her. "You are a Sutton, Anne. You are not to sympathize with this degenerates. There are people meant to serve people like us. That is how it has always been."

"Yes ma'am," Anne reluctantly agreed, trying to hide her disgust.

They ascended a hill and could now view the entire estate. Anne took in the enormity of the amount of land, hundreds of acres covered in bright, green sugarcane. There was a large windmill to the left, slowly turning its blades with the help of a stiff breeze. To the right, a large warehouse with numerous puncheons of rum stacked up on their sides. Men carried them into the warehouse with others supervising the work.

"That is the still house," Miranda said proudly. "No one is allowed in there except the men in charge... and even then I do not trust them."

"Why?"

"Because all men debauch if given the chance."

Anne realized what she meant.

They will drink all the rum if they were allowed. Including my uncle?

"The West Indies can be brutal," Miranda led her forward. "We must forever be diligent Anne. Men and women come here with intentions of making their fortune, soon to become overwhelmed by the life that one can lead here. They are unaffected by the customs and class system back home in England. They become rich with alcohol and loose morals. You can see that your Uncle Randal is too loose with the drink and that causes his tongue to also become unguarded."

They walked over to another structure. The heat was so intense from the outside, Anne could only wonder what the temperature could be like inside.

"The boiling house." Miranda waved her hand forward. "Only the most unruly are punished by having to work in there."

Miranda nodded her head slightly. Anne realized her aunt wanted her to take a look. Anne reluctantly stepped forward and timidly peered around the corner. There were large, copper cauldrons with steam rising from boiling cane juice. Men and women with large ladles skimmed the liquid from one cauldron to another. The smell was strong and pungent. If not skimmed properly, the cane juice would pop upwards, causing a spray of scalding liquid.

The place seemed to be hell on earth.

Anne pulled back, happy to be in the cooler air, even if the temperature was still very hot.

When they walked up to the sugar mill, Anne stared at the three large cylinders as tall as a man and thick as a horse's body. She watched as men and women fed large cane pieces in between the rollers. The cane juice was then extracted.

Suddenly, a scream jolted Anne. She watched as a few of the men pulled a woman away from the grinder. The woman held onto her hand in pain. From the distance, Anne could see the woman had hurt her fingers, blood pouring down the middle one.

"She is lucky," Miranda said with no sympathy in her voice. "If she would have lost her hand, she would be of no more use to us."

"What would have happened to her?"

"We would toss her out of course."

Anne was mortified. Was her aunt that cold and callous? She seemed the opposite of her brother.

"Do people often get their hands caught?" Anne timidly asked.

"Yes."

What a terrible thing to be constantly afraid of!

"How do you get the people... detached... if that happens?" Anne reluctantly asked.

Miranda pointed to the side of the cylinders. "With that, of course."

Anne's eyes widened. There was a nail protruding from the post, holding a rope attached to— an ax.

～

Dinner was a splendid feast but Anne could not stop thinking about the men and women in the fields. Those who were forced to live here as property of her aunt, most likely mistreated and abused.

The thought alone disgusted her.

People forced to grow their own food which consisted of nothing more than yams and potatoes. How did they get enough nourishment to survive the long, punishing hours in the heat of this island, toiling away at a job they were forced to do? And the indentured? How many of them thought they had made the wrong choice? That perhaps the gallows would have been a quicker solution compared to a dangerous, pitiful existence on this plantation?

Anne had never really thought about where her family's riches had come from. She knew that her family had always been well off but in the last twenty years, according to her father, the family fortune had grown due to the investment in sugar in the West Indies. Miranda had married into the Langdon family, and in turn, combined family investments created this plantation. Miranda had run the plantation for years almost by herself. Uncle Randal had little interest, except to 'taste' the rum that Rosewood produced.

Miranda and Randal have no children, so the actual heirs to the family fortune are—

Myself and Michael?

Anne had a hard time eating her pudding, slow to realize that the sugar in this dessert and all she had consumed her entire life had come from a plantation like this. It came off the backs of men and women subjugated to work for little or no money.

"May I go riding sometime?" Anne asked, trying to think of something else instead. Anne had noticed the large stable, and wanted to take a tour of the island soon.

"You may," Miranda said, looking at her with friendly eyes. "But not unaccompanied."

"Of course. I would never leave without a guide," Anne nodded. "May Zara go with me?"

"I would be all right with that Anne," Miranda spoke, then took her spoon and dipped it into her own dessert. "However, you must maintain your distance."

Anne cocked her head slightly, suddenly concerned. "Umm... I don't understand,"

Miranda looked up. "Zara is the help young woman, not a potential friend. I know you might be in need of one since you are the only other young person in the family right now."

Anne was slowly coming to realize her aunt believed in class distinctions, and Zara, as well as Elizabeth were not to be included in theirs.

"There are many fine young ladies as well as men on this island I will introduce you to over the coming weeks. Perhaps you will find a suitable companion and... maybe more."

"You are not going to force me to find a match are you?" Anne blurted out. She dipped her head low, keenly aware she had no right to question her aunt, especially at such an early stage when they were just getting to know each other.

"Do you not want to get married Anne?" Miranda asked, eyebrow cocked in curiosity.

"No," Anne was frank. "I have no desire to be a wife or a mother."

Anne did not know why she had suddenly confessed this to her aunt. Perhaps she felt this woman, another strong willed female like Elizabeth, might see her role as more than the one expected of her by society?

"What do you desire then?" Miranda asked.

"I do not know Aunt Miranda... I have no idea."

"Well, we are Sutton women and we have certain expectations we must fulfill." Miranda ate another spoonful. "Do you think I wanted to marry that insipid fool of a husband?"

"I... I have no idea ma'am. I do not know anything about him or you."

"Well, I did not want to marry him. I was shipped off to this island and expected to marry into his family. I have loathed him since the day I have met him. Thankfully we have no children."

Miranda smiled at her. It was a wild smile, deep with hidden meaning etched in the lines. "Love is a fickle thing Anne. You will find it in the most — *unexpected* of places."

Anne nervously rubbed her napkin and played with the cloth. She had no idea what her aunt was hinting at. *Does my aunt know what happened back home with Sarah? Has my father told her about the kiss?*

Why would he want to do that? So that he can be assured I am kept away from other females on the island? But she just offered for me to meet other girls as friends.

Or is it— something else?

Will she be open to allowing me to love whom I want?

Somehow, Anne had a strange feeling her aunt knew of her love for girls.

No matter how hard Anne wanted to tell someone, she also knew that it would be a bad idea to share with this woman.

Aunt Miranda truly frightened her.

ANNE KEPT to the grounds and enjoyed the gardens. Everywhere, cabbage palms grew into great heights as well as other tall palms with sharp black spikes down the trunk. There were many plants and vines with beautiful blooms and fruits. Vibrant birds sung tunes as they flew from branch to branch amongst other palms. She was enthralled with all the sights and sounds, so different from back home in London. The only common bird on those streets were the pigeons and loud mouthed crows.

Even the smells here were pleasant.

Blossoms of orange trees and other citrus fruits gave off a sweet smell. The fruits themselves were more delicious, even the sour lemon could be tamed into a delectable drink.

A small object darted in front of her face, then buzzed in midair. Anne swatted away the pest, sure a bug was trying to make a feast of her.

In the islands, the bugs were big— scary in fact!

The batty little blue creature flew towards her face again. It hovered for a moment, then darted to the left and right, quick to show its annoyance. Anne giggled to herself when she realized it was not a bug but a humming-bird, quite upset that she was too close to its nest!

"Okay little one," she snickered. "I will go another way."

He seemed to understand, for he swiftly buzzed up into the orange tree and out of sight.

"Anne?" A deep voice said.

She turned around quickly then bumped into someone. Anne pulled herself back and straightened herself. In front stood her Uncle Randal. His jacket was stained with dirt and his neck sash was falling off. He opened his mouth then grinned with yellow stained teeth. He quickly spit a piece of tobacco on the ground inches from her feet.

Anne stepped back farther, extremely uncomfortable and wanting to leave.

"Enjoying the morning?" he asked as his eyes focused on her chest for a little too long.

A sudden call from the house alerted them both. Someone was calling for Anne.

"Good day to you sir." Anne never felt so thankful to be rid of someone's company. She pulled her skirt up slightly and made for the house. Her body was shaking slightly. Every time her uncle looked at her, her skin crawled.

Anne did not know if she should mention anything to her aunt. The woman knew he was a drunk but did she also realize he was also a little too free with his eyes?

Miranda was talking to one of her house servants when Anne walked into the hallway. Her aunt looked up for a moment then continued her conversation. Anne sauntered over to a side table and waited. She moved her legs apart slightly and balanced back and forth, trying to imagine what ship movement felt like under her feet once again. Her toes curled within her stiff boot, hardened from all the salt water they had been subjected to, and now the dirt from the outside gardens.

"Don't stand like that Anne," Miranda's voice said from behind.

Anne turned. She did not even notice that the servant had left.

"Sorry ma'am," Anne said. "My legs are still wobbly from the ocean."

"You should have gotten over that by now."

Anne nodded. She watched as her aunt looked her over then glanced at her worn boots and clicked with her tongue.

"Why are you wearing those tattered things? Where are your other pairs?"

Anne looked down. She realized her boots were worn but they were also the most comfortable. "I like them. They are most agreeable for my walks."

"They are disgusting. We need to replace them."

"But?"

"No butts," Miranda chastised, then turned on her own and began to walk to the kitchen. "Come with me."

Anne nodded her head in compliance once again then followed her aunt. She had heard her aunt was a strict disciplinarian. Anne felt this was odd, considering the woman had no children herself.

"You brought all your shoes from London I assume?" Miranda asked.

"Several."

"Are they all worn?"

"I have not had a new pair in a while."

"Did Miss Barton not take you to shop?"

"No, she did not..." The sudden question startled her. Anne cocked her head slightly, confused. "Umm... how do you know of my governess?"

Miranda's eyes hardened. "I know all about you Anne. Do you think I did not know to ask your father questions before he left you in my care?"

"No," Anne swallowed hard. "I guess not."

"We will go into town and remedy this situation. You could also do with a few new dresses."

Anne frowned.

New dresses and shoes usually meant frilly things like a ball. Anne forced herself to remain optimistic. *If I can meet a new girl or two, then maybe it will be— worth it?*

They stopped in front of the kitchen door. Inside, servants were busy preparing a lunch time menu. From the looks of the frantic action, they were expecting to serve a fancier meal.

"Is someone coming?" Anne asked.

"Just an auditor from a neighboring plantation. I am trying to gauge if I want him to come work for me."

"Are you poaching someone?" Anne inquired.

"I am." Miranda narrowed her eyes, the familiar stare that Anne was becoming all too familiar with. "Randal used to take care of the books but now his time is spent in other endeavors."

Zara appeared in the corner of the kitchen. She began to speak to another when Miranda cleared her throat. Zara immediately came over and bowed her head.

"Yes ma'am?" Zara asked.

"I have business I have to attend to this afternoon," Miranda said with a sniff.

"Yes ma'am."

"Pack a lunch."

"Yes ma'am."

"Am I going somewhere?" Anne blurted out.

"Zara will take you up to the hills to ride. I would prefer to be alone with the auditor. Not that I think you would not make good company at the table. It is just that I need to discuss sensitive matters."

Anne nodded, happy to finally get to see something other than this plantation.

THE STABLES WERE NOT FAR from the main house. Anne had been given a tour yesterday but she had not been allowed to ride until now. She followed Zara to the stable area and immediately walked over to a fine horse. He was a large beast, with black coloring and a white mane. His nose was also white. When Anne put out her hand to touch the back of him, another hand reached out and pulled it back.

"Do not touch the mistress' horse," Zara chastised.

"Why?" Anne challenged. *If I were a cruel person, I could have Zara punished for just touching me.* "I know well enough to not stick my hand near his mouth. I only wanted to feel his coat."

"This horse has bad manners. He may rear up and kick at his stall,"
Zara said. "He has done this on many occasions."

"Sounds like he needs some better training."

"He needs to be left alone." Zara followed the stable boy. He led two
horses out of the gate. Anne took the reins to a chestnut mare.

"Thank you," Anne said to him as she patted her mare. "I did not even
think to ask her name."

"Bonnie," he said sheepishly.

Anne put her feet in the stirrups and easily got on the horse. Still,
because she wore a dress, she had to ride side saddle.

Zara had on trousers and sat on the horse like a man would. She stood
up in the saddle and let her animal trot slightly.

Anne patted her mare once again. "Well, Bonnie... I hope you are a
good ride. Anne leaned back slightly, trying to adjust herself to the saddle.
"Where are we going anyway?"

"To Mount Hillaby."

Anne cocked an eyebrow. "Isn't this island essentially flat?" Anne
maneuvered the mare to stand in front of the girl. When she saw a grin on
Zara's face, Anne took a slight offense. "I do not see what is so funny?"

"Do you always assume you know before you see?"

Eyes narrowed, Anne was baffled by the question. "What does that even
mean?"

"It means do not presume to know what you believe without first seeing
to discover."

Before Anne could react to what she assumed was verbal nonsense,
Zara clicked her mouth and kicked her horse to move. Zara was quick to
trot away. Anne nudged her horse forward, letting the mare follow behind
her guide.

Anne carefully watched the way Zara rode.

She rides with skill.

Zara appeared confident and she had a natural grace. Anne could not
help but stare at the girl's exquisite beauty. Anne had never seen someone
with a skin color like hers before, until coming to Barbados.

Anne was fascinated.

She was also troubled by their relationship.

Anne finally gulped hard, *I have to ask.*

"Are you a slave?" Anne hesitantly asked.

"No," Zara said bluntly much to Anne's shock. She turned her head and grinned. "Did you assume I was?"

"Well... yes," Anne stuttered.

"I am only a servant to mistress and no one else."

They rode north for some time. Zara told her that the island was around twenty three kilometers in diameter, thirty four north to south.

Anne followed her guide. Her horse easily walked over the sandy path that was littered with crushed sea shells. Nowhere were any type of dark, obsidian rock Anne had heard about in the West Indies.

"There are no volcanoes on this island?" Anne asked, curious.

"It is a coral island," Zara answered.

"But the coral is dead."

"Skeletons of the oceanic creatures have built this island."

Anne looked down at the sand and wondered how many millions of years it had taken for the little creatures to be pushed up, layer by layer on top of each other to create the mass they now walked on.

"I saw the coral reefs when we docked," Anne said. "They are beautiful."

"They are much more beautiful up close."

"You swim near them?"

"I dive for pearls sometimes."

This was not something Anne had ever thought of trying to do. Zara seemed so adventurous. "Are you not frightened?"

Zara looked at her sideways. "Of what?"

"What of sharks?" Anne asked. "Would they not eat you?"

Zara started to laugh. "Those are tales meant to scare readers in silly stories. A shark has little interest in you humans."

Anne raised an eyebrow, slightly thrown of by the phrase. *What does Zara mean by that? Surely it is just a slip of the tongue?*

When they reached the highest point of the island, Anne carefully got off her horse and looked out towards the horizon. The sky was a beautiful mix of radiant blues. In the far distance, a purple and dark set of clouds crept inwards from the east. Anne could see flashes of lightning within the forebidding clouds. She took a telescope out of her side pack and studied the formation.

"Will it storm?" Anne asked, concerned. She wiped sweat off her forehead, slightly nervous. She had heard of the storms that traversed these islands but had yet to really experience one.

"It will," Zara nodded. "I think we should head back. Besides..." Zara clicked her tongue, making her mare turn around. "You look a little dehydrated."

"I think you are right," Anne nodded in agreement. Her throat was parched once again.

Why am I always thirsty?

Anne retrieved her canteen, opened it and quickly drank the rest of her water.

Wiping her forehead once again, Anne stopped for a moment and stared out into the direction of the port and Elizabeth's ship. The HMS Defiant, was still in dry dock.

Anne put the small telescope to her eye and began to gauge its progress. The holes on the side of the ship were already patched up and currently there were men on deck struggling with lifts and pulleys, trying to get the new mainmast installed. Anne scanned the area below the ship. On the sand Elizabeth was standing there with her arms crossed, staring at the work as it was being done.

Anne put down her telescope.

She had lashed out at her friend a few days ago. Anne felt a knot in her stomach, followed by sudden regret. *Can I ever forgive Miss Elizabeth?*

Should I even try?

"We should go," Zara said impatiently.

"Of course," Anne agreed. She quickly put the telescope away and got back on her own horse.

Soon, they were cantering back home to the plantation side by side.

15

———————

nne folded her dress and placed it in the top drawer. She touched the fine fabric. She quickly turned when she heard footsteps.

"I can do that," Zara stood behind her.

"It is no problem," Anne smiled.

The servant girl nodded then walked over to the small side table and began to pour a drink. Anne did not notice that she had brought in the refreshment.

"I do not need any more, but thank you," Anne said.

"You must drink." Zara held the crystal glass up. "Mistress has said I must keep you hydrated, lest you get sick."

"Then I will have water instead."

"The water is not very good this week. Besides, only the field hands are given stored water."

"But what about the storm last night?" Anne asked, confused.

"They failed to secure the water barrels properly," Zara said, shaking her head. "The wind was so violent, the barrels were knocked over."

Anne inhaled sharply, remembering last night's storm. She had never experienced weather like that before. For a while, Anne thought they were being hit by a hurricane. Her aunt assured her otherwise. Anne sat in the dark, unable to have any candles lit. She was told that it was very dangerous to do such a thing in the tropics. The harsh wind and rain was so intense, it actually blew sideways! Anne's shutters had flung open on two occasions. Anne had gotten soaked trying to secure them.

Tonight, Anne was happy it was just humid and sticky, as opposed to life threatening.

She also did not want to drink any more punch. The alcohol was strong and made her lightheaded.

Still, it was better than stagnant water.

Elizabeth had told her of times that the ship had been becalmed, with no fresh water for days. Water was kept in casks that were not always well sealed. Algae, especially in more humid climates, could contaminate the water and make people sick. People had to remain hydrated in order to survive but sometimes the cure was worse than the condition.

Anne took the drink and thanked Zara once again for her consideration. The attention Zara showed was not a form of kindness but more of a duty. As Anne drank, she wondered if her aunt had told Zara to keep her distance, or if the other girl simply did not like her— *or maybe she is just indifferent to me?*

The punch was a different blend than what she had at dinner. This was more of a mixture of orange and grapefruit, the latter being a new flavor she had just been introduced to this afternoon. The grapefruit was a spherical fruit, enclosed in a semi-tough rind, that when peeled revealed distinct sections filled with soft flesh. When squeezed, the flesh produced a juice at once sweet and tart.

After she drank the delicious mix, Anne handed the crystal glass back to Zara, who put the drink down and began to pour more.

"No thank you," Anne put her hand out, insistent. "I do not want any more."

Zara nodded and put down the pitcher. "Mistress has told me you wish to see the gardens at night?"

"Yes," Anne said, remembering her conversation at dinner. She was afraid to walk through the gardens at a late hour, wary her drunken uncle might be lurking in the shadows. "I would like to see the splendor under the moonlight."

"You are lucky then, for tonight we have a full moon and the grounds will be lit." Zara picked up the tray and began to walk to the door. "Put on a shawl... it is slightly chilly outside."

"But it was so hot today."

"This is the way of the tropics. Best to know the emotion of the island, lest it have dominion over you. I will meet you in the courtyard."

Before Anne could ask her what that meant, Zara walked out of the room. Anne quickly retrieved another dress. She put it on and stood in front of the full length mirror. Suddenly, she felt an urge to apologize to Elizabeth for reacting so rudely the other day.

We should at least be able to talk. Will I even be able to do that? Surely my aunt will not allow me to go alone to the town without an escort.

Then Zara will have to go with me.

Will my aunt even entertain that idea?

Her aunt seemed to detest Elizabeth and Anne had no idea why. *Surely it cannot be just because my aunt deems Miss Elizabeth 'lower class'?*

No, they must have a history. Perhaps, if I write a letter instead, Zara can deliver it?

I'm not ready to forgive... but I can at least have a civil discussion.

Anne followed Zara down the path as they walked towards the edge of the garden. The grounds were beautiful at night. The moon was radiantly full. It gently illuminated the long fields of cane. The light that bounced back produced a soft, green hue that seemed to glow.

Her aunt had only shown Anne this section for a quick moment last week. The older woman seemed more concerned with the monetary side of things as opposed to the actual beauty of the plantation.

Anne skipped forward as she tried to keep up with Zara. Her stomach suddenly felt unwell, her head began to spin. As Anne stopped, her guide turned.

"Are you not feeling well?" Zara asked.

"I am." Anne looked at the girl, only to see a slight blur, followed by two of her. "Slightly dizzy."

"The heat can be deadly."

Anne froze for a moment, startled. Those were the same words her aunt had used when she spoke to Elizabeth in the courtyard a while back.

"Follow me," Zara commanded.

Anne did not know why but she felt compelled to follow her guide. What Anne's mind thought and what her legs did seemed to be in opposition. She shook her head and tried to will the muddy feeling to go away.

Anne kept pace as best she could. Now her legs were beginning to feel wobbly and pained in places she had never felt before.

The path was starting to get more rugged. She had to keep from tripping over large stones that blocked the footpath. It was obvious that few people walked this way. Weeds crept around her feet. Anne had to use large steps to keep from getting snagged by the unruly foliage.

"Where are we going?" Anne finally asked, concerned. "This can't possibly be the way to the gardens?"

"Come," Zara ignored her. "Over this hill and we will be there."

Anne finally willed her legs to stop. "I do not want to go any further Zara."

"Why?" The other girl turned with eyes that bore deep. "Are you frightened?"

Anne did not want Zara to see how truly scared she really was. Anne had a bad feeling. *Whatever Zara is insisting on showing me, it can't be good!*

"I just want to go back," Anne confessed.

"As you wish." Zara turned around and glided by Anne.

Relieved, Anne spun around and suddenly, could no longer see her guide!

"Zara?" Anne said, panicked. "Where are you?"

There was no answer.

The moonlight illuminated the path for many yards. *There is no way Zara could have disappeared so easily?* Anne gulped hard.

Now angered, Anne yelled louder. "Zara? Where did you go?"

When there was no response, Anne exhaled sharply. "Bloody hell," she whispered under her breath. Anne looked straight ahead. *Now I have to find my own way back!*

Suddenly, the laughter of children caught Anne's attention. She looked around, trying to find the location of the high pitched sounds.

"Who's there?" Anne practically begged, her voice beginning to crack. Her body was chilled to the bone with fear.

Again, the tittering echoed through the bushes.

A shadow darted across the path. Anne jumped backwards and quickly realized that it was too small to be Zara. *If that is a child, why are they running around the plantation so late at night?*

"Hello?" Anne desperately tried to get some type of response. "Don't be frightened. Are you lost?" She stepped into the bushes and pushed back some of the leaves.

She had a hard time seeing where she was going. Through the corner of her eye, another shadow darted by. A sudden wave of panic hit her hard once again. *Why am I even attempting this? Shouldn't I just run back into the main house and tell the staff to send someone else out to find this— lost child?*

Her foot caught on a root and she fell. Anne's hands were now muddy and her index finger scraped. She got to her feet and trudged forward. When she pushed back a large branch, she stumbled upon an open section of flat terrain. In the center sat a huge tree, bigger than anything she had ever seen back home.

The trunk had to be at least eight feet in diameter, with a height taller than her three story house back in London. There were large buttressed roots that protruded out of the bottom, giving the illusion that the tree had sprouted into a snake and could easily walk away.

The tree was a frightening site. Anne should have known better than to be scared of something like this but she had heard stories as a child, back in England, of haunted forests— places people dared not go into for fear of being lost forever.

Were there similar stories here in Barbados? Did the people who lived on this island also hold with ancient superstitions?

Anne heard a low laugh, followed by another, higher in pitch. Anne swore she definitely now heard the sound of children.

Against her better judgement, she continued forward.

What appeared to be a child crawled onto one of the buttressed roots and sat. Anne could not make out any features since the younger one was drenched in shadow.

"Do you need help?" Anne asked, hand out as she walked forward. "Do you want me to take you back to your parents?"

There was no sound from the child.

Anne's whole body shivered. She had a bad feeling about this. Despite her fear, her feet slowly shuffled forward once again.

"*Anne?*" The deep voice seemed to emanate from the ground, muffled and barely audible.

Anne whipped around and scanned the area. She was convinced she heard nothing but her heart was beating fast, her imagination running away wildly.

"*Anne?*" The voice was more pronounced this time.

That is not coming from the child! Anne gulped hard. She realized that this was not her imagination. As she stepped back, getting ready to run she made the mistake of looking where the child had been sitting.

He was gone.

Anne turned quickly, then screamed.

The child was right in front of her!

Anne quickly realized this was no ordinary child. He had to be a specter, some type of supernatural being. Deep set red eyes glowed, but there was no face. The body was a dark hue that was slightly transparent. A sudden mouth appeared with a set of long, sharp teeth.

Anne lost her footing as the creature leapt onto her chest and made her fall. As she hit the ground, she struggled to get the monster off.

A pair of hands grabbed her. She struggled to no avail. They simply pulled her arms over her head and reached down to stop her thrashing.

"Anne!" a lighter voice yelled this time. "Settle down!"

Scared out of her mind, Anne pushed forward and jumped up, her hands now unrestrained and out of control. She felt something fall on her — a net of some sort? *Has this thing caught me? Is it going to eat me?*

"Stop this!" Miranda's voice yelled. A slap on Anne's face brought her back slightly.

Anne, wild with savagery, pushed back. She looked at the other face in front of her.

Zara!

"You left me!" Anne accused harshly. "You left me there!"

"What?" Zara blinked, shocked. "Left you where?"

"In the garden!"

"We never made it to the garden." Zara shook her head. She pulled the fallen mosquito netting away from Anne's face. "You passed out on the floor here in the room."

Anne tried to understand what the girl was saying to her. She touched her own forehead and realized she was drenched in sweat.

"You were having a nightmare Miss Anne."

"I was?"

"Yes." Miranda was standing above her, arms crossed looking clearly annoyed.

"I don't know what happened." Anne rubbed her forehead and began to feel the fool. "I swear I felt like I was out in the garden. It seemed so real... the tree... the child—"

"What child?" Zara asked with an eyebrow bent in concern.

"Something that looked like a child. Red eyes, dark skin... sharp teeth," Anne shuddered.

Zara glanced at Miranda. "Duppies?"

"There is no such thing," Miranda brushed off the suggestion with a wave of the hand.

"What is a duppy?" Anne asked, frightened.

"Silly superstitions that these islanders have." Miranda walked to the door. "Leave her now Zara. She needs to go back to sleep."

As Miranda left, Anne grabbed Zara's hand before she could get up off the bed. "Zara, what is a duppy?"

"Supernatural beings that feed on unwilling humans," Zara smirked.

She seemed almost proud of the fact. "Stay out of the garden and away from that tree Miss Anne. Please."

"But I thought you said it was a bad dream?"

Zara got up and looked at Anne. "Was it?"

Anne swallowed hard, now terrified. When Zara left the room, Anne looked down at her finger.

It was bleeding from a small scratch.

16

After her harrowing night, Anne was unsure if she ever wanted to leave the main house again. She felt that her dream was more than it appeared. Anne felt like she had entered into a nightmare that was all too real.

Anne looked down at her hand. She had put some salve on the scratch this morning. It was small, but still alarming.

Did I scratch it on my bed post? Or, did that creature really harm me?

Anne sat on the veranda and stared ahead into the distance. Now that she knew her surroundings better, Anne could see the top of that tree within the canopy of foliage. Anne had asked what kind of tree she had 'imagined'.

Zara told her it was a silk-cotton, the oldest one on the island.

Anne sighed.

Not only did she feel mentally unwell, she also felt physically unwell. Anne had stayed to herself in her bedroom for hours. She did this a lot these last few days.

Her stomach was also upset.

Anne did not know if she was depressed or had an actual illness of some kind. She was told that the West Indies had the reputation for being a place that was defined by sickness and the people it claimed as victims.

Later that afternoon, Anne was forced to go out. She followed her aunt through the town of Bridgetown. She had not been here since her carriage trip with Elizabeth two weeks before.

Two weeks already? Has it really been that long?

Soon her friend would sail away and Anne had yet to talk to her.

Anne strained to see the shipyard. The HMS Defiant was no longer careened, but in the harbor, moored to a pier. She could not see well enough to know who was on deck supervising.

The smell of the town was, well, rude; that was the best she could describe it. Similar in nature to the streets of London but instead of large bustling buildings, the streets of Bridgetown were filled with dilapidated houses.

Anne did not understand what she was seeing. She swore that the sights she had seen with Elizabeth had been more vibrant in color, happier than today. Because it was late afternoon, Anne thought perhaps that without the bright sunlight, this is what the town of Bridgetown looked like at this time.

"Keep up," her aunt demanded.

Anne picked up her pace and ran to Miranda's side.

She barely got out of the way of a cart that dashed by. Her aunt grabbed her by the shoulder and pulled her in tight. "Watch where you are going! Why are you so complacent?"

"I am not feeling well ma'am... I feel dizzy."

"You are being affected by the heat. You will get used to that. That is why I brought you to town at this hour."

"Miss Elizabeth told me I would get used to the heat. I wonder when that will happen?"

Miranda stopped cold. She turned to the young woman with ice in her eyes. "Do not say that woman's name in my presence."

Anne swallowed hard. She knew she shouldn't have said Elizabeth's name the moment she uttered the words. She also didn't realize how defensive her aunt might get.

"In fact," Miranda sneered. "Do not say that woman's name ever again."

"Yes... yes ma'am," Anne stuttered, frightened.

Miranda turned on her heel and lead the way. Anne had a hard time keeping up, her breath ragged as she sweated profusely.

Anne had wanted to ask her aunt if she could visit her friend. After that outburst, Anne's heart deflated. *Even if I wanted to talk to Miss Elizabeth about what I had witnessed, Aunt Miranda will never let me visit my friend.*

Anne sighed.

She might have to be resigned to writing a letter instead.

When they turned a corner, Anne jumped back when she practically ran over a dead animal carcass being torn to shreds by a group of black crows.

"They are just as nasty and fowl as the creatures in London. Only these do not freeze in the winter." Miranda did not even pay attention. She just shooed them away by walking too close to them and at full speed. "Pity."

"It does seem as disgusting as these creatures are, they have a purpose."

"And what is that? Please enlighten me."

"They are eating the pestilence in the street. If not for them, we might be overrun with the carcass of dead animals and street filth. Like rains that clean the streets."

"Hmm... you may be smarter than you look."

Anne did not know how to process a comment like that. As she followed the woman, she noticed people darted to get out of the way.

In their eyes— *is that respect? Or fear?*

A few other pedestrians darted across the street instead of being forced to walk by her aunt.

Miranda opened the door to a dressmaker. Anne walked to the corner and waited as a few customers scooted by her aunt without saying a word. Miranda closed the door and locked it. She grabbed Anne by the arm and dragged her over to the counter.

The man behind practically jumped out of his skin when he saw who his next customer was. He was a bald, portly figure with a tight fitting vest. He held a bolt of cloth and a tape measure.

"Mrs. Sutton?" he nervously said. "How nice of you to be here."

"Drop the formalities Mr. Lorey, I need not the fake kindness you bestow on your other customers."

"Of course. What may I do for you today?"

Anne found it odd that despite being married, her aunt chose to use her maiden name Sutton instead of Langdon. Apparently she only used the hyphenated name, Sutton-Langdon when entertaining or entering into official business for the plantation.

Miranda touched a roll of fine fabric on the counter. Her fingers caressed the cloth before looking directly at him. "I will need a number of dresses made for my young niece here."

When the man smiled formally at her, Anne returned the gesture. She was uncomfortable and she sensed he realized this. Her aunt was a very threatening presence and meant to intimidate anyone who questioned her.

"When do you need them Mrs. Sutton?"

"This weekend. We are having a series of dinners and lunches."

Anne widened her eyes.

Had her aunt also planned a ball? Was she going to show off her newly arrived niece to the planters' sons? Anne narrowed her eyes, angrily.

"How many do you need?"

"Three."

"Three?" Mr. Lorey started to fidget with his ruler. He put down the bolt of cloth on the counter. "I do not know if I can make them on such short notice."

"Why not?" Miranda asked dryly. "You are a very able tailor."

"But Mrs. Sutton? I have other customers to whom I promised dresses who are ahead of you," Mr. Lorey protested. "Surely you cannot ask me to put them aside?"

"If you need more money than I normally pay, I can take care of that easily."

"But my word?"

Miranda touched a spool of fine lace sitting on the counter. "Such fine work I must say. The detail, exquisite. The London crowd lost a fine craftsman when you left them, did they not?"

"Yes," Mr. Lorey agreed sullenly.

"And your wife's work?" Miranda's lip twisted slightly. Her fingers caressed the embroidery, then turned the stitching over. "Such intricacy."

This time he said nothing, only stared at Miranda with fear and resentment in his eyes.

"Field work is much harder on the hands, is it not?" Miranda asked, eyebrows bent.

"But?"

"And the possibility of such hands being crushed in the sugar cane grinder? It would be a terrible loss not only to this settlement but to your children."

Mr. Lorey glanced at Anne then the floor.

"You have two children now?" Miranda asked with a sniff.

"Yes ma'am."

"Children do not last long in the fields."

Mr. Lorey quickly pushed aside the bundle of cloth, whipped out a paper and quill and put the items on the counter. He then dashed over with measuring tape and whipped Anne's arms upwards. "I will get right on your order Mrs. Sutton."

"Good," Miranda said with a smile that did not reach her eyes. "Your cooperation is much appreciated."

Miranda took a few more planned steps around the room as she pretended to admire the cloth, then turned. "Anne, I will be across the street attending to some business. I will be back soon. Do not go anywhere without me, do you understand?"

"Yes ma'am," Anne swallowed hard.

Miranda opened the door, triggering the small bell that announced she had left.

Anne was stiff as she allowed the dressmaker to measure. There was complete silence between them. The air was hot and stale but the perspiration on the top of his bare head was not the result of heat. She was afraid to ask him anything or even partake in polite conversation.

Mr. Lorey was terrified.

But surely he is not frightened of me?

When he glanced at her then quickly went back to his work, Anne sighed.

He is terrified of me! But why? I am nothing like my aunt!

Her aunt had told her one night at dinner that strong women were to be revered, and rightfully so. But had she forgotten to tell her the part about threatening people to get something done?

Anne felt a wave of nausea hit her stomach.

Maybe I am just like my aunt, I just haven't realized it yet.

Anne was afraid that her aunt was not all she appeared to be.

In a world she previously thought of as black and white, Anne was slowly discovering the gray shades in between.

ZARA LED Anne down the long hallway. Ever since the terrible dream, Zara avoided Anne unless attending to her. The servant girl had been mostly absent for a few days. Anne was afraid Zara had been warned to stay away.

What if it was worse?

What if my aunt is physically cruel to the poor girl?

She wished she had the courage to ask Zara if this was true but Anne was more frightened of her aunt.

"How are you feeling?" Anne asked her guide. If she could at least get the other one to open up a little, maybe Zara would start to trust her?

"I am fine miss," Zara nodded, looking straight ahead.

"You have been gone for a while," Anne said, skipping ahead to join her side. "Were you sick?"

"No." Zara shook her head firmly. "I had duties to attend to."

"For my aunt?" Anne asked, eyebrow cocked.

Zara glanced at her for a quick second, her expression hard. "Please do not ask me what I do for your aunt." Zara caught their reflection in a hall mirror. Quickly, she diverted her eyes from her own reflection. "She has eyes everywhere Anne. You would be wise to keep your own council."

Again someone speaks of mirrors. Miss Elizabeth had mentioned mirrors as if someone were watching her.

How is that even possible?

They stopped in front of the portrait room. Anne nodded as Zara led her in then closed the door behind.

"You wanted to see me Aunt Miranda?" Anne asked. She stepped forward and looked around. There were dozens of portraits on the walls, so many that they reached almost to the ceiling. Her aunt was standing in front of a particular painting. Anne remembered a similar painting of the same subject back at her London home.

Anne had been in this room before but never with her aunt until now.

Miranda turned, hands together as if she were praying. The older woman inclined her head towards the piece of art. "Do you know who this is?"

"I believe that is my grandmother."

"Very good," Miranda smiled. "Yes... my mother. She was a formidable woman."

"I do not remember her," Anne sighed. "I think I was three when she died."

"Yes you were."

Anne turned her head for a moment. "Was that when I met you?" She asked remembering her father mentioning the only time she had actually met her aunt.

"Yes," Miranda sighed. "I had come back for the first time since being sent out here to marry... that..." The way the word stop short Anne could sense her aunt was suddenly irritated. Miranda shook her head for a second removing the thought that was certainly ready to leave the tip of her tongue. Instead she forced a saddened smile. "Regardless of the circum-stances that is when my mother took ill."

"At least you were with her when she passed."

"I wasn't." Miranda shrugged looking at the painting once again. "I was on my way back to Barbados. I did not find out for a few weeks but I knew she was dying."

Anne creased her lip suddenly aware her aunt seemed aloof and uncaring to what had happened. *Is she truly that cold hearted? To leave when her mother was dying? Or was she just happy to not have to face a hard truth? Did she even get along with my grandmother?*

Anne stepped closer and examined the painting. Her grandmother was in her late fifties when she sat for this portrait. She held no smile nor expression of happiness. Agnes Sutton's eyes were stern with deep faded blue eyes that projected wealth and superiority. Her dress was exquisite, finely tailored purple embroidery etched through delaine fabric. The subject was wearing a pendant with a large, amethyst stone. As Anne looked at the jewelry, Miranda pulled the same necklace from around her own neck and dropped it in the girl's hand.

Anne pulled the chain up and examined the stone. This was the same crystal amethyst that was painted on the neck of her grandmother Sutton. She let the candlelight hit the surface from various angles. The reflections produced made a wondrous dance on the wall and floor. She was entranced by the beautiful display.

"It is stunning," Anne gawked. She flipped the stone slightly once again to produce new patterns.

"May I see yours?"

Anne didn't realize what the woman was saying at first.

Mine?

But, I only have a small ring. Anne gave the stone back to her aunt then retrieved her own jewelry off her neck and handed the item to the older woman.

Miranda took the ring off the chain and began to examine it. She turned the item. "Do you know anything about crystals?"

"No... just that they are pretty and create a light show."

"What kind of light show?"

Anne was not going to tell her about the visions she had seen on the wall in the parlor back home, nor the fact her mother stepped off the roof when she swore she saw something in that same piece. "Light shows... I made small trinkets to put in the window in my old workroom that my father made. When the sunlight shown in, it hit my art and produced the most wonderful of shows. So many colors all over the walls and floors."

Anne pointed to Miranda's stone. "Just like that did."

"Yes, they do make wonderful prisms."

"Would I be able to make some here?" Anne needed some release from the last few weeks. "I do love them so."

"My dear girl… crystals are not to be played with."

"Oh…" Anne felt a deep feeling of regret for suggesting her passion to her aunt. Of course the woman would probably find her hobby— juvenile, something only a young girl played with.

"Your mother learned that lesson the hard way did she not?" Miranda said.

Anne looked at her with a pained expression. Her face flushed red as she quickly looked down at the ground. She had tried not to think about her mother's death. Why had her aunt brought up the subject so callously? Anne bit her lower lip desperate to keep herself from bursting out in tears.

"Crystals are meant to be used to harness energy." Miranda held up the ring and let the light hit the stones. As she let it turn, Anne watched the show once again. "Simply letting light hit this is like only enjoying a painting for the brush stokes… you have to look deeper at the whole picture to enjoy it and understand its meaning."

Anne thought it disquieting that the older woman could say something so hurtful and not bat an eyelash while continuing the conversation.

Now angered, Anne pursed her lips. "I do not know what you mean Aunt Miranda."

"All crystals harness energy Anne. What you are seeing is not just light… but an energy that is given off," Miranda said. "What do you see right now?"

"I still do not understand," Anne said.

"Try and look deep."

Anne was fearful of what she might see. She knew she had seen something that night in the parlor.

Blue.

I had seen movement, like waves.

The ocean.

"I have seen the ocean in my own crystal," Anne confessed as she looked toward the floor.

"And you crossed one to get here, did you not?"

"How would that happen?"

"Some crystals can predict the future if you look deep enough... a form of clairvoyance," Miranda said. "Where is this crystal that you speak of?"

"I threw it in the ocean."

Miranda widened her blue eyes in disbelief, then wrinkled her nose. "Why would you do that young woman?"

"It scared me."

"I see." Miranda focused in on her niece. "Is that the crystal your mother held?"

"Yes," Anne confessed now trying to understand this sudden revelation. *My mother had seen something in that crystal. She said she saw paradise.* Anne looked at her aunt. As much as Anne wanted the answer to her questions she thought otherwise. *I don't fully trust my aunt and I do not know why.*

Miranda gave Anne back her ring. While Anne replaced her jewelry, Miranda held up her own amethyst and let the light bounce onto the wall. "Tell me what you see in this."

"Must I?"

"Yes."

Anne focused on the crystal first then looked to the wall. The pattern danced, a wild motion of reds and deep purples. "I see... great power... a person whom others fear... people cowering... a tree... that—" she gasped. "That tree I was at in my dream! The silk-cotton!"

Miranda snatched up the amethyst and quickly put it on her neck. She seemed to be suddenly enthralled, with a smile on her face that scared Anne even further.

"What does that mean Aunt Miranda?"

"I believe we are destined for great things."

"What does fear have to do with that?"

"Our family has always been able to see and manipulate what we want or need to our own betterment. Through the ages since the time of the celts, we have always been powerful."

Anne did not want to believe she herself had any type of power. She just wanted to be a regular girl. She had seen visions on the wall. Now her aunt was telling her wild tales.

"I do not want to be feared," Anne confessed.

"Fear is addicting Anne, once you feel its power, you will never step back from it." Miranda's lip twisted into a threatening smile. "You are family... and family must be loyal at all costs."

Anne swallowed hard.

A knock at the door alerted Miranda. She turned and sighed. "What is it Zara?"

Zara cleared her throat, nervously. "Ma'am. Mr. Style has requested your immediate attention."

"What has happened?"

"Runaways."

Miranda cracked her neck, annoyed. "And did he find them?"

"Yes ma'am," Zara said.

Miranda looked at her niece, eyes hard. "Come with me Anne. It is time for you to learn what being the mistress of a plantation means."

Anne stood by her aunt's horse and began to stroke his mane. Anne had always loved these animals and of all the things she missed from her home in London— was the horse she had to say goodbye to. Despite what Zara had said, the horse was not ill behaved. Maybe it was because her aunt was nearby?

"What's his name?" Anne asked.

"Thermador." Miranda mounted her horse then turned and held out her hand. "Come— we have work to attend to."

Anne put her left foot in the stirrup and let her aunt help her up. She gently grabbed her aunt by the waist as the horse was commanded to turn around. Anne held on tight, the horse in full gallop and heading towards the fields. Her aunt did not force her to ride sidesaddle. In fact, she had made Anne change into riding breeches and a fine jacket, as did Miranda herself.

Anne wondered if her aunt was putting them on display somehow?

"May I ride him some day?" Anne asked.

"Best not. He tolerates only me," Miranda said holding the reins. "There are many other fine horses in the stables for you to ride."

The horse slowed down. When they were over the small hill, Anne could see a gathering of people. She counted at least twenty. As they got closer to the scene, Anne realized there were two people on the ground, on their knees with hands bound before them.

A man and a woman, both young.

The female had ebony skin that glistened in the sun. She looked to be no older than Anne herself. When the confined young woman sunk her head low, the man next to her spoke in her ear, trying to reassure her. He had pale skin the color of most recent indentured arrivals from England. His hair was blond, but covered in dirt.

When he caught the eye of their mistress, he refused to look away.

"What is this all about?" Miranda let the horse trot around the circle of people, a move meant to intimidate. "Why have you wasted my time?"

An overseer stepped forward, whip in hand. The leather was wrapped around in a perfect circle, ready to be snapped out and used on anyone he saw fit. "These two decided to try and run away."

"I see," Miranda said low with an almost sympathetic tone in her voice. She dismounted and helped Anne behind her. Her aunt held her riding whip close to her breeches and walked towards the frightened couple.

Miranda tilted her head and smiled at the young girl. The way her aunt's mouth creased, Anne knew that the gesture was not one of kindness. The sheer terror on the groveling girl tore at Anne's heart.

"Now why would you run away?" Miranda reached out her hand and touched the girl's chin. Roughly, she pulled it forward, forcing her victim to look directly into her eyes. "When you have everything you need here?"

"It's my fault my lady!" The young man finally spoke up, his Irish lilt quivering with anger. "I wanted to marry her."

"And why could you not be married here young man?" Miranda turned her attention solely on him. "Do I not give you enough?"

"We *were* trying to run away!" The girl spat harshly. "Away from you, you witch— you are devil himself!"

Miranda slapped the girl hard across the face. Anne could not believe what she was seeing.

"You ALL belong to this plantation!" Miranda stood up and swung round with furious eyes. "You ALL belong to ME!" Every eye on her now was filled with terror and loathing. No one in this crowd would dare speak up. "Do you understand?" Miranda yelled once again.

One by one, they nodded. Some even fell to their knees begging for mercy.

Anne felt sick. She was horrified to see the terror in these people's eyes but even more ashamed with herself for being here. There was nothing she could do. It was not her place to question her aunt especially in this setting.

Who was to say that the woman would not turn around and strike her next?

"What do you say mistress?" The overseer asked.

"Let's start with him." Miranda pointed to the young man. "Twelve."

Twelve? Anne thought. *Twelve what?*

He was seized up by two strong men. As he was tied to a post, Anne realized the poor boy was about to be whipped.

Anne started to walk back but a firm hand grabbed her arm. Her aunt stared at her with a deep, menacing look. One that said, don't you dare walk away.

If I do, will I be perceived as weak?

Anne had never had the intention of witnessing a flogging and now she would be forced to watch one!

The heavy whip snapped in the air and landed on bare skin. The sound of the victim's screams and the crackle of leather twisting in the wind hurt Anne's ears and heart. She closed her eyes as the other eleven were given.

The victim was dragged away and dropped right in front of the girl whom he loved. The poor girl's eyes were filled with tears and rage.

When the overseer gave his mistress a nod, Miranda spoke up once again. "She shall have two dozen."

The poor girl screamed in sheer terror. She wallowed in misery before she was even brought to the post. To further her sorrow, Miranda had the girl stripped naked for all eyes to see. Every single whip snap and piercing scream buried itself in Anne's psyche.

By the time the deed was done, Anne had to turn her head and try to contain her tears. She could not bear to watch the blood seep from the victim's back, nor the limp body being dragged away.

Anne did not know if the girl was dead.

How can anybody survive such a terrible punishment?

The overseer yelled a command and the crowd began to disperse.

Miranda turned around and pulled Anne to the side.

"Do not cry girl," Miranda ordered. "We are the mistresses of this plantation and it is our duty to supervise punishment of these indentures and slaves. I brought you out here so that you may be broken into the—business."

Anne looked horrified. *Am I expected to do such a thing when the time comes?*

"I do not want to hurt people!" Anne protested.

"It is not a question of hurting people!" Miranda yanked Anne by the shoulder and pulled her closer. "We must maintain order and discipline lest these people cut our throats in our sleep."

"They will?" Anne squeaked, horrified.

Miranda stepped into her stirrup and swiftly got back on her horse. "I need to attend to something else, alone." Miranda looked down at her terrified niece. "Run along back to the house. I am sure lunch will be ready shortly."

Anne waited for her aunt to gallop out of sight. When she disappeared over the hill, Anne darted into the bushes and threw up. Her hands on her knees and her head dipped low, she could not imagine how cruel life could have been in this so called paradise!

Was this really what I wanted?

Does my father even know what happens here?

Anne wiped her mouth and stood up, trying to maintain her balance for her head was spinning.

How will I even attempt to eat lunch when I just lost my breakfast?

17

———

Captain Elizabeth Spencer had been on this deck for weeks now since the Defiant was finally put in the water, but this was the first time she would be officially read in. Wearing her newly tailored dress uniform, she stepped forward as the coxswain blew a pipe. The sailors, themselves wearing their very best, quickly got in line. A few stragglers were pushed between them by fellow crew, eager to show the newbies how it was done.

She was slightly nervous, her pulse unsteady.

Elizabeth breathed in for a quick moment. She focused on her center, letting her body and mind relax. Elizabeth remembered the lessons she learned from her teacher years ago in Siam. Many hours Elizabeth had spent meditating under the sun. The warmth of its rays made her smile inside.

Slowly, she exhaled as she felt her unease dissipate.

Her hand reached down and touched the tip of her cutlass, always a reassuring feeling for someone in charge. *We must always remain strong,* she kept reminding herself. *Respect and authority must be instilled at once, otherwise the crew will interpret weakness.*

Elizabeth was proud. She was the first female in the Royal Navy to command a ship in the fleet. And being such, she would make sure this ship was kept up to standards by any means necessary.

Lieutenant Hicks saluted her as she walked up to him.

"Have we still not filled the ranks Mr. Hicks?" she asked him.

"No ma'am," he shook his head. "We had little luck securing the needed men. We were only able to pick up three last night."

"Where are they?"

"Still sobering up."

Elizabeth rolled her eyes slightly.

The press gang.

She abhorred the practice but sometimes it was the only way to stock a crew. If they happened to snag a few drunks with nothing in their life but debauchery, serving a Queen's ship made her sleep a little better at night. She discouraged her men from taking others who had families or women they had to support.

"Bring them up then," Elizabeth ordered.

A trio of men, hardly dressed and with bare feet, were brought up from below deck. One swung his arm. He barely missed the coxswain, who was a beast of a man. The attacker was thrown down easily and smacked in the head with the back of a hand.

"Get up you piece of filth!" The coxswain ordered. "Do that again and you will find yourself on a grate. You try that with an officer and you will swing from the yardarm."

The offending man was pulled up quickly and pushed amongst the others. He made a double take when he saw Elizabeth. His friends also looked surprised, their eyes wide with lifted eyebrows.

Elizabeth watched their facial expressions for a moment then turned back to Lieutenant Hicks. "So, I am assuming these dregs did not know their captain would be female?"

"No ma'am. We were lucky to even get them sober enough to be brought on board this morning."

"Hmm," Elizabeth muttered as she began to size up her new additions. The lone attacker was a scraggily, short man who seemed to have enjoyed his drink more than eating actual food. His teeth were mostly missing, others already showing signs of distress. This was most likely a sign of scurvy, a remedy they would have to fix immediately with the abundant citrus of the West Indies.

Then there was the tall, muscular man with a bald head. He seemed to be a welcome addition to the crew, someone who could easily be trained to hoist large sails and perform other backbreaking work.

The last looked like a man but despite burly physique had a boyish face. He was most likely a young man in his teen's who did not want to be here.

Elizabeth stepped up to him. "How old are you?"

"Thirteen," the boy said timidly. His eyes quickly glanced down at the wooden deck and stayed there.

Elizabeth sighed, her disapproval evident.

Many ships carried ship's boys, but unless they were destitute or wanted to join, she would not force a youngster.

Elizabeth turned and eyed her lieutenant.

"Why is he here?" she demanded.

"Sorry Captain Spencer." Lieutenant Hicks grabbed the boy by his scruff and began to pull him away. "Little devil looks older in the dark. Now that we got him on deck I see that's not a beard but dirt!"

There was slight laughter as Elizabeth cocked an eyebrow, then smiled. "You are free to go back on the island," she told the young boy.

"No!" The boy pleaded as he broke free. "I want to stay!"

"You do?" Lieutenant Hicks asked with a slight grin. "You do know where you are, right? You are not still drunk?"

A slight hint of laughter started once again but Elizabeth put her hand up and commanded them to stop immediately. "Why do you want to stay?"

"There is nothing left for me 'ere. My mum's dead, father I never knew," the boy softly pleaded. "I would rather try my chances on the sea, than die penniless in the streets."

"You may still die penniless sir," Elizabeth said. "There are no guarantees you will not die before a prize is found."

"I am willing to take that chance."

Elizabeth took a moment to size him up. "What is your name sir?"

"Avery Fulton."

"Well Mr. Fulton…" Elizabeth held out her hand. "Welcome aboard."

The boy eagerly shook Elizabeth's hand. When he was done, he walked over to the side and joined a group of sailor's who greeted him with a few pats and smiles.

"Well then—" Elizabeth stopped when she heard one of the other men grumble. She walked forward and cocked her head, pretending to hear. "What did you say sailor?"

"I ain't no *sailor!*" The would be attacker sneered. "And I will not be *sailing* under no woman! So you best let me leave."

The sudden, rude revelation left Elizabeth stunned for a moment. This was not the first time she had been insulted in front of crew, but this would be the first and last time she would allow this man to challenge her as captain.

A simple flogging will not do.

I have to do something more dramatic.

"What is your name?" Elizabeth asked him in a low pitch meant to instill fear.

"My name is Jackson, girlie," he whipped back his dirty brown hair and smirked, sure he had won. "And I will be leaving now."

"Yes, you will," Elizabeth smiled at him, then pointed her hand to the side railing and gave a sly look to her lieutenant. "And I hope you can swim."

Before Jackson had a chance to respond, Lieutenant Hicks seized him up and threw him over the side. There was a scream, followed by a large splash. Elizabeth waited to see if the man would start to struggle. She took a gamble by tossing him overboard.

If he knows how to swim, I will look the fool.

If he does not…

Hicks signaled to her that the man was drowning.

Elizabeth's gamble had paid off.

"Do not presume to think I will treat you any differently because I am a woman," Elizabeth said loudly to the crew. "And do not assume that you may treat me with any less respect because I am one."

None of the men dared step forward to help the man who was pleading for his life. Jackson was slowly drowning, and everyone on deck knew that to be fact.

"I am your captain whether you like it or not. I have been appointed by the Admiralty in Her Majesty's Royal Navy and you will obey my commands without question, do you understand?"

Most of the crew nodded, some had grins on their faces that showed they respected this female captain, others were just entranced by the gall she had shown to throw one of them overboard.

When Elizabeth was satisfied, she turned back to her lieutenant.

"Retrieve the soggy bastard," she ordered.

Once Jackson was fished out, he was tossed down in front of her. He continued to gasp for air. His hands clawed at his neck as if he were trying to remove a phantom noose that strangled him. On his knees, he grasped his chest and fell to his side. He was pulled up to his feet by fellow seamen and forced to stand.

The coxswain blew his whistle.

Elizabeth then turned with paper in hand and began to read in her commission.

When the task was finished, Elizabeth did not dismiss the crew. She needed to inspect them before allowing their duties to commence. The nearly drowned man was thrown at her feet once again, an act of fealty that said take him and do with him what you please.

Elizabeth had little sympathy for a man such as this. Jackson would be a troublemaker, someone she would have to discipline more than once. *But I need the body. A ship my size cannot function without men to drive her forward.*

In the meantime, I will have to make do.

Jackson will either comply or swing from my yardarm.

Elizabeth's experience told her whatever this man had done before and whatever he was destined to do on her ship— his fate was most likely death.

"Seize him up and put him in irons," Elizabeth ordered. "Let him dry out for a few days."

"Yes ma'am," Lieutenant Hicks picked up Jackson and dragged him off.

Elizabeth walked down the stairs and disappeared into her cabin.

ANNE HAD FEIGNED sickness yesterday and today to keep from eating at the grand table. The truth was, Anne was not feeling well. She was also afraid. Anne had never seen a flogging before.

It was everything Miss Elizabeth warned me about.

A bare back ripped open by whipping is an ungodly sight!

Anne wanted now more than ever to meet with her friend one last time. She secretly wanted to run away to the ship and sign on as a midshipman. Anne feared that her wish to be free from her life back in London had led her to hell on earth with no escape.

If she could at least have lunch with Elizabeth, perhaps a kind word or two would help her through this situation? It was obvious Elizabeth did not get along with Miranda. *Would Miss Elizabeth be able to give me some advice on how to handle this new life?*

How to handle my aunt?

Anne sighed. There was no use fantasizing about running away to the ship. Elizabeth would never allow her to do such a thing, even if Anne was unsure about staying here.

Miss Elizabeth said herself that something was— off? Surely, if I got a letter to her perhaps we could at least talk?

But how can I do that without raising my aunt's suspicions? Zara cannot do it. Surely she would refuse for fear of punishment!

After what Anne had witnessed she would never ask Zara to risk her own well being. *I will just have to figure out something myself.*

Anne continued to wander the hall. She was half convinced she was walking around in a haze.

It was almost dusk.

There was a lone light coming from the portrait room. Anne carefully peeked around the corner, trying to avoid her aunt. She had also been careful to keep away from her uncle.

Zara had been kind enough to check on his whereabouts tonight. He had not stumbled into her room drunk yet but after what Zara had told her he might think her body was also plantation property. Zara might be a little standoffish but the young girl was fiercely protective. She said she would never allow that man into Anne's quarters.

Zara was loyal to Miranda Sutton and in turn loyal to Anne Sutton.

Zara also seemed not to be afraid of him.

Of all the servants, she said she had special permission to keep him away through any means necessary— including at the point of a knife, which she said she had to pull a few times this year, Randal thinking she too was *his* property.

Zara is only about fourteen years old. What kind of deviant tries to molest a girl that young?

Now Anne was really fearful of running into her uncle alone again.

Tonight, Uncle Randal was *visiting* a woman in the indentured servant's quarters. Just the thought made Anne recoil in anger, sure the woman did not abide his company willingly.

Anne walked into the room and spun around slowly, taking in the spectacle of all the portraits on the walls. Something about the room felt soothing. The pictures seemed to whisper in a way. Anne closed her eyes and tried to listen.

Are they talking to me?

Opening her eyes quickly, she darted to her left then her right. Voices in her head began a chorus of speech. What were they trying to say?

What door?

A wall?

The light by the wall?

Anne whipped her head towards the eastern wall. She saw a lone sconce, the only one that was lit in the room. It was the lone *light* by the wall.

But no door.

Anne walked over and pushed a brick.

Nothing happened.

She pushed again, still with no reaction.

Intrigued, Anne carefully pushed her hand on the sconce. She was afraid she might burn herself but there was no heat. Her fingers felt for a lever. She touched a round surface then quickly pulled down.

The bricks that seemed to be a wall revealed a door instead. Carefully, she poked her head inside.

Anne's eyes lit up. She opened her mouth and gawked at the beauty lining the mirrored shelves in the small room.

Crystals— *everywhere!*

Anne realized there was no actual light in the room. *Are the crystals producing their own light?*

Is it harnessed energy?

Black obsidian, citrine, rose quartz. Every kind of crystal Anne had ever seen or read about were on these shelves! Most were large and bigger than a fist. Blue, green and yellow apatite, aquamarine and carnelian.

And then there were the ones Anne did not recognize.

"Every crystal has a different purpose," Miranda said from the doorway.

Anne did not look back. The light show was too amazing to be disturbed by her aunt's intrusion. "They are all so beautiful!"

"Who told you how to get in here?" Miranda asked as she stepped in front of the amethyst and admired it.

"I thought I heard whispering."

"Hmm... you also have the ear."

"Ear?"

"Your ancestors... they still communicate through the harnessed energy."

Anne finally looked at her aunt. "The paintings? They are alive?"

"Not in reality. They are just paintings." Miranda picked up a ruby and held it to her eye. "Our familiar energy continues to move to and through the crystals we harness for power... education... soothsaying. Some crystals can record the past. They can remember."

Anne noticed a few buckets of dirt on a lone table. She walked over and put her finger on the dirt.

"Those are recharging," Miranda explained.

"In dirt?"

"The earth's vibrations."

"Why not just put them in the garden?"

"That dirt," Miranda pointed to the bucket on the left. "Is from Pompeii. The one in the middle is from the Caves of Zugarramurdi. And the one you have your finger on," Miranda walked over and put her own on. She pulled out a blue topaz. "This is from Northern Ireland. The lands from which our ancestors came."

"Celtic?"

"Very good." Miranda moved around Anne, and faced the girl directly. "You have much to learn of our family."

Anne walked over to another set of mirrored shelves and stared at the wonders. Her eyes were entranced by the colors. "You said all crystals have energy?" She lifted her necklace and held her mother's ring. Ever since her last discussion with her aunt Anne was even more curious about the piece of jewelry. "Even this?"

"Yes." Miranda walked over. "This ring was once your grandmother's."

"It was?" Anne said, surprised. *Why then was it given to me instead of to my aunt?* "Father... he gave it to me before we left."

Miranda huffed. "Your mother should have given it to you on your seventeenth birthday."

Anne looked at her oddly. "Why seventeenth?"

"Because that is when we start to develop our gift Anne."

Anne looked around, uncertain. "What do you mean by that?"

"Feel into the gemstone and you will understand."

Anne raised her eyebrows, slightly amused. *Why is my aunt being so cryptic?*

Anne finally did as she was told.

"Close your eyes," Miranda said, touching Anne's hands. When their skin made contact, Anne felt an electric charge. She tried to pull away, but her aunt held a firm grip.

"My hand hurts," Anne whimpered.

"Ignore the pain," Miranda's eyes hardened.

Anne tried to pull back once again. This time, her aunt squeezed harder.

"You're hurting me," Anne complained.

"Your connection is strong," Miranda ignored her protests. "But your mind is weak."

Anne could not concentrate. Her arm felt like it was on fire. Finally, she had had enough. She let her body lean backwards, forcing the connection to end.

Angered, Miranda went to grab her niece's hands once again, but Anne stepped backwards.

"Leave me be," Anne warned. She did not know where she'd found her sudden confidence but her aunt heeded the warning. Miranda actually stopped, her own eyes a little frightened.

She's scared of me? Anne thought, intrigued. *But why?*

"You should have come to me sooner," Miranda snarled. "Your mother refused, and now you are without discipline."

What does she mean by that? She thinks me a hellion?

"Lara kept you from ever learning because she wanted nothing for you but a boring, mundane life," Miranda said with a sniff. She turned her head for a moment, looking at her own wall of treasures.

"My mother was nothing but loving to me." Anne felt the blood rush to her face, her mask of politeness now gone. It appeared there was no longer room for social niceties in this house. "You speak cruelly of a woman whom you never visited, let alone really knew."

"I did not have to visit to understand you were never meant to stay there. I can give you more than she ever offered."

"You whip people bloody Aunt Miranda. Is that what you are planning to teach me?"

The older woman folded her fingers around her amethyst pendant and locked eyes with Anne. "You have a destiny girl, whether you want to accept it or not."

"I would like to go to bed if I may be excused? I am not feeling well." Anne hoped to remove herself from this situation before she said something really off putting. Would her aunt dare try to strike her? Or whip her like a field hand for telling her true feelings?

Miranda sighed then narrowed her eyes once again. Anne was sure she had insulted the woman and was about to get a tongue lashing; instead, all that was given was a wave of the hand.

"Go to bed if you insist," Miranda said. "But this conversation will continue once you are feeling better."

Anne nodded her head. "Thank you Aunt Miranda."

Quickly Anne left the room.

18

─────────

Anne was almost recovered from her last bout of sickness before she lay ill in bed once again! Her head hurt tremendously and she could hardly move. Legs that were swollen and a stomach that kept trying to decide if it wanted to empty itself, Anne was bedridden for two days straight.

Why am I always so sick?

Am I cursed here in the West Indies?

Anne could not help but think of what her aunt had said to her days before.

I have no special powers. I am no one to be feared. I am just an ordinary, boring girl— right?

Who sees things in crystals? Anne huffed.

Anne had finally insisted to her aunt that she wanted to see Elizabeth before the ship sailed. Of course, her aunt said no and then forcefully insisted the sickness would keep Anne from going anywhere anyway.

Her aunt had instructed Zara to keep her hydrated. Anne did not want to drink any more. The beautiful cocktails she had come to know had turned into a nauseating nightmare. She didn't know if the drink itself was causing the distress.

Or my aunt's words?

Miranda told her that people sometimes reacted differently when given nourishment from another part of the world. She had insisted Anne keep drinking the cocktails to keep up her energy. The more Zara poured, the more Anne felt sick.

Thankfully tonight, Anne had begun to feel a little better.

Zara had brought her soup earlier in the evening. The liquid had a little kick to it. Anne had never had such spicy food in her life until she moved to this island. This time it was Zara who explained that spicy food was a staple in a tropical region like this. She had assured Anne her palate would get used to the hot food in time.

Anne forced herself to sit up and swing her legs over the side. She put her left hand to her throat and touched her mother's ring. The cold sensation was a welcome feeling.

She missed her mother.

She missed her father and brother.

And Lord help me, I miss Miss Elizabeth the most!

No matter what the woman had done, Elizabeth had been nothing but kind and generous. No one else would have paid so much attention to her except her own mother. If she confessed to Elizabeth what was really going on, would the other woman try to intervene?

In reality, what could Elizabeth really do? She was not family and had no right to interfere.

Anne had also come to believe her Aunt Miranda was pretty much— insane.

Was this the affliction Elizabeth had questioned her father about that night?

Will I too slowly go insane one day?

Anne stood up and dressed. She put her boots on carefully and walked to the veranda and stood in the open air.

The night wind was breezy.

She was thankful the heat had been a little better these last few days. The combination, along with her sickness, had not helped her mood much. She didn't know if a walk would help, but she was determined to try.

Anne looked towards the harbor and exhaled softly. If she weren't so sick, she might actually have tried to go down to the port herself.

I did it once before in London. And see how well that turned out? Miss Elizabeth might not be there to save me this time.

I'm such a stupid girl!

Anne knew she should not venture into the garden alone this night but the weather was so nice. And, she desperately wanted to smell the garden in bloom.

Anne carefully walked through the garden. She made certain to make little noise.

She disappeared into the line of jasmine trees and put her hands out. Softly caressing the flower, Anne put her nose to the sweet blossom and inhaled. She would make sure to bring some back to put in her room. Perhaps it would help alleviate the smell of sickness in the air there?

Suddenly, a rough hand reached out from the side and pulled her back. Anne tried to yell, but another hand quickly muffled her mouth.

"Anne?" Uncle Randal's raspy voice whispered. "What are you doing out here so late? You seem to like to wander... unattended."

He is drunk— again!

The smell of hard spirits emanated from his whole body. Anne had come to know that the man did not settle for simple cocktails with small amounts of alcohol. He liked his spirits hard and drank them with as much gusto as a drunken sailor.

"If you promise not to scream," Randal lied. "I will let my hand down."

Anne frightfully nodded her head in agreement. Anne did not know if she could escape but she was pretty sure he had enough liquor in him that she might be able to knock him over.

It was only courage she needed to muster.

She was terrified.

"That's a good girl." Randal released his hand from her mouth, but not her arm.

"Let me go," Anne insisted, trying to find her strength. Unfortunately, her voice only sounded weak. "Or I will scream for my aunt!"

"Your aunt? Do you think your aunt actually cares about you?"

Anne blinked, confused. "Of course she does?"

"Stupid child. Why do you think you have been so sick? Miranda has been keeping you drugged, haven't you noticed?"

Anne would not believe his accusation. "You're lying. Why would she do that?" *What possible reason can my aunt have to drug me?* "I have been sick because of the weather and my exertion from travel, nothing more."

"Is that what she has been telling you?" Randal slurred, his tongue loose from the alcohol.

This Anne recognized.

She had seen this before in men, and women. Anne had witnessed loose talk at balls and dinner tables filled with guests. The more they drank, the more they were free with their thinking and actions. Her brother Michael had told her a few tales of sailors who had lost their whole pay by drinking too much then fighting and landing in a jail cell.

Anne did not know much of her uncle's history but she was pretty sure this must have happened to him more than once in his lifetime.

"Let go of me!" Anne forcefully demanded once again, this time her voice more steady.

"Nonsense." Randal pulled her close. "Let us have a dance!"

His breath was so close, Anne could hardly keep from gagging. She looked around, panic stricken. She did not know what to do.

Silently, Anne prayed he would let her go if she had one dance with him. Her body shifted as she allowed him to lead.

Her uncle hummed a drunken tune.

Anne closed her eyes. If she imagined she was somewhere else— *perhaps in the arms of Sarah, maybe this will end quicker?*

Suddenly, his hands pushed up against her breasts. As Anne went to scream, he put his left hand over her mouth once again.

This time she had no room to move.

The more Anne fought, the tighter his grip!

"Stay still!" Randal cursed.

When his hand reached under her dress and caressed her genitalia, Anne pulled back as hard as she could. He reached for her neck with both hands and forced her closer. Anne's necklaced ring was caught in his fingertips as he began to choke her. She knew that in his mind, Randal did not care if she was unconscious to get what he wanted!

If he violates me, will my aunt believe me? Or will she blame me instead for wandering around so late at night?

Anne was now angry.

I will not allow him to rape me!

I want him off— now!

Anne's rage became focused. She did not realize that her anger had channeled through her body and into the crystals in her ring. A bright, blue flash of energy shot out from the jewelry and hit Randal hard. He flew backwards several feet before hitting the ground.

Anne gasped, trying to catch her breath. She did not know what had happened. She touched her neck and nervously looked around.

Where did that blue flash come from?

Anne looked down and saw her uncle on the ground. His eyes were wide open. There was no movement from his body.

Is he even breathing?

Anne stared at him. She could hardly catch her breath as her hand, as if by instinct, touched her ring.

Anne wanted to scream in anger and pure terror!

Instead, she kept her mouth shut. She did not want to draw unwanted attention.

Did I do this?

Did I kill him?

"Anne? Where are you?" A loud voice yelled from the distance. "Where the bloody hell have you gone off to?"

Anne widened her eyes, once again terrified.

Somehow, Anne sensed her aunt had felt the energy in some way. Anne looked around, panicked. She knew she had to get out of here and flee despite how weak her body was.

She could hear rustling of foliage and yelling voices in the distance. People had been ordered to find her.

Anne bolted to the stables.

She had only one place she could flee.

Anne prayed her savior had not yet set sail!

IF THERE WAS one thing in life that Anne was taught as a lady, it was the ability to ride. This mare was fast, one of the best on the plantation.

As a lady, Anne was also expected to ride side saddle when wearing a dress. This was neither the time nor the place. She had always switched when her coach was out of sight. Her brother would chastise her but always laugh. They had great races, many of which she won. How could she be expected to win like a man if she could not ride like one?

Anne looked out towards the port, which was still a good distance away. She squeezed her legs and made the horse go faster.

When she had gone into town with her aunt, she was careful to have studied the path. Her horse's hoofs beat quickly on the dirt road as she remembered the way. The night was dark and thankfully few pedestrians were on the streets. The horse almost knocked her off as she quickly pulled to the side to keep from running over a drunk. He cursed at her as she continued to race forward.

In the distance, the most welcome site lay in front of her.

The HMS Defiant.

This was the ship her father and Elizabeth had laughed at and joked about weeks earlier.

Will it be my refuge? Anne hoped. *Even if it does not sail tonight, surely Miss Elizabeth will not allow me to be returned to my aunt?* Anne would demand she be allowed to stay. *I will plead and cry if I have to!*

Anne steadied the horse and stopped near the dock. Quickly, she jumped off and slapped the animal, so the great beast would run back from whence it came. When the horse did not move, she ran towards it.

"Go!" Anne yelled as the horse bolted.

She lifted her skirt and ran as fast as her legs would take her. She did not care that she had been sick with little energy. If she passed out, she would do the deed on Captain Elizabeth Spencer's ship!

As Anne tried to walk up the gangway, an officer put out his hand and demanded she stop.

"Where do you think you are going young woman?" Lieutenant Hicks asked roughly.

"Please! I have to get on this ship!" Anne begged.

"I am sorry if one of these lost souls married you or did— whatever? But you cannot just run onto a Queen's ship," Lieutenant Hicks said. "You can wave like all the other strumpets when we leave tomorrow morning."

Anne could not wait that long.

Tomorrow?

I have to wait until morning? Where else might I hide in the meantime? And what about my aunt? Will she try and storm the ship if Miss Elizabeth does take me on board?

"Please sir!" Anne pleaded. "I must speak to Miss Elizabeth!"

"To whom?"

"Captain Spencer!" Anne corrected herself quickly. "This is her ship?"

"Yes, this is her ship young woman but Captain Spencer has turned in for the night. Perhaps you can come back in the early morning."

"No!" Anne shook her head roughly. "You don't understand! Just let me speak to your captain?"

Abruptly, Lieutenant Hicks turned his attention away. He looked over her shoulder at the commotion heading down the road. A black carriage was moving at full speed, surrounded by numerous men on dark steeds.

"Now what is this?" Lieutenant Hicks murmured to himself. His hand reached down towards his chest belt as his fingertips gently touched a flintlock.

Anne turned and gasped. Quickly, she felt her heart drop. She knew exactly what this was. *My aunt is determined to bring me back!*

Panicked, Anne started to yell at the ship.

"CAPTAIN SPENCER!" Anne's voice screeched. "CAPTAIN! PLEASE!"

Lieutenant Hicks grabbed her by the arm and pulled her inward. "Be QUIET young woman! I told you the captain is—"

Anne did not care. She continued to scream louder. "MISS ELIZA-BETH! PLEASE— HELP ME!"

The carriage pulled up. As the horses neighed and screeched, a door forcefully swung open. Miranda jumped out and headed straight for her.

"WHAT are you DOING you stupid child!" Miranda accused.

Frozen in place, Anne swallowed hard. Her aunt was mad as a hornet.

Anne shook her head for a moment, trying to shake off her anxiety. She needed to find her courage. Anne dug her heels into the sand then tried to bolt up the ship's gangplank. Lieutenant Hicks reached over and held her tight.

"Let me go!" Anne pleaded.

Lieutenant Hicks refused to release his grip. Anne was sure he had no idea what was going on but an older woman yelling at a young girl meant only one thing!

He probably thinks I am trying to run away with a sailor.

With a wicked snap of the wrist, Miranda pulled Anne away from him. She leaned into her niece's ear. "I will lash you harder than you have ever been when we get home."

Anne looked into the older woman's eyes. She inhaled sharply. They appeared to be completely black. Anne tried to pry herself loose but the other woman's grip was like a vise— almost inhumanely strong.

"WHAT is going on Mr. Hicks?" A deep, yet feminine voice bellowed from the distance.

Anne turned her head and caught the attention of Elizabeth. Anne said nothing, pleading only with her eyes.

"Anne?" Elizabeth quickly ran up the steps and over the gangplank. She put her hands gently on one of the younger woman's arms, ignoring the fact Miranda was practically strangling the other. "What is the matter? Are you okay?"

"She is fine Elizabeth." Miranda's tone had completely changed to kindness, as well as her eyes back to normal. "We had a slight misunderstanding. I think Anne got frightened from her fever. She has been very unwell."

Elizabeth eyed her old enemy then turned her attention only to Anne. "Is that true Anne?"

Anne wanted to tell Elizabeth the truth but the vise-like grip on her arm got tighter, the pain more intense. Her eyes slightly watered from the pain. Her mouth would not work, even as she willed her muscles to move. It was as if something were keeping her from speaking.

"See... she is not well," Miranda said. "She needs to go back to bed." The woman turned her attention back to the carriage. Zara was dutifully standing outside the door, waiting for orders. "Zara... help Anne back into the cab. She needs to be hydrated, I feel she has been fevered."

The suggestion of more cocktails jerked Anne back into reality.

"No... please!" Anne screeched.

Elizabeth tilted her head in concern. She wrinkled her brow as she studied Anne's face for a split second.

Anne was beyond frightened. Her breath caught in her throat. She was unable to properly find her words. She wanted to cry but no tears would form.

Is my aunt controlling me somehow?

Elizabeth carefully watched the young woman's eyes. Anne wondered if her friend could feel the utter horror at the idea of going back to the plantation.

"Miranda?" Elizabeth finally said. She turned to her old foe. "I think that Anne should stay with me. If only for the night. Something has truly frightened her. Perhaps in the morning you can come fetch her."

"No." Miranda was stern. "She will come back with me now. You have no right to this child."

"I am NOT a child!" Anne snapped loudly, happy she had finally spoken up.

Miranda turned and eyed her niece. "You are a silly, insipid little nit. You need to be taught your place and I will do that whether you like it or not!"

Elizabeth moved forward. She stood in front of Anne and put her own hand up in a defensive posture. "Release her arm Miranda— immediately."

Miranda laughed loudly. "And what will you do if I do not... captain?"

"I will order Lieutenant Hicks to shoot you."

"You would not dare."

"Try me."

Miranda looked over at the ship. Sailors stood at the side railings, eager to join the fight if need be. Miranda turned to her own men. They were also ready to fight.

Anne glanced around the scene. Her aunt only had four men. Elizabeth's crew numbered a good dozen this late night. *Are they to have a bloody fight? I do not want to be the cause of such violence!*

Anne felt the grip on her arm release. She looked at her aunt.

She must accept she is vastly outnumbered?

Elizabeth leaned inward. "Get on board the ship," she quietly told Anne.

Anne quickly bolted up the gangway and ran onto the quarterdeck.

Miranda stepped forward and harshly glared at her enemy. "I would severely advise you to rethink this Elizabeth."

Elizabeth inhaled sharply, her own breath caught for a brief moment. She tried not to be frightened by the sudden change in Miranda's eyes, but how could she not? They had turned dark as the night sky.

"This will go very badly for you," Miranda added.

Elizabeth stepped back onto the gangway and drew her saber. Collective gasps ensued as she moved close and put the tip to Miranda's throat. "If you try to take Anne by force... I shall end you."

Their eyes remained static for a long time. Finally, Miranda's eyes returned to normal as she stepped back. "You will regret this... captain."

"Most likely."

Miranda whipped around like a whirlwind and stormed towards her carriage. Her door was opened for her as she entered then she slammed the door behind her. Only when the carriage and men began their long journey home did Elizabeth finally lower her weapon.

"What have I just done?" Elizabeth softly whispered to herself.

Not knowing what to do, Anne rubbed her hands together nervously and paced back and forth.

What have I done! Anne cried inside. She quickly decided her decision to flee might have been wrong. *Maybe I overreacted?*

Anne didn't have time to ponder. The cabin door opened and shut with a bang. Anne stopped abruptly. Her breath caught in her throat. Frightened, Anne slowly turned to see Elizabeth. The woman's eyebrows were bent harshly. Anne had never seen her friend so displeased before.

Before Anne could open her mouth to explain her actions, Elizabeth crooked a finger and pointed toward a chair instead.

"Sit!" Elizabeth firmly instructed.

Anne sat down immediately in front of the desk. She could not even look at her savior.

Captain Elizabeth Spencer walked around her desk, pulled out her own chair and sat down. She did not speak.

Anne waited for her to start a lecture but nothing came. The silence was deafening. Anne finally lifted her head and acknowledged the person that had helped her. Anne knew she was expected to explain.

"Miss—"

"Ah!" Elizabeth cut her off. She crossed her fingers and leaned forward. "Before you speak, be mindful of what you are about to say. Please tell me why I might have just thrown away my career. Please tell me you didn't just force my hand over some childish tirade or misunderstanding."

Anne was afraid to open her mouth. She had never heard her friend use such a harsh tone.

Maybe I did overreact? Anne worried. *Do I even fully understand what happened? Maybe I should have just stayed back at the plantation and told my aunt what happened! Let HER deal with her husband!*

But her eyes... so dark and black.

And drugging me? Is it true what Uncle Randal said?

"Can you not speak anymore Anne?" Elizabeth demanded.

"I'm sorry miss... I'm..." Anne stopped mid-sentence. She could not find her words.

Elizabeth studied her, watched her— almost to the point of making Anne feel uncomfortable. When Anne tried to look at her own feet, she was instructed not to.

"Look at me Anne," Elizabeth ordered.

Anne did as she was told.

"He attacked you, didn't he?" Elizabeth questioned.

"Yes miss." Anne wasn't surprised that her friend could guess that was what happened. She had a feeling that Elizabeth had known this to happen before.

"What did he do?"

Anne stared at Elizabeth. The whole situation happened so fast Anne didn't really know what to tell her friend. *And the flash of energy? How can I even explain that?* Anne couldn't even describe to herself what had transpired.

"Did he... " Elizabeth chose her next words carefully. "Violate you?"

"I don't know!" Anne gasped. "He put his hands on my breasts and embraced me!" Deeply she inhaled, trying not to burst out crying. "He stuck his hand under my dress and... he touched me there!"

"You did nothing wrong Anne. You did nothing to deserve this." Elizabeth reached her hand across and held the younger one's in her own. "Randal is a disgusting creature, into whom I should have put a lead ball years ago. If I would have been there I would have shot him dead. I still may."

Anne opened her eyes wide, shocked by the comment.

"Does that bother you?" Elizabeth continued. "That I would kill to protect?"

"No."

"We never should have left you there." Elizabeth shook her head in disgust. "You were violated, and I am deeply sorry for that— but thank God you were not raped," Elizabeth said softly.

"Women who are not virgins are not marrying material."

"Unfortunately in our society, a woman's worth is based on stupid customs." Elizabeth got up from her chair and walked over to a side table. She grabbed a decanter and a goblet. She sat down and poured herself a drink of rum. After Elizabeth took a long sip she placed the goblet down. "However horrible this experience has been for you, know that your first sexual experience should be one of love, not violence. One that you would carry with you for the rest of your life..." Elizabeth paused for a moment as if a memory had entered her mind. "Believe me."

Elizabeth drank another large portion of the rum then exhaled. She put the goblet down once again. This time she leaned forward and started to rub her own temples.

"My mother never spoke to me like you do," Anne confessed.

"Your mother was brought up believing that the less girls know, the better," Elizabeth smiled. "As I once was." Anne watched Elizabeth carefully as the woman drank some more. "I was raised in a similar way but the older we get the more we learn about life and hopefully become wiser."

Elizabeth caught her gaze. She tilted her head, slightly intrigued.

"What is it you want to ask me?" Elizabeth inquired.

Anne hesitated for a moment. She did not know if she really wanted to ask the question. *Will Miss Elizabeth find my question too intrusive?*

"You said believe me?" Anne finally asked. "Did something happen to you?"

Elizabeth emptied her goblet then stared at the wall. She made no eye contact or speech for a long moment.

"I was attacked when I was younger than you," Elizabeth finally confessed.

"Like me?"

"No... I should have been more specific." Elizabeth looked directly at her subject. "I was raped when I was much younger than you."

Anne put her hands to her mouth and loudly gasped.

"For a long time I let it define me... shape me..." Elizabeth shook her head. "I was angry, very angry... It still hurts, but no longer has the control over me it once did."

"I'm sorry that happened to you," Anne didn't know what else to say.

"I am sorry too," Elizabeth said as she got up. She walked over to the younger one and held out her hand. Anne accepted the kind gesture. "I will get you settled and we will talk about your next steps in the morning."

Elizabeth walked Anne over to the corner. Anne sat down on the small cot.

"Will my aunt not come back tonight?"

"I would not put the idea past her. She is an awful woman." Elizabeth headed for the door. "That is why we are setting sail immediately. Which is what I need to attend to. As for you, you need to rest. You really do look horrible from your sickness."

Anne laid down as Elizabeth left the cabin. She was thankful that she had escaped but fearful of what her aunt might do. Anne had to tell Elizabeth the truth— but how?

Will Miss Elizabeth even believe I might have magical powers?

PART III

19

As Miranda paced back and forth she mumbled to herself incoherently. She was in the portrait room surrounded by her family of yesteryear. She swore they were laughing at her. Always they watched with scornful eyes mocking her feeble attempts at greatness. Another Sutton that was destined to destroy herself through her own stupidity!

The voices never stopped. They spoke to her within her mind. She knew she was not imagining things. Her mother had conversed with the paintings many times before.

Miranda put her hands to her ears and screamed. She could not take their shaming anymore. She began to yell back at the portraits in a series of insults as they continued to mock.

"Shut up!"

"Go to hell!"

"I know!"

"You have no idea!"

"You never understood!"

"I am NOT like you!"

Miranda screamed once again and threw a candle at them. She wanted the paintings to burn.

Nothing happened.

The candle simply fell to the ground; the wick sputtered and died. The paintings would never burn, no matter how hard she tried.

"What happened?" another voice said.

This voice was different, soft— consoling.

Miranda walked over to the full length mirror. Her reflection gave way to Miss Barton, Anne's former governess who smiled back.

"My blasted husband, that is what happened!" Miranda started to pace once again.

"You need to calm down."

"Easy for you to say; you are four thousand miles away!"

A hand reached through the mirror as the surface rippled. Miranda walked over and pulled Miss Barton out. Miss Barton now stood in front of Miranda in the flesh.

"Tell me what happened," Miss Barton calmly requested.

Miranda shook her head. She snapped her head angrily as another painting mocked her. Miss Barton came from behind with open arms. The woman leaned inward and nuzzled her chin in the crook of Miranda's neck. Miranda enjoyed the embrace for a second until she remembered her dilemma.

"Not now Selina," Miranda chastised.

Selina Barton ignored her command choosing instead to kiss Miranda softly on the neck.

"My deity will not be happy," Miranda said calmly as she gave into the sensation. She turned and allowed the kiss to transfer to her lips.

"He will understand you need to calm down first to think clearly. Let me — help calm you down."

They enjoyed each other for a long moment before Selina pulled back gently. She touched a loose strand of Miranda's hair and softly stroked her fingers through the locks.

"Where is your infernal husband?" Selina asked.

"Where he can't interfere ever again."

Miranda took Selina by the hand and walked her into the bedroom. In the corner, Randal sat straight up in a chair, eyes wide as he appeared to be catatonic. Only when he flicked his eyes towards Selina, did a show of fear appear on his sullen face. Selina smiled in delight as she examined him closer, like a circus animal on display for her amusement. She turned to her lover and smirked.

"You left him somewhat conscious." Selina stuck out her finger and poked his forehead, forcing it back slightly. "Your work is exceptional my dear... much better than mine."

"I did not do this," Miranda bit. "Anne did!"

"She did?" Selina poked him with her finger once again. She smiled wickedly. Randal might be enraged but one could not really tell. After she had her fun she turned towards her lover. "Hmm.. she is more powerful than you thought."

"Yes— and I need her back here!"

"Then send Zara to bring her back."

"I already have but I do not have faith that Zara can accomplish the task."

"Why? You have taught her well." Selina crept closer and caressed the other woman's face. "And you are an... excellent teacher my dear."

Miranda closed her eyes and enjoyed the touch. She was finally beginning to settle down. Selina was always able to calm her in the most perfect way.

Miranda returned the favor and touched Selina's face. "Anne overheard her father say she had an... affliction."

"Were you spying on your brother and his whore again?"

"Elizabeth suspected something. That blasted woman has always had a way of getting under my skin."

Selina's expression suddenly hardened, angered by the comment.

Miranda stroked her lover's cheek this time trying to calm her. "Ignore thoughts of Elizabeth. You must learn to forgive me."

"I hate that woman."

"As do I."

Selina took a moment then finally nodded her head in agreement. "So an affliction? Is that what we are calling our gift these days."

"No." Miranda let out a small chuckle. "The silly little nit probably thought her affliction was a preference for girls."

"How interesting... our little Anne is becoming more intriguing by the moment," Selina cooed. "I always suspected." She wrapped her arms around Miranda and softly whispered in her ear. "As the saying goes... the apple doesn't fall far from the tree...or family tree I should say."

They both laughed as they sauntered towards the bed.

Selina turned and stared at Randal.

"What about him? Are you going to help him?"

"No. His libido has caused enough unwanted attention to my plantation."

Selina walked forward as Miranda sat on the bed. She patted the bed encouraging her lover to sit. Selina glanced at the husband for a second, unsure.

"Are you simply going to leave him there?" she asked.

"Yes." Miranda didn't even look at him. "Let him watch."

STANDING ON THE QUARTERDECK, Anne breathed in the ocean air. She had slept well despite all that had happened to her last night. Anne remembered what Elizabeth had said... that she would have shot Uncle Randal dead if she would have been there.

But what about that flash of energy that came out of my ring? Anne thought nervously. She touched the piece of jewelry hanging around her neck. *How can such an enormous amount of power come from such a little object? Aunt Miranda bragged about our family's lineage and abilities. Did I call on the crystal to protect me?*

Anne wanted to tell Elizabeth what really happened but she was too frightened. *What will my friend think? My aunt talks to crystals? I can harness a power I cannot explain— or have any idea how I did it?*

Miss Elizabeth will laugh in my face.

Anne decided she was not going to say anything to her friend.

Whatever happened has to have been a fluke. Sometimes in nature odd things happen that cannot be explained, Anne tried to convince herself.

"Anne?" A timid voice said from behind.

Anne turned and saw the young man whom she had met at the ball and who had walked with her in the garden a while back in London, Midshipman Finlay Travers.

"Finlay!" Anne leapt forward and placed her hands around his neck. She happily hugged him.

Behind her Anne heard a throat clear to announce another's presence.

Finlay looked up and quickly changed expression to one of embarrassment as his face flushed red. Captain Spencer stood right behind them. Finlay quickly pulled back from Anne's embrace.

"Sorry ma'am," he apologized to the captain then nervously pulled on his jacket afraid his uniform might have gotten out of order.

Elizabeth glanced at him, then at Anne. "While I am glad you may have found a lost friend Anne— let's keep the touching to a minimum."

"Of course." Anne dipped her head slightly. "I am sorry to have done that Mr. Travers."

"It was... my—" Finley tried to speak but was at a loss for words. "I'm fine— I mean..." Another glance from his captain helped him along. "I must get back to my duties Miss Sutton," Finlay nodded to them both. "Captain."

When Finlay bolted down the stairs, Elizabeth chuckled. "Young men have the worst time finding their words around pretty girls."

"Me?" Anne guffawed. "No... he is just a nice boy who walked me through a garden once."

Elizabeth cocked an eyebrow.

Anne knew what her friend was getting at. "We are just friends!"

"Well please keep it at that while you are on this ship. The young man needs to learn about sail and navigation, not the ways of the heart."

Anne smiled. She was confident she would not be getting too *friendly* with him.

THE JOURNEY to Jamaica took less than a week. The winds were good and the ship managed to stay afloat. Anne was slightly concerned when Finlay had told her that men had to take turns on the bilge pumps for water had been seeping into the hold. He assured her that Captain Spencer would surely get the problem fixed once in port. Since the HMS Defiant had been careened for such a long time, there was no way to see how sound the ship would be until she was let loose on the high seas and tested to her limits.

Thankfully they made it to Kingston harbor and did not sink.

Anne stood at the railing and watched as they sailed by the island. Jamaica had tall mountains that pierced through dark, foreboding clouds. Rows of sugarcane snaked up the hills producing dark, green reeds that were taller than a person.

The ship docked in the harbor. All around, there were many other ships, including two Royal Navy frigates and a cutter. Anne did not see her father's ship.

"My father is not here," Anne said as Elizabeth walked over to her.

"No... I did not think he would be. He was headed for the Leeward Islands."

"Oh— "

"Don't fret Anne, we will get word to him."

"I have no idea what he is going to think when he gets a letter saying I ran away!"

"You technically did not run away. You asked for help and I took you from that island."

"That is what you are going to tell him?"

"That— and a few choice words about your Uncle Randal."

Anne knew in her heart that her father would never have wanted her to be in danger. What would her father do to her uncle when he found out? Would he shoot him dead like Elizabeth had threatened to do?

The coxswain yelled loudly to a group of men. Anne watched as they maneuvered the pinnace over the side.

Slowly, they lowered the boat.

"Do I have to get into the basket again?" Anne asked.

"Yes," Elizabeth said.

Anne sighed and did as she was told.

Once she was safely in the pinnace and on her way she watched the sights roll by as the coxswain encouraged his crew to keep pace. They rowed in unison as they started to sing.

Anne smiled, listening to the tune.

Finally, the pinnace pulled up next to a pier. A young boy in torn clothes and bare feet grabbed the line that was tossed to him. He wrapped the rope around a post and pulled forward, tightening the grip around the beat-up wood. The HMS Defiant's coxswain got out first. Next, Elizabeth stood up and easily stepped off the boat. She turned and looked at Anne, who was having a hard time balancing as the pinnace bobbed back and forth. Elizabeth held out her hand and helped the younger woman onto the pier. Anne barely kept from tripping as her foot caught her skirt bottom on the rough wood.

"Thank you," Anne said politely as she straightened out her dress.

The coxswain placed a set of small bags onto the pier and nodded to his captain. He stepped back into the pinnace and barked another set of orders. The crew quickly untied the rope, grabbed their oars and headed back to the ship.

"Anne? Would you find trousers more suitable as we travel?" Elizabeth asked.

Anne had only worn trousers once in her life. She had put on a pair of her brother's and joined in a neighborhood game of rough play. Not only was she scolded for wearing such a thing, she was punished for rough-housing with the boys.

Ladies did not act in such a manor, her mother had yelled.

When her father found out, he just laughed, much to her mother's dismay. Anne believed her punishment was worsened because of his aloof reaction.

"I would like that," Anne answered.

"Excellent." Elizabeth smiled. "I do not want you to take a dip in the water by accident. I do not want to cause you undue harm before I deliver you to your father!"

Anne grinned. She imagined herself being *delivered* to her father in a pair of trousers with a tanned face and salt scorched hair. What kind of reaction might he have but shock, then laughter?

"Balancing in a pinnace takes a little practice," Elizabeth continued. "Of course... the bay is unusually choppy this morning." She looked at Anne. "You also need your own incidentals."

Anne nodded. She had run away without anything but the dress she wore and the boots on her feet.

Anne smiled at her older friend. "Thank you miss."

They both looked at the darkened clouds as they rolled in off the mountains. The sun radiated bright hues of red and yellow, as it softly mixed within the dark purple and deep blue of the oncoming thunderstorms.

"We will most likely have a nasty storm soon," Elizabeth said.

Anne had already experienced a few of these *nasty storms* with wind so harsh that the rain blew sideways. The shutters in her aunt's house would be closed by the servants as quickly as the storm would approach. The weather could be beautiful one second then minutes later a violent gale would roll in. She was always afraid that the storm could turn into the worst thing imaginable.

"Hurricane?" Anne hesitantly asked.

"No," Elizabeth half answered as she nodded to the young boy. He snapped up the bags and waited. "Most likely not."

"But are we not in hurricane season? How can you be so sure— " Anne stopped, unsure if she should continue. Maybe it was not wise to question a woman who had not only taken her in but was obviously capable enough to have become a captain on the high seas.

Elizabeth smiled as they walked forward. The young boy quickly followed by their side. "The barometer did not indicate a low enough pressure when I checked it this morning but that does not mean the weather cannot change at a moment's notice. We must forever be vigilant."

As wood turned into dirt, Anne looked at the sights. She quickly realized how much bigger Kingston was in comparison to Bridgetown. Large, wooden buildings with huge, open shutters lay on both sides of the main streets. They bustled with as much activity as back in London. Carts filled every available space, pulled by horses and donkeys, their hooves kicking up dirt on the hot day.

Many of the local population were similar to those in Barbados. Beautiful women with skin the color of coffee walked with baskets on their heads while lean, muscular men worked the docks, unloading and loading goods.

Everyone was busy this morning including the small boy who struggled with the luggage he had in tow.

They stopped in front of a large courtyard entrance. The young boy put down the bags and waited as Elizabeth handed him a few coins. As he thanked her, he quickly darted down the street and out of sight. Elizabeth picked up the bags as they walked through the courtyard. There were large trees covered with fruit. Anne walked up and smelled a large orange colored flower. The sweet scent tickled her nose.

After the bags were settled, and their hotel room secured, Anne accompanied Elizabeth once again down the street. The morning was turning into early afternoon and they both were hot. The glare off the sand reflected a bright, unmerciful streak of light that blinded Anne's eyes. She repositioned the bergère Elizabeth had given her so that it sat slightly below her scalp to help keep the rays out. Anne watched Elizabeth's feet as a guide.

They hiked for a good distance before stopping. Anne lifted her head and put her hand in front of her eyes. Before her was a large, two story building, painted white but without the touch of island life. The front had stone steps and five columns and was built in the style of many in London. Anne knew immediately this was most likely the Admiralty.

As they walked up the steps, Elizabeth turned to her.

"Wait here… and stay out of the sun," she ordered.

Anne nodded as Elizabeth opened the door and disappeared.

~

EVEN IN THE SHADE, the heat was unmerciful. Anne fluttered her hand in front of her face to try and stir up a breeze. There was little relief from the pitiful movements. Anne wished she had a fan to cool herself with. She quietly hoped Elizabeth would hurry up.

It was hot as Hades out here!

Anne leaned against a column and watched the traffic go by. There were a few women carrying parcels or with children in tow. A man snapped his whip forward, frightening the donkey that was supposed to be hauling the dray cart.

The animal slowly moved forward.

Anne shook her head. She never liked to see animals mistreated.

As she lowered her head, she swore she heard a snicker come from the corner. Anne looked up but saw no one. Curious, she walked to the back of the columns and peeked for a quick second.

Again, the noise occurred but not where she stood.

Anne returned to where she had been. She looked left, then right. There was a boy leaning against the farthest column staring at her. His arms were folded inward and his feet were crossed. A small, tricorn hat sat on his head. His scalp was wrapped with a red bandana, his brown hair pulled back with ribbons and long braids. He wore a dark leather plackart with matching gauntlets. A sword hung from his side.

He looked like a pirate.

Anne could not see his face clearly. A piece of sugarcane was in his mouth. As he lifted his hand to adjust the stick, Anne could finally see the color of his skin— a rich caramel.

The boy began to walk towards her.

Anne watched how he walked, sauntered in fact. His hips were slightly bigger than expected.

Then it hit Anne.

The boy was not a boy— but a girl!

Anne put her hands on her hips and faced down the girl. "May I help you with something?"

"Nope," The pirate girl laughed as she leaned against another column.

She rolled the sugar cane stick around in her mouth again, then spit on the ground.

Anne curled her lip. "Then why are you staring at me?"

"Little presumptuous to think I am staring at you love."

"Then what were you doing?"

"Trying to comprehend why you would be with Lizzy."

"Who?"

"Lizzy?"

"I have no idea who that is."

"The tall, black haired strumpet you just arrived with."

"You mean Captain Spencer?" Anne sniffed, insulted.

"Captain?" The pirate girl laughed as she spit on the ground again. Anne turned her nose away at the disgusting habit. "Guess our little curd has gone up in the world."

"I will ask you kindly not to refer to my captain in that manner!"

"Your captain?" The pirate girl chuckled. "What on earth could you be to her... a maid perhaps?"

"Steward," Anne lied.

"Glorified maid... washing her unmentionables and other... items?"

"Excuse me!" Anne stepped forward, ready to smack the offender. "You have insulted my captain and now me. I take offense to your comments. Take them back immediately!"

The girl spit on the ground once again. "And you will do what if I do not?"

Anne hesitated. She really did not know what she would do. This girl looked like she could fight. Anne had no idea how to defend herself.

"Then I... I... I will report you to the governor!" Anne blurted out.

The pirate girl bent over and started laughing. When she had a good chuckle, she leaned back on the pillar. "For making fun of your cap— ee— tan? Ha— no one cares!"

Anne crossed her arms and stewed in her own annoyance. She could not do anything and now this little scalawag was laughing at her.

Anne did not know how else to react but to just be plain rude. "You need to leave."

"You do not own the streets."

"No I do not, but Captain Spencer arrests pirates. You better run along before she puts you in a gibbet."

Anne realized she may have gone too far.

Her gut was right.

She backed up when the pirate girl spit out her sugarcane stick and walked forward. Anne put her hands on her hips and straightened her back, defiant.

The pirate girl circled her. Anne held her head high. A sudden push to the back of her head caught Anne by surprise. Anne turned around and swung her fist. The pirate girl ducked then started to laugh.

"Leave me alone you little— " Anne was so angry she could hardly catch her breath. "You... you trollop!"

The pirate girl leaned in then suddenly stopped. She looked towards the door and cocked her head to listen for a moment.

"Must be going." She quickly stepped backwards, bowed with her hat extended and then took off down the road. "Many things to do this fine day!"

"What is your name!" Anne yelled at her.

"I shall remain..." The pirate girl barked from the distance. "But a mystery to you my dancing queen."

Anne snarled and slapped her hands to her side. Just as she did, the door opened.

Out stepped Captain Spencer.

"To whom were you talking?" Elizabeth asked, concerned.

"An annoying troublemaker!" Anne spat.

"There are many troublemakers around these parts Anne. Watch yourself."

"Yes miss." Anne followed her friend down the steps. She looked at the satchel the older woman held. "Were you successful in what you needed to do?"

"I was."

As Anne kept pace with the captain, she could not stop thinking about that girl. Why had that *person* bothered her in the first place? What could that *pirate* have possibly gained by annoying her?

Anne swiftly touched her neck.

Her necklace and ring— they were gone!

"That little scalawag!" Anne spat as her legs froze. "She stole my mother's necklace!"

Elizabeth looked at her oddly. "Your necklace is gone?"

"Yes! That girl who was bothering me. She must have taken my necklace when she— ugh!"

Elizabeth leaned on her left leg and scanned their surroundings. "I thought that little devil was following us."

"You know her?" Anne cried, shocked.

"Well, I haven't seen her in a few years." Elizabeth smirked as if she already knew. "Tall, mixed complexion... Spanish accent?"

"Yes!"

"Yep. That is Éndira."

"We must find her!"

"Do not worry yourself Anne. I know exactly where to find her. I am meeting with her father later in an open tavern. She will not be far."

"What if she sells my necklace? Or loses it in a game of cards tonight? Or God knows what?"

"Anne, settle down."

"My mother's ring is on that necklace!"

"I suspect Éndira was only having a little fun with you. I can guarantee I will see her tonight. If she has lost your ring, her father will have a hefty sum to pay you."

"Who is her father?"

"The Pirate King Diego de la Cruz."

Anne had no idea who that was but the title sounded frightening.

20

Elizabeth made good on her promise to buy Anne incidentals and now a pair of trousers. As Anne stood in front of the full length mirror she could not take her mind off of the theft. She thought of nothing but her mother's ring so easily stolen.

I was too careless, Anne sighed wondering if she would ever get the item back.

When Elizabeth put a tri-corn hat on Anne's head the younger woman gasped feeling happy for the first time in a long while.

I look like a pirate, Anne giggled inside.

"If only my mother could see me like this," Anne said, remembering how her mother loathed anything not considered feminine. Her mother even fought her father over Anne's artful creations.

If not for my art, mother might still be alive, Anne sighed. *Perhaps she was right. I should have just concentrated on preparing for marriage and not being so difficult all the time.*

"Well— " Elizabeth snaked a vest through the girl's arms. "You might as well have a little fun before you get sent away."

Anne blinked, suddenly aware her serious thoughts had turned into serious questions. "What do you think will happen to me?"

Elizabeth sat down on the corner chair and crossed her legs. Anne could not help but admire the fine leather boots. Anne realized at that very moment how much she would like a pair herself.

"I am really not sure Anne." Elizabeth rubbed the vamp and removed a spot with her fingertip. "If it were up to me, I would place you with an upstanding family for the time being... but I am afraid your aunt would force you to return before Trevor— I mean your father can decide."

"What do you think he will do?"

"Send you back to London I imagine."

"NO!" Anne squealed. "I never want to go back there... there is nothing for me there anymore."

"What about your friends?"

"I said goodbye to them. I am never planning on going back... ever." Anne wrapped her arms around her chest. "I would rather stay with you."

"Anne, that cannot happen."

"Why not?" Anne threw her hands down, exasperated. "That *pirate* girl thought I was your steward! Why not let me do that?"

"And have you get killed or maimed when we go into battle?" Elizabeth said firmly then shook her head. "No, I will never put you in danger like that. We will find your father, or I will put you with people I trust who can defend you against Miranda."

"Like who?"

Elizabeth chuckled slightly. "Let's just say, these women know how to defend against... anything."

Anne was confused. *Does Miss Elizabeth suspect my aunt of nefarious things? Does she know if my aunt is indeed powerfully skilled?*

Anne shook her head, trying to keep from over thinking when she should be pleading her case.

"Why did you run away to sea?" Anne asked, then paused. The question was so abrupt, Anne was afraid she might have offended her friend.

"I was desperate," Elizabeth said honestly. "I had no other options."

"Have I no other options?"

"Anne... you have a father and brother that love you, a large house back home with servants... you have—"

"— money you mean?" Anne interrupted.

"Well, yes... you have money."

"I care little about money anymore."

"Only a young person with *money* would say something like that. You have no idea how the world works, how cruel life can be."

Anne wanted to ask her more about how she had gotten to this place in life. Elizabeth had said she had been desperate, *but how is my life any different now? Aren't I too in a desperate situation?*

The shopkeeper walked up to them. He did not seem to be enjoying dressing a girl in men's clothing. He curled his lip when he saw that a vest had been added and sighed.

"Are you buying that too?" he sneered.

"Come now!" Elizabeth slapped her boot then stood with a sly grin on her face. "I am making your purse heavier sir... so let's have a pair of boots while we are at it!"

"Really?" Anne's eyes lit up.

"You have to complete the outfit."

"Very well then," the ornery man said as he walked away. "I have a few small sets in stock."

When Elizabeth winked at her, Anne started to laugh. This was a day she was always going to remember.

ZARA PULLED off her coat and laid it by her side. She sat down at a small table outside a tavern and positioned her hat low over her forehead. The sun was strong, but not enough to block her vision.

The heat was not as intense as back home.

Still, she was parched.

Zara quickly looked around, trying to see if she could sneak away for a moment to grab a pint. Anne was in the tailor shop across the street, no doubt getting new clothes that did not consist of a dress. Zara had to laugh. Anne wanted to be more like a boy than she would let on.

Zara did not care what the girl was doing she only wished that Anne would hurry up.

How am I ever going to get her away from that blasted woman? Zara sniffed, looking over at the counter once again.

Her throat begged for a drink.

If I fail, Miranda will make my punishment worse than anything Anne might suffer.

Zara shook her head, now angry.

Anne Sutton might be a spoiled rich girl but she certainly did not deserve to be treated harshly. Zara had not been told exactly why Anne was needed.

But Zara was not stupid.

Miranda wants Anne for what the girl is.

Anne does not even know how powerful she might be— not really.

Swiftly, Zara got up and pushed her chair in. She left her coat there, not caring if someone stole it. It was that damn Randal's anyway. Just his smell made Zara want to retch.

Miranda had insisted she appear to be a man therefore less likely to be spotted by Anne. Zara touched the amulet hanging from her neck. Created by her great-grandmother, Zara's mother had eventually passed the charm down years ago.

When Miranda needs me to spy, Zara sighed. *She makes me use it.*

She walked over to the counter and rapped her fingers onto the wood. The attendant turned. She was a young woman with breasts ready to pop out of her bodice. When she smiled, Zara realized it was meant to be more than friendly.

"What can I do you for?" The woman said through darkened teeth.

Zara closed her eyes for a moment. She prided herself on her own appearance and it bothered her that others did not.

But, she realized that was not fair.

Others most likely did not have access to a mage or magical being to help them— *nor have it in their blood like I do.*

"Pint," Zara said, slightly surprised at the lilt and deep resonance in her voice.

"Coming right up," the woman said, winking for effect. "My name's Celestia by the way."

Zara waited for her to turn away but the long delay was understood completely.

"I'm…" Zara stopped, tongue tied. She had not even come up with a false name before embarking on this mission. She realized, by her stutter, Celestia would find this… alluring.

"My name is Oliver," Zara lied, turning her head on purpose and stared at another woman, trying to put a quick end to whatever she had unwittingly started. When she looked back, Celestia was no longer intrigued, her back now turned and retrieving the pint. When Celestia swung back around, pint in hand with a sour face, Zara realized she felt a little bad.

"Two farthings!" Celestia slammed the pint on the counter, splashing ale and foam on Zara's hands. Zara pulled back, ready to snap at her, but stopped herself quickly. She did not need to cause a scene.

Imagine if I got myself arrested and put in a cage? Zara thought, quickly closing her eyes and remembering something worse. *If I come back without Anne? I would rather be in an English cage instead of Miranda's!*

Zara reached into her pocket, wet fingers and all.

I better give her three.

She pulled out the coins, only to drop one on the floor. Zara bent over quickly, knocking into someone's arm. Zara stood up fast, hand bent outwards.

"I apologize," Zara said, then stopped dead. Her eyes focused in on the woman she had bumped.

Elizabeth Spencer.

"Not a problem," Elizabeth said. She bent down and retrieved the coin. When Elizabeth caught Zara's eye, she stopped, handing it gently back while never looking away.

"Do I know you sir?" Elizabeth continued, eyebrow cocked.

She can feel me? Zara thought, panicked. *What do I do?*

"No miss," Zara lied. "I do not think so."

"You seem familiar." Elizabeth suddenly winced, then started to rub her own left shoulder as if she had been bitten by a mosquito.

Zara swallowed hard. She did not know what to do or say. *Can Elizabeth Spencer see through my deception? How will I lie to this woman if her senses have already been piqued?*

Celestia cleared her throat, annoyed. "Right gentleman 'e is," she sneered, hand on her hip with breasts on high alert. "Bumps you over, then makes you pick up 'is coin," Celestia nodded to Elizabeth.

Elizabeth smirked, then handed the coin to the woman. Quickly, the attendant swooped it away, tucking the coin into her breast pocket.

"And what can I get you?" Celestia asked Elizabeth, no longer in a flirtatious mood.

"Two," Elizabeth said as she rubbed her left shoulder gently for the second time.

"Did I hurt you?" Zara said. She reached out to touch but pulled back wisely.

I look like a man, not a woman. If I go around touching without permission, I will really end up in jail.

Or— knocked out!

Elizabeth Spencer can most likely defend herself.

"I'm fine," Elizabeth said, shaking her head. "Do not worry yourself."

"That will be one farthing." Celestia put two pints on the counter, this time gently with a smile.

Elizabeth reached into her coin purse, eyebrow cocked in surprise. "Four you mean?"

"No." Celestia looked at Zara, then gave a wryl smile. "We are 'aving a special."

Zara opened her mouth to protest then realized she had brought this on herself. She ignored them both, quickly downing her pint while Elizabeth nodded and carried her own away.

Zara slammed down the empty pint onto the counter and shook her head. She tried to ignore Elizabeth's eyes, which were now staring at her with curiosity from a nearby table. Zara darted her vision, only to catch Anne staring back at her, her own eyebrow cocked in intrigue. Zara hoped that the girl thought a feud over a potential tryst had caused the display of unease.

Zara quickly scooted over to her own table, snatched up her jacket and scurried out of the tavern.

"Shite," she whispered under her breath.

THEY HAD SPENT a good portion of the afternoon and early evening at the hotel while they waited out a storm. Anne realized Elizabeth had become very protective of her. In fact, they were staying in the same room, Anne behind a privacy screen with the bed, Elizabeth perfectly happy on the couch. The whole time, Anne had been secretly fidgeting and worrying about her ring. Her hand would instinctively touch her neck from time to time, always realizing the necklace with the treasured item was not there.

Later, they had supper downstairs in the small dining room. Anne did not have much of an appetite but Elizabeth insisted she eat everything. Sometimes, Anne felt like the woman was her mother. Elizabeth definitely had a maternal streak.

Perhaps that is why she is so adamant about not taking me on her ship?

Anne wondered how her father would react if he knew his daughter was sailing on Elizabeth's warship? Most likely he would feel betrayed and anger would be his only reaction. Anne realized she might be the catalyst that broke his and Elizabeth's friendship— relationship apart.

Anne was no longer angry with Elizabeth over the affair. Yes, Anne understood what they had done, what they were doing was wrong. But... Anne desperately wanted to see her father happy again.

Elizabeth had been nothing but kind to her; not an insincere kindness to get close to the daughter to get close to the family, like Sarah's infernal mother.

Elizabeth was genuinely kind.

"Stay by my side," Elizabeth quietly ordered the young woman. "I am meeting with some rough people tonight."

Anne nodded her head in compliance and stepped to.

"I would have left you at the hotel," Elizabeth continued. "But I did not like the looks of that innkeeper's son. He best keep his distance or I will stick my knife in his gut."

Anne gasped.

"Well," Elizabeth corrected, quickly hiding a smile. "I would frighten him enough that he would probably wet himself."

They turned the corner and walked into a large patio area. The tavern was open with many tables littered with men and women laughing and happily drinking. Anne scanned the area then looked back at her friend.

Miss Elizabeth has guessed this situation right. These people looked like they have seen a rough life on the high seas. So many hardened sailors who fought to stay alive then come here to enjoy nights like this.

There were other men dressed in garb that did not fit the Queen's men. Anne quickly realized they might be pirates *and* privateers. Why were there so many *bad* people on a British island?

"Don't we hang these types of people?" Anne asked, curious.

"We used to." Elizabeth led her to the back area. "That was before we realized we needed them."

Anne did not understand. "How?"

"Well... if you are at war with the Spanish, who do you think will fight if the navy is stretched to the limits?"

"I guess other Englishmen."

"We give them license to plunder our enemies with a letter of marque of course."

"This gives them legal right?"

"Until Queen Anne no longer has any use for them. Then all hell will break loose and they will plunder anyone they choose again."

"So right now, the enemy of my enemy is my friend?"

"Exactly."

Elizabeth spotted her contact. She walked over to a table filled with men and a few women on their laps. One man eyed Elizabeth and whistled. The bigger man in the group got up.

"Shut your mouth Rico," the bigger man said. "You know Beth here will slice you in half before you can even draw your sword."

"Ha!" Rico chuckled. "How about we take a go at it Beth? Or, if you want, I can take you upstairs and have a go at— you."

Elizabeth leaned across the table, right in front of him and grinned. "You could not handle me big guy... I'd make you cry."

Anne listened to the sudden way Elizabeth talked and realized, the woman had a little pirate in her. Anne crossed her arms and chuckled herself. When Rico turned and smiled at her, Anne stepped back, repulsed by his dirty, gold plated teeth.

"And who do we have here?" Rico raised his shifty eyes and began to get up. "I—"

A sudden crack caught everyone's attention. Rico looked down, only to see a knife wedged in the wood between his middle fingers. Rico snapped his head up and growled. "What the hell Beth? I was only going to give her—"

"What Rico?" Elizabeth leaned in, eyes ablaze. "What were you going to give her?"

Sudden laughter at his panicked expression circled the table. He got up, waved his hand down in anger and left. The girl he had been with snarled at Elizabeth then followed him.

The large man who had teased Rico snapped his fingers. The rest of the table cleared. Anne knew right away this must be the Pirate King Diego De La Cruz.

"Beth?" he said as he hugged her. "How are you?"

"Doing the best I can." Elizabeth held the embrace for a second then pulled away, all business. She turned and held out her hand to introduce. "This is Anne— Anne, this is Diego."

Diego held out his hand. "Nice to make your acquaintance Miss Anne."

Anne looked at him. Diego was a tall man with broad shoulders and a wide nose. His skin was mocha with a bronze glow under the patio candles. His face was angular with features that could have easily been sculpted by a master artist. Diego was exquisitely handsome and very exotic to Anne's eyes.

"And yours." Anne accepted the gesture. She was pleasantly surprised how well-spoken he was through his thick accent. "Umm... I do not mean disrespect sir, but are you Spanish?"

"I am from the Cuban island," Diego answered as they sat down. "Not from Spain herself."

"But you are fighting against your government?"

"I am an enemy to the Spanish government Miss Anne. I am considered a pirate."

"But aren't you? I mean," Anne shook her head, confused. "You *are* a pirate, right?"

Elizabeth started to laugh. "Diego was once a navigator in the Spanish navy... he... disagreed somewhat with his captain and had to flee."

"If you mean I punched him bloody, yes. Instead of hanging me, he had me imprisoned at San Carlos de la Barra, but I escaped and joined a pirate ship. Eventually they made *me* captain."

"Made you captain?" Anne asked, curious.

"Pirates pick their own captain," Elizabeth said. "They have a quarter-master who represents the crew."

"A captain can be removed if the crew overwhelmingly agrees," Diego added.

"Not like the Royal Navy."

"Lucky for Beth here."

Anne said little more as Elizabeth and Diego talked. The conversation was mostly about convoys and ships that had been tracked but when the discussion turned to the Bruja del Fuego, Anne's ears perked up.

"Where was she last spotted?" Elizabeth asked him.

"Near Trinidad. I heard she set fire to two English merchant ships last week... no one survived."

"She set fire to the ship with people on it?" Anne swallowed hard, horrified at the thought.

"The Fire Witch gives no quarter," Diego said, clicking his tongue. "She has been on a murderous rampage these last few months."

A fire witch? Is that who my father is in charge of taking down?

"Who is she?" Anne timidly asked.

"We do not really know," Elizabeth said, shrugging. "All we do know is that she has been allied with the Spanish for quite some time.

"Why do they call her a fire witch? She can't possibly be a real one."

"She is. The Bruja del Fuego is a witch," Diego looked solemn. "I have seen her destroy a village with my own eyes. She is able to manipulate fire at her will and she loves to burn Englishmen alive."

Anne gasped.

Witches are real?

Am I one?

And what of my father and brother?

She closed her eyes for she did not want to even think about that horrendous possibility. When she opened them, Anne suddenly caught a glance of the pirate girl who stole her ring!

The girl named Éndira.

Near the corner of the coral rock wall, the pirate girl laughed at a group of men, gave them a slight nod and skip, then headed up a coral side walkway and out of sight.

"Miss?" Anne suddenly interrupted.

Diego and Elizabeth both stopped talking and looked at her. Anne had not realized she had stood up so quickly.

"What is the problem?" Elizabeth looked confused.

"Privy. I need to use the privy," Anne blurted out.

"Can you not wait until we get back to the inn?" Elizabeth asked.

"No miss," Anne lied hopeful that her older friend would not follow her to the bathroom.

Diego snapped his fingers at a young man standing near the bar. The boy nodded and walked forward.

"I will take her," Elizabeth stood up.

"No Beth," Diego said, then nodded slightly. "We need to talk."

When Elizabeth nodded in agreement, Anne knew they had a private conversation in mind.

"Sir?" The boy said as he walked over. When he saw Anne, he grinned.

"This young lady needs to use the privy," Diego said forcefully. "Make sure she is not bothered."

"Watch her with your life." Elizabeth made sure to warn him severely with eye contact. She gripped her sword's handle for added effect.

The young man nodded then put his hand out to lead Anne away.

HER MIND WAS TOO focused to have listened to anything the boy said. Anne knew what she wanted and she was damn well going to do it.

Anne had to admit he was handsome having a soft face with barely a hint of stubble but the way he carried himself, he must have thought he was the biggest and baddest pirate on the high seas.

Anne had to laugh.

He wore his britches too big and he looked like he struggled under the weight of multiple guns and knives strung across his large, leather strap that hung across his chest.

"The privy is over here, in this shack," he pointed to a small structure.

Anne curled her nose.

This wasn't a shack.

This was a beaten up mishmash of wooden planks strapped together. The wood barely hit five feet, and between the fence that was missing, and those positioned at weird angles, one could peer right in and see the whole show!

Anne turned the corner and held her nose. What constituted a toilet was actually a pit, carved out of coral in about a one foot circumference.

And God knows how deep it is!

She could not possibly fall in, but a misplaced leg might quickly be covered in a mess of unspeakable disgust. She turned to her guide and just stared at him.

"Let me know if you need any help in there," he winked at her.

"Will you please go over there sir?" This was more a command than a request. Anne needed to make him leave, not that he might care if she slipped away. Then again, Elizabeth did threaten him.

"Can't. That navy woman told me to keep an eye on you."

"Where am I going to go? If I fall down the hole, I will call on you to rescue me."

"Now you're teasing me," he sniggered, then tilted his hat as he moved out of her line of sight.

Anne rolled her eyes.

Were all boys this disgusting?

She waited a few moments before darting towards the stairs. Carefully, Anne walked up and studied her surroundings. That pirate girl Éndira had hopefully not skipped down the other side of the structure. There were multiple breezeways and stairs that connected many residences. The gangways did not look stable, but these steps were at least made of solid, coral rock.

Anne moved quickly past a room that had open, full length shutters. She peeked inside and saw no one. She then glanced into the next room.

There, she spotted Éndira.

Anne watched the young woman closely. Her target wore the same hat, dark and black, curled at the front like the beak of a bird. The tip was tilted downwards, hiding eyes with hair tied up in the back with a red ribbon and braids that hung loosely. When Éndira walked over to a nightstand, Anne slipped in carefully and stood behind the silk dressing screen and quickly scolded herself. If this girl was turning in for the night, surely she would need to undress!

Anne quickly glanced around. If she could sneak back out, would it be wise to just simply wait till her target went to sleep?

But it is so early.

Surely, this *pirate* would not be turning in while the party raged outside? Then again, for a girl like her there was probably a party every night.

Anne tensed as Éndira walked over to a full length mirror. For a moment the target stared at herself, then reached into her pocket and retrieved the ring. Anne clenched her fist in anger and waited. Éndira balanced the ring on her finger, then placed the item on a hook by the mirror. The ring swung back and forth as it dangled.

Anne's irritation intensified as she closed her eyes for a brief second.

The necklace was missing. *The blasted thief must have broken the chain when she snapped it off my neck!*

Anne was determined. She would have to be patient if she were to retrieve her stolen property.

Éndira began to pull off the thick, leather plackart she wore over her chest and back. Next, she removed the guard braces that covered her shoulders. When she began to unfasten a double breasted, leather bodice, Anne quickly tilted her head away, not wanting to invade the young woman's privacy. Éndira might be a thief but she did at least deserve some dignity.

Through the corner of her eye, Anne caught the sight of Éndira's loose-fitted blouse made of a soft, slightly transparent material. Anne wanted to close her eyes, but her curiosity was too strong to fight.

When Éndira pulled the ribbon out of her tied back hair, Anne gasped as quietly as she could.

Éndira looked like a goddess!

The soft breath of moonlight on high cheekbones, long flowing hair the color of chestnuts, highlights of dark reds, caramel skin that seemed to glow from reflections of candles that lit the room.

Slowly, the goddess reached for a brush and began to caress her hair with soft strokes. She ran her fingers along her scalp, brushing back loose strands with care. Her left hand found a bottle of perfume on the vanity, the right hand quickly took her hair in a clump and tilted her head to the side. She removed the stopper, tipped the fragrance so only a small bit lay on her fingertip. She then rubbed the perfume on her clavicle, tracing all the way down to the top of her breasts.

Anne shook her head and tried to stop her daydreams. She quickly reminded herself that this *pirate*, not goddess, stole her necklace which held a treasured ring.

A voice from afar called to the goddess. Éndira turned, quickly acknowledged, then left the room into the adjacent breezeway. Now that the thief was distracted, Anne knew she could do something.

Anne swiftly darted over to the mirror and swiped the ring off the hook.

Let that little scalawag wonder where it went. Serves her right!

When Anne turned around, she was pushed back roughly into the wall, an arm pressed hard against her throat.

The goddess had her tightly pinned.

21

Anne could not breathe. Pain tore through her throat as her eyes began to well up with tears. She dropped the ring as she suddenly began to panic. Her hands reached out and tried to pull her attacker off. Anne tried to scream but her voice was rendered silent.

She could not release the arm's pressure. Anne desperately felt around for some type of weapon to use. Her fingers searched the table near her but nothing sat on the wooden surface.

"Is a piece of jewelry worth dying for?" Éndira taunted as she pushed harder.

Anne kicked forward in response. Her feet tried in vain to hurt her attacker but nothing would connect.

Slowly, sounds around her began to die. Anne could hear only the soft pumping of her heart as it beat faster. Anne opened her mouth again to scream but nothing came out.

Staring into her attacker's brilliant green eyes, Anne was convinced she was going to die horribly and no one would hear her cries for help.

Unexpectedly, Éndira released her victim.

Anne fell to the floor and grabbed her throat. She coughed uncontrollably as she tried to breathe. Her hands touched raw skin and gulped the air violently. As she inhaled she slowly found her breath.

Anne rolled onto her tailbone and sat against the wall. She glanced near her feet and saw the ring. Her hands picked up the item and held it out. She looked up at her attacker who stood above her.

"You stole..." Anne coughed for a moment. "You stole this from me!"

Éndira said nothing as she bent down and looked at Anne. For a moment, their eyes met, two people locked in a battle for dominance.

Anne lowered her eyes. She did not want to fight. "Please... I just want my ring back. I'll give you anything else of value I might have— just... I beg you."

For a long moment, Éndira watched her. Anne had tears in her eyes from being almost strangled but now they had turned to ones of supplication.

"Why is it that important to you?" The thief asked.

"It was my mother's," Anne's voice was hoarse. "It is the only thing I have left of her."

Éndira stood up and walked to her vanity. She pulled out a chain. Walking back over, she offered the item.

Anne reached out and allowed the girl to pull her up.

"Here... I broke your chain," Éndira said as she handed over the item. "You may keep it."

As Éndira made her way back to her vanity, Anne folded her arms. "That's it?— no I am sorry?"

"You must be confusing me with someone who cares," Éndira chuckled, then turned. "You are lucky you are leaving here in one piece."

"I want an apology," Anne said, then quickly regretted the statement. If she were smart, she would just get the hell out of this room.

When the thief said nothing, Anne got testy. "Why did you steal it anyway?"

"I wanted to see if Lizzy taught you anything."

"Like what?"

"How not to get robbed on the streets," The thief laughed. She walked back over. "Why are you with her anyway?"

"That is none of your business."

"I can throw you on the floor and make you tell me."

The threat actually made Anne consider the option. The girl was so beautiful and so... dangerously attractive. Before Anne could even answer, Éndira put up her hand to silence her. The girl searched the room with her eyes.

"What is it?" Anne asked, concerned.

"Beth... are you even listening?"

Elizabeth was half paying attention to what Diego was saying. Her focus was on the corner of the building.

How long does Anne need? Elizabeth wondered. *Shouldn't she be back by now?*

Elizabeth wanted to respect Anne's independence but she also needed to keep her safe.

"Hmm?" Elizabeth asked. "What were you saying?"

"I said, I don't think you can rendezvous without a minimum of seven men."

"I'll have it covered... besides, I have Hicks."

"What if you have separate prizes?"

"I should be that lucky." Elizabeth suddenly stood up. She grabbed the hilt of her cutlass out of instinct as she stared at the boy who had been left with Anne. He was busy talking to a group of girls at a table.

Anne was nowhere in sight.

Elizabeth quickly darted towards him. She pulled him away from the table by the scruff then held him by the collar of his jacket. Eyes wide, he looked terrified. A group of men ran forward and drew their cutlasses. Others had their pistols drawn.

"Where is Anne?" Elizabeth demanded.

"Who?" He stammered.

"The girl you left here with!"

"Still in the privy I think... over there!" he pointed to where the shack was.

Elizabeth threw him off, unconcerned that she had quickly been encircled by a group of confused pirates. She ignored them and pushed through. They seemed stunned that she couldn't care less that they were threatening her.

Diego ran up and waved his hand for them to lower their weapons. As the boy straightened out his jacket, then his hair, he quickly flushed red. He was mortified that his own captain was standing right in front of him with a look of amusement on his face.

In a huff, the boy walked away.

Elizabeth pushed her way through the crowd near the bar. A woman yelled an obscenity but Elizabeth did not care. She ran over to the shack and turned her head away quickly at the sight of a drunk man trying to stand over the hole with his pants down and are out in full view. He seemed to be more concerned with keeping his drink balanced in his one hand than hitting the right spot with the other.

Just as she walked away from the scene, a scream from upstairs caught her attention. Elizabeth bolted forward to the steps. A large, blue flash blinded her eyes for a moment. She covered them with her arm.

A loud noise was heard then a crash as the door blew outwards.

Éndira was flung through the doorway onto the landing. She slid down the top steps on her back. She reached out her hands and stopped herself quickly.

Éndira grabbed Elizabeth's leg before the woman could get by.

"The... mir..." Éndira was not fully coherent because of the blow.

"The what?" Elizabeth tried to listen. She was too concerned with Anne to care. The sharp hold on her forward movement caused her to give a second glance.

"The mirror!" Éndira finally got the words out. "Keep her away from the mirror!"

Keep her away from the mirror? Elizabeth was confused for a moment, then it clicked.

Miranda?

Is the witch traveling through the mirrors?

Elizabeth drew her cutlass and ran into the room. Just as she did, a sudden, hard wind violently threw her back. Elizabeth turned over onto her stomach and put her arm forward to try and block the blast of wind. Her hair came undone and whipped into her eyes, snapping like cords against her face. She could barely see but an outline of a foreign hand pointed towards her. Elizabeth's body slowly began to be pushed back.

"Éndira!" She turned towards the steps and yelled. "Go around the other side! She can't fight us both!"

Éndira stumbled to her feet and ran down the steps.

Elizabeth forced herself to move behind the coral wall entrance but a sudden blast of wind blew the rock away. She grabbed her head and barely kept from getting hit by the flying debris.

The wind suddenly shifted. Elizabeth scrambled to her feet and saw the attacker. This was the man she had seen in the bar, the one who bumped into her. Elizabeth knew what he was.

He has to be a witch or mage. One who can travel through the mirrors.

He was fighting Éndira, who had no weapons but her wits and fists. The attacker was frustrated as her target darted quickly around the back breezeway. The man's hand was wrapped around Anne's neck and was dragging her backwards towards the mirror.

Elizabeth watched as Anne struggled. The girl was putting up a good fight but she would never be able to wiggle away from the grip of a witch.

"What is going on?" Diego had crawled up the steps.

"Witch!" Elizabeth held out her hand. "I need your flintlock."

"You can't shoot a witch Beth," he said as he pulled the pistol off his leather strap that was around his chest. "They never get hit."

"I'm not going to shoot him." Elizabeth took the flintlock. She looked at him. "Is this thing primed?"

"Always," Diego smirked as if she could doubt him.

Elizabeth stepped up and drew the pistol. She walked carefully to the side and listened. The wind was still blowing towards the back door.

"You're a strong one," the attacker yelled at Éndira. "But your fight will soon be done."

Anne reached backwards and grabbed the man's amulet accidentally. Fingers entangled, when Anne broke the cord, Zara lost the form of the man she had been.

Zara turned towards Elizabeth, who now stood in the doorway, mouth agape. Zara pulled Anne forward and dived towards the mirror with her hostage.

Zara was not fast enough. She hit broken glass and fell, releasing her hostage in the melée.

Anne turned and saw Elizabeth standing, arm drawn with a smoking flintlock in her hand.

She had shot out the glass.

The attacker had nowhere to escape now.

"Zara," Anne said to them all. "Her name is Zara."

Zara sat in a chair; her arms were bound behind her. Elizabeth tightened the ropes securely. Once Zara's hands were fixed Elizabeth pulled up a chair and sat in front of the captive.

"I remember you," Elizabeth said calmly. "Did Miranda send you?"

Zara ignored her, choosing to look at Anne instead. Zara's eyes were sharp and focused. Uncomfortable, Anne unconsciously wrapped her arms around her chest and tightened them. Zara smiled then began to study the other people in the room. Her eyes flicked from Diego to Éndira. When Zara stopped on the pirate girl and grinned, Éndira walked forward with her fists clenched.

"I can make her talk," Éndira bragged.

"No." Elizabeth snapped her head around and glared at the young woman. "Stay back— I will take care of this."

Éndira folded her arms and looked away.

Anne raised an eyebrow, wondering why Elizabeth was suddenly so forceful.

Is she upset that Éndira stole my necklace?

Zara started to laugh, taking pleasure in the pirate girl's sudden degradation. As she did, Éndira tightened her fists even harder. Anne was waiting for Éndira to start swinging and Elizabeth would be the one to have to physically stop the attack.

"I knew I felt something when you touched me." Elizabeth leaned into her captive, intrigued.

Zara lost interest in Éndira, instead turning her attention back to her interrogator. "You have no idea what you are getting yourself into," Zara warned. "Miranda can destroy all of you easily."

Elizabeth pushed her chair closer. "I know Miranda is a witch but what does she want with Anne?"

Anne blinked at the sudden revelation.

My aunt is a witch? Anne swallowed hard. *Does that also make me a witch?*

"She misses her," Zara lied.

Those words broke Anne's thoughts. Anne stepped forward, a new found sense of confidence in her bones.

"Liar," Anne accused. "She was drugging me."

Zara let out a small snigger, amusement and irritation all in one breath. "So what?" she said.

"So what?" Anne repeated. Her face flushed red. "Why would she do that to me?"

"To make sure you gave no trouble."

"How can she give trouble?" Elizabeth accused, looking sideways at Zara. "She is a seventeen year old girl. Where was your mistress when her husband attacked Anne?"

Éndira glanced at Anne, concerned. Their eyes met for only a moment, Anne quickly diverting her own in shame.

"She cannot control the impulses of her husband," Zara spat with anger in her voice. "He is a swine."

Anne remembered how protective Zara had become. Anne thought that Zara was becoming a friend and not just a servant. *She was told by my aunt to watch and protect me,* Anne theorized. *There was nothing more between us.*

"How can she expect me to return after what happened?" Anne accused.

"He has been... taken care of."

Anne inhaled sharply. *Does that mean Uncle Randal is dead? Did Aunt Miranda kill him or... did I?*

"Anne will be staying with me until I can find her father." Elizabeth stood up and pushed her chair back. "She will not be returning to the plantation."

"You have no right to her!" Zara snarled.

"And neither do you," Éndira said forcefully.

Zara snapped her head around and glared at the girl. "You know nothing of this— Dago!"

Éndira jumped at the insult. She lunged forward and tried to punch the girl, but her father's hand stopped her mid-stream.

"Don't," Diego said calmly in a low tone. "She needs to speak."

"After that may I thrash her?"

"Depends on whether or not she cooperates."

Elizabeth was not so kind. She grabbed Éndira by the collar, pulling her back towards the wall. Anne jumped back, frightened at the sudden display.

"I told you to stay out of this," Elizabeth snarled.

"Get off me!" Éndira pushed her arms up and released the older woman's grip. Éndira looked at her father, eyes ablaze. "Do something!"

Diego shook his head and looked away from his daughter. He folded his arms and leaned back against the neighboring wall. When Éndira knew she would get no help from her father, she slapped her hands to her side. "I will never understand why you always take her side!"

Anne watched the exchange. She was no longer focused on the girl who tried to kidnap her. This was much more entertaining.

"Why is she even here?" Elizabeth snapped at Diego. "Consorting with these men?"

Diego opened his mouth but Éndira spoke up first. "Who I consort with is none of your business Lizzy," Éndira said, irate. "You're not my mum."

"If I were," Elizabeth crooked a finger. "You sure as hell would be back on your island, not here."

Diego cleared his throat. They both looked at him, daring him to interrupt their fight. He nodded his head towards Zara, reminding them there was a bigger issue that needed attention.

Elizabeth focused her eyes on Éndira as a warning then turned back to the captive.

"You're going to help us Zara," Elizabeth said. "Whether you want to or not."

"My deity would never forgive me if I helped you," Zara said.

"Who is your deity?" Elizabeth asked. "Whom do you serve?"

"I serve no one that you know of— witch."

That caught Anne's attention.

All this talk of witches? My aunt, now Miss Elizabeth?

Anne touched the ring on her necklace. She felt the crystal, trying desperately to understand these powers her aunt claimed the family had.

Elizabeth snaked her jacket off. She handed the item to Anne then sat back down. Anne put the jacket on the back of the chair.

Anne watched Elizabeth pull down the neckline of her blouse and push the cloth back, revealing a small patch of skin on her left shoulder. Anne turned her head for a better look but Elizabeth shifted her body so that only Zara could see.

"Do you recognize this?" Elizabeth asked the girl.

"Yes," Zara said.

"Is this whom you serve?"

"I serve no water deity," Zara spat.

"You serve someone... tell me who."

"Is that how you sensed me?" Zara accused. The girl was still defiant. She stared at Elizabeth, the loathing in her eyes withering. "I shall say *nothing.*"

Anne caught a glimpse of skin as Elizabeth replaced the sleeve. Anne could have sworn her friend had a tattoo of some sort. Anne wondered how a tattoo could be used as a warning.

And what has it got to do with a water deity?

Does Miss Elizabeth serve one herself? Is she marked on purpose?

"The vial please," Elizabeth instructed Éndira.

When Éndira handed the item to the older woman, Zara perked up with sudden terror etched on her face. Her hands desperately tried to untie her bonds. She stopped and stared at the small bottle that Elizabeth held in front of her face.

"You know what this is?" Elizabeth asked.

"Yes," Zara swallowed hard. "But I will still not say anything."

"There will be pain then."

"I know."

Eyes wide, Anne tensed. What was Elizabeth going to do to her attacker? Surely she would not kill her!

"Wait!" Anne spoke up, hands out in protest. "Don't hurt her."

"Anne," Elizabeth said, shaking her head. "We have to know why your Aunt Miranda is so desperate to get you back."

"But what are you going to do?" Anne asked, concerned. "Poison her?"

"It is a truth serum," Éndira interjected calmly. "It causes a person's nerves to react when nothing is spoken— or lies. She will only be in pain if she causes her own."

"Oh," Anne softly said. She did not want to cause undue harm to Zara but she desperately wanted to know what her aunt wanted.

Elizabeth opened the vial, sprinkled out the dust onto her palm then blew it in Zara's face. The girl coughed for a moment and closed her eyes. The group watched as Zara twitched slightly. Pain began to creep into the lines of her face. Zara closed her eyes and leaned her head backwards.

"Don't fight it," Elizabeth whispered. "You know that eventually everyone gives in."

"I... have lasted," Zara whispered through clenched teeth. "Been trained for this... I can... outlast you."

"Did Miranda train you or torture you?"

Zara opened her eyes as if the older woman knew the real truth. "I... I cannot tell you... she will *punish* me if I do."

Anne pushed forward. "Then don't return to her," she implored. "What could my aunt possibly give you that we cannot?"

Zara's eyes began to tear.

Anne, caught off guard by the sudden display of emotion, kneeled next to the captive girl and touched her knees.

"She will hurt me," Zara said, shaking her head.

Anne looked straight at Elizabeth. She had more questions than answers. The older woman sighed. Anne wondered if Elizabeth was now doubting herself for what she had just done.

Éndira was the only one in the room to try and question the captive's sincerity. Éndira smacked her lips to accuse. "She's lying! Hang her over the side and threaten to drop her on her head. That always does the trick!"

Anne glared at Éndira. She was really starting to get annoyed with the *goddess*. Everything seemed to involve violence in some way. *Does Éndira not know any other solution?*

Elizabeth did nothing. She waited to see if Zara would choose truth or pain. When the girl started to sweat profusely, Elizabeth looked Zara dead in the eyes studying her closely.

Anne wondered if her older friend was truly worried about Zara or took some sort of sick pleasure in this torture.

If she is, she is really good at hiding behind that stoic facade.

Zara turned her head and rolled it back. Every twist and turn that the victim made ripped at Anne's heart. Anne glanced at the others in the room. Diego was looking at the floor. His daughter Éndira had her arms folded and was leaning back on her left leg. By the creases on Éndira's face, Anne could see that the pirate girl appeared slightly disturbed by this process.

If she is, she is trying to hide it.

Éndira caught Anne's eye. Anne did not look away but Éndira quickly glanced at the floor.

She is disturbed by this! Then why doesn't she try and stop it instead of accepting the situation?

When Zara let out a small groan, Anne decided she had had enough.

"Give her some water at least?" Anne finally spoke up, not knowing what else to do.

"You get it," Éndira said harshly. "I'll stick the rag over her nose— might help."

"No!" Anne turned, angry. "What is wrong with you? Do you enjoy watching people suffer?"

Maybe I was wrong about her.

Éndira exhaled and rolled her eyes with a wry smile on her face. "Depends on who is getting the treatment," she added.

"Enough of this!" Anne walked over to the washstand and retrieved the jug. She poured water into the basin, grabbed a towel then dunked it in and wrung it out. She poured more water into a cup. Anne walked over to Zara, put the items down onto the floor and began to untie Zara's hands.

Elizabeth put her hand out to stop Éndira from interfering. The room watched as Anne helped Zara to the floor. Anne looked at Elizabeth then signaled towards the jacket. Elizabeth nodded, retrieved the item, then rolled it up nicely. She handed it to Anne. Anne kneeled and placed the wet rag on the girl's forehead while putting the soft cloth under her head.

"Just tell them," Anne implored. "Why go through all this pain?"

"I cannot betray my mistress," Zara replied, swallowing hard.

"But how long can you truly last?"

"Days," Zara said as she drank. After a large gulp, she looked at Anne. "If I come back without you, she will punish me severely."

Anne believed her. Anne knew what her aunt was capable of after seeing that poor girl and boy whipped bloody. Anne also knew she would not be returning with Zara, despite the girl's impending punishment.

"Will she whip you?" Anne asked, concerned.

"No," Zara inhaled, letting out a small breath. "She has other ways for those like me."

Anne wanted to believe Zara meant those with special abilities, not because of the color of her skin. Anne shook her head in doubt, questioning what might become of this poor girl.

Zara is so beautiful.

Anne had watched her in silent wonderment admiring the rich coffee hue of her skin.

Does Zara know how beautiful she is on the outside?

But, the inside?

Zara is being used, she is only fourteen years old! Anne insisted to herself. *She cannot possibly be evil like my aunt.*

"Do you mean because of the color of your skin?" Anne hesitantly asked. "Or because of what you are?"

"Because of what I am," Zara confessed. "I would rather be whipped than what your aunt has in store for me."

Anne wanted to cry, to scream— anything to help this poor girl! Zara was a prisoner. *My aunt keeps her around because of her supernatural abilities.*

What if my aunt is denied this help?

Will Miss Elizabeth risk more wrath from Aunt Miranda to save another?

"Stay with us then," Anne said compassionately, looking at Elizabeth for a decision. "Why let her go back to my aunt?"

Elizabeth exhaled, then nodded. "If she wants to stay with us... she can."

Anne glanced at Éndira, waiting for an explosive response. Nothing was said. Éndira simply stood and stared at them all.

"I can't," Zara confessed. "I am bound to her. I will die if I am away from her side for longer than four days."

Anne did not know what to do. The empathetic side of her said to try and save this girl but the logical side said she needed to stay as far away from her aunt as possible.

Anne looked at Elizabeth once again. "Do you have any sleep elixir?"

"I do," Éndira interjected, answering the question first. "But we need her awake, not asleep."

"Zara?" Anne softly asked the captive. "If you fall asleep, how will she punish you for saying anything?"

"She will know."

"Does it matter if you are asleep?" Anne asked Zara, then looked at Éndira. "How long would it last?"

"Depends on the dosage," Éndira said.

"How about a week?"

"That is a long time," Elizabeth muttered. "I do not know if that is healthy."

"I would be happy with that," Zara said softly. Her breathing had returned to normal, now that she was cooperating and no longer fighting the potion.

"Can you make it take effect after a few minutes?" Anne asked Éndira once again.

"Why?"

"We can send Zara back through a mirror." Anne stopped for a moment, not believing her own words. How had that even happened? Traveling through a mirror? Despite her questions, Anne plunged on. "Let her tell my Aunt Miranda she was powerless to stop us. Then she can fall asleep as if we had drugged her."

Zara pushed herself up, now able to speak more coherently. "Your Aunt Miranda worships Dge," Zara revealed finally. "He is a deity trapped in the silk-cotton tree you passed out in front of."

"I felt... something in that tree," Anne said, swallowing hard, remembering her supposed dream with the creature that looked like a child with no lower face. It had red glowing eyes and a mouth that had suddenly appeared with long, sharp teeth.

Was that Dge?

"He was already outside of the tree," Anne's skin prickled. "In my dream at least."

"It was not a dream."

Anne shivered. "So you lied to me and left me out there to be attacked by him?"

"No... and yes," Zara confessed. "Miranda put a spell on you."

"Why would she do that?" Anne said, worried that Zara might reveal the secret that Aunt Miranda had bragged about.

Power over crystals.

"I wish I could tell you more but I am simply a vassal to her, nothing more," Zara went on. "What you saw was not Dge, but a duppy. They are attracted to the tree because of the power it leaks. They... feed off of it."

Anne rubbed her own shoulders, wondering if she were currently in a dream. "Then why me? What do I have to do with releasing Dge?"

"You have something to do with the process... but I do not know what."

"How was Dge trapped?" Diego said from behind.

Anne glanced at him. She had almost forgotten he was in the room.

"I believe the Tarits tricked him," Zara said. "Supposedly he has been bound there for more than a century."

"Right around the time the Spanish started to colonize the new world.

"And wiped out the Tarits." Elizabeth wrinkled her nose, frowning. She looked at Zara. "Do you know when this is supposed to take place?"

"When Anne turns eighteen."

"That is in one month," Anne whispered to herself, knowing the others in the room could hear.

How would my aunt know I would be coming to the West Indies in time? A terrible thought hit Anne in the gut. *What if my aunt caused my mother's death?*

Anne shook her head.

That is impossible.

What could she possibly do from 4000 miles away?

"If we keep Anne away," Elizabeth said, looking at Diego. "Miranda will not be able to use her."

"But for how long?" Diego asked, concerned.

Elizabeth looked at Zara for the answer.

The captive simply shrugged. "I do not believe there is a time limit. Only that Anne is an adult."

"Aunt Miranda knew my mother was sick," Anne confessed, knowing her mother was not long for this world even before the accident. "It was only a matter of time until I came to live with her."

"Miranda wants Anne," Zara revealed. "She has been promised immortality and great power by Dge. She wants to rule the island as a goddess, and she will let nothing stand in her way."

Elizabeth looked at Diego harshly. They both seemed to understand right away how severe this whole situation was.

Anne, on the other hand, thought the whole thing— *bizarre.*

"Do you know how stupid this sounds?" Anne chuckled, wanting to believe this was a dream. "My aunt worships a tree that may hold a god of some type?" she nervously laughed, wanting the others in the room to join in.

No one did.

"It is fact," Zara said, serious.

Elizabeth got up and helped Zara to her feet. Zara took a moment to find her balance.

When Éndira handed the girl a small cube, Zara eyed her.

"You are not trying to poison me, are you?" Zara asked.

"No..." Éndira sniffed. "If I wanted you dead— you would be dead already."

Zara took the cube and put it in her mouth and chewed.

"Go back to Miranda, and you tell her," Elizabeth spoke forcefully, "I will do what it takes to protect this young woman. I will gut her if she tries to take Anne. Do you understand?"

Zara nodded in affirmation.

Elizabeth turned to Éndira. The pirate girl reached out her hands and slapped them together. As she did, some of the shards of glass on the floor moved around, slowly reforming the breaks that had shattered. Anne looked on in amazement as Éndira lifted her hands up and pushed forward, making the newly reunited pieces float, then reform the mirror as before.

Anne froze with wide eyes not understanding what had just happened.

Elizabeth directed Zara to the mirror and stood her in front. She handed the girl her amulet back.

Zara regained her confidence and lifted her chin. "I will deliver your message witch, but know this: Miranda is more powerful than any of you. She will not stop until she gets what she wants."

Zara stepped into the mirror and disappeared.

22

———————

"So— let's just burn down the tree!" Éndira said with a grin.

Anne blinked at her, still trying to understand how the pirate girl had reformed the mirror with only her hands. *Now this thief is suddenly concerned with my safety? So she can rob me of more belongings?*

"Why do you care?" Anne said dryly, remembering how easily Éndira took her necklace then threatened her life.

"I don't," Éndira snorted. "I just want to see this magical tree myself."

"The tree is not magical," Elizabeth sighed, irritated. She rubbed her temples as she sat down. "Just the deity inside."

"Thank you for that correction." Éndira looked down her nose at the woman. "I am sure your vast knowledge of witchcraft makes you an expert on the subject."

Elizabeth turned to Diego, eyebrows bent. "Why is she even here?"

"I've been training her," he confessed.

"And how does your wife feel about that?"

"She's not happy as you can imagine."

"Will you two stop talking about me like I am not here!" Éndira huffed.

The repeated claim of witchcraft crawled up Anne's spine once again.

How did Zara jump in and out of that mirror? If I hadn't seen it with my own eyes I would never have believed it!

Anne started to shake.

These sudden revelations began to upset her mind. She didn't know what was real anymore, being thrown into chaos by her aunt or finding out that Elizabeth was more than she seemed.

Anne stood frozen, looking Elizabeth dead in the eyes.

"Are you... really a witch?" Anne could barely get the words out she was shaking so hard now. Elizabeth was about to stand up but Anne stepped back in an act of self preservation. Hands up, Anne quickly backed into the farthest corner and stared at them all.

"She's not a very good one," Diego said, trying to diffuse the situation.

"Shhh," Elizabeth chastised him, finally standing up. "You are not helping." Elizabeth put her hands behind her back to show she meant no harm. "Anne... please, do not be afraid."

Anne unconsciously started to play with the ring on her necklace. Elizabeth did not know of her powers... *yet.*

Am I able to strike down Miss Elizabeth to escape?

Do I even have it in my heart to hurt the one who rescued me?

When she noticed Éndira staring at her with a worried expression, Anne stopped playing with her jewelry.

Does she know?

Can she feel me?

"Are you one too?" Anne accused the girl.

"No," Éndira shook her head. "I'm not."

"But... but how did you make that mirror reform itself?"

"Éndira has a sixth sense regarding some supernaturals and the way they travel," Elizabeth said. "Because the mirror was enchanted, she could see the portal and manipulate it. The glass was not actually glass, but plasma... a fluid of energy on another plane."

Is that what I am?

Some type of supernatural freak?

Anne diverted her eyes afraid Éndira would discover her secret.

Hopefully I will be rid of this girl's company soon. But what of Miss Eliza-beth? Can she sense me also?

Anne walked over and touched the glass. The surface began to appear to melt. She stepped back as it slowly began to liquify and drip to the floor. The fluid then swiftly evaporated leaving only wood behind.

Anne closed her eyes. She felt like she was going to pass out.

What is going on!

How did I even come to be in this situation?

Elizabeth took another chair and placed it in front of Anne. Elizabeth sat down once again, crossed her legs and put her hands in her lap in a non-threatening posture. She raised her left hand and suggested with the motion that Anne sit. Anne hesitated, looking around the room for a quick exit.

Eventually, Anne gave in and sat.

"You have questions," Elizabeth said rhetorically.

"You're damn right I have questions!" Anne snapped as she folded her arms, then pointed at the mirror. "First, how did Zara walk through that thing in the first place?"

"Like I said before... the mirror is on another plane... only certain supernaturals can do that."

"Then she is a witch?"

"No," Elizabeth said. "I think she is most likely a pythoness."

"She plays with snakes?"

When Éndira snorted Anne turned and glared at her.

"It means she may be able to conjure spirits," Elizabeth said kindly.

Anne closed her eyes and waited for a moment, hoping that this was all a bad dream. She exhaled and opened them back up. Before her was the same scene.

"So... my psychotic aunt wants to feed me to a tree," Anne then pointed at Éndira. "You're not a witch, but something even stranger," Anne said bluntly, earning Éndira's irritation. "Zara's a python.... or... whatever, who is bound to said psychotic aunt," she then threw her hands up and looked at Elizabeth once again. "And you are a witch who does what exactly? Do you sacrifice chickens and dance around naked under the blood moon?"

Anne huffed loudly while Éndira started to laugh.

Elizabeth ignored the taunting and smiled. "Not exactly."

"She is not a blood witch Anne," Éndira interrupted, giggling. "She is only an earth witch."

"A very poor earth witch, as Éndira's father has kindly added," Elizabeth smirked at the man in the corner. "My skills were taught to me when I was about your age Anne. They were taught to me for self-preservation. I was very sick at the time and a kind sept of women helped me learn enough to keep myself healthy."

"You cannot defend yourself?" Anne asked, curious now.

"Only with my wits, pistol and cutlass." Elizabeth rubbed her own leg. "My potion skills are extremely limited. About the most I can do is make a few sleep elixirs and a *mélange* of herbs to control pain."

So maybe she cannot sense me, Anne thought somewhat relieved.

Anne remembered that night in the cabin. "Do you smoke something like that?"

Elizabeth blinked surprised by the question. "Why yes... it is best used that way."

"So that night, when I was sick in the cabin... is that what was in your pipe when you stayed with me?"

Elizabeth nodded. "Yes. I had a very severe injury when I was a midshipman. The pain bothers me to this day."

Diego walked over and put his hand on his daughter's shoulder. "I am thinking that perhaps Éndira should join you... to help protect Anne."

"On my ship?" Elizabeth shook her head. "How will I explain two young females not of the Royal Navy?"

"Well, you certainly cannot leave Anne here on this island. Your ship is the only place without large mirrors," Diego said, then smirked. "Unless you installed a full length in your cabin? Your vanity is almost as pretentious as your wardrobe."

"Oh, be quiet," Elizabeth chastised.

Anne raised an eyebrow. *What is the man talking about? Doesn't Miss Elizabeth only own uniforms? How on earth would one keep a set of dresses in that tiny cabin anyway?*

Unless, of course... *Diego is teasing her.*

Miss Elizabeth is a beautiful woman. Does she not think this about herself? Anne wondered silently.

While Elizabeth seemed to be contemplating the idea, Anne stepped up.

Now is my chance!

"What about being your steward?" Anne asked sheepishly.

Elizabeth rubbed her chin, thinking, then looked at Diego. "Perhaps Anne could pose as my steward for the time being... and Éndira..." Elizabeth stared at her subject, who was looking back with a scowl on her face. "Can be a liaison."

"That may work," Diego said.

She's coming with us! Anne fretted, shuddering at the thought. *Will I have to sleep with one eye open?*

Éndira huffed but said nothing. She crossed her arms and frowned.

Elizabeth ignored her. She turned back to Anne and sighed. "If your Aunt Miranda intends to hurt you, I will keep you under my protection and away from her at any cost."

Anne smiled.

She no longer cared who was a witch... or pythoness. She just wanted to feel safe.

"Once we get word to your father," Elizabeth added. "I have a feeling this situation is only going to get worse."

"Why?" Anne asked. "Will my father not believe me? Or you?"

"We have no idea how far Miranda's powers go. Some witches are able to harness energy and amplify powers of persuasion."

Anne felt her heart skip a beat.

Powers of persuasion?

Aunt Miranda told me of an ancestor who did this. Does my aunt also have that ability?

"Beth," Diego said. "We do need to finish our conversation and..." Diego glanced at his daughter for a moment. "Since we have new arrangements?"

"Yes... yes, you are right." Elizabeth nodded as she picked up her jacket and started to put it on. She looked at Éndira. "Keep an eye on Anne until your father and I come back." Elizabeth glanced at the hollow mirror. "And stay away from mirrors."

"Of course my lady," Éndira mocked, bowing for effect.

Elizabeth rolled her eyes and left with Diego.

Great, Anne huffed. *Now I am stuck with this annoying girl! Can this situation get any worse?*

THE CABIN WAS small enough for one person, now Anne had to share it with this thief!

First, Éndira had the gall to steal Anne's necklace and ring, apparently just for fun. Now, to annoy Anne further, Éndira was rummaging through her own bag and tossing items everywhere.

"What are you looking for?" Anne complained. She propped her feet up on her own cot and crossed them. *Thank the Lord I got to keep the better bed! She might have stolen that too if given the chance.*

Éndira did not hear Anne's question. She was too engaged in her own task. Swiftly, she pulled out a black bone dagger and watched the candlelight as the rays bounced off the sharp steel edge.

Anne inhaled sharply, mortified at the sight. She pulled her legs closer and moved back slightly. When Éndira smirked at her, Anne's eyes widened. *Is this girl going to kill me in my sleep?*

Éndira took the knife and placed the item under her pillow.

"Are you serious?" Anne finally chastised. "Who are you expecting to stab tonight?"

"You— if you continue to annoy me."

Anne hoped her bunkmate was joking, but still— *Éndira frightens me.*

"Do you always sleep with a knife under your pillow?" Anne hesitantly asked.

"Yes." Éndira pulled out a flask and offered a drink to Anne. "Every woman should."

Anne shook her head. "No, thank you."

Éndira shrugged her shoulders and drank. When she was satisfied, she let out a loud belch, which shocked Anne.

"You are rude!" Anne said bluntly. She needed to tell this *pirate* she had no manners.

"Don't care." Éndira threw the flask onto her own cot and began to take off her shoulder guard braces. She threw them onto the bed, followed by her chest plackart. She started to struggle with her wrist gauntlets. After a few moments she huffed in frustration.

"Would you help me with these please?" Éndira asked as she stepped towards Anne.

Anne was pleasantly surprised Éndira had used the word please. *Perhaps she can be tamed,* Anne giggled to herself.

With nimble fingers, Anne loosened the leather straps on the gauntlets, then the small belts. She carefully unlaced the thin cordage. The criss cross pattern was similar to a bodice— something Anne was all too familiar with. She thought it funny that this pirate girl needed help in the same way a proper girl needed someone to lace her up in the back.

"Thank you love," Éndira said as she took the gauntlets and tossed them onto her cot.

"I don't mean to be rude," Anne said. "But what nationality are you exactly?"

"How is that not rude?"

"I mean— you speak with a Spanish accent, but you occasionally have an English lilt?"

Éndira bent down and began to throw her items back into her sack.

"Your father is of Spanish descent, is he not?" Anne continued.

"Yes."

"And your mother?"

"She's dead— don't know— died giving birth to me."

Anne suddenly felt pity for the girl. They were both without a mother. Anne pulled her knees close to her body and hugged them tight.

"My birth mum was from Europe, that I can tell you," Éndira said. "And the reason why I talk with this English lilt," Éndira mocked. "Is because I was raised by a proper English woman."

"Really?" Anne was intrigued. By the tone of her voice, she realized she may have just insulted her bunkmate.

"Does that shock you in some way?"

"No," Anne lied. Now she was at a loss for words. Why did she suddenly care if she offended this pirate girl? "I am just curious... you are very exotic."

Uggh— Why did I just say that out loud?

"Am I?" Éndira chuckled.

Anne was suddenly aware she might be projecting too much. Yes, Éndira was beautiful, but she was also annoying and so... *beneath me?*

Why would I instantly think something like that? Had I not recently chastised my aunt's thinking that some people were meant to serve and others were lower class, even Miss Elizabeth?

"I... I only mean you look like you are mixed race."

Éndira put her hands on her hips. "I am. Does that bother you?"

"No..." Anne leaned back slightly afraid she might have offended. "It is just that... there is no one in London that looks like you... or anyone I met in the West Indies."

"You must not have gotten out much," Éndira taunted.

Anne wanted to be upset by the sly comment but the truth was she did not get to see many people in Barbados. *My aunt kept me hidden, like a figurine never to be handled.*

Until it was time to feed me to a tree, Anne sighed, then chuckled slightly.

"What is so funny?" Éndira asked, quick to become upset.

"Nothing." Anne shook her head. "I am just remembering something in my past." Anne looked up, wanting to continue the previous conversation. "The reason why I asked about your lineage, is because... I find it fascinating."

"Great for you," Éndira snorted.

When Anne didn't react, Éndira huffed, then continued. "I am African and Spanish, with some Purépecha in my background... from my great-great-grandmother apparently."

"Purépecha?" Anne knew a little about the history of the native people who once lived on the Central American peninsula. "My you are a goddess."

"What?" Éndira started to remove her boots, half hearing what was said.

"Nothing." Anne thought it comical that her bunkmate did not sit to do this. She sort of hopped around like a little rabbit.

Anne watched the show, silently laughing to herself. When the hopping stopped, Anne realized she herself was very tired. She did not want to press any further conversation with her new bunkmate. She did not want to accidentally say again, in so many words... *you are the most beautiful woman I have ever seen!*

Too bad her personality is so abrasive.

She could be beautiful inside and out.

Anne's eyes quickly widened in shock. Éndira had taken off her blouse, revealing her bare breasts.

"What are you doing?" Anne turned her head towards the floor. "Give me some warning!"

"What is the matter with you?" Éndira chuckled. "Have you never seen a naked girl before?"

"Just myself, thank you. And there is such a thing as modesty!"

"Don't be such a gnashnab."

Anne looked up, insulted. Before she could respond, Éndira threw off her trousers and tossed them to the floor.

She was now completely naked.

Anne's eyes were wide. She could not help but stare, not only out of shock but intense curiosity.

Éndira is a goddess.

Her body was perfectly sculpted with breasts not too large, but ample enough with a wide space in-between. Her nipples pointed slightly outwards. A long, sleek torso showed a muscular stomach.

When Anne eye's followed a path that ended between Éndira's legs, she only got a glimpse of a small patch of brown hair before turning her head in embarrassment.

Anne wanted to see more. She wanted to study the beautiful body in front of her but she was afraid.

What would she think if I just stared?

Would she think me strange?

Curious?

Would Éndira even mind?

Éndira suddenly crawled into her own cot and threw the thin sheet over her naked body.

"You sleep naked?" Anne gasped, again mortified by this girl's behavior.

"Yes," Éndira turned over. "Now douse the candle— goodnight!"

Anne did not know what to do. She was stiff with anger and what may have been... arousal? Her lower half had a tingling feeling she did not understand. She knew little of sex but this naked girl had stimulated her senses in some way.

"Good night," Anne said softly. She put out the candle and rolled over, gently putting the cover over her shoulders and wishing she understood more about her own body.

23

———

nne's morning did not start off well. First, Éndira had managed to leave the cabin a mess so that Anne had a hard time finding her own boots to put on. Second, when Anne went down to the galley to fetch Elizabeth's breakfast, Jolly, the cook, took offense and refused to make food that was not hand delivered by him. He said he acted as Captain Spencer's steward, not a lanky seventeen year old girl who was playing sailor. When he walked off to attend to some other duties Anne was left alone to stare at a pot of boiling water. Determined to make the breakfast herself she reached over to a bowl and picked up an egg.

"You need help there twiggy?" an annoying, familiar voice said.

Anne curled her lip. "No, I do not need your help— go away."

As she dropped the egg in, she could hear the other one snicker. With both hands on her hips, Anne turned in anger. "Please, leave me alone. It is bad enough I have to room with you."

"Oh, I would like nothing more either than to string a hammock below deck away from you, love... but I have to watch you whether you like it or not."

"There are no large mirrors on this ship. You heard your father. So, go up on deck and go... play with the birds or something!"

Anne grabbed a pair of tongs and pulled the egg out. She placed the item into a wooden egg cup. Next, she took some butter and spread the stuff on a piece of bread. When she put the slice on the cast iron skillet, the butter sizzled quickly and started to burn the bread. Anne tried to pick the piece up quickly with her fingers then pulled back before she got burned. She looked frantically around for a spatula or knife. Out of the corner of her eye, she spotted a fork. Frantically, her hands tried to pick up the piece of toast. After numerous tries, she flipped it quickly for a moment, then tossed the bread onto a small plate. One side was burned, the other barely cooked.

"Oh, that looks palatable," Éndira snickered.

"Shut up." Anne placed the egg holder on the dish and quickly pushed her way towards the exit.

She knocked gently on Captain Spencer's door.

"Come in," a voice said.

Anne balanced the plate with one hand and managed to open the lock with the other. She closed the door behind her and walked over to a small table. As she placed the items down, Anne suddenly remembered she forgot, "Coffee."

"Don't worry about that Anne," Elizabeth said from behind her desk. "I had some earlier."

"You did?"

"Jolly brought me some." Elizabeth raised an eyebrow and looked oddly at the table. "Did he have something else to attend to?"

"No, he asked me to bring this to you," Anne lied.

"Did he now?" Elizabeth smirked as she got up and walked over. "How are you getting along with Éndira?" She sat down and picked up a fork. She cautiously lifted the bread, Anne keenly aware the burned side was on the bottom.

"She sleeps naked!" Anne blurted out.

Elizabeth laughed as she put down the utensil and picked up a spoon. She hit the top of the egg.

A small splash fell onto the plate as the egg shell top sank into the liquid yolk.

The egg was raw.

Anne closed her eyes.

"You made this did you not?" Elizabeth asked.

Anne opened one eye and felt like she had shrunk two feet. "How can you tell?"

Elizabeth gently put the spoon down, picked up the tray and handed the items back to Anne.

"When you have properly apologized to Jolly for... whatever this was," Elizabeth said nicely, "Tell him I would like him to make another breakfast and you will assure him you will not be replacing him any time soon."

"Yes miss." Anne scooted out of the cabin, tail between her legs.

MIRANDA BUSIED herself in her work. If she allowed herself one minute to rest, the damnable voices would begin to drive her mad. The paintings never rested, always taunting her whenever the opportunity arose. She threw another batch of comfrey into a bowl and started to grind the herb with her pestle. Miranda sniffed angrily. She pushed the pestle down too hard, causing her hand to slip and crash into the side of the bowl.

"Dammit all to hell!" Miranda snapped. She lifted her finger and licked her wound. Behind her, she felt a hand on her waist.

Miranda shook her head quick to chastise the source of the touch.

"Leave me," Miranda ordered.

"You are trying to spell while angry," Selina said from behind, a slight giggle in her voice. She tried to reach for the uncut herbs. "Let me help."

Miranda quickly pushed her lover's hands away. "Do NOT touch this."

"I am tired of your anger Miranda!" Selina crossed her arms then huffed.

"You're tired?" Miranda glared at her then motioned towards the back of the room. "I'm tired of being surrounded by incompetents!"

Near the wall was a large cage.

Inside, Zara was fast asleep.

The blasted girl had been sent with one mission; to return Anne to the plantation where she belonged. Zara had been gone for three days with instructions to bring Anne back through the closest mirror possible. Miranda had also instructed Zara to kill Elizabeth if the chance arose. In fact, Miranda had strongly encouraged the young servant to take the initiative and rid the world of that vexing woman.

How dare that low-class slag interfere with my mission, Miranda thought angrily of Elizabeth.

"You've interfered for the last time." Miranda threw a dash of salt into her mixture. "I will gut you like the fish-wife you were meant to be."

Selina's eyes widened, scared. She let out a slight whimper.

Miranda turned and rolled her eyes then clicked her tongue. "Not you Selina."

Selina opened her mouth to speak but closed it quickly, keenly aware she should not press her luck.

Miranda was glad her lover was lucid enough tonight to keep most of her running thoughts in her own head. In these last few days, Selina had begun to get on Miranda's nerves. Instead of anger Selina had tried to dispel Miranda's growing frustration with physical exertion.

But even that could become tiresome with time.

Selina will never truly understand what is at stake. What will happen to me... to us if I fail?

Miranda would never tell Selina she had bargained both of their lives to Dge. She didn't understand what he would want with a half-wit like Selina anyway but that was the bargain he demanded.

Miranda growled inside. She wanted her blasted niece back here and nothing was going to stand in her way!

Miranda continued to chop her herbs with intense movements. She ignored the woman at her side. Miranda stopped for a moment and wiped her forehead. She was exhausted from stress and tired at this late hour. Her mind and nerves had been going non stop for days.

Three o'clock in the morning will work best. My victim will be fast asleep.

"That Elizabeth is still a gnashnab," Selina said sternly. "This is all her fault."

For once, she speaks with reason.

"Yes, she is," she turned to Selina and nodded. She reached for a bunch of lavender and pushed it towards the woman.

"Start with these," Miranda said, softer this time.

Selina giggled. She grabbed a long knife and began to chop carefully. They worked in silence for a long while before Selina started once again.

"I hate her," Selina sniffed.

Miranda stopped her work and looked at her for a second. She actually did not know which person Selina was talking about.

"Anne or Elizabeth?" Miranda asked.

"Both of them!"

Miranda shook her head and returned to her work. She did not want to get involved in one of Selina's rants. The woman could go on for hours talking about those she could not stand. Many times, Selina would talk to her through the mirrors in Anne's London home. Miranda had been afraid Selina would be caught doing this. She also understood that she had to be there to listen to Selina in her moments of madness, so that the woman could be talked down. If Selina had been found out, the whole plan to get Anne to Barbados would have been ruined.

"Do not worry about Elizabeth," Miranda said while pressing the pestle hard. "She will be gone after tonight."

"How?" Selina asked, eager.

"I am doing a possession spell."

Selina squealed, catching Miranda off guard. Almost dropping her tool, Miranda closed her eyes for a moment to calm her nerves. *I might have to make another calming batch for her if she continues to agitate me.*

"Will it be Anne?"

"What?" Miranda looked at her, confused.

"Will Anne kill her?"

"No." Miranda shook her head. "That would cause too many problems. We just need to get the ship back to land. A dead captain will ensure this."

"That is no fun," Selina whined then perked up. "Am I allowed to fetch the little beast once that happens?"

"We will see."

Just then, a sound in the corner alerted them. Selina and Miranda turned and looked at the cage. Zara turned slightly.

She was still fast asleep.

"Poor little birdy," Selina snickered.

"Ignore her." Miranda stopped, letting her head stretch backwards. She cracked it side to side, trying to relieve the stress that had been deep in her muscles. When gentle hands started to massage her tired neck, Miranda allowed the caress.

"I wish you would let me," Selina snickered. "I would love to slit that woman's throat!" Her hands reached forward, ready to touch the tip of the potion.

Miranda yanked her lover's hand away, pulling it up close to her own eyes.

"No one is killing Elizabeth except me!" Miranda spat, her eyes reddened with fury. She slapped Selina's hand down roughly. "Go outside and find some more sage!"

The tip of Selina's mouth quivered. No longer happy to be by her lover's side, Selina turned on her heels angrily and stormed out of the room.

When a loud slam of the door shook not only the table, but Miranda's nerves, she took a deep breath and closed her eyes.

Her hands touched the top of the wooden table. Slowly, her fingers felt for the object in question. When her skin touched a cold metal surface, Miranda smiled. Slowly, she lifted a kitchen knife to her eye and looked at the surface.

When she dropped the knife into the bowl, Miranda began to hum a tune from childhood.

This sound will lull you to sleep. And the tip of cold metal will end your life.

"You deserve death," Miranda whispered, thinking only of Elizabeth, the woman who had interfered for the last time.

"I WIN," Anne declared as she threw down her cards and happily touched their surface. "Again!"

Finlay cocked an eyebrow and said nothing. He simply touched the winners and turned them slightly. He had no reaction, instead picking them up and placing them back in the deck.

Anne crossed her arms and started to laugh. She was unable to keep from rubbing salt in the wound. "We should play for money. I believe you might buy me a grand dress with your skill."

As he shuffled, Finlay could not help but smile. "You are a wily one Anne Sutton," he said, then looked at her. "I fear if I played you for money, I would be in debtor's prison and no longer on a queen's ship."

Anne smirked.

"Besides," Finlay added. "I would be happy to buy you a grand dress, if you would let me take you to a grand ball?"

Anne gulped hard, realizing she had suddenly caused her own unease. *Why did I throw out such an easy target?*

I'm always trying to be quick with my words. And instead, I cause myself to become entangled by my own tongue.

"There are no balls as far as I can see," Anne said confidently. "So there will be no need for dresses or dances, thankfully."

The way Finlay looked at her, Anne immediately regretted her words. He seemed deflated, choosing to return to his job of shuffling the cards instead of verbally dancing with the girl before him.

Anne sighed. "Not that I would not enjoy your company at one Finlay, it is just that... I do not enjoy things like that anymore."

He looked at her. "You do not miss your life back home?"

"Oh, heavens no. I much prefer to be on this ship and away from all that nonsense."

"Even if your aunt has nefarious reasons to want you back at the plantation?"

Anne blinked at him, unsure exactly why he said those words.

"Everyone knows Anne," Finlay continued. "I mean... about the strange things that happen on that island."

"Like what?" Anne asked as she leaned closer.

"Just that many of the men on this ship have been in the West Indies for years. They have heard or spoken of things. I don't know if it is just their own superstitions but they claim that many of the people working or enslaved by your aunt are bewitched."

Anne remembered those poor souls bound to her aunt. Many of them seemed devoid of life or any personality. Their eyes were absent of spark as they mindlessly did the chores they were ordered to do.

Suddenly, the door flung open, scaring both occupants. Anne grabbed her chest and looked at the sight in the doorway. Éndira stood there with a smug smile on her face.

"So…" Éndira walked over and touched the table gently. "What are you two going on about?"

Finlay looked up, words ready to leap off his tongue.

"Nothing," Anne said, sternly looking at him then at the intruder. "Nothing that concerns you."

Unexpectedly, Anne was startled as Finlay leapt out of his chair and pulled another one out before Anne could figure out what happened. She watched the way his face seemed to light up around the pirate girl.

He is smitten with her. Anne smirked then felt a twinge of jealousy. *He just sat here and told me about wanting to take me to a ball and now he is flustered over her?*

"Thank you… love," Éndira said with a soft voice then sat down, not before touching his hand gently, making him turn slightly red in the cheek.

Anne could feel herself become angered.

Over what? This bloody pirate girl?

I don't even want him.

"So?" Éndira eyed her for a moment then turned and looked at him softly. "What are we playing?"

"WE are playing piquet," Anne huffed. "There is NO room for a third."

"Unless of course you want to play ombre, Éndira," Finlay cleared his throat, looking at Anne for correction. "Now that we do have a third."

Anne glanced at him then narrowed her eyes and watched the way Éndira was looking at her. The girl wore a confident smirk, more than sure of herself and what was going on.

She wants to play with me?

A game of wits and class?

I will eat her alive.

Anne handed her cards back to Finlay. "Sure, why not. We can liven up the night."

They spent the next hour trying to outwit each other. Anne was a confident card player and sure she might easily take Éndira on.

Confidence and actual play were two totally separate things.

In her first three hands, Anne easily beat them all. After that, everything went downhill once they changed to basset.

Éndira was able to outmaneuver on every counter trick Anne played. The more Anne grew frustrated, the more she made stupid mistakes.

Anne could see how much her irritation made Éndira happy.

On the last hand, Anne finally had had enough.

"That is not possible," Anne huffed. She reached forward and took Finlay's cards from him instead.

"What are you doing?" Finlay asked.

"Counting."

While Anne pulled the deck in front, Éndira started to laugh. Anne eyed her for a moment then turned back to her task at hand.

"What *are* you doing?" Finlay asked again.

"She's counting because she thinks I cheated," Éndira snickered. She took her flask and drank a sip.

"You didn't?" Finlay hesitantly asked. "Did you?"

"No. I did not." Éndira shook her head, not at all offended then pointed to Anne. "Of course, I suspect this one just stinks at playing this game."

Anne stopped and glared at her. "How would you know how I fair at basset? And besides— how do you even know HOW to play this game? It is only played among society and those with..." Anne looked down her nose at the girl. "Class."

The way Éndira scrunched up her face, Anne knew she had hit a nerve. Without thought, Anne went in for the kill. "Unless you were a servant in someone's household?"

Éndira stood up and slammed her chair then looked at Finlay. "The company you keep has left a bad taste in my mouth. I will leave you to your princess."

Finlay stood up, mouth agape. His hands were held out, not knowing what to do nor what to say to either of them.

"Let her go," Anne said bluntly. "She can go cheat somewhere else."

Éndira whipped around, furious. "I did not cheat. I have no reason to cheat. You think just because of who I am I need to do that?"

"Yes, because you ARE a thief," Anne snapped.

Éndira glared at her, turned on her heels and stormed out.

Finlay and Anne sat in silence until he finally decided to speak up.

"Why do you have to be mean to her?" Finlay asked.

Anne opened her mouth, aghast. *Did he just have the gall to suggest I am being the unkind one?*

"Because she is a nightmare!" Anne huffed, throwing down her cards. "You do not have to share a cabin with her."

Finlay cocked his head to the side and shook it. "I share a berth with several officers on this ship and I can guarantee you... even if we are supposed to act like gentleman, some of them are far from it."

"Well, Éndira is certainly no lady... and is far from being a gentleman, though she tries to dress like one."

"Is that the reason why you dislike her?"

"Because of the way she dresses?" Anne looked down at her own attire. She wasn't far off from resembling the pirate girl. Anne looked up at him. "No, why would you suggest something like that?"

Finlay chuckled loudly. He started to deal out a new hand. As he threw several cards in front of her, Anne pushed them to the side. She was not happy to be mocked.

"What is so funny?" Anne demanded, sure her pride was going to take a hit in some way.

"You're acting just like all those snobby girls at the ball." Finlay started to look at his hand. His eyes glanced at her then back to the cards. "You told me in the garden that you abhorred the practice of being put on display like cattle at the auction. You then spoke for a good ten minutes about how class difference was a sin of our society and how you would long for the day all women would be treated as equals."

Anne glared at him, not fully understanding why he was bringing up her own words. "Yes, I did say that. But what does that have to do with Éndira?"

Finlay put down his cards and exhaled. "Anne. You are treating her as less than you because of the color of her skin and the accent she has."

"— I am not!" Anne screeched, offended to be called out like this. "She's a bloody pirate, that's why!"

When Finlay put up his hand, Anne crossed her arms and let him continue.

"Back home in London, Éndira would be less than a scullery maid," Finlay continued. "But in this part of the world I see an independent woman who can do anything. She's the daughter of a pirate king for God's sake! I would imagine someone *like you* would admire someone *like her*."

"What do you mean by that? Someone like me?" Anne asked, afraid to hear the answer.

"I mean... you have a fierce independent streak. I admired that from the moment I met you Anne." Finlay looked at her and smiled. "I would think you might admire that in another," he laughed. "I fear you are both more alike than you think."

Anne was about to protest but stopped herself to think about those words.

More alike than I think?

Finlay is right.

Éndira is someone I would like to be. Someone who does not accept a woman's ordained station in life.

Anne shook her head and smiled at him. "You are right. I should have seen it earlier." She looked at her hand. Two aces and a few throwaway cards. Anne nodded to him to deal a new set. "And, just so you understand I am not put off by the color of her skin," Anne looked at him. "I actually think she is quite beautiful."

The words flew out of her mouth before she could stop them. Anne felt her heart drop as her hands suddenly felt clammy. *Why would I confess that so easily to a boy who is obviously in love with Éndira?*

Or me?

Am I trying to put him off?

Or am I just hoping to reveal myself so he will just concentrate on friendship instead?

"I think she is very beautiful too," Finlay said while looking at his cards, much to Anne's relief. When he stopped and looked straight at her, Anne knew what was coming next. "But not as beautiful as you."

Anne gulped hard, automatically thinking of the words taught to all young women her age from doting mothers and governesses alike.

"Thank you kindly sir," Anne quickly said before burying herself in her cards.

Anne did not know what would be more awkward, the next hour with this young man, or returning to a cabin with a girl whom she had insulted.

Miranda gasped and quickly grabbed her chest. She looked around her surroundings, trying to figure out if she had made the journey.

My consciousness at least.

Her eyes had yet to focus properly, Miranda concentrated on using her nose instead. All around, stale scents of sweat and seawater infused the musty old wood.

I'm on the ship. On the lower deck with the sailors.

Now who am I in?

Miranda looked down at her hands. Slowly, a pair of stubby, calloused palms came into focus. She allowed them to touch her chest. It was flat, no indication she was in the body of a woman. Miranda felt her consciousness jerk suddenly. She closed her eyes and concentrated on the body she barely hung onto.

He's trying to push me out.

Miranda drove herself in deeper, grabbing hold of his psyche.

Go to sleep, she commanded.

After a few seconds, the man inside surrendered to her will.

Commoners, she sneered. *So easy to understand. Give them a taste of what they crave, and they will do anything for it.*

Miranda had always had the ability to bend others' will with her magic.

She always focused herself through her crystals, using that power to manipulate and find the path she desired. Men like this, a simple sailor with little means? He would easily be lulled into submission by inner dreams of his wildest desires. Once their minds were put into a fantasy state, it was hard for her prisoner to ever awaken to reality.

Miranda had left many catatonic after her intrusions.

She wanted to put Elizabeth into a catatonic state that would ensure a lifetime of mental torture.

I want Elizabeth to suffer but I do not have the luxury of time.

Instead, Miranda would have to settle for a quick death at the end of a blade.

Which reminded her— *I need a knife!*

Miranda commanded the sailor to awaken but keep silent. She then had him slowly step out of the cot; she could feel the feet touch the bare wood floor. She always found it fascinating that when she possessed a body, every inch of a person's being was hers to control. She felt everything, down to what the possessed had eaten for dinner. Miranda scrunched her nose, reliving the disgusting salt pork stew that this sailor had for dinner. Thoughts of food turned her plan around.

She would not have to search for a knife in the kitchen.

This sailor had one in his belongings.

Miranda searched for the weapon. She carefully dug in between the hammock rolls. She found a well made five inch knife. It was a magnificent weapon, most likely won in a card game or purchased on shore. She tucked the weapon in the back waistband of the trousers and left the berth in search of her target.

Miranda easily found her way. To her left side, locked doors held weapons and purser supplies behind them. To her right, she could feel her blasted niece Anne rooming with the Dago. Miranda was tempted to go in and knife the interloper dead. Despite what little Zara revealed before falling under a sleep spell, Miranda had a feeling that this Dago interfered or helped Anne in some way.

"Oye," a voice said from the shadows. "What are you doing up 'ere?"

Miranda turned and looked at the marine sentry. He was standing in front of the captain's door, protecting the occupant from the rest of the crew. He also was most likely protecting the girls.

How noble, Miranda sniffed, looking at the rifle that was now pointing at her.

"Sorry mate, got lost looking for the 'ead," Miranda lied, knowing the body she was in might not make it past the long bayonet inches from her chest.

Thankfully, Miranda could still channel her magic even though she was hundreds of miles away. She reached out her hand and shot a blast towards him. The marine was temporally paralyzed. Miranda swooped in to slit his throat ear to ear. She felt a rush of exhilaration as the man fell to his knees, clutching his neck in vain. Blood poured down his hands. The marine fell to the ground, dead.

Miranda smiled.

She stepped over his body, careful not to slip in the warm blood that now dripped over the cold, damp wood floor. She had not murdered anyone like this in a long time.

Oh, how I miss the thrill of taking another's life.

Miranda looked around carefully. No one had come to the man's rescue. She was momentarily fearful that one of the girls would burst out of their cabin and try to stop her. Miranda had no idea what the Dago was but she felt some type of energy come from behind the wood. Miranda walked over and touched the surface near the door handle. She pulled back quickly and licked her fingers.

This girl tastes— good.

Perhaps after I am done with Anne, I might hunt this one down. She might be of future use to me.

Miranda turned and walked over to Elizabeth's door. She did not even try to open it. She knew that it would be locked. Captains did not sleep without some security. Mutiny could happen anytime, even on the best of ships.

When they are so free with the use of the cat-o-nines, what else can one expect?

Miranda had no idea if Elizabeth was a kind captain. She was not going to ask her blasted brother about his mistress's temperament. Besides, the bitch would die tonight whether kind or cruel.

Miranda touched the lock, letting a small flow of energy pierce the metal. The lock slowly began to melt. She watched the now molten metal drip onto the floor. She turned the handle and quietly entered.

Her bare feet made no noise as she carefully walked over to the small cot where Elizabeth lay. Miranda stopped and looked at her prey.

Elizabeth was sound asleep on her back. Her hand was on her upper chest.

Miranda watched the movement of breath. She waved her hand. A small flow of green energy left her fingertips and danced over Elizabeth's body. The energy spun like a tiny cloud then dropped onto the sleeping victim.

I am being kind. I would rather you see my blade as your last view on earth but I cannot risk your screams.

Miranda stepped over her victim and gently pushed Elizabeth's hand away.

You've always been nothing but a bane to my existence.

She lifted her knife high and aimed carefully. Miranda channelled all her fury in one motion, plunging the weapon toward the heart of her enemy.

24

As the tip hit skin, Miranda was suddenly blown back by a blast of blue energy. Her borrowed body flew across the cabin and hit the wall hard. Dazed, Miranda focused what little strength she had left in keeping herself inside the sailor. He tried in vain to escape but Miranda fought back with all she had. Once he was secure, she looked at her other victim.

Elizabeth sat upright, her eyes wide with astonishment.

Miranda scanned the floor for the knife. She saw a glimmer in the corner. Filled with rage, Miranda leapt forward, barely touching the weapon as a weight fell with force on her back.

Elizabeth was fighting like hell to survive.

Before Elizabeth could yell for help, Miranda turned and hit her intended victim hard in the throat. Elizabeth lost her balance and fell backwards.

Miranda found the knife and turned quickly, slicing Elizabeth in the hand. Elizabeth crawled backwards and kicked hard. The blow hit Miranda in the face. Miranda yelped, feeling every bit of pain that the borrowed body did.

"Give me back my niece, you bitch!" Miranda growled.

Elizabeth stopped and looked at her. As she registered the words, Miranda leapt at her once again. This time, the door swung open and Miranda was hit hard on the head with a blunt object. She fell to the floor and lost her weapon. Her vision was groggy. She turned and looked at her attacker.

A naked girl stood in front of her, skin the color of rich caramel. Miranda was frozen for a moment, unable to find her focus except on the heavenly beauty facing her. Her admiration was momentary, as a pair of hands pushed her down and locked an arm upwards.

"Get off!" Miranda commanded to deaf ears. No one was coming to her rescue. She looked up again and saw another step from behind the naked girl.

It was Anne, dressed in a night shift and looking at the scene in shock.

"What is going on?" Anne asked, horrified.

Elizabeth stood up and tried to catch her breath. She leaned inward and put her foot on Miranda's back. Softly Elizabeth rubbed her bloody hand on her own shift. As she did, Anne walked over and went to examine it.

"Never mind that Anne." She pointed to the weapons cabinet. "Find me a cutlass while I hold your bitch of an aunt down."

Anne raised an eyebrow and looked at the possessed sailor then shook her head, confused.

"Now," Elizabeth added forcefully.

While Anne did as she was told, Elizabeth nodded to Éndira.

"Thank you both for coming in," Elizabeth said. "I fear I might have lost this battle."

Éndira motioned towards the captive. "I felt something... off."

Anne walked over and handed Elizabeth her sword. Her older friend put the tip at Miranda's throat.

"Sit up, but do not otherwise move or I will slit your throat." Elizabeth glanced at Éndira then quickly diverted her eyes. "And you... please put some clothes on."

Éndira looked down at herself and shrugged.

Anne sighed. "I told you she sleeps naked."

"Go in my dresser and find another shift."

Elizabeth turned her attention back to Miranda. "Trying to kill me in my sleep?" Elizabeth clicked with her tongue as she leaned over. "Really Miranda? Are you that desperate?"

Anne looked at the attacker. "Umm... that's not my aunt miss."

"It is," Éndira interjected, now clothed. She held a rag. Elizabeth put out her sliced hand and let Éndira quickly bandage it.

Anne could easily still see through the thin cloth Éndira wore. She was too shaken up to even care anymore about looking at her roommate's naked body.

"How?" Anne asked.

"Possession spell," Elizabeth answered, moving closer and putting her tip into Miranda's neck. Blood dripped down the small prick. "Isn't that right?"

"How did you do that?" Miranda sneered. "I had you under control. You were asleep. How did you force me off?"

Elizabeth looked at her oddly.

Anne had no idea what they were talking about but Elizabeth also seemed confused.

"Your energy!" Miranda snapped. "How did you channel that energy?"

"I have no idea what you are talking about," Elizabeth said. "What I do know is you will release this man and return to your home and promise to leave Anne alone."

"And why would I do that?"

Anne shifted her eyes around the room. Each of them was standing frozen in place, the shock of events keeping them still. Anne realized, if her aunt had possessed this man, she cared little for his safety.

Miranda started to laugh then turned to her niece. "I will find you. If you do not return to me soon, your punishment will be so severe, you might never see the sun again."

"Why?" Éndira snapped. "So you can—"

Anne pulled her cabin mate back hard.

"What?" Éndira glared at her. When Anne shook her own head quickly, Éndira realized she should not say anything more.

If my aunt finds out I know what she has in store for me she will hurt Zara.

"So you can let your husband attack me again?" Anne said, trying to steer the conversation quickly. "How many women does he rape on your plantation?"

"That... was an unfortunate event."

"Unfortunate? Is that what you call it?" Anne said, her anger coming out. "And how do you suppose you will protect me from him?"

Miranda stared at her. "He's dead."

Anne widened her eyes and put her hands to her mouth. Zara had spoken the truth.

Was it me? Anne cried inside. *Did I kill Uncle Randal?*

"You need to come home," Miranda said softer this time. "You need to learn your... place. If you do not, how will you ever learn how truly *powerful* you can become?"

When Éndira and Elizabeth glanced at Anne oddly, she crossed her arms. She had to think of something quick.

I can't tell Miss Elizabeth. What will she think of me if I tell her I have powers over crystals and I killed my uncle in defense of myself?

And Éndira? She herself has strange powers and a sixth sense.

Can she sense me?

Has she already and said nothing?

Or has she already told Miss Elizabeth?

"I have no desire to be mistress of a plantation," Anne spoke true words even though her intention was to deceive. "No matter how *powerful* I might become."

Miranda started to laugh. Anne stepped back, afraid that the woman's power would come out and kill them all.

"I will find you Anne." Miranda looked at the others in the room and nodded. "These feeble dalcops cannot save you."

"Do not listen to her," Elizabeth said to Anne. "She is a madwoman bent on becoming something that long ago was lost." Elizabeth leaned inward, making sure to drive her point deep. "Isn't that right Miranda? You lost your identity years ago, did you not?"

Anne had no idea what Elizabeth was referring to. She only knew that those words seemed to sting, for Miranda had eyes that screamed betrayal and hate all in one blink.

Unexpectedly, Miranda jumped up and ran into Elizabeth's sword. The pain crept into the victim's face, a look of shock on the other. Elizabeth held Miranda upright.

"I shall... end *you*," Miranda sneered, speaking the same words Elizabeth had threatened a week ago.

The unfortunate victim's body went limp. Elizabeth let the weight fall, watching Miranda slide off the sword and fall to the ground— dead.

She wasn't dead, however... this Anne knew.

The unfortunate sailor whom Miranda had possessed was the one who had been murdered.

The three females stood in silence and shock. Elizabeth threw her bloodied cutlass down and sat on her cot. Anne feared that her older friend's legs might have given way if not for the readily available seat. Anne thought she herself might collapse. Anne stepped backward and leaned against the bulkhead, taking in the sight of death. She closed her eyes and inhaled deeply.

"Are you going to pass out?" Éndira asked kindly.

"I think I might be sick," Anne confessed, eyes looking away now.

"Take her outside," Elizabeth said, glancing at Éndira only for a moment. "And find Hicks and Travers. We need to keep this from the crew... for now."

Anne shook her head. How would they keep this murder from the crew? Would the crew mutiny over a sailor who appeared to try and assassinate his captain?

As Anne turned to walk away, something near the desk caught her attention. A sharp bounce of light glimmered off of an object on the floor.

"Wait," Anne said, walking over to inspect.

She picked up a small pendant. Attached was a broken chain. Anne turned and looked at them both. Elizabeth stood up and walked over.

"This must be yours," Anne said as she touched the small turquoise gemstone. Suddenly, her fingers felt hot. She quickly handed over the jewelry and unconsciously put her fingers to her mouth. When Elizabeth looked at her oddly, Anne put her hand behind her back.

"Odd," Elizabeth said as she held the pendant. She touched her chest and winced. Carefully, she pulled down the neckline and inspected her skin.

Anne widened her eyes.

Elizabeth had a small impression of the pendant indented into her skin. Surrounding it, the skin had been slightly scorched.

Éndira walked over and raised an eyebrow.

"How did that happen?" Éndira asked the woman.

"I..." Elizabeth glanced at both of them, confused. "I... haven't the slightest idea."

Anne wanted to say something but she could not.

"It must have repelled that crazy woman's attack," Éndira said.

Elizabeth looked at her, still bewildered. "That is not possible. It is nothing but a piece of jewelry."

"Who gave it to you?" Anne asked, intrigued, not knowing if Elizabeth herself carried crystal powers.

"My mother, years ago," Elizabeth said, shaking her head. "When I was very young." She put the pendant on the desk and turned to them both. "Never mind that. Go find Hicks and Travers."

Éndira nodded then touched Anne on the shoulder.

Anne wanted to stay but how would she question the woman without revealing her own secrets?

"Let's go," Éndira said.

Anne nodded, walking away with the other girl. Anne turned before exiting. She watched as Elizabeth touched the jewelry, obviously still confused by the revelation.

Miss Elizabeth must have a way with crystals, Anne thought, perplexed. *How else could she have saved herself?*

~

In the morning, Anne had remained below deck while the unfortunate sailor and marine where committed to sea. As captain, Elizabeth had the sad task of presiding over the service. Anne was not too keen to watch more death rites, especially after her mother's funeral. It was bad enough Anne had witnessed another person take his own life.

Two suicides in such a short period of time.

Only Anne, Éndira and Elizabeth knew that the unfortunate sailor had been possessed by Miranda. Elizabeth assured Anne that she would not write the cause of death in the ship's log as self-inflicted due to a failed assassination attempt.

The sailor would have been deemed to have been in a fit of mental incapacity, an unfortunate side effect due to a prescription of medicine he had been taking. Elizabeth and the surgeon explained to the crew what had happened, and once the sailors were assured it was a freak accident and no others would come under that spell, most were satisfied they would also not die from that cause.

Hours later when she was finally able to go back onto the quarterdeck, Anne was less than happy. She was stuck on this ship, watching from the distance as four other ships sat waiting. One by one, they began to unload cargo and bring it to the docks where a lone warehouse stood.

This was a long process and very boring to the casual observer.

Anne cocked an eyebrow, suddenly confused.

What on earth were they doing anyway? Cargo in the middle of nowhere made no sense. Surely they needed to go to a real port? Anne did not even know if the other ships were privateers, pirates or Royal Navy.

Anne sighed, no longer caring what was happening vis-a-vis the cargo.

What made Anne upset was the fact that this long day could be spent walking or admiring the foliage and birds on the small, isolated island. Anne craved some fresh fruit. Even one measly orange would be satisfactory.

Surely there can be no mirrors on this island? Anne huffed, putting her elbows on the railing.

Éndira had assured her that no more possession spells could overtake any members of the crew. Elizabeth and Éndira had used salt and herbs as a simple potion to protect the ship and all its members.

Éndira had gone ashore to help, as well as three quarters of the crew. Finlay was assisting on one of the other ships. Both lieutenants and Elizabeth were on shore directing the traffic.

Only the carpenter was left in charge on deck.

Where would they go anyway? Anne knew enough that the ship needed a certain number of bodies to function. As for her safety, Anne was left in the care of the Jolly the cook.

She had finally managed to get him to warm up after a rocky start. She had made a deal with him— to at least allow her to attend to cabin duties and he everything else.

Anne needed to feel useful.

She refused to be a pampered child any more.

Anne asked him to go on deck for some fresh air. Jolly only agreed to allow this if she remained on the quarterdeck, where only officers were allowed.

She crossed her arms and stood up.

"Left ye all alone I see," a deep voice suddenly said from behind.

Anne whipped around quickly, only to see a short man near her side now. When he grinned, his crooked, mostly missing yellow stained teeth made her step back. Something about the way he smiled at her made her tense up.

Anne touched her necklace and began playing with the ring. She did not know how she had stopped her Uncle Randal, but hoped the same energy would repel this man if he tried to touch her.

Is this man possessed? But... that cannot be possible.

Unless, Éndira lied to me?

Can't be. Miss Elizabeth told me she had helped assure this.

"You are not allowed on the quarterdeck," Anne said, voice stiff. She needed to project the confident socialite, even if she were shaking down to her bones.

Jackson ignored her command, instead choosing to lean on the railing. He sniffed, then spit into the water.

"What do ya think they are doing out there?" Jackson sneered, then looked at her.

"I..." Anne shook her head. She realized she should not engage in conversation with this man. "I... have no idea, nor do I care."

"I think I know," Jackson chuckled.

"I really do not care." Anne stepped back away from him. When she went to leave, he grabbed her roughly by the arm. "Let go of me sir!" Anne snapped, her voice steadier.

"Don't run off too far lass," Jackson said. "I 'ave a feeling this ship might sink or... burn." He licked his lips. "What if I 'ave the only life boat?"

Anne blinked, face red. She was angry that this man had the gall to threaten the people on this ship. Would he be so bold as to set fire and risk killing everyone, including himself?

Anne pulled her arm away roughly. She glared at him before storming down the steps and disappearing. She needed to tell someone what just happened. Jolly would be in the galley. Anne bit her lower lip, trying not to tear up as she started to shake.

25

Elizabeth stood careful watch and observed her crew with hardened eyes. She had not expected to be in this position so soon. Elizabeth watched as Lieutenant Hicks scrutinized the men who stood in the front line, while Mr. Travers inspected those in the back.

A flogging was a terrible but necessary thing.

The crew had to be reminded of punishment that would be inflicted if they broke any of the articles of war. Elizabeth had assured herself she would not be heavy handed as captain but now that she was in the actual position things were different.

Jackson deserves this punishment, Elizabeth groaned inwardly.

Usually, men who were sentenced to the cat deserved the lash for drunkenness, fighting or other general offenses. Yes, it was true that some captains used flogging as a general tool of terror but most sailors thought of the punishments as just the way of life on a queen's ship; this, however, was different.

Elizabeth closed her eyes for a moment, not wanting to blame the man who was supposed to have kept an eye on Anne.

This is not Jolly's fault, Elizabeth sighed, her eyes now focused on the grate. *Jackson had no business on my deck, no business... bothering Anne.*

Elizabeth tightened her hands behind her back, twisting leather within leather. The cut on her hand hurt badly but she wanted to hide the injury from prying eyes. She waited for Lieutenant Hicks to nod her way. Elizabeth looked at him, turned and signaled to her boatswain.

"Hands, witness punishment!" the boatswain piped. He turned and listened as each section verbally announced their attendance.

Elizabeth waited for the culprit to be brought up. She wished the sun would hide behind a cloud. She was broiling in her full dress uniform.

Two marines pulled an unruly Jackson up by his arms. His hands were bound but he was putting up a hell of a fight. He screamed a slew of obscenities at them. The larger marine hit the prisoner hard with his fist, sending blood onto Elizabeth's clean deck.

Jackson needs to shut his mouth. Men like him never learn. She was thankful both Anne and Éndira were below deck. Elizabeth refused to allow either one of them to witness this flogging.

When he was pulled in front of Elizabeth, the prisoner stopped struggling for only a moment.

"Ya wench," Jackson snarled. "Ya think you are going to punish me? For what, I ask ye?" he looked at the front row of unsympathetic seamen.

Elizabeth just stared at him, knowing he would get no assistance from the crew. *Jackson is a troublemaker about to be given what he deserves.*

"I will make this short and to the point," Elizabeth said directly to him. "Your offenses were being on the quarterdeck without authority and touching Miss Sutton." Elizabeth turned and nodded to Lieutenant Hicks. "Twelve lashes."

Jackson jumped forward just as Lieutenant Hicks lost his grip. Elizabeth stood her ground, only to be spit in the face by Jackson.

"You've just assaulted Captain Spencer," Lieutenant Hicks said, grabbing the prisoner by the scruff. He punched Jackson hard in the stomach, then added, "Shall I hang him from your yard arm ma'am?"

Elizabeth looked down at the pathetic man withering on the floor. She shook her head then glanced at her lieutenant. "No, that would be too easy."

Mr. Travers handed her a handkerchief. She nodded in thanks, then began to wipe her face. Elizabeth was disgusted with what had just happened but would never show that she was also physically sickened by the act.

Spitting is such a degrading thing to do. Only those of the basest class would stoop to such a repulsive act.

Elizabeth waited for Jackson to be pulled up once again, this time farther away from her.

"For that," Elizabeth calmly said. "You will receive a dozen more."

More insults were spewed, as well as attempts to spit once again. Twice Lieutenant Hicks hit the offender in the stomach, trying to make him stop. Only when Jackson was finally tied to the grate, did the prisoner stop fighting.

This time he began to laugh.

A piece of leather was put in his mouth to bite down on but also to shut him up. Many who received this type of punishment were thankful not to bite off their tongues should they convulse from the pain.

The boatswain pulled a cat-o-nine-tails out of a green bag. He firmly held onto a thick wooden handle while nine pieces of rope dangled precariously. The boatswain waited for the carpenter to announce Jackson was properly secured. The surgeon then stepped forward to feel the offender's pulse.

"He is fit to receive punishment," the surgeon said, turning on his heels and moving back to his post.

"Boatswain," Elizabeth said sternly. "Do your duty."

The boatswain stepped backwards, hand held high and swung the cat. A loud crack, followed by a muffled scream rung though the deck. Elizabeth did not flinch but she darted her eyes momentarily to see the crew's reactions.

Her hardened officers had no expression of remorse or pity. The carpenter even looked a little bored— or tired? Elizabeth could not tell. Another snap of the whip alerted her. This time she looked directly at Mr. Travers.

Finlay looks a little green around the gills. If he passes out, he will be teased by the crew.

Just like Trevor.

He told me he passed out his first time while I stood upright with no problem.

Does that make me heartless?

Another snap of punishment and Jackson was no longer laughing. By the end of his first dozen, Jackson was openly weeping. The last set was to be doled out by the boatswain's junior, giving temporary rest to a hearty arm but not to the back being lashed.

Halfway through, Finlay did pass out. Elizabeth waited patiently for them to remove the young man. She ordered that he be brought to the officer's berth and to remain below deck until he felt better.

When the boatswain reached back to finish the job, the surgeon called the punishment off for a moment. Jackson's head was hanging low. The thought was that he had passed out.

The surgeon touched the man's cheek. Another check, and the physician looked at the second in charge of this ship.

"Is he fit to receive the remainder?" Lieutenant Hicks asked, eyebrows narrowed in annoyance.

"Yes, sir," the surgeon said in a neutral voice.

When Lieutenant Hicks looked at Elizabeth, she simply nodded. "Continue!" he said sternly.

When the punishment was finished, the sorry man was cut down from the grate. Blood pooled around his feet and dripped down his back.

Jackson was carried down the steps and out of sight.

Elizabeth nodded to the surgeon, who followed and would attend to the man in the sick bay. She gave one last stern look at her crew then disappeared herself.

I need a stiff drink, Elizabeth sighed.

ANNE STOOD at the railing and watched the horizon. The weather was cooler today. Anne took off her jacket and let the breeze flow through her blouse. When she turned, she realized she should put it back on. The cloth was thin and comfortable, but also slightly transparent. After what happened with Jackson, she did not want to encourage any other wandering eyes or hands.

Not that any of Elizabeth's officers would act in such a manner. Anne just understood that as a lady she should not encourage a display unbefitting someone of her upbringing.

Even if I am dressed like a man on a ship, Anne chuckled inside.

When the bell on deck rang, she watched as Finlay stepped forward and walked over to the mate of the watch who held a log line. The mate turned, then cried to another to turn the sand glass.

The log was tossed into the water. They watched as the rope attached to the spool was reeled out; all the while the mate's hand touched the line to check its progress. He could feel the knots on the rope which measured the distance.

"Stop!" yelled the man in charge of the glass as the last of the sand ran down.

Quickly multiplying the distance by the length of time measured by the sand glass, the mate arrived at their speed.

"Seven knots!" The mate cried out as he began to pull the log in.

Finlay walked up the stairs and onto the quarterdeck.

"Seven knots sir," Finlay reported to his superior.

"Thank you," Lieutenant Hicks smirked, then added. "And... try not to fall on your face today."

Finlay gave a weak smile. "Yes, sir."

Anne tried not to laugh. She had heard the exchange clearly and quickly darted her head when Finlay walked up to her. When she looked back at him, his face was flushed with embarrassment.

"I guess you heard about me passing out?" Finlay asked her, uncomfortable.

"I did," Anne answered politely.

"My father will be ashamed."

"Why?" Anne asked, puzzled. "Surely he cannot expect you to witness something as horrendous as a flogging without some emotion?"

"My father served for many years as a lieutenant before being wounded." Finlay shook his head. "He told me to keep my head high when I witnessed my first flogging because a captain must dole out punishment to maintain order. An officer who retches or passes out is essentially undermining his authority."

Anne crossed her arms to her chest, remembering how her aunt doled out such punishment to her indentures and slaves. She warned stiffly that a mistress of a plantation must be harsh, lest those whom she oversaw murder them in their sleep.

"I threw up," Anne confessed.

Finlay looked at her oddly. "Surely... you were down below?"

"No." Anne shook her head. "On my aunt's plantation. She made me watch two runaways get whipped." Anne felt her stomach turn slightly. "She forced me to watch it."

"She should not have made you watch," he growled.

"I wish she hadn't," Anne sighed.

Their conversation was interrupted when they heard boot heels running up the steps. Both turned, only to see Éndira coming to join them. Anne wanted to express tolerance towards the girl but the way Éndira sneered at her— Anne's magnanimous mood evaporated.

"Yes?" Anne asked stiffly, cutting Finlay off before he could make his own salutations.

He gets so tongue tied around her, Anne had to snicker.

Éndira said nothing. She leaned against the railing— waiting.

What does she want anyway? To overhear our conversation and laugh?

Anne was about to protest the intrusion. As she opened her mouth to chastise, Éndira nodded her head towards the stairs. Elizabeth walked up quickly. The woman wore no jacket nor sash around her neck.

In fact, Elizabeth had on a loose fitting blouse Anne had never seen before. It was light red with a long v neck. The bottom had an angular border that dipped downward with a triangle cut on the right side. Anne walked over and began to admire the tunic.

"That's so pretty," Anne admired. "I have never seen anything like that before."

"It's from Siam," Elizabeth said proudly.

Anne reached out then looked at her for permission to touch. "May I?"

"Of course."

Anne felt the intricate embroidery decorating the bottom hem. She did not recognize the pattern but understood that it must represent something in the Siamese culture.

"My father told me about Siam," Anne said, inquisitively. "He said that the people there have almond shaped eyes and are very beautiful."

Éndira walked over. "You should see the dress she brought my mum once. It is a brilliant green with a cloth that drapes over the left shoulder." Éndira smiled at Elizabeth. "Of course mum feels a little strange with her other shoulder bare."

"Bare?" Anne asked. "What type of dress has one shoulder covered and another one bare?"

"It is called a 'Chut'," Elizabeth said. "Siamese women wear it as part of their culture."

Anne cocked an eyebrow. "Do you own one?"

"I do actually. But it is back in London with a lady that keeps my possessions safe for me."

"I can draw you a picture," Éndira said politely.

Anne turned and looked at her. Éndira had actually said something nice for once.

"I would like that very much," Anne said.

Elizabeth slapped her hands together. "Okay, enough talking for now," she nodded to Anne. "I have a tunic in my cabin waiting for you. I think it will fit."

Anne looked at her oddly.

"We are going to train," Elizabeth added with a smirk.

"Train what?" Anne gulped, looking around at the other's watching her. She whipped around, frightened. "Me?" Anne squeaked.

"You need to learn how to defend yourself."

Anne waited to see if this whole conversation was in jest. When she realized it was not, Anne disappeared into the captain's cabin. Laid out on the bed was indeed another tunic. This one was a bright green and also intricately embroidered. Anne picked up the tunic and admired the work.

"I can't wear this," Anne said quietly. "What if I ruin it?"

Knowing Elizabeth was waiting Anne ignored her worries. She quickly changed and ran back up on deck.

This time, the deck had been cleared of everyone but Elizabeth and Éndira.

Great, Anne huffed. *Does she really have to be here?*

"Stand in front of Éndira," Elizabeth said.

Doing what she was told, Anne walked over and placed herself within striking distance. She swallowed hard, afraid she might get hit by the pirate princess.

Elizabeth stood behind Anne. "Now, grab Éndira's wrists."

"Okay," Anne hesitantly said, doing again what she was instructed.

"Now... hold on as tight as you can."

Anne formed a good grip. She looked at Éndira, worried. The girl just smirked then quickly snapped her own wrists away.

Anne sighed. *I must hold on tighter. I refuse to let this pirate show me up!*

Again, Anne tried to grip hard and again she failed.

Elizabeth stepped in, took Anne's wrist and touched the thumb.

"Your thumb has little strength when your opponent snaps out of the hold correctly," Elizabeth instructed. She took her own hand and gripped Anne's wrist. "Do not try and pull back to get out of the hold. Instead, lean forward a little then bend in your elbow and snap outwards."

Anne just looked at her, confused.

"It takes practice," Elizabeth assured. She reversed hand positions. "Grip me hard."

Anne complied.

Elizabeth snapped her hand out so quickly, Anne did not even know what happened.

"She's faster than you," Anne taunted, knowing this would annoy Éndira. A roll of the eyes confirmed Anne's petty comment.

Another demonstration occurred, this time slower. Anne watched but still did not understand. Elizabeth gripped Anne's wrist this time.

"Slow motion first," Elizabeth instructed.

Anne followed her direction carefully. Anne tried to snap out of the grip but failed on numerous attempts. Finally, on her eighth try, Anne succeeded.

"Brilliant!" Anne gasped. "Can my father fight like this?" she asked, curious.

Elizabeth shrugged. "I imagine he knows fist-a-cuffs, but this is much more fluid."

"How did you learn?"

"I spent eight months overseeing a small port with very little to do," Elizabeth smirked. "I was bored."

They practiced the move over and over again, until Anne was sure she could do it by learned memory and not by having to think it through.

The next move proved to be equally entertaining. Anne was taught how to kick inwards onto her attacker's kneecap. This time she had to keep herself restrained for fear of hurting her opponent. Elizabeth was well skilled but even a well placed kick to the front of the knee would incapacitate.

After an hour, Anne was confident she would be able to escape a bad situation if needed. Elizabeth told her the first line of self-defense was to get away from the attack. Anne was taught another skill, hitting an attacker with the heel of the palm into his or her nose.

Anne had to laugh.

I am actually enjoying this!

"I want to learn how to use a cutlass," Anne suddenly blurted out. When Éndira laughed at her, Anne narrowed her eyes, unamused. "What's so funny? Do you think I cannot learn?"

"Shouldn't you stick to riding for pleasure instead and leave the defense to us?"

"And where shall I find a horse?" Anne said stiffly.

Elizabeth ignored the exchange. She walked over to a small table that had been set up. On it, was a jug with three mugs by its side. Elizabeth poured herself some water and drank. She offered another to Éndira, who drank quickly. Anne came over and gulped down her own. When she was finished, Anne looked around instinctively for a napkin.

Éndira chuckled while she used her own sleeve to wipe her face.

"Don't you have any manners?" Anne said stiffly.

"Sorry we do not have a butler here for you your highness," Éndira snickered then walked away.

Anne was unamused.

Elizabeth handed her a towel.

"Use this," she said. "It's clean."

Anne thanked her and wiped her mouth.

"Do not worry about her Anne," Elizabeth said. "We should be close to finding your father's ship. I spoke to one of the captains yesterday. The Latitude was spotted near Antigua."

Anne felt her heart deflate. Once they found her father, this wondrous journey would end. Despite being frightened by that Jackson character, Anne still wanted to be on this ship with all on board.

Including Éndira.

Despite Éndira's harsh exterior, Anne still found her— fascinating.

"How long until we get to Antigua?" Anne asked.

"A day."

Anne crossed her arms and hugged her chest. *Only a day left?*

Elizabeth put down her drink. "Let's finish with one other move," Elizabeth looked towards the distance and shook her head. "I fear we will be getting bad weather soon."

Anne did not care. She shrugged and walked over to the center of the quarterdeck once again. Elizabeth instructed her to stay still. When a sudden grip came from behind, Anne froze. She felt as if her Uncle Randal had subdued her.

When Elizabeth began to speak, Anne could not hear her friend's words.

Everything was muffled.

The tighter the grip became, the more Anne began to panic.

Anne closed her eyes and tried to concentrate on what was happening. *This is only a test. Miss Elizabeth is not my uncle! She is not trying to hurt me!*

Anne's ring did not care.

Suddenly, the area around her neck began to feel hot.

"No! DON'T!" Anne yelled as she pulled away. She turned and barely kept herself upright. She closed her eyes.

When Anne finally found the courage to open them, both Elizabeth and Éndira were staring at her with concern. Elizabeth was flicking her own hand up and down slightly.

Did I hurt her?

Oh God, Anne sighed. She watched her friend snap her hand down once again and grimace.

"What happened?" Éndira said to them both. She tried to take Elizabeth's hand but the older woman pulled it away.

"Nothing, I just caught my finger on Anne's necklace," Elizabeth said. "I should not have done that to you. I apologize."

Anne shook her head.

She knew better.

I burned her, Anne thought bitterly.

"No... I did it," Anne whispered. "It was my fault."

Éndira walked over to Elizabeth as they both watched Anne disappear down the steps.

"Her fault?" Éndira asked, confused. "I do not understand."

"Neither do I," Elizabeth softly said.

26

———

Anne did not understand what had happened this afternoon.

Is it my ring that holds the power?

Or is it the crystals in the ring?

Am I channeling my own energy through it?

Anne shook her head, annoyed. If her crazy aunt were not trying to use her for nefarious reasons Anne felt she might have found answers to these questions.

I have no one to tell me, — whatever this is!

Anne did not know if she should confide in Elizabeth. Anne suspected that Elizabeth's pendant somehow saved her from Miranda's attack. *But how can I even approach the subject? Miss Elizabeth might think me mad.*

She might even throw me off this ship.

Anne sighed. She looked out at the distance and admired the view.

Just stop thinking about this craziness. Just enjoy what you have left of this time.

Anne returned her attention to the sky. She had never seen such vibrant colors swirled within magnificent clouds. Vivid hues of crimson red and orange mixed with purple and dark blue. The sun peeped through heavy clouds, trying to keep from being shuttered away.

Was this a thunderstorm trying to gain strength?

Anne had not seen a West Indies storm form on the ocean. She had only the knowledge of what one felt like, for her father had kept her below when they had passed through a gale the day before arriving in Barbados. And when she was on the island? She had never clearly seen what a West Indies thunderstorm looked like. Her aunt made her stay in her room, with the shutters closed when storms hit. Still they crashed open under the stress.

This storm was now clearly on the horizon for Anne to see.

Something about the wild colors dazzled, yet frightened her.

Anne walked to the rail and leaned over to look at the ocean. There was little movement of the waves as the ship easily sailed along. Small splashes of mist spat up and hit her in the face. Even with her lack of experience, Anne knew the ocean to be unusually calm.

She pushed herself back up. When she looked to her side, Éndira was standing in the shadows.

Anne grabbed her own chest, frightened.

"I scared you?" Éndira chuckled.

"Yes..." Anne folded her arms, annoyed. "I don't like people stepping out of the darkness."

"Sorry." Éndira leaned her back against the rail.

Anne was pleasantly surprised that Éndira had simply apologized instead of giving a smart response.

"What happened anyway?" Éndira asked with a curl of the lip. "This afternoon?"

"What do you mean?"

"Lizzy's finger? Did she really catch it on your chain?"

Anne glared at her. "I do not know. Why don't you ask her?"

"She won't tell me."

"What do you think happened?" Anne snapped.

Éndira cocked an eyebrow, amused. "I think you bit her."

Anne shook her head, dumbfounded. Was the girl trying to make a joke, or was she actually serious? Anne opened her mouth to protest but a sudden crack of thunder made them both jump. Next came a low rumble that seemed to sing like a men's choir.

Anne noticed the look of concern etched on Éndira's face. Now Anne was worried. Next, they both watched as Elizabeth walked over to the barometer. She whispered something to the officer of the watch and boatswain.

"It is sinking fast," Éndira whispered to herself.

"What is? The ship?" Anne asked, quickly panicking.

"No, the barometer. It measures the air pressure. And the wind is dying down."

"Isn't that a good thing?" Anne protested. "I mean no wind means no storm... right?"

Éndira looked at her somewhat amused. "What are the storms like where you come from?"

"I do not know what you mean?"

"Don't you feel some type of eeriness before one hits?"

"I guess," Anne shrugged. "Sometimes the air... smells different?"

Éndira looked up at the sails. They were beginning to lose momentum as the wind no longer pushed the canvas. "Not a good sign."

Anne inhaled.

The air did smell different. Even— *hot?*

She took her blouse and snapped it forward a few times to try to cool herself down. As minutes turned into half an hour, Anne's stomach turned sour.

It has to be my nerves.

It cannot be sea sickness... the ocean is so calm!

A sudden whip of hot air brushed by Anne's cheeks. She touched her skin. A quick gust snapped a sail like a switch on a piece of laundry.

"How bad will this be?" Anne hesitantly asked.

"Bad." Éndira raised her eyebrows as she watched Elizabeth go below deck. "Now where the bloody hell is she going?"

Anne felt the urge to run after her older friend and hide. She silently hoped Éndira was just teasing and playing a joke.

The sky darkened some more as thunder growled low in the distance. All around them, sailors stood and waited for orders. When Elizabeth appeared back on deck, Anne noticed that she had a flintlock attached to her waist belt.

Why does she need a weapon for a storm? Anne wondered.

Suddenly, some of the crew darted toward the forecastle, yelling in fear. Others slipped on the deck as they tried to crawl away from what had frightened them. Anne stepped back as soon as she looked up. On top of the mainmast, a fireball danced wildly. The glow it emitted was a violet, ghostly apparition that hung, suspended on the tip of the wood.

"It's a corposant," Éndira said, pulling Anne back.

"A what?"

"A corposant."

Before Anne had a chance to ask for clarification, the fireball slid down the mast.

It crashed on the deck and disappeared.

The rush of energy had struck the wood so hard, the two girls, as well as the bosun and a group of men were thrown backwards. Anne pushed herself to her side. The ship pitched hard as a sudden rogue wave hit the deck and drenched them all.

"We are going to be in for it captain!" The boatswain yelled as he struggled to get to his feet, his words clear for no wind was there to drown them.

Anne brushed her wet hair out of her face and stared at the mast. She had once heard of this phenomenon from her brother Michael. Sailors feared the sight of *St. Elmo's fire* as a foreboding that the weather would bring terrible plight.

Anne looked forward and gasped.

Standing on the deck was a woman.

She had a long face with round cheekbones, her skin a deep coffee color. Her clothes, as well as hair, were sopping wet. Multiple necklaces hung around her neckline. Some were made of shells, others were gold and silver. The long dress the woman wore was ripped and torn in many places. Seaweed was wildly draped around her arms and shoulders. When Anne looked closer she realized the dress was not made of cloth but... *seaweed itself.*

Anne gasped.

The wicked creature scanned the deck and laughed as the sailors near her feet cowered in fear. As she grinned, she revealed white as snow teeth with some sharp like an animal's.

"What is she?" Anne whispered as she pushed back with her feet and sat next to Éndira. She turned and looked at the other girl's face. Éndira curled her lip as she stared at the unwanted visitor and sighed.

Anne realized that Éndira did not look scared.

How can she not be scared of this— this— dead woman standing on the deck!

"Mama DgBaba," Éndira whispered. "These are her waters."

Just as Éndira spoke her name, Mama turned and looked down at them. Anne pushed backwards, frightened to the core by the eyes that stared back. Silver flecks in parts of dark purple irises. Mama reached out her hand and motioned for them to stand.

Anne wanted to refuse but her body seemed to be under Mama's control. Anne stood up and waited as Mama DgBaba glided forward. Mama's hand reached out and began to caress blond locks.

Anne could not move.

Now that the woman was standing face to face Anne got a better look at the intruder. Mama DgBaba might look dead from afar but up close Anne could make out the soft beautiful face of a woman no older than thirty.

"Let go of her," Elizabeth said forcefully, a cocked flintlock inches from Mama's face. "This one is not for you."

"But you have already stolen one from me." Mama released Anne's hair and touched the tip of the flintlock. She pushed the metal away slowly and stepped back. "Have you not?"

Mama smirked as she looked at Anne then locked eyes with Éndira. Elizabeth positioned herself in front of both girls.

Anne was frozen in place. She watched Mama walk slowly around Elizabeth as if she were seducing her into a dance. Elizabeth put the muzzle closer to Mama's head. The creature shook her own and snickered. "Please do not tempt dear. A ricochet of your weapon would be most disastrous don't you think? Who might you hit? Surely not me?"

Mama's voice was soft and pure. Her island accent danced off the tongue like tinkling bells in a gentle afternoon rain.

This woman had come from the deep without warning or somehow manifested out of the corposant. Either way, Anne had to believe a musket ball would do no harm to this creature called Mama DgBaba.

Elizabeth lowered her weapon and uncocked it. She put the flintlock in her waist belt.

"What do you want Mama?" She asked sternly.

The creature sauntered once again. "Your ship is most impressive Elizabeth."

Anne glanced at Éndira and raised an eyebrow. *This Mama knows Miss Elizabeth by name?*

"You have not paid penalty to travel in my waters woman," Mama said. She grinned at a frightened sailor. He turned and ran towards the forecastle of the ship. "I have been needing new blood lately." Mama eyed Anne. "Young preferably."

Blood?

Anne could feel herself tense.

Does this creature feed on blood?

Mama suddenly disappeared, then materialized behind Éndira. Anne quickly stood in-between and immediately regretted the decision. She had thought herself brave, but the way those silver flecks flushed in dark purple eyes made her knees want to give out.

"I have been granted passage to travel these waters." Elizabeth did not falter. She quickly patted her own left shoulder with two fingers. There was no hesitation in her voice. "I would advise you to leave us alone."

"Is that a threat?"

"Just a warning."

"Hmm." Mama sauntered around Elizabeth then whispered something else in her ear. Elizabeth had no reaction. When Mama pulled back, Anne stepped away. Mama had a mischievous grin. The woman snapped her hands and simply— disappeared.

The clouds suddenly evaporated and revealed a beautiful nighttime sky.

Anne could hardly catch her breath. Never had she seen anything as scary as Mama DgBaba!

BACK IN THE CABIN, Anne hesitantly asked, "What was she exactly?"

Éndira was on her own cot, busily trying to take off her last boot. "Mama DgBaba?"

"Yes." Anne leaned forward. "Here, let me help you."

Her hands firmly grasped the leather. When Éndira pushed backward, the boot slipped off, making Anne fall on her rump.

Éndira could not help but chuckle. Anne picked the boot off the floor and tossed the item at her. She herself started to laugh at her not so graceful assistance.

"Thank you." Éndira shoved the footwear under the bed. She pulled her ribbon out and let her long hair loose. As she brushed back the strands with her own hand, Anne could not help but stare.

Éndira did not notice.

"Is she a water spirit?" Anne asked, trying to keep her focus on questions, not on studying her bunkmate's body.

"She's the trickster god of these waters."

Anne gasped, "I thought only our god existed."

"The christian god?" Éndira sneered. "Throughout all these centuries and cultures, do you think only one survives?"

Anne huffed for she took offense. "I do not know, I never met him... or any other god until tonight." She started to think about this. "I wonder if the greek gods are still here. I always found those myths so fascinating."

"If they are then those are not myths but factual."

"How does Miss Elizabeth know her?"

"I do not know." Éndira began to undress.

"Miss Elizabeth tapped her own shoulder."

"Who did?"

"Miss Elizabeth." Anne tapped her own to show. "The one with the tattoo. She tapped her own shoulder as a warning. When she showed Zara and asked her if she served a water deity? Does Miss Elizabeth serve this Mama?"

Éndira didn't react, turning her attention to fussing with her plackard. Anne waited, finally realizing that the other girl was purposely ignoring the question.

"Éndira?" Anne pressed, annoyed.

"What?" Éndira glanced up.

"I am asking you a question."

"I have no idea." Éndira waved her off and returned to her clothing.

Anne crossed her arms, irritated. "How do you know her?"

"I do not know her."

"You are lying to me," Anne accused, keenly aware of the other girl's tone. *Why would she not want me to know the real story?* "Tell me the truth."

Éndira stopped and glared at the other girl. She threw her shirt down. This time, Anne's eyes did not focus on the other girl's naked chest. "If I told you the truth about Mama DgBaba," Éndira said. "You would never sleep another night after the horrors you learned."

"I am not a child," Anne snapped.

"Are you not?— You act like one!"

The way Éndira said the words so bluntly, so without care— Anne wanted to hit the girl! Instead, she got up off her bed and headed for the door. Anne heard laughter as she slammed it shut behind her.

Anne wanted to scream.

Éndira could be charming one second and a brash hag the next!

Maybe I just should have slapped the girl! I would have most likely gotten a black eye but the pain would have been worth it.

"I'm not a child," Anne whispered to herself as she stood on the quarterdeck and leaned on the side railing. The wind was crisp tonight. She shivered slightly and realized she should go back to the cabin and retrieve a wrap. *No, then I will have to see Éndira too soon. I will wait until the other girl is fast asleep before returning.*

Anne secretly wished the trickster known as Mama DgBaba would make another appearance on the deck. This time she would be brave and ask the woman what she was and what she wanted. Anne was convinced, now that she had seen Mama's face, that perhaps that was the woman she had seen in the shadows so many weeks ago on her father's ship.

When I threw my crystal into the water.

Did I call on Mama DgBaba somehow by doing such a thing?

Anne twisted the ring on her necklace.

"Aren't you cold Miss Anne?" Finlay asked from behind.

Anne turned and smiled at him.

"Slightly, but I will be okay," she answered.

"Here." The young midshipman took off his coat and put it around her shoulders. "I do not want you to catch a sickness Miss Anne."

Anne curled herself into the jacket. She smiled, happy that someone at least had some manners. Éndira could learn a few things from this young man.

"Thank you," Anne said.

He nodded then stepped up to the railing and scanned the horizon.

"How are you enjoying the cruise so far?" Finlay asked her.

"Besides my bunkmate? I am enjoying it quite well."

Finlay took humor in the remark, for he chuckled slightly. Anne knew he was happy to have her company, and she considered him a friend. She glanced down at his hands. They were bandaged across the palms.

"What happened to you?" Anne reached down and held his hands in hers.

"Slight mistake on my part." Finlay adjusted himself to allow her to see better. "One of the seaman thought it funny to trick me into holding a rope that sailed quickly into the ocean. My palms got burned."

Anne gasped. "Why did he do that?"

"Because upsetting young officers is what some men do Miss Anne. It makes them feel superior."

"Did you punish him?" Anne asked, aware that a flogging might be in order for such an offense.

"No," Finlay said. "I am sure he expected me to commit him to the cat, but I think it upset him more that I did not care."

"You didn't?"

"No, of course I did. I just did not want to show him. Men like that get a thrill from annoying others."

Anne turned her ear to the ocean and listened to the soft waves. *I should take a lesson from this young man. Maybe Éndira will not be so brash if I show her little attention?*

"Perhaps I should just ignore her," Anne whispered to herself.

"Your friend?"

"She's not my friend."

"No?" Finlay asked. "You seem to have finally warmed up to her."

Anne straightened up. "Why would you say that?"

"You seem more engaged by her presence. I confess, I am a little too. I've never actually met a female pirate before. I find her interesting."

Interesting?

Does that mean he truly has an interest in Éndira?

And if he does would I care?

The deck bell rung.

"Well Miss Anne," Finlay bowed slightly. "I must tend to my duties this evening. I am officer on deck tonight."

Anne returned his coat and blushed when he kissed her hand goodbye. She quickly glanced around, trying to see if any spying eyes had seen what had just happened.

And why do I secretly wish Éndira had?

ELIZABETH QUIETLY SHUT the cabin door. She walked behind her desk and slowly sat down. Exhaling softly, Elizabeth looked at them both with stern eyes.

"I am no longer worried about finding your father Anne," Elizabeth said.

Anne took a second to process the comment. She shifted uneasily in her seat.

"Because of Mama DgBaba?" Anne hesitantly asked.

When Elizabeth snapped her eyes towards Éndira, the other girl simply shrugged and sat back like she was bored.

"You told Anne her name?" Elizabeth said sharply.

Éndira waved her hand down unconcerned. "I told her nothing important."

"Liar." Anne turned, upset. "You told me she was the trickster god of these waters. You then called me a child for wanting to know more."

"You *are* a child."

"Go to *hell*," Anne snapped.

"Enough!" Elizabeth ordered. She laid her elbows on the table and slowly rubbed her temples. "I have enough of a headache without listening to the two of you squabble."

Anne huffed then leaned back and folded her arms to her chest. Éndira rolled her eyes and did the same thing.

Elizabeth shook her head, exhaling once again. "Mama has taken an interest in you Anne... and I have no idea why."

"Because she is vastly... *interesting,*" Éndira snickered.

When Anne glared at her, Éndira smirked, most likely feeling she had scored another hit.

"Éndira?" Elizabeth calmly warned. "You are on my ship as a liaison, but you are still under my command. Unless you want to be peeling potatoes for the next several days, you will refrain from being a pain in my arse? Do you understand?"

"Yes," Éndira reluctantly agreed. She refused to look at Anne whose smile was wide with triumph.

Anne waited to be chastised next but that did not happen.

Miss Elizabeth is taking my side? Anne thought happily then quickly realized that it might not be a good thing. *Éndira will simply hold this against me and get her insults in when we are in private.*

"As I was saying," Elizabeth continued. "Mama DgBaba has taken special interest in you Anne. The only thing I can think of is that your Aunt Miranda has made some sort of deal with her."

"What?" Anne gasped. "Is that even possible?"

"Yes," Éndira calmly said. "Mama makes deals all the time."

Anne looked at Elizabeth directly. "Did she make one with you?"

Elizabeth blinked, somewhat blindsided by the question. She sat still for a moment and said nothing. When Éndira leaned in, curious, Elizabeth shook her head.

"I..." Elizabeth slightly hesitated, "I have... never made a deal with Mama."

"But you know her?" Anne asked.

"Yes, I do know her," Elizabeth said softly. "Unfortunately."

Anne glanced at Éndira, confirming the question that the girl refused to answer yesterday in the cabin.

Why would Éndira not want me to know?

"Then what does Mama want with me?" Anne sighed. "Just to bring me back to my aunt?"

"Well..." Elizabeth unconsciously rubbed the back of her neck. "I cannot answer that question Anne but I know who might."

Both girls looked at her with inquisitive eyes.

"I am diverting the ship to Mayreau... where I plan to leave you Anne."

Anne opened her eyes wide, concerned. She didn't even know where Mayreau was.

"Why?" Anne asked, aghast.

"I told you about my limited potion skills," Elizabeth said to them both. "I was taught by two women who practice obeah."

"Obeah?" Éndira screeched, startling Anne. "Are you kidding me?"

Elizabeth narrowed her eyes. "Do I look like I am kidding?"

Éndira nervously moved in her seat. "You never told me you know obeah."

"I don't know obeah... really."

Anne leaned forward. "Um? What is obeah?"

"It is dark magic," Éndira huffed.

"It can be dark magic," Elizabeth said. "And there is also white magic. These women know the dark arts but they do not use them unless they must."

"And they told you this?" Éndira protested.

Elizabeth sighed and sat back in her chair, looking now directly at Anne. "I believe they can protect you Anne."

"And you trust them?" Anne hesitantly asked.

"With my life."

There was silence in the room as Anne watched Elizabeth's face. Anne realized that her friend was indeed very serious.

There is no way she would leave me alone with people that she did not trust. How would she explain that to my father?

He would never speak to her again.

She loves him, Anne sighed looking at her. *I know she loves him deeply.*

"I still say we should burn down the tree," Éndira said stiffly.

"No one is going back on that island until we can figure out how to stop Miranda."

"But you are planning on stopping Mama DgBaba with dark obeah?" Éndira said sarcastically.

"They will use what they can."

"No one is powerful enough to stop Mama," Éndira insisted. She leaned forward in frustration then sighed. "Maybe I should go with Anne?"

Anne blinked, surprised. *Why does she want to come with me? She actually wants to help me?*

"They have stopped Mama in the past," Elizabeth insisted.

"How?"

"They saved my life."

"That is why you have that sigil!" Éndira slapped the table hard startling both women. "I knew it!"

Again, Elizabeth seemed blindsided by the statement. She said nothing, just turned her head and glanced at the wall.

"You must have really angered Mama somehow woman!" Éndira added.

Elizabeth glared at her accuser.

"Umm... what is a sigil?" Anne asked innocently trying to break the tension.

"A ward against evil," Elizabeth said, turning her head and looking at them both.

"It's not a tattoo?"

"It is a tattoo," Éndira said. "But a sigil is placed on a person to ward against something in particular, like..." Éndira looked at Elizabeth with interest in her eyes. "Mama DgBaba."

Elizabeth stood up and walked to the door. The conversation was over as far as she was concerned.

"I have much to do this morning," she opened the door and looked at them both.

Once they had both exited the door Elizabeth sighed and walked to her desk. She sat in her chair and leaned back, deflated.

"What else can I do," Elizabeth whispered to herself. She rubbed her arm and closed her eyes for she was tired and spent. She reached for her goblet and took a quick drink. Elizabeth decided she would empty the rest of the decanter this evening.

27

Miranda had trekked for a long time over the uneven path. Few, if any, traversed these walkways; there were many reasons to be afraid here.

This was a dark and foreboding place.

The wind howled in a frightening low hum; the shadows made by the trees could send chills up one's spine. Others could swear they heard blood-curdling laughter in the distance.

Duppies and jumbees ruled the area, many locals would say. A decent, law abiding citizen, would never traverse this part of the island.

If they did, they had only one thing on their mind— their own possible demise, or that of another.

She was tired from her walk. Her horse was able to go only so far before she was forced to continue on foot. The bag she carried contained heavy gold pieces, payment for the action she needed to ask for.

Miranda reached her hands out and used her feet to climb the steep precipice. The first time she made this trek, she scratched her hands and injured her legs, the thorns of the bougainvillea cutting into her skin like a butcher slicing into a piece of meat. Now she wore her riding breeches, long boots and leather gloves. Thankfully, there was not a drop of rain to be felt or seen, and the dew was only just beginning to settle.

No one would bother her on this journey.

No one would admit to having seen her.

If they had, they would simply ignore the mistress of the grand plantation that most of the populace on the west side of the island knew. Others out east had heard of her, and did their best not to gossip fearful that Miranda Sutton-Langdon could hear their thoughts and would fly in the night to frighten them in their sleep like the night hag.

Miranda laughed inside.

Idiots! If only I could fly!

But those were often silly superstitions that peasants told themselves.

The people of the island had grown up believing their own tales. Whites from Europe brought tales of fairies and leprechauns. Africans told stories of witch doctors and soul-eaters. Those on the islands for multiple generations believed in soucouyants, duppies and jumbies as well as many others.

Miranda knew how to scare people into submission. Even if it was technically in her blood, she never considered herself a simple witch.

She was a Crystal Astrid.

A very powerful one.

And so was her niece which is what brought her out at this godforsaken hour in the first place.

I need her back!

Miranda pushed some bushes aside and forced her way forward. She was unafraid of the bottles that clinked overhead in the trees. Put there as a warning, any stray traveler would know that an obeah man or woman was close. Some of the bottles contained liquid of various colors, others held rusty nails and feathers. They swung in the trees with the wind, like tiny dancers twirling and rocking back and forth.

She stopped in front of a chasm, a small opening to the mouth of the cave. Her body was lean, but still the fit was tight. With her hands up, she scooted along the rocks and entered.

The cavern was small. Miranda put her hands forward and willed light to be shown. A small, glow of energy released from her pendant and lit the room.

In front were three more chasms to choose from. The spell on the entrances made sure all flames would suddenly be extinguished, and the explorer would fall to their death, the depth of the hole unknown to even the obeah man.

Only one, each time different, led to the cavern itself.

"Baka!" She yelled out, her voice reverberating on the rock walls. "Make yourself known!"

A blast of wind blew out of the chasm to the left. Miranda stepped forward and once again had to maneuver her body through the tight space. The farther she went, the brighter the light of flames could be seen. She snuffed out her own light since magic was no longer needed.

A tall, lean man with smooth ebony skin stood in front of a fire. The flickering light from crackling flames bounced from beneath him, giving his deep set eyes a haunting look. He held a walking stick in his hand and wore nothing but loose trousers, his bare, well chiseled chest and bare feet glistened with sweat.

"To what do I owe the pleasure for this visit Miranda?" Baka purred.

Miranda cocked her head. He had always fancied her and as much as he wanted the pleasures of her flesh, she refused him, not because of the color of his skin, but because she loathed having any relations with men.

"I have come for your help," Miranda tossed him the small sack.

He caught it with ease then jiggled the bag. His fingers carefully opened it as he felt the coins. Satisfied, he tossed the bag on his bed and motioned with his hands to come forward.

She watched him place a small bench in front of her. Baka waited until she sat before he sat on his own.

They stared at each other over the fire. Both their faces were illuminated from beneath. The light danced on their skin in such a spine-chilling way, any witness to this exchange might die of immediate fright.

"I need my niece back," Miranda demanded.

Baka threw a stick in the fire. "She ran away already?"

"You knew this would happen?"

"I told you the fire never lies."

"You told me she would be difficult!"

"And do difficult children not run away?"

Miranda turned her head and looked at the corner of the room. There was a small table that held more bottles, each one filled with a different liquid and parts of animals. On the floor near Baka's feet, a cat's skull, beads and powders in multiple calabashes, egg-shells and feathers. Hanging from a stick on a tripod of wood were human skulls woven with twine. Feathers stuck out from smashed parts of frontal and parietal orifices. To the left a pair of small cannonades sat complete with boxes of ammunition and muskets.

"Are you getting ready for a war?" Miranda sneered as she looked at him once again.

"We must always be prepared for the worst."

"You have nothing to fear from me."

"It is not you I must protect myself from," Baka said. "Spells take time, curses even more— you should know that. But a white man with a rifle charging a man like me must defend himself with more."

"Who has been threatening you?"

"No one," Baka laughed. "Do you think I would leave them alive if they did silly woman?"

"That is why I make them cower, lest they get any ideas."

"You are a white woman, and a rich one." He put more kindle on the fire. "I do not have that luxury. I may be free but I am still not of your color."

"When I rule this island, they will quiver at your feet."

"But you have lost your key."

"That is why I have come back to you... help me."

"You do not need my help Miranda."

"Are you trying to acquire more money from me?" Miranda sneered, looking at the wall of weapons once again.

Baka laughed much to her annoyance. He reached down and picked up his walking stick. "I fear my skills will not help with a body so far across the islands and sea."

"This would not have been as hard if your sister was still alive!"

Baka tightened the grip around his stick unnerved by the comment. She turned back to him immediately regretful of what she had just said. Miranda knew deep down that the man was still grieving over his loss.

I cannot agitate him. If he refuses to help me anymore then I do not know what I will do.

"I apologize Baka," Miranda said sincerely. "I am just... frustrated."

"I understand that Miranda."

"I know I have promised to help you with..." Miranda said, remembering their other deal made not too long ago, "I... I... will not go back on my word."

"I know you will not," Baka nodded without anger. He reached over to his side and picked up a calabash filled with a grey powder. His fingers took a pinch and tossed it in the fire. A sudden, quick flash of bright blue flame lifted up then fell into a swirl of beautiful blues that sparkled. In the mix of circulating magic, an image of a woman appeared.

Miranda peered closer, but could not make out who she was.

"That is who you must ask to help you," Baka said.

A face appeared, followed by a smile with teeth slightly sharp, a grin most sinister.

"How do I contact her?"

"You must simply call her name and tell her your wishes." Baka leaned forward. "If she feels your plight is something worthy she may help you, but remember..."

Miranda impatiently waited.

"She will always ask a price," he continued. "You must be willing to give whatever she wants. There is no room for one to ask and then back away."

Miranda nodded and looked further into the fire. "I am willing to give what is needed."

Baka flipped his wrist and made the vision disappear. He reached for a bottle, took two mugs and poured each a drink.

Tonight they would celebrate Miranda's impending victory.

AFTER SHE HAD DECIDED Anne was to go to Mayreau Elizabeth presided over the Sunday service. Anne attended this but Éndira chose to stay below.

Elizabeth did not care.

Éndira's wildness and lack of respect for any authority only enhanced Elizabeth's irritation.

Elizabeth then read the Articles of War out loud. Each and every seaman, including the officers, were required to listen. This was the law of the Admiralty, and every captain was required to do this at least once a month.

As a lieutenant, and now as captain, Elizabeth would take mental note of who was paying attention and who was half-listening. She looked straight at her newest addition, Jackson, and observed him. He stared out at the horizon until he turned and caught her eye. When he sneered at her, Elizabeth tightened her fist, angered. She was surprised that Miranda had not possessed him.

Jackson would not even have needed any help if Miranda had simply asked him. He would have enjoyed slitting my throat.

He still might.

After the service, she sent Anne below deck to read. Since Anne had expressed the desire to have as little contact with the other girl as possible, Elizabeth agreed the great cabin would be private enough.

"Sail!" The look-out suddenly cried from the crow's nest. "Port bow!"

"Flag?" Lieutenant Hicks asked from below.

"Union Jack I think?"

"Hmm..." Elizabeth turned to Finlay. "The signal book!"

Finlay glanced at the side then turned quickly in the other direction not knowing where he was supposed to go. The coxswain rolled his eyes and tossed him the signal book. The young man unskillfully juggled the item before getting a firm grasp. Quickly he started to flip through the pages.

He seemed lost.

"Any day now Mr. Travers," Elizabeth firmly encouraged.

Finlay put a telescope to his eyes and began to read out the colors. He looked down in the book and began to translate what they meant. Elizabeth had been training the young midshipman to be able to read any signals under pressure. He was only interpreting the international signal that civilian ships used to communicate by distance. If this was another English ship-of-the-line, there was a separate, secret set of signals that could never fall into enemy hands. They had ways of ensuring their safety.

Elizabeth crossed her arms behind her back as she stared ahead, eyebrows cocked in doubt.

Lieutenant Hicks moved next to her. "Ruse?"

"I am thinking so."

Finlay read off more flags. The ship was saying that she was friendly and heading to Saint Croix.

"Does he think we will not board him as a precaution?" Hicks asked her.

"I think he wants to distract us until he can make a run," Elizabeth said. "If he hits a patch of wind, we will lose him."

"What do you want to do?"

A deep, uneasy feeling hit the bottom of Elizabeth's stomach. She knew that the ship in question was not friendly. Somehow her intuition was telling her that it was a Spanish brig, not an English merchant which the signal flags were claiming.

"Shall I order a response Captain?" Hicks asked.

"No," Elizabeth said as she walked forward and snatched the telescope out of Finlay's hand. "I will take a look myself first."

Quickly, she traversed up the rigging with a skill only shown by one with much experience. Careful to take each step in the right place, her boots were built for such ease, a slight heel to ensure a proper backwards grip. She easily grabbed the netting with her hands, her upper body strong as she searched for the easiest path.

Captains rarely, if ever, stepped foot in the rigging if they had others to command. Elizabeth had always been hands on. She sometimes needed to see with her own eyes the dangers that lay ahead.

Elizabeth pulled herself up.

"Where?" she asked the lookout.

"Port bow ma'am," he smiled, seemingly impressed that she made the trip so fast.

Elizabeth's left leg entwined itself in the netting. She wrapped a loose rope around her right arm and leaned forward, letting herself dangle slightly above the deck. Carefully, she put the telescope to her eye and searched the horizon.

The light was very bright. The sun bounced off the water and produced a wicked glare. Elizabeth strained to see. She had to compensate for the ship's pitch and roll before finally finding the object in question.

Was it what she feared? Somehow she knew that the ship was a Spanish brig luring them into a trap.

What do I do? Elizabeth pulled back the telescope and wiped her forehead. Her nerves were already on high alert. *Engage or not?*

How do I justify my actions if I choose not to?

Elizabeth was no coward. She had always been steadfast in the heat of battle. She watched men cower when presented with death while she quickly took their place to continue the fight. She always cared for the safety of her crew and never took that fact lightly.

This is what we have trained for.

We each might die for Queen and country.

But not Anne! Not this girl I am sworn to protect!

"Dammit!" Elizabeth cursed under her breath thinking equally of Éndira's safety.

I knew this might happen. Mama threatened as much.

Anne and Éndira are onboard and now we are going to go into a BLOODY battle!

Elizabeth sighed. She knew she had to engage.

There was no other alternative.

Any captain who refused to engage or, worse yet withdrew, risked repercussions under the Articles of War. Elizabeth knew them all too well. She had just read them off to her crew no less than an hour ago.

The tenth Article of War: "Every flag officer... upon signal or order of fight, or sight of any ship or ships which it may be his duty to engage, or who... shall not make the necessary preparations for fight, and shall not in his own person, and according to his place, encourage the inferior officers and men to fight courageously, *shall suffer death!*"

The twelfth Article of War: "who through cowardice, negligence, or disaffection... or not come into the fight or engagement... or shall not do his utmost to take or destroy every ship... every such person so offending... sentence of court martial, *shall suffer death.*"

The list went on and on.

Elizabeth jumped from line to line as she descended to the quarterdeck. When she landed, she handed the telescope back to her midshipman and silently conversed with Lieutenant Hicks.

"That is a Spanish brig," Elizabeth stated. "I would bet my life on it."

"Don't be rushing to fill the butcher's bill yet ma'am," Hicks said. "Shall I beat to quarters?"

"No, she is still too far off." Elizabeth looked up at the sails. "This wind will not hold. We may be in for a long day." She rubbed her hands together behind her back again, a nervous tick she had long ago acquired. "Send the hands to lunch early. Let them have a hot meal before we have to douse the fires."

"Yes ma'am." Hicks walked over to the bell and rang. The early call for a meal had the crew excited. They knew that there was a potential prize ship in the distance. Why else would the captain suddenly run up the rigging like a newly minted midshipman?

They smell prize money.

They did not care that some of them were more than likely to die in the process. The loss of life and limb lay little on the mind of a man who desired to pounce on a ship, especially a Spanish one that could be holding bullion that made some rich.

"The Fire Witch?" Hicks stood once again at her side.

"I doubt it." Elizabeth shook her head. "Last I heard she had a convoy of ships... the ones she did not burn."

"What about your charge?"

"She will have to hunker down in my cabin. I know not what else to do with her."

"What if we put her in a pinnace with the Spanish one?"

"No. I will not risk that. Their chances are better if we keep them on the ship." Elizabeth looked at him directly in the eyes. "If the worst happens, I will not allow either of them to fall into enemy hands and be..." Elizabeth did not want to say the words "— and neither will you."

Violated.

Either of the girls.

I will have to end them both.

It would be horrible— yet the only honorable thing to do.

Elizabeth started to nervously rub her hands together once again.

28

Captain Elizabeth Spencer reached into her desk and pulled out a log book. She turned and pointed to the corner. "Éndira hand me that canvas bag."

Éndira did as she was told. Elizabeth took the sack from her and threw in the book. She ran over to the cabinet and rummaged through a stack of rolled up navigation charts. Her hands found what she was looking for, the master signal book, never to fall into enemy hands.

Elizabeth tossed the item in. She continued to rummage through papers and added those she deemed important to the mix.

"What is she doing?" Anne asked innocently.

"Papers, correspondences," Éndira answered. "Anything that could be deemed useful to an enemy must be dumped overboard if the ship is captured."

Elizabeth tossed a bar of lead into the bag, then tightened the rope and secured the top. She handed the bag to Éndira. "Take this to Lieutenant Hicks right away. He will know whom to give it to."

"Okay." Éndira bolted out the door.

Anne was starting to get more nervous. She didn't really grasp the reality of what was happening till Éndira said in case of— *capture?*

Are we really going to do this? Anne swallowed hard. *Am I actually going to be involved in a battle?*

Panic hit the pit of her stomach.

"Anne, come here," Elizabeth ordered.

Anne's feet moved as quick as a body filled with fear could do. She said nothing as she watched.

Elizabeth dug into the cabinet, pulled out a wrapped piece of cloth as well as a wooden box and placed them both on the table. With a flip of the wrist, the cloth uncovered two flintlocks, fine wood with white bone engraved handles.

Elizabeth picked up one of the pistols. She reached into the box and pulled out a smaller sack. Holding the weapon, she pointed the muzzle towards the floor and half-cocked it. Elizabeth tore open a paper cartridge that held a ball and powder. She pulled back the frizzen, placed powder in the flash pan, then carefully flipped it closed. Her hands poured the rest of the powder down the barrel, carefully placed the ball into the paper wadding, pulled the ramrod out and packed them tight. She put the weapon back on the table and repeated the process with the other one.

Anne watched each step carefully.

Elizabeth swiftly pulled another set of flintlocks out of the cabinet and placed them carefully on the table.

"I want you to load these," Elizabeth said.

"What?" Anne stepped back as if the weapons would turn into snakes and bite her.

Elizabeth leaned on the desk, her eyes deeply serious. "I want you to load these Anne."

The younger woman reached out her hand and timidly picked up one of the weapons. The piece was heavier than she imagined. Her fingers almost lost their grip. Anne snatched up the weapon with her other hand and held the handle tight.

"Here." Elizabeth proceeded to instruct on how to hold and point the flintlock.

Anne's hands were shaking as she followed her captain's instructions, careful not to spill the powder, making sure cloth was wrapped around the ball. When she had the ramrod firmly in place down the barrel, the door to the cabin opened suddenly, making her drop the weapon.

Elizabeth caught the pistol by the butt before it could hit the table.

Éndira, wide eyed, stepped away from the door once she realized the muzzle was pointing right at her. Elizabeth turned the weapon quickly towards the floor.

Éndira cocked an eyebrow and surveyed the scene. "Are you sure that is a good idea?"

"Go in my bureau and retrieve my guards," Elizabeth forcefully instructed Éndira.

The girl rolled her eyes and opened a wood drawer. She rummaged through a few pieces of clothing and snickered when she lifted a fine, silk dress.

"Put that away and hurry up!" Elizabeth snapped then started helping Anne once again.

Eventually, Anne managed to finish the correct steps.

Éndira handed Elizabeth a pair of black gloves. Elizabeth snaked them on, then allowed help to fasten the guards firmly onto her wrists. Elizabeth dived into her cabinet once again and retrieved a sword and belt. She pulled the sword out and looked it over for a moment. Her hands swiftly cut the air sideways then down.

Anne watched as Elizabeth twisted the hilt of the sword in opposite directions. The sword turned with her movements, separated like a pair of scissors, then snapped into two weapons!

Before Anne could comment, Elizabeth rejoined the swords and put them back in the scabbard. She took Anne by the arm and walked her over to the windows. She then pushed hard against the desk, pushed it slightly upwards and quickly flipped the wood onto its side.

Anne stood still afraid to do anything that might upset the pacing in the room. She continued to watch as Éndira sharpened a sword near the door. Elizabeth placed three of the flintlocks on her own shoulder belt. Anne stepped back slightly when she was handed a cutlass.

"What am I supposed to do with this?" Anne's hands were shaking as she unwillingly accepted the item.

"Keep this next to you." Elizabeth did not wait for a response. She grabbed the last flintlock and kneeled by the underside of the now tipped over desk. She motioned for Anne to come join her.

Anne slowly kneeled down.

Elizabeth inhaled deeply for a brief moment. "Listen to me Anne. You are safest here in my cabin, but if something happens... if anyone comes in that is not supposed to be here..." Elizabeth put the flintlock in the girl's hand. "You use this, do you hear me?"

"I've never shot anyone before!" Anne squealed. "I've never even shot a pistol!"

Elizabeth tightened her grip around Anne's shoulder. "Listen to me Anne. You can do this."

Anne's eyes were wide with panic but she knew she had to do what was right. "Yes miss."

"Good girl," Elizabeth smiled.

Anne knew she had to learn to defend herself. She nodded in agreement and placed the pistol down slowly. She looked up to see Éndira standing above her.

"You'll do fine love," Éndira winked. "Lizzy will not let anything happen to you."

Anne nodded in agreement once again.

"If anyone besides Éndira or I come in through that door," Elizabeth said firmly. "You shoot them— understand?"

"Yes... yes miss."

Anne closed her eyes and turned. She let her back hit the inside of the desk top. Only when Elizabeth touched her shoulder gently once again did she open them. Anne motioned with her head that she understood and was ready. She watched as they both left and locked the door with a key from the outside.

She was now alone with an unspeakable terror she was not ready to face.

~

HOLDING THE PISTOL TIGHTLY, Anne sat stone-faced and stared straight ahead at the windows. Slowly she counted them.

Seven perfectly fit windows with nine panes layered between rows of muntin. Slightly frosted glass the color of light blue was the result of sea water spray. It gave the light that seeped into the cabin a deep tint. Dust danced in-between the rays, a cosmic show that entranced Anne's vision.

She had always tried to focus her negativity and fear into the positive. That is why she created so many pieces of glass and crystal art.

Light and crystals fascinated her.

She loved the way light bounced off the gemstones. So many refracted rays created multi-colored lights in vast arrays of patterns. Patterns that could swirl within each other, creating a sense of motion.

Only now did she understand why she had been so attracted to crystals.

Anne nervously played with the ring on her necklace with her free hand. Her other was shaking as she gripped the flintlock. She was afraid if she let go something bad might happen. She felt the grooves carved in the silver part of her ring and the sharp facets of the jewels that were embedded in it. Her fingertips caressed their surfaces.

Beneath her, Anne could feel the motion of the ship. She could feel the cannons as they were cast loose. Slowly, Anne put down the flintlock and placed both her hands on the wooden floor.

I can feel... within the ship?

Anne concentrated harder. Someone ran down from the quarterdeck, barely able to hold onto the railing.

Anne turned her head to listen more carefully.

As her hands searched the wood she sensed another pair of feet. These were light steps that paced back and forth. Soft boots that barely made a sound but still Anne could hear them.

Captain Spencer?

Anne could feel Elizabeth pacing back and forth. She felt Elizabeth's heart beat as the woman tightened her gloved hands within each other, leather scraping against leather.

Fast footsteps ran towards Elizabeth. Worn leather soles with raised heels?

Éndira?

Anne sensed Éndira suddenly stop and turn.

Does she feel me too?

Finlay was on the lower deck in charge of gun crews. He was nervously pacing back and forth. Anne could feel his unease. He had never gone into battle before.

The noises got louder the more she concentrated. Other cannons were cut loose. The bare feet of sailors were heard as they ran and retrieved tampions and rammers. A key dropped. The gunner picked the item up and unlocked the magazines. Cartridges were handed to men who ran back up the stairs. Anne could feel which men were running and to whom they had given the ammunition.

How can I feel all of this?

Anne quietly listened for minutes that seemed like hours. The heart-beats of sailors who knew they might not survive. Men who were crouched at cannons waiting for a signal.

All was quiet for a while until—

Elizabeth jumped forward and gave her command.

In that instant, it was like hell itself had opened.

Anne grabbed her head and tried to block out the massive rumbling of the cannons. One after another, they screamed loudly, then jerked back and recoiled, each time scraping on the deck. The pounding was constant and no longer the entertainment Anne had once grown to love.

A sudden crash into the side of the ship made her jump. The enemy was firing back. Again and again they came, one hit after another, bending and scarring the wooden planks that held the ship together.

Anne could almost feel the ship's pain.

The relentless fighting went on and on, neither side letting up.

After a while of constant bombardment, Anne no longer knew what time it was.

How long have we been fighting?

Who is winning?

Who is still alive?

Anne felt beneath her fingertips and pulled back as if she had been stung. She felt blood on the wooden decks above.

She felt bodies laying on the planks.

Some were no longer moving. There were others that did not belong on the ship.

Have we been boarded?

She frantically searched for Elizabeth's footsteps. Anne could no longer feel them. *Has Miss Elizabeth fallen?*

Just the thought made Anne frantic. She nervously grabbed the flint-lock and got to her feet. She herself started to pace back and forth.

Something is wrong!

The cannons are no longer firing.

Anne touched the wood around the windows. She closed her eyes and listened for a moment. Only the sounds of feet running back and forth could be heard. Metal scraped on deck. Bodies fell.

So much screaming!

A pound on the door alerted her. Anne raised the weapon. Her hand shaking uncontrollably. She tried to steady the weapon with her other hand and waited. Her legs wobbled slightly as she stepped forward.

Someone is playing with the lock?

Oh God what do I do? Anne swallowed hard. *If they get in here?*

Suddenly, the door swung open.

Anne pulled the trigger. The blast threw her off balance as she skipped backwards. Smoke engulfed her face. Anne waved her hand and coughed. Frightened, she tried to see if she had shot anyone.

"Good thing you are a lousy shot." Éndira crept up from the shadows and closed the door with a key.

"What is happening out there?" Anne squealed, frantic.

Éndira walked over. "It is not going well."

"We've been boarded, haven't we?"

Éndira crooked an eyebrow. "How do you know that?"

"I... I just know," Anne confessed.

Éndira took the flintlock out of Anne's hand. "I'll load this— "

"No, wait!" Anne pulled the weapon back. "I can do that."

Éndira opened her mouth to protest but stopped herself. She watched Anne begin the process. After Anne did all the right steps she handed it back.

"I am duly impressed," Éndira smirked as she pulled out her other weapon.

"Good for you," Anne chided. She turned her back and leaned against the inside of the table.

Éndira kneeled next to Anne.

"Why are you down here anyway?" Anne objected. "You should be up there helping Miss Elizabeth!"

"Miss Elizabeth can take care of herself," Éndira sniggered. "It is you she is concerned about."

"I can take care of myself."

"No you can't."

"I almost shot you dead, didn't I?"

"You missed— "

"Really?" Anne swiped the hat off Éndira's head and put her finger in a small hole in the brim. "Then what is this?"

Éndira snapped her hat back and put it back on. "Beginners luck."

Anne was about to protest once again when Éndira pushed her downward. She watched as the pirate girl pointed her weapon at the door.

"Someone's coming," Éndira whispered.

29

———

Anne remained very still. She reached down and picked up her loaded weapon. Firmly gripped in her hand, the flintlock seemed to be made for her small fingers. She waited patiently next to Éndira.

A swift kick of the door produced nothing but a slight budge. Again and again the door held tight as someone on the outside wanted it down.

For a moment, the girls thought the intruder might have given up. Éndira peeked her eyes higher and waited like a panther ready to attack.

Another loud crash and this time the door was kicked in. A man with a red bandana and harsh suntanned face ran forward with cutlass in hand. Éndira calmly stood up and shot him. He jerked back and fell, dead before he even hit the wood.

Another ran in behind him. Éndira dispatched him also with ease. She turned and tossed her weapons down then snatched Anne's loaded flintlock.

"Need this," Éndira said.

Anne nodded then quickly began the task of reloading the other two.

Another shot popped off.

Anne tried not to think what was happening. Éndira would need the weapons to be filled as quickly as possible. Just as she finished loading one flintlock, Anne saw her spent weapon hit the side of the dresser. Anne finished loading Endira's second then leaned over and retrieved the third.

Another scream, then swords clashing.

Anne peeked over and saw Éndira fighting with a large attacker. Her sword was tiny compared to his, his huge biceps bigger than either girl's head. Anne locked eyes with Éndira.

Éndira could speak words with only a look.

One that said... *I need your help!*

Anne leaped forward and tossed a loaded flintlock towards the girl. Éndira quickly countered the attacker's movement, turned her body low and swept sideways. She jumped up and snatched the weapon. Before he could hit her again, Éndira swept in the opposite direction, kicked him in the leg and dropped him with a blast of the flintlock. As he fell down, Éndira jumped out of the way.

"Thanks love!" Éndira winked at her. She tossed the spent weapon back just as Anne gently tossed a loaded one to her.

A quick flutter hit Anne in the stomach. The sensation was not unwanted at all but this girl who had annoyed her from the beginning had suddenly made Anne feel— wanted.

"What?" Anne didn't realize Éndira had yelled to her. She had been too busy daydreaming at the most inappropriate time.

"Where is the other one!"

"I— " Anne tried to focus. "Yes, I— " she reached down and quickly tossed the other loaded weapon.

Éndira grabbed it easily.

Anne began to load when another shot rang out immediately followed by a second.

Éndira was out of shot once again!

Anne knew she had to be quick but her hands were shaking.

"Anne!" Éndira yelled in frustration.

Anne heard steel hit steel. She shook her head and tried to finish her task. Once she got the flintlock loaded, she jumped and froze. Éndira was frantically fighting with cutlass in hand. Both of her spent flintlocks had fallen to the floor out of Anne's reach.

"Here!" Anne yelled.

Once again a weapon was tossed. Éndira managed to grab it and shoot her attacker.

As Éndira continued to fight, Anne ran and slid downward behind the girl. She took the spent flintlock out of Éndira's hand. Anne tossed it high and threw it behind the desk. Quickly Anne did the same with the other two.

Anne returned to her cover. Now that she had all the weapons, she started to panic.

Do I load them all at once? Or do I load one and toss as I go?

As Anne frantically tried to load the first weapon, a loud groan was emitted and a loud crash on the floor. Anne realized Éndira was too small to make such a noise.

Stop panicking!

One!

Just finish one!

Anne managed to get her fingers to work. She finally finished the first and jumped up.

"Éndira!" Anne realized she should not have yelled the other girl's name without looking. Éndira suddenly turned, unaware that the remaining attacker had already retrieved his saber. Éndira did not see the way the metal twisted with his sudden movement and was about to drop on her head.

Anne fumbled with the pistol and tried to point. She did not know if she could even aim. The weapon was sideways in her hand. Frantically she tried to find the trigger; her hands were covered with sweat making it hard to grasp.

The attacker was about to drop his weight down for a perfect cut but he jerked upright for a moment, eyes wide. Two blades were sticking out of his chest, perfectly aligned and both dripping with blood. As they were pulled out, his massive weight fell to the floor with a huge thud.

Anne barely held the flintlock while she stared ahead. Éndira turned quickly and had the same view.

Elizabeth was standing there holding two bloody swords in her hands. Her legs were braced in a fighting stance, her head was dipped low so that her eyes were barely visible beneath her wild hair; blood trickled down her face. She said nothing, quickly bolted up the stairs and ran back onto the deck.

Both girls looked at each other for a moment, amazed and frightened at what they just witnessed.

THE DECKS WERE STREWN with bodies and coated in blood. There were a few pained movements from some figures, others were dreadfully still, now nothing but corpses. Anne stood at the top of the stairs and stared with wide eyes at the gangway.

Horrified, she put her hand on the railing to help keep her balance.

Will I pass out? Anne thought sadly.

She watched as sailors with blood dripping down their own faces tossed buckets of sea water on the decks to remove the sticky mess. Others used hoses and mops to frantically clean, their eyes hard, their long-suffering, yet unflappable constitutions as hardy seamen put to the test. The sand, which had been placed to keep feet from slipping, was now coagulated with gore. Bodies were soaked wet from blood and sea water.

Anne choked for a moment, not on the stench, but the sudden realization she could 'feel' the death of the dead men drenched in that salt water. She suddenly knew the Spanish soldier who fell near the railing, shot dead before his feet landed, had three children back home and a wife who was forever worried about his safety. He had a doting mother who would not survive the news once it was learned. The ship's mate on the Defiant who was only here because he had been pressed. A deacon's son who wanted more options in life than would be available back home.

She grabbed the side of her head and pulled her hair down, hoping to drown out the sounds of death all around. Closing her eyes, Anne concentrated. A small pause from her tumultuous thoughts that gave little consolation.

How am I hearing all this?

What kind of strange power do I have?

Anne saw Finlay walk by. He looked stunned, but alive. She wanted to run to him and see if he was okay but another led him down the opposite steps.

She scanned the deck, suddenly aware she did not know if Elizabeth and Éndira were still alive. Éndira had run back on deck once the cabin had been secured. Anne's eyes searched and searched as her legs moved from stairs to deck. She walked forward, almost tripping on a body. Hands reached up for help but she backed away in fear. Another set pushed her away, the coxswain telling her it was not safe to be on deck.

Anne looked forward and finally saw Elizabeth. Éndira stood at her side, as well as Lieutenant Hicks.

Anne realized immediately something was wrong.

Elizabeth hugged her left side with her arm. Her face was contorted with deep lines etched in a face full of pain. When the woman stepped forward, she barely kept herself up. She looked like she was going to pass out. Éndira reached out her hands and caught her before she fell.

Miss Elizabeth has been wounded.

Anne choked on her own breath.

"PUT HER OVER HERE!" Lieutenant Hicks pulled a fallen chair up. He turned it around quickly.

Éndira and Anne carefully helped Elizabeth. They made sure she sat with the back to her front and leaned her arms forward so that she would be able to grasp the wood.

"Mr. Hicks— go back on deck," Elizabeth said through clenched teeth.

He nodded and left, keenly aware that his duties came first.

"Hot water!" Éndira ordered Anne then quickly pulled Elizabeth's jacket off.

Anne could not move. She was frozen as she watched Éndira examine the wound.

A sword or knife had cut deep across the torso, a large gash that was flowing blood at an alarming rate soaking Elizabeth's blouse. Éndira took a towel from Elizabeth's wash stand and pushed it hard against the wound, making Elizabeth cry out in pain.

Anne gasped loudly.

Éndira quickly turned her head. "Dammit!" she yelled. "Get some hot water and stop gawking!"

Anne bolted to the kitchen. She frantically looked for the cook who was nowhere to be found. Panicked, she ran to the stove. Anne snapped open the cast iron door and peered into the oven.

Nothing but ash.

Then Anne remembered why.

All fires were doused in bad weather or before any type of engagement. The most dangerous thing on the high seas was not dying by cannon fire or getting stabbed by a cutlass.

It was the ship catching fire.

Anne scanned the kitchen. She spotted the wood in the corner and grabbed a few pieces. Once in the firebox, she found the flintlock match and tried to light the wood.

When nothing happened, Anne started to panic. She had never lit a fire in her entire life. The stoves back home as well as the fireplaces had always been lit by her father, brother or servants.

What a stupid time to understand that women of her class were kept from doing basic chores because of custom.

Customs are going to allow my friend to die!

Anne began to use a ladle to put water in a large pot. She then continued to try in vain to light the fire. She brushed back hair from her face. It was glued from the sweat beginning to accumulate on her forehead.

I have to go and ask someone to help me light the fire.

Quickly getting to her feet, Anne stopped for a moment and looked at the salt box. She did not know why but she grabbed the item and dumped some of the crystals into the water. Her hands touched the side of the metal pot as she closed her eyes and concentrated. Her hands began to feel warm. Anne held them there until she could no longer stand to feel the heat. When she looked down into the water, her eyes were wide as she realized the water was boiling!

"What in the bloody hell?" She whispered to herself.

Quickly, she glanced around the room, careful to see if anyone had viewed what she had just done.

Anne grabbed a lid, placed it over the rim, grabbed some pot holders and swiftly scooted out of the galley.

Elizabeth was still in the chair with her head down. A sheet was now draped over her back, replacing the torn blouse. Anne placed the pot next to Éndira. The girl nodded in thanks then dipped her rag in the water. As she wrung it out, she turned to Anne. "How did you heat this up so quickly?"

Before an explanation could be made up, Elizabeth groaned again and cursed, the first time Anne had ever heard her do such a thing.

Éndira placed the hot water on the wound. Elizabeth grimaced once again and bit her lower lip.

"This is going to need stitches," Éndira whispered.

"Anne?" Elizabeth turned her head slightly. "I need you to wait outside."

"Beg pardon?" Anne was taken aback.

Surely Miss Elizabeth needs me to help in some way?

"I need you to wait outside."

"But? I can help you. Just tell me what to do," Anne protested.

"No— "

"Why?"

"Anne!" Elizabeth was more forceful then she had ever been to her young friend. Elizabeth's pain had manifested itself into a temper. "Go outside— NOW!"

Hurt, Anne turned on her heels and headed back to the galley.

30

Holding another pot of hot water in her hands, Anne stopped in front of the cabin door. She put the pot down and was about to knock, before she suddenly stopped herself. Anne desperately wanted to know what was happening with Elizabeth. But she did not want to entertain the possibility that the woman could die. Anne did not want to be selfish but wondered what would happen to her if Elizabeth did die?

Will I be stuck with this annoying girl?

A pair of footsteps came from behind. Anne turned quickly, afraid Jackson had taken the opportunity to harass her once again.

It was only Finlay.

Anne breathed a sigh of relief, happy to see her friend.

"Will she be okay?" Finlay asked, concerned.

"I do not know," Anne said honestly. She knew nothing about wounds nor how bad one had to be to be life threatening.

When he touched her gently on the shoulder, Anne suddenly felt like crying. She turned and looked at him, thankful for his kindness.

Suddenly, the door swung open, startling them both. Éndira eyed the two of them. "If you two are done being all dewy eyed, I need more water."

Finlay cleared his throat then quickly excused himself.

Anne pointed at Éndira's feet. "There is plenty right there."

Éndira took the water and put it in the room. She bent over again and picked up another pot. She roughly handed the item to Anne.

Anne barely kept the bloody water from splashing up onto herself.

"What the hell is wrong with you?" Anne snapped, ready to toss the water back onto the girl.

Éndira just glared at her.

"What is happening?" Anne snapped.

"Nothing we can't handle," Éndira bit.

"Let me see her."

"She doesn't want you in there right now."

"Why not?" Anne pointed her finger. "There was no reason to kick me out. I know she is modest, but what am I going to see? A breast?"

"That is not the reason. "

"Maybe she is embarrassed by me." Anne was unsure she should say something. "My father probably told her."

"Told her what?"

"That is none of *your* business."

"Whatever." Éndira pushed the pot. "We need more. If you can be bothered to stop whining about yourself."

"I am not— whining about myself."

"Yes you are! Since I have met you, I have never seen such a self-centered, egotistical girl in my life. And I have met a lot of terrible people!"

Anne's mouth was agape.

"Stop making this about you!" Éndira spoke low, but firm. "Lizzy is hurt worse than she will let on. If we do not sanitize her wound it will get infected and she will be in worse shape than she is in now... so shut the hell up and get some more *BLOODY WATER!*"

Eyes wide, Anne could not respond.

"Knock on the door and leave it outside!" Éndira turned and slammed the door shut.

～

Éndira walked into the galley and continued to wipe her hands on a towel. Her hands were still bloody. She would need to wash them in hot water and soap in order to get them properly cleaned.

Elizabeth was now on deck surveying the cleanup. Éndira wanted her to stay below but the older woman insisted she needed to make an appearance on deck simply to prove she was still in command. A captain could not show weakness, and even though she was fatigued, a simple walk on deck would appease the crew and her own mind. Thirty minutes maximum before she would go back down to her cabin and lay her head to rest.

Thirty minutes to get the cabin clean.

Éndira did not want Elizabeth to have the scent of blood permeating the air— neither her enemies' nor her own. Éndira had given her a clean shirt and pants, and washed her face and torso as best she could. The crew had disposed of the enemy's dead men immediately after the fight. Their own dead were respectfully laid along the rail, covered with sheets.

Now all that lay on the floor were blood soaked rags and puddles of water and blood.

Éndira walked over to Anne, who was sitting quietly in the corner.

"Anne?"

The girl looked up.

Éndira did not want to feel bad but Anne's eyes were red.

"Yes?" Anne answered.

"I could really use your help in the cabin... it's a mess. I don't want her to have to come back to that."

Anne stood up. "You let her back on deck?"

"I did not let her do anything. She does what she wants, you should know that by now."

"Fine."

Once they had the supplies they needed, Anne followed Éndira back to the cabin. When the door was open, Anne stepped back slightly. She had not noticed the smell before.

Now that the bodies were gone, blood was all that remained.

It was everywhere.

Éndira touched her shoulder gently.

"Will you be all right?" Éndira asked, concerned. "I know it is over-whelming but blood is something you must get used to on a war ship."

"I will be fine." Anne stepped over a puddle. "I just didn't realize there was so much."

"Some of it is Lizzy's."

Anne nodded then dropped a pail on the floor. She grabbed a large rag and began to mop up the mess. Éndira kneeled and started to do the same thing.

They were quiet and silently engaged in the work at hand. Anne found the task not as horrendous as she first thought. People lived and died—they bled when they were hurt. *Some of this blood could have been mine if Éndira and Miss Elizabeth had not had the bravery to fight,* Anne thought sadly.

"Will she be okay?" Anne asked.

"Lizzy?" Éndira chuckled. "Will be a long time before Davy Jones claims her."

Anne rolled off her knees and onto her bottom. She wiped the sweat off her forehead and took a slight break.

"Why do you call her that?" Anne asked.

"Just a name I gave her once. She yelled at me about something stupid. I called her that and I could see how annoyed it made her. So I guess, I just enjoy goading her sometimes."

"Do you dislike her?"

"No." Éndira stopped and placed her hand on her knee, her other one hitting the floor. "Never have disliked her... never have gotten along with her much though."

"How long have you known her?"

"Guess all my life really." Éndira rubbed the sweat out of her own eyes. "She has been around here and there... but I know she has spent a great deal of time in the East Indies... that is where she learned her arts."

"Art of what?"

"Defensive arts."

"How is that an art?" Anne said, trying to understand how that was 'classical' in some way.

"Not what you think Anne," Éndira chuckled slightly. "Art of swords, hand to hand, stuff like that."

"Oh."

Éndira smiled when she realized Anne still looked confused. "Like what she taught you on deck. Fending off an attacker with only your body." Éndira leaned down and began to scrub once again. "Of course, her sword work is the most impressive."

"She saved me from being attacked on the London docks. She used her sword to disarm a man."

"Which one did she use?"

"Umm..." Anne stammered. "A pointy one?"

When Éndira began to laugh, Anne smiled.

"I did notice she has a lot of swords." Anne pointed to the wall cabinet in the corner. "I thought that was just normal for a captain."

"No— nothing is normal for Lizzy," Éndira softly sighed. "Listen Anne... I am sorry I yelled at you."

"No, you are right... all I have been thinking about is myself. I've forgotten how much Miss Elizabeth has sacrificed for me. She might lose her career over me."

"She told me about your uncle. Piece of filth." Éndira shook her head, then pointed at her. "Nah, she did the right thing. She will not be punished for it."

"You think so?"

"Especially with your father defending her."

They worked in silence for the next few minutes. For the first time, Anne was not completely repulsed by her cabin mate.

"I did not bite her by the way," Anne said with a smile. "In case you were wondering."

"I know, I was just teasing with you," Éndira said, grinning.

"Do you enjoy... teasing people?"

"I like to see uptight people get their knickers in a twist."

"I am not..." Anne gasped, almost offended by the comment. "I am not 'uptight'."

"You are sooo... uptight," Éndira snickered.

Anne ignored the quip. She wiped the perspiration off her forehead. She stopped and stared at the open door.

"What is it?" Éndira asked.

"She looked like a mad woman... covered in blood like that."

"When one needs to survive, the animal inside takes over," Éndira said.

Éndira got to her feet and went over to the bureau. She pulled out a small box and pipe. Anne joined her by her side. "Do you want to prepare this or do you want me to?"

"Why didn't you give her this before?" Anne picked up the pipe. "She must be in extreme pain."

"Because it also makes her sleep. That is why she is attending to things now."

Anne knew what the captain was attending to. Besides making sure the ships were secure, the woman had the dreadful task of committing the bodies of her fallen crew to the sea, the final resting place of all sailors who died at sea. "She said she had a terrible accident when she was younger. Do you know what happened?"

"Yes... she never told me the whole story but she was on a fire ship. She was in charge as a midshipman actually. They managed to achieve their goal, but Lizzy did not get off in time. Her whole back was burnt, most of her breast. She should have died."

"My God," Anne gasped as she took the story in. "Is that what she did not want me to see?"

"Yes. She is embarrassed by the scars."

"She shouldn't be. She is a hero! She probably saved many lives that day."

Éndira nodded. "Even though deep down she knows that, she feels the pain every night and the scars on her back still haunt her. She still has nightmares."

"I've heard her before," Anne said, remembering that night in the Kingston hotel when Elizabeth had suddenly cried out in her sleep. Anne had pretended not to hear. She kept her eyes closed. When she could finally catch a glimpse, Anne saw Elizabeth drenched in sweat.

"Nightmares never go away Anne," Éndira said. "No matter how hard we try— but we must carry on."

Anne nodded, for she had her own nightmares and scars that plagued her every night. She truly appreciated what the other girl had said. As brash as she appeared, Éndira was kinder than she let on.

31

M iranda was not keen on standing out in front of the silk-cotton tree on this humid night. She touched the neck of her blouse and shook it slightly, allowing a little bit of warm air to circulate. Her other hand held her favorite fan. It was intricately decorated with a picture of a sunset somewhere in the East Indies.

Someplace I have never been, Miranda huffed.

Miranda had always dreamed of traveling to India to view splendid sights of elephants and other wild creatures she had only seen in picture books. Her whole life had been in the service of another, or tied to that degenerate Randal as a means to better the family standing.

Not anymore.

I've been promised great power and I mean to have it.

Have you? A deep male voice suddenly entered her head.

Miranda froze. She should have been used to this by now. This is how Dge communicated with her. She fell onto her knees and put her head down in submission.

"Great Dge," Miranda said out loud. "I come to offer my services to you."

You foolish woman. You have done nothing but disappoint me, the voice inside her head snarled.

"I cannot... lie to you," Miranda said, eyes fixed on the tree, her voice dripping with fear. "But... I refuse to fail. I will find my niece."

Is that whom you are looking for?

Miranda pulled herself upwards and looked at the tree, confused. Surely Dge knew this already?

"Stand up woman," a female voice said from behind. "You look like a mess wallowing in the dirt."

Miranda turned around and gasped.

Behind her stood a woman with mocha skin and hair that seemed untamed to her eyes. The woman's eyes glistened with silver flecks in purple irises. As she smiled she showed her sharpened teeth. Slowly she sauntered over, her dress alive with strands of seaweed and gulf-weed. Salt water dripped down onto bare feet.

Frightened, Miranda felt her heart drop.

"Are you?..." she gulped. "Are you Mama DgBaba?"

A deep guttural laugh came from within the trickster. She put her arms out and looked up to the sky. A crackle of thunder and a quick bolt of purple lightning shot down and hit the silk-cotton tree.

Miranda jumped back in fear and clutched her chest.

The tree was on fire!

"What did you DO?" Miranda screamed, looking at Mama with desperate eyes.

Mama shrugged then flipped her hand down nonchalantly. A large chair appeared. It was made of intricately carved tropical wood and red plush velvet cushions. Mama sat with her legs draped over one of the arms. Mama rolled back her head and continued to laugh.

Miranda had the opposite reaction. She was scared and now angry.

Do I dare become irate with this deity?

"Help!" Miranda yelled, scooping up dirt in her hand and throwing it towards the tree. "Water! Someone get some water!"

Miranda pulled back, burned by the fire as it roared even louder. She held her hand tightly and watched her future go up in flames. Miranda screamed once again but no one was coming to her aid.

"They cannot hear you dear," Mama sung in her island lilt. She leaned back in her chair, now drinking a red and purple punch.

Miranda turned. Her face was red with anger. No longer frightened, she yelled at the trickster. "Why? Why would you do this?"

Mama ignored her cries. Instead, she stirred her drink before sipping it. After taking a long sip, Mama put the glass down onto nothing. It just simply floated in midair.

"I would offer you some," Mama said. "But I believe fruit from the Manchineel tree is deadly to you humans?"

"Please!" Miranda ran over to her, fell on her knees and started to beg. "Please put out the fire!"

Just then, a rumble came from within the tree, followed by a pained scream. Miranda's eyes became desperate.

She is killing him!

Mama leaned over and looked at her. "What has my infernal brother promised you besides great power?"

Miranda shook her head, not wanting to answer the question. When the screams got louder, Miranda started to shake. She looked back at Mama DgBaba and shook her head even harder.

"TELL ME!" Mama yelled.

The words were loud and inhuman, a reverberation that tore into Miranda's ears.

"Immortality," Miranda said quickly then gulped. "He promised me immortality!"

"And?"

"To become queen of this island."

Mama raised an eyebrow, amused.

"That's it?" Mama snickered. She leaned back in her chair and sipped her drink once again. "Immortality is overrated woman," she taunted. "And as for great power... there is always someone vying to take it from you."

Miranda did not know what to do. The tree was still on fire, and the deity inside was slowly burning to death.

"Would you rather not have untold riches?" Mama asked.

Miranda knew she should not lie to this woman. Dge had promised her both. But if he died?

Can I make a deal with this trickster?

"Can you offer me the same?" Miranda asked bluntly.

Mama blinked at her then smirked. "You dare make a deal in front of my brother? Do you know what he will do to you once he gets out of that tree?"

"I do not know," Miranda confessed. "Can he hear us?"

The words seemed to amuse Mama. She stood up and began to laugh once again. Her hands brushed downwards, making the chair and drink disappear.

"Depends," Mama snickered. She motioned for Miranda to stand. Once the subject did as she was told, Mama walked around her as if she were inspecting her. "I have been wanting to release my brother for centuries," Mama sighed. "But alas, even I do not have that power."

Miranda looked at her strangely.

Even she cannot do this? Then how does Dge expect me to release him only with Anne?

He's always been full of himself.

Miranda gasped and stepped backwards. The voice was the same as spoken moments ago. *She can make herself sound like her brother?*

Was that you before, not Dge speaking to me in my mind?

Mama smiled. **Of course silly woman.**

So he cannot hear us, can he?

No.

Mama touched Miranda's hair. **Now, you know not what to do?** Mama cocked her head to the side and watched the way Miranda squirmed.

"I just want what I was promised."

"And how do you plan on releasing him?"

"My niece," Miranda said. "She is the key."

The fire in the tree suddenly disappeared. Miranda looked at it, realizing the flames were only a facade. The tree was unburnt.

"Tell me of her," Mama said.

Miranda began to tell Mama of how she brought Anne to the island. She described a little about the history of what power was in the family and why Dge believed Anne was the only way to release him.

"Only the essence of pure vitality may do," Mama said, nodding her head with confidence. "I have met this Anne. She smelled... interesting."

The way Mama smirked, Miranda was reminded how much she herself had little power against the will of a deity. If Mama wanted Anne for her own there was little Miranda could do to stop the trickster.

"She is much more powerful than you," Mama added.

Those words stung.

"She is not!" Miranda snapped. "She is but a child who knows nothing of her history or power. She is simply a vessel."

"Is that what you think?"

Suddenly, there was a loud scream coming from the pathway that led up to the silk-cotton. Both turned, only to see a woman with wild eyes run full force with a sickle. As she swiped down violently towards Mama, the deity simply laughed and disappeared.

"Stop!" Miranda yelled to the attacker. "You don't know what you are doing!"

Selina looked at her with confusion. She did not listen, searching instead for the woman who had vanished.

"Where is she?" Selina cried. "Show yourself!"

Mama appeared in front of her. The trickster flicked her finger and threw Selina onto the ground. She walked over and stood above the crazed woman.

"You dare challenge me?" Mama sneered.

Miranda jumped in front of her lover. She put out her hands in protest. "Leave her be. Please."

Mama looked at Selina helpless on the floor. "She's a half-wit?"

The words stung the would-be victim. Selina yelled angrily as she tried to get up to attack once again but Mama laughed and pushed her to the ground with another flick of the wrist.

"Shall I take you with me?" Mama taunted once again.

"Not her," Miranda said stiffly. "You will only grow tired of her antics."

"I think I might have some entertainment out of her before... I dispose of her."

"Miranda?" Selina whimpered. She looked at her lover for protection.

Miranda pointed to the side instead. "You can have her."

Mama whipped around and cocked an eyebrow. She looked at a young girl standing in the shadows. When Zara tried to run, Mama closed her fist and dragged the girl in front of her. Zara narrowed her eyes, angry.

Miranda thought it odd that Zara was not frightened of the trickster.

Mama observed the girl for a moment then easily dismissed her with a shake of the head.

"And what will I do with her? She will fly off the first chance she gets," Mama snickered. "Only my foolish sister deals in her kind."

Zara was able to free herself from the trickster's invisible grip. She got to her feet and ran as fast as she could, disappearing down the cobble pathway and out of sight.

Mama laughed once again.

"You have nothing to offer me," Mama said, disappointed.

"I do," Miranda pleaded. She looked at her surroundings with desperate eyes, trying to come up with a solution to her problem.

Then it hit her.

"My people," Miranda said quickly. "I will offer you my slaves and indentures."

This seemed to intrigue Mama, for she put her palm to her chin and appeared to be contemplating the idea.

"All of them?" Mama said, licking her lips.

"Yes," Miranda nodded.

"Hmmm..."

"Do we have a deal?" Miranda asked.

Mama smiled then snapped her fingers.

In a flash she was gone.

Miranda stepped forward, looking around wildly.

"Do we have a DEAL?" Miranda yelled to no one.

ANNE SAT BACK on her cot and began to read a borrowed novel. She tried to concentrate but all her mind would return to was thoughts of Éndira.

The girl wasn't so bad. She had finally shown a softer side, which Anne took to easily.

Anne shut the book and closed her eyes.

Now that she was all alone, Anne could not help but also think about her ring. Leaning back on the wooden slats that lined the small cabin, Anne listened to the quiet hum of the ship. She touched the ring on her necklace and put her other hand on the wood. Her ears focused in on the ship at it sailed over the gentle waves.

They were going fast. Anne did not need to read a log line to tell her that.

Anne felt her ring heat up slightly. She pulled her hand away from the wood and started to examine the jewelry. What a strange sensation to seemingly 'understand' what was going on around her? She'd questioned her aunt about being a so called 'glorified soothsayer'.

Was this what the power was?

The ability to look deeper?

Aunt Miranda said I can harness a crystal's energy. Is it only the ones in my ring? Am I feeling the salt on the decks and around the ship?

But what about the men I could read?

Were they also wearing a gemstone?

Anne huffed in frustration. She was afraid to even mention her ability to Elizabeth, let alone Éndira. Sure, the girl had special powers, but nothing like— *mine?*

My aunt is dangerous.

Miss Elizabeth might fear me— but wasn't it her own pendant that repelled the attack from my aunt as I did with my uncle?

Anne closed her eyes and wondered if these obeah women could help her. Surely, if they had their own magics, they could at least help her in some way.

Or at least keep Aunt Miranda at bay?

A rush of loud voices and heavy footsteps alerted her. Anne opened her eyes and listened to the commotion. Briskly, she ran over to the door and swung it open. Just as she did, Éndira stopped in front.

Anne's heart dropped.

Something was wrong.

"Are we sinking?" Anne hesitantly asked, quickly realizing that was a stupid question. *I think I would feel it,* she thought.

"No," Éndira said, shaking her head. "Just... I am not sure."

When Éndira took her hand, Anne felt her face flush. She enjoyed the touch, even when being dragged towards the stairs. When they both were on the deck, Anne gasped.

There was a small island village on the port side engulfed in flames.

SLOWLY, Anne helped attend to the survivors. She had been put in charge of making sure the young children had soup and bread. At her side, Éndira was comforting a small girl who was crying.

"It will be all right now." Éndira touched the girl's cheek and wiped away the tears. When the little one would not stop, Éndira reached in and gave her a hug. Only then did the child begin to settle down. Éndira held her tightly then nodded towards Anne. "Would you please fetch me an extra blanket?"

"Of course." Anne got up and went to retrieve the item. She walked over to the side rail and stopped. The sheer horror of the carnage had not hit her until this very moment. She could feel her legs begin to give way. A firm hand grabbed her by the arm and held her upright.

"Steady now," Elizabeth said at her side.

Anne brushed back loose hair, ashamed to have lost her footing in front of the woman. She could lie about losing her balance but there was no reason. She turned and looked at Elizabeth.

"How can anyone do something like this?" Anne asked, troubled.

"People with nefarious intentions are capable of great evil," Elizabeth sighed, squeezing Anne's shoulder tighter.

The HMS Defiant had arrived at the small island near Mayreau just hours ago. The lone village was still smoldering. Elizabeth had the guns run out. As the sailors waited for orders, Anne watched Elizabeth weigh her options. The lone schooner in the harbor had been burnt to the hull. Elizabeth had her ship lay anchor and cautiously waited, her eye looking at the two scenes through her telescope.

Anne had watched Elizabeth row to shore with three of the long boats. Each sailor had a rifle and cutlass. Anne had been scared for her friend. Whatever had happened to that town could still be waiting for them!

According to one of the survivors, the two obeah women had left years ago. When asked who had attacked the island, the name Bruja del Fuego, or Fire Witch came up.

Anne had heard the name many times in the last few months. Now that she had seen the carnage, Anne suddenly worried for her father. He had orders to find the bruja and stop her. Did the woman really shoot fire out of her hands? Or had Éndira's father embellished the story to make the tale more interesting?

Now that Elizabeth was by her side, Anne could not help but question. "Was it the Fire Witch?" she asked.

Elizabeth turned away for a moment and glanced at the carnage. She finally looked back at Anne and sighed once again. "Yes... she did this."

"But my father?" Anne gasped. "How is he to stop this madwoman?"

"Do not worry about your father Anne. He is a very capable sailor. If anyone can bring down this bruja, your father can."

Anne nodded in agreement but still she was not sure. *If the Fire Witch has magic, how can he fight something like that?*

Can I fight someone like her?

Anne bent down and retrieved a small blanket. She left Elizabeth to her duties and attended to her own. She kneeled next to Éndira and handed the soft cloth over.

"Thank you," Éndira smiled, taking the blanket and putting it around her young friend.

Anne felt something in her chest. She had not realized how Éndira had begun to grow on her.

Is this a small crush? Surely a girl as adventurous as Éndira would never be... interested in someone like me?

Besides, Anne huffed inside. *She thinks me a snob.*

32

Elizabeth sat at her desk and stared at her half filled decanter. It was early in the evening and she had already retired for the night. Elizabeth picked up her glass. She swished the alcohol from side to side, looking into the deep, caramel hue. She'd grown accustomed to drinking rum while in the West Indies. Elizabeth preferred brandy, and she had hoped they would find some bottles amongst the cargo seized during their recent battle. Being a Spanish ship, the prize had turned up none of her preferred spirits, only a few caskets of rum and wine.

Elizabeth exhaled before taking a long gulp. She put the empty glass on the desk and reached for her decanter. Soon the goblet was filled once again.

She kept mulling over and over in her mind what to do with Anne. Elizabeth had wanted to leave the girl in the care of her friends but now that they were gone— *where can Anne go?*

Surely I cannot continue to keep her on this ship.

Perhaps the only safe place is Éndira's island? Despite their constant bickering, Elizabeth was sure that Éndira would try to protect Anne.

Elizabeth thought about the destruction they had recently come across. Was anywhere in the West Indies safe anymore?

When she and Trevor arrived in London from a three year sail in the East Indies, they had only heard scuttlebutt about this so called— *fire witch.*

Many of the officers laughed off the notion of a witch terrorizing the West Indies. Only low class people and common sailors believed in superstitions they would say.

Even Trevor thought the idea preposterous— at least, in front of his crew.

"There is no such thing as witches," he would argue, shutting down any mention of occultism at the officer table.

Elizabeth did not press the matter. She let the crew believe what they wanted. There was no use in arguing with them about such things. They might believe but if she had interjected and confirmed their truths, they might actually think her mad.

It was one thing to entertain the thought, a whole other thing to believe!

Elizabeth had experienced witchcraft first hand.

Miranda Sutton was a practitioner. She had been since Elizabeth first came into that house to be a servant. Elizabeth had seen Miranda spell. Often, she had to clean up the mess the girl had made.

The scary thing was, Miranda's mother seemed to encourage the practice. Elizabeth often wondered why the older woman would entertain such things. Surely witchcraft went against the church's beliefs?

Elizabeth was brought up Catholic, a heathen in the eyes of people like the Suttons. She and her mother attended the Anglican church along with their employers every Sunday. Of course, Elizabeth and her mother had to sit in the back row with all the other household servants of the distinguished families.

Elizabeth never took much to religion after her father died.

She didn't see the point.

And once her mother passed Elizabeth lost all faith.

Quickly, she emptied her glass. This time, she put the empty goblet on the desk. Her body had already begun to feel the effects a while back. If she continued to drink, her hangover would be miserable tomorrow.

"So early in the evening Elizabeth?" a deep voice said.

Elizabeth closed her eyes. She did not even act surprised. She was sure another visit from this woman would happen soon.

She opened her eyes and glared at Mama DgBaba.

"What do you want?" Elizabeth sneered, rubbing the pain in her own arm. Whenever she was near the trickster, her sigil would heat up severely. *Like a brand.*

Mama walked over and sat on the edge of Elizabeth's desk. Water from the creature's seaweed dress dripped down. Elizabeth grabbed her decanter and pushed it to the other side.

"I want to know what you owe Miranda Sutton?" Mama asked, eyes eager.

Elizabeth abruptly pushed her chair back and sprang to her feet. Her fears had rung true.

"How do you know Miranda?" Elizabeth asked, concerned.

"That is not your business woman," Mama purred in her island lilt. She touched the sextant on the desk. A finely polished brass surface instantly turned green, then turned into dust.

"Anne is not going back to Miranda." Elizabeth did not even bother to look at her destroyed equipment. "Despite what she has promised you."

"And why do you think she has promised me something?"

"Because," Elizabeth leaned inward and put her hands on her desk. She should be frightened, but many years of dealing with the trickster had made Elizabeth impervious to Mama's threats. "No one deals with you unless you get something from it."

Mama moved so quickly, Elizabeth did not see until the trickster was standing right in front. Elizabeth stepped back slightly. Mama leaned inward. She took her hand and roughly grabbed Elizabeth by the chin.

"You know nothing of deals Elizabeth Spencer," Mama threatened. "Whoever breaks one with me shall *forever* incur my wrath."

Suddenly, Mama pulled back her hand and hissed. She looked down at her palm. It was slightly burned, a green smoke coming off the fingertips. When she glared at Elizabeth, the captain returned a hardened smile.

"Anne Sutton is in my care Mama," Elizabeth's brown eyes warned. "I will do everything I can to keep her from Miranda."

Mama clicked her tongue, slightly entertained. "There will come a time when you need me." Mama wagged her finger at her foe. "I suspect it will be— very soon."

She cocked her head and smiled. "And when you call on me, you know what the price will be."

Elizabeth reluctantly nodded. "I do."

And with that, Mama vanished— leaving Elizabeth alone with her drink and her regrets.

THE HEAT in the cabin was stifling. Anne took a fan and waved it in front of her face, trying in vain to cool herself. The ship had dropped off the survivors of the dreaded Fire Witch's attack a few hours ago. Most of the remaining victims had family in Mayreau. The small girl whom Éndira had comforted had none. She was immediately taken in by another who promised to raise her as one of their own.

When Éndira finally returned to the cabin, she immediately started to give Anne a hard time.

"You prefer to bake down here like a pie?" Éndira chastised.

Anne eyed her. "And where else can I go?"

"Up on deck." Éndira grabbed her own pillow and blanket, then turned with a smile.

Anne raised an eyebrow. "You want me to... sleep on deck?"

When Éndira did not respond, Anne quickly realized the girl was serious. Anne shrugged her shoulders, got up and retrieved her own items.

Holding her blanket and pillow tightly Anne scanned the room for a moment. Would she need her shift? Was she expected to sleep in her trousers and blouse?

"Come." Éndira nodded to the hallway.

Anne dutifully followed.

When they made their way up to the quarterdeck, Éndira led them to the far end. In the corner, she had already set up a trio of barrels for privacy. Éndira threw her blanket on top of a mess of canvas. She took Anne's blanket and repeated the process.

Anne looked down at the makeshift camp and had to smile. She used to build small forts with her friend Sarah when they were younger. As they got older, Sarah would still partake in such 'foolishness' as their mothers would say. Many times both she and Anne would spend a night talking of frivolous things. *The most wonderful thing of all was being close to Sarah.*

I loved that so much.

Anne watched Éndira plop down on her section and stretch out. Anne could not help but take in the beautiful girl. She'd been slowly coming to terms with wanting to know her bunkmate better. Anne had been cruel at first, thinking of Éndira only as a thief and low class.

Finlay was right, Anne sighed. *You are taken by her.*

"Why is there no wind?" Anne asked as she laid down next to Éndira.

"It happens sometimes," Éndira said. "Mostly in the doldrums. Near the equator where the prevailing winds are calm."

"You've been past the equator?"

"Yes, many times."

Anne smiled. "My brother told me of some silly ritual he had to do when he crossed the first time."

Éndira pushed herself upwards and leaned on her elbows. "The line crossing ceremony?"

"I guess?" Anne said. "He wouldn't tell me everything. Just that someone dressed like King Neptune presided over the ceremony, or something like that."

"I'm sure there was more to it than what he wanted to share with his sister."

Anne looked at her, concerned. "Why? What did they do to him?"

"Could be a number of things," Éndira shrugged. "I don't know what they do in the Royal Navy."

"Maybe we should ask Lizzy?" Anne said, keeping her face hard.

When Éndira looked at her with a pained expression, Anne quickly changed her demeanor and chuckled.

"For a moment, I thought you were serious," Éndira snickered.

"I'm sure she would never tell us," Anne sighed. "If it was bad for my brother, it was probably worse for her."

"Being a sailor is hard enough," Éndira agreed.

Anne nodded. She had seen enough of the life so far to realize one had to not only be physically strong but mentally fit as well. Anne rubbed her shoulders and leaned against the wood slats. "I do not think I could be a sailor."

"Why not?"

"Because I'm feeble."

"Who told you that?"

Anne blinked for a moment, surprised that Éndira had not agreed immediately. "It's what I am. I'm a spoiled girl from England who needs others to protect her!"

"That's rubbish." Éndira waved her hand down. "You just need to be taught how to defend yourself better. You've already got a good foundation."

"What do you mean by that?" Anne asked, intrigued.

Éndira pulled herself up completely. She wrapped her feet inward and leaned forward. "You were able to defend yourself in the cabin. You didn't burst out crying and hide in the corner like a coward."

"I had no idea what I was doing!"

"Yet you followed orders. You watched how Lizzy loaded her flintlocks. When I needed them, you had them ready for me."

"I guess." Anne swallowed hard. She hadn't really thought about what had happened during the battle. She wanted to survive.

Anne smiled at Éndira. She wanted to reach over and hug her but was afraid.

"So you don't think I am a... horrible person?" Anne asked, hoping for a small touch of kindness.

"No," Éndira chuckled then laid back down. "You're not so bad."

"Neither are you," Anne said softly.

Anne closed her eyes and could think of nothing but the beautiful girl beside her.

THE NEXT DAY'S heat was worse. Anne sat on deck with Éndira, both under a canvas awning and trying to keep cool. Éndira had assured Anne that the ship was not doomed.

Losing the wind often happened.

There were plenty of water casks on board to keep the crew hydrated for a few weeks. Anne did not want to even think about what might happen if they ran out.

Éndira slowly peeled a kumquat with the knife she carried everywhere. As the skin pulled back, she put the peel in her mouth and chewed. She cut another piece and handed the fruit skin to Anne.

"I do not like those," Anne politely declined.

Éndira chuckled as she pulled back another layer.

"How can you not like these?" she asked.

Anne quickly flashed back to the 'cocktails' her aunt used to make her. Supposedly the concoctions were to hydrate her body and make her feel better. Only later did she find out that the juices had been laced with potions that played havoc with her mind as well as her intestines.

"They remind me of a place I would like to forget." Anne's thought trailed off as she watched a seagull fly overhead. As the bird hovered, she admired how graceful the creature soared. The seagull chirped loudly. Éndira tossed a rind in the air. The bird swooped and caught the offering.

"See, she knows what tastes good," Éndira said.

Anne rolled her eyes then held out her hand. She was not going to let a feathered creature show her up. Her new friend cut another slice and handed the skin over. Anne ate the skin. The sweet, delicate rind was actually refreshing.

"So?" Éndira asked.

"Good."

When Éndira had managed to peel off all the skin, she tried to offer Anne a piece of the meat. Anne shook her head no. Éndira shrugged then bit in. She sucked in deeply as the tartness hit her cheeks. Her lips puckered and eyes slightly watered.

"Aahh—" Éndira bit. "Love it."

"You're strange."

"You love me."

I think I do, Anne thought fondly.

Anne turned away quickly, not sure if she said that out loud. Her emotions had been on high alert these last few days. She did love to see Éndira enjoy everything and anything. She only wished Éndira would confess she wanted— *to enjoy me?*

Anne's heart ached.

The closer Anne got to Éndira as a friend, the more she thought she wanted more.

She did not notice Éndira jump off the barrel she had been sitting on. "Let's take a swim," the girl declared.

When Anne did not respond, Éndira called her name.

"Huh?" Anne had quickly stopped her daydreaming.

"How about a swim?"

"Um— no," Anne said. "No, I am fine."

"Oh, come on." Éndira pulled her up by her arms and walked them over to the railing. "The sea is calm as glass."

"Sharks?" Anne sheepishly asked, not wanting to jump into the water for an embarrassing reason.

"No sharks anywhere for miles." Éndira cocked her eyebrow and smirked. "Are you menstruating?"

"No," Anne quickly bit then immediately chastised herself for answering the question so abruptly.

As Éndira continued to interrogate Anne for reasons as to why they should not enjoy a nice dip in the ocean, Elizabeth walked towards them. They did not notice her presence behind them.

"Well the hell with you," Éndira said in a playful tone. "I'm going for a dip."

Anne watched in horror as Éndira took off her vest. Next came the left boot, which had the girl hopping comically onto the deck. As the other one came off, stockings were next. Anne looked at the seamen in the rigs and stepped forward.

"You are not going to strip out here, are you?" Anne asked, horrified.

"No, she is not," Elizabeth interjected. "Or I will lock her in the aft cabin until we get to land where I will promptly sell her to a nunnery and rid my ship of her for good."

Anne was mortified that Elizabeth had witnessed their exchange.

Éndira only shrugged and tied her pants string tight. "No skinny dipping for me captain, I swear... I reserve that for my water hole back home where only the fish may see my nether regions."

Anne was quickly consumed with visions of Éndira slowly coming out of the water, dripping wet with a slight hint of coldness hardening the nipples of her dark breasts. Anne shook her head quickly as she tried to remove the thoughts entering her mind.

Éndira was about to jump in when a hand stopped her. She turned and realized Anne had a firm grip on her. Éndira was confused for a moment as she glanced down in the water.

"What is it?" Éndira asked with concern.

"I cannot swim," Anne blurted out.

Éndira smirked, stunned for a second. "Really?"

"Yes, really."

"I should have realized this," Elizabeth said. "Anne had no reason to learn in London. Most people do not know how."

"Then I will teach her," Éndira happily declared.

"What?" Anne squealed in panic. "No, I'm fine!"

"Come on, it will be fun!"

As Anne began to slowly creep backwards, she bumped into an immovable mass standing right behind her.

"I think that's a marvelous idea," Elizabeth said. Anne turned around as her older friend began her lecture. "The crew of English ships are not taught to swim for fear that they might escape easily in port. I, however, have never felt that a smart idea. I've always encouraged my men to learn to keep themselves from drowning. I think it is high time you learn the same."

"I really do not want—"

"— It is not a suggestion," Elizabeth said in a tone reserved only for direct command.

Anne knew she was sunk.

Literally.

The sea was not something she ever wanted to be in. She only wanted to glide over like the seagull that flew overhead. Who would ever want to actually be soaked in seawater like a piece of salt pork? Anne preferred to remain as is, dried to the bone as wizened as a piece of hard tack biscuit.

A snapping of fingers from Éndira instructed Anne that she would have to remove her boots, socks and vest. Anne slowly leaned against a wooden barrel and began to commit to her fate.

Anne had wanted to get close to Éndira, but not like this!

33

———————

As Anne sat in the pinnace praying that she would not drown, the coxswain yelled his orders to his men to start the boat's decent. Behind her sat Éndira, towards her front, Elizabeth with her back turned to them both. The older woman had also taken off her boots, stockings and jacket.

Anne peeked her head over the wooden side and stared down into the bright, blue water that could possibly seal her doom.

When the boat gently hit the water, Éndira and Elizabeth removed the ropes. They pulled a pair of oars up and began to row to the stern of the HMS Defiant. Anne was at least thankful that the crew would not see her flounder like a porpoise, half naked while water shot out of her mouth in a fit of drowning.

As the pinnace arrived at the stern, the coxswain threw down another pair of ropes. Elizabeth easily took them and secured the boat once again. Even though the sea was calm, the water was still in perpetual motion. Elizabeth did not want to lose her pinnace to a sudden swell or current.

"All right," Elizabeth turned and declared as she stood upright. "Time to get wet."

Anne was horrified and amazed at the same time by Elizabeth's sudden and perfect head first jump into the water. Another splash behind jolted Anne once again.

Both teachers were now in the ocean!

Anne laid down in the boat and exhaled. Her nerves were on high alert. *Maybe if I just lay here out of sight, maybe they will forget all about me?*

A sudden, wet head popped up over the side.

"Hiding is not going to get you out of this," Éndira giggled.

"I hate you," Anne whined. "Go away."

Another set of hands reached onto the side of the pinnace and pulled up. A very wet Elizabeth held tight as she took her right hand and brushed salt water out of her own face. She reached in and retrieved the oar closest to her. After she handed the wooden paddle to Éndira, she turned her full attention to Anne.

"I'm not going to let you drown, you know that... right?" Elizabeth said kindly.

"Yes."

"We will be here every step of the way," Éndira added.

Anne slowly sat upright. She turned and looked at the two drenched faces in front of her.

"I know."

Elizabeth slowly, and patiently instructed her student to move her body over the edge of the boat and dip into the water. For a slight, panicked moment, Anne went under and struggled until she was brought up by two pairs of hands. She coughed and struggled until her own hands were firmly placed on the shaft of the oar.

"Kick your legs," Elizabeth ordered.

Anne realized after a few, sudden, scary moments, that she was indeed not drowning.

Her arms were firmly gripped to the shaft.

After a while, Elizabeth started to maneuver her in the water so that her kicking was now behind her, thrusting her forward. The encouraging words Éndira gave helped Anne build her confidence.

For the next few days, Anne worked feverishly at becoming a proficient swimmer. The ship was still becalmed. Anne had realized she actually liked swimming in the tepid salt water. It was much better than sweating in the small cabin, or sitting on deck without a soothing ocean breeze.

Anne was able to kick forward for small distances as her legs became stronger each day. After the third day, Elizabeth no longer joined them, for she had her own duties to attend to.

As Anne slowly eased into her front stroke, she could not help but hear the words Elizabeth had told her on her first day of instruction. How she, herself, had been taught to swim by being thrown right into the ocean!

Sink or swim was the motto.

Anne was very grateful, as strict and rigorous the captain might be on her crew, she was grateful Elizabeth was also kind and caring. Yes, she made her crews work hard, but as she had explained to Anne, better a well drilled crew learn whilst practicing than learn the hard way in battle.

The same thing could be said for learning to swim, Anne thought. She was thankful, even after the initial twinge of fear, that she would be much better for the experience.

Anne had also become something of a secret flirt, making herself 'vulnerable' on purpose so that Éndira had to come close to help her float... or whatever she was trying to reinforce that day.

Yesterday, Éndira had to hold Anne by the waist with one arm, her other holding tight to the pinnace as they both had to catch their breath. Anne had challenged Éndira to a race. She knew better than to try and exert herself so early in her training but she could not resist getting the other girl close to her as much as possible.

The action might be considered a coy move on her part but Anne could not resist trying.

Today Anne was just waiting for the right opportunity to try it again.

"Hey, you!" Éndira said as she popped her head up. "How are you doing over here?"

Anne smiled. She had been treading water for over a minute now and was beginning to get a little winded.

"Just trying to keep my head above water."

"Good," Éndira teased. "If I drown you, I am sure Lizzy will be upset."

"Don't call her that."

"Why, what are you going to do about it?"

Anne splashed Éndira in the face and took off. Her victim laughed then gave chase. They both rushed forward at full speed, the pinnace at least twenty-five yards away. As Anne gained her confidence at being able to finally beat her teacher, a rush of water entered her mouth and she began to choke.

Éndira did not notice the other one struggling to stay afloat. She reached the boat, and turned ready to gloat but Anne was nowhere to be seen.

"Anne?" Éndira said, then yelled as she realized her opponent might be in trouble. "ANNE!"

Éndira backtracked as quickly as she could, then dived. The salt water stung her eyes as she scanned for her friend. Éndira pulled herself up as she gasped for air. She ignored the loud splash behind her, knowing that was not whom she was looking for.

A rush of bodies came up as Elizabeth, in full uniform and struggling herself under the weight, pulled Anne up. Éndira tried to help as Elizabeth roughly brushed her off.

"Get in the pinnace!" Elizabeth snapped.

Éndira swam to the pinnace, and threw herself in. Elizabeth pulled Anne to the side as they both helped hoist Anne in. Éndira smacked her student's face.

There was no response.

Elizabeth pulled herself in the pinnace and pushed Éndira off. She then took her hand and slapped Anne's chest hard. The girl finally spit up water. Anne turned and vomited, then coughed for a few moments before being finally able to breath.

As her eyes adjusted, she only saw the look of concern on Elizabeth's face, followed by anger as the older woman turned and glared at Éndira.

"We were only—" Éndira tried to explain before she was harshly cut off.

"Quiet!" Elizabeth snapped. "I will deal with you later."

～

ANNE STOOD PATIENTLY OUTSIDE of Elizabeth's cabin and tried not to overhear what was happening inside. She stepped away and leaned against the edge of the stairs. As she closed her eyes, a strongly worded argument could still be heard clearly.

The door opened abruptly, startling Anne. She jumped back and caught the eye of Éndira. Her friend was red in the face from what appeared to be anger.

"Lizzy wants to see you," Éndira snapped then pushed on by.

Anne opened her mouth to speak but Éndira quickly disappeared around the corner.

Inhaling deeply, Anne shrugged her shoulders and waited in the doorway.

Elizabeth was pacing behind her desk. She turned and nodded.

"Close the door," the captain ordered.

Anne did as she was told. Her legs moved slowly, afraid of incurring the same wrath Éndira had just been subjected to. Anne didn't wait to be told to sit down. She sat then obediently waited for her turn in the proverbial hot seat.

"I'm not angry with you," Elizabeth said. She pulled her chair out and waited a moment. Looking straight at her subject, Elizabeth sighed. "This wasn't your fault."

Anne was about to speak up but stopped. She did not know why she was suddenly gripped with a feeling of trepidation. *But it is my fault for almost drowning, not Éndira's!*

"Éndira is going to move to the aft cabin for the time being," Elizabeth said as she sat down. She leaned back and rolled her head slightly, looking at the planks above.

"But miss?" Anne cleared her throat, concerned. "Why?"

Elizabeth leaned over and placed her hands on the desk. Her eyes narrowed harshly as she looked at Anne; the severity of her anger was etched in the lines around her eyes and mouth. "Because... Éndira *expressly* defied me."

"How?"

"I told her not to engage in any roughhousing. You are to novice a swimmer to engage in such activities."

Anne swallowed hard, her throat now dry. She needed to speak up for her friend but could not find her courage.

Elizabeth stood up abruptly and walked over to her. She put out her hand as a gesture to leave. Anne got up and followed the motion. When a soft touch fell upon her shoulder, Anne bit her lower lip, saddened.

"You should remain in your cabin for the rest of the day," Elizabeth said softly. "Now that we have the wind in our sails, we will be making landfall soon."

Before she knew it, Anne was led out of the cabin. When the door closed behind, Anne turned. She touched the wood and put her head on the surface. Feeling like a coward, Anne closed her eyes.

She gathered her strength and walked to her cabin.

The door was wide open.

Anne stood in the doorframe and watched her friend. Éndira was collecting her meager belongings. When the girl looked up, Anne walked over to her.

"I'm sorry Éndira," Anne said softly.

"No you're not," Éndira stood up, eyes ablaze. "You knew *exactly* what you were doing."

Has Éndira figured out I fancy her? Anne swallowed hard. *Were my attempts that obvious?*

Éndira pushed herself right into Anne's space. Even if Anne had wished for this closeness, Éndira's anger broadcast too much negative energy. Anne stepped back into the wall. Her hands touched the wooden planks.

"I didn't mean to," Anne lied. "I just thought we were having fun?"

Éndira stood still for a moment.

"I like..." Anne swallowed hard once again, afraid to say the words she wanted to. Instead, she chose a cowards way out. "I like being with you."

Éndira snorted. She bent down and snatched her bag. Tossing the satchel on her shoulder, she turned back to Anne, her eyebrows narrowed in irritation.

"Well, do me a favor," Éndira bit. "Stay away from me from now on."

Anne watched her friend storm out of the cabin. Another door was roughly opened, followed by a loud slam. Anne sighed and flopped onto her cot. She rolled onto her back and closed her eyes.

MIRANDA LEANED over her table and pulled the tip of the map closer. This was not the first time she had studied the parchment. She'd spent many hours looking at the locations of all the islands in the West Indies. Miranda had fantasized about being mistress of them all. Her little island of Barbados was just a start.

Dge had promised her much more than this small spit of land.

And now Anne is threatening to destroy all of it!

Miranda inhaled and let out a small grunt. She hadn't slept in days. All she could think about was how to get her blasted niece back!

A small knock in the open doorway made her grimace. Miranda did not want to entertain anyone at this moment, including her vexing lover Selina. She closed her eyes, hoping her lack of response would be enough of a hint to go away.

"Are you coming to dinner or not?" Selina said harshly.

"I'm not hungry." Miranda did not even bother to turn around. Her hands were starting to burn in irritation. She gripped the table surface with her fingernails and started to dig.

"You need to— "

Miranda spun around eyes ablaze. "LEAVE ME!"

Selina froze. Her face turned white, her own eyes wide with fear. Instead of fighting back, Selina spun on her heels and quickly left the room.

Miranda turned her attention back to her table. As she leaned over once again, her thoughts focused on the task at hand. She needed to figure out a way to force Anne back to the plantation.

One that involves my own magics.

Calling on Mama DgBaba provided nothing worthwhile.

Miranda had essentially promised the trickster her indentures' and slaves' souls in exchange for much needed help. Mama had appeared to like the proposition but had not given a definite answer. She had tried in vain to appeal to the trickster— to at least have another audience to discuss the matter.

Nothing had transpired.

Miranda was now starting to get desperate. She had no idea if she could even release Dge at this point.

He has stopped speaking to me.

Miranda had spent the last five nights by the silk-cotton, trying to get him to communicate with her. She did not know if Mama had muted her brother in some way.

Why would the trickster do that? Mama said she has wanted to release her brother. She was even curious on how this would happen and how Anne was to be involved— but still no word from the blasted woman!

Miranda watched the candles by her side flicker. The flames danced within the gentle breeze. Quickly, she snapped her head towards the patio. The shutters were wide open, allowing more island sea breeze to come inside.

Suddenly, a strong gust blew in and extinguished all the candles in the room. Another rush of wind and she was thrown to the floor. The shutters then violently slammed shut. Miranda grabbed her chest in fright and tried to calm herself.

What just happened?

Miranda lay on the floor for a brief moment. Eventually, she forced herself up. She carefully walked over and opened the shutters. Her hands secured the latches so the shutters wouldn't blow shut.

The cool island breeze hit her skin once again.

Miranda walked onto the patio and leaned against the railing. Closing her eyes for only a brief moment to try and build her courage, she slowly opened them and looked out towards the silk-cotton tree in the distance. Its leaves were still despite the heavy island breeze.

Miranda did not want to trek out to visit it tonight. She was tired of having to explain to something that probably could no longer hear her. Dejected, Miranda went back into the room.

She leaned over her desk. She was about to start to roll up the map, when something odd caught her attention.

Miranda quickly replaced the candles upright and lit them all. Now that she had better light, she could see clearly.

The spilled candles had left trails of dried up wax. One path in yellow led straight from Mayraeu to Martinique. Another in blue, crisscrossed from Dominica straight to St. Lucia, but ended abruptly in the middle of the ocean. Even more strange, another path, but in red wax this time cut that line perpendicularly.

Miranda stared at the map for a long period of time. Some in the family were masters in divination. She had experimented with the practice on occasion, but it was never a strong skill. As she continued to study the lines on the map, Miranda wondered if this was indeed some type of sign or direction?

Have I done this?

Confused, she nervously touched her pendant and looked again out towards the patio.

Maybe Mama DgBaba is going to help after all?

34

Anne could no longer allow herself to hide from her responsibility. She enjoyed Éndira's company immensely. These past few days, getting not even a smile from her friend, made Anne's heart hurt. It was her own selfish actions that caused this rift.

Anne put her spoon in her stew. She dabbed it a few times before taking a small bite.

"This is the third night you haven't felt like eating," Elizabeth said softly.

Anne looked up. The woman could be enormously strict but immensely gentle when needed. The two of them ate alone in the great cabin. Normally Éndira would be in attendance, along with many of the officers.

These last few nights it was only she and Elizabeth.

Anne sighed as she put down her utensil. "I have a confession to make."

Elizabeth raised an eyebrow. She swallowed what she was drinking then put the glass down. "And what might that be?"

Anne took in a deep breath sure she would make a mess of things.

Just get it bloody over with.

"It's my fault miss," Anne finally confessed. "The race. I started it."

"I know," Elizabeth said nonchalantly then began to pour herself another drink.

Anne blinked, unsure of what was just spoken. Had Elizabeth just said she knew the whole time?

"Then why?" Anne said, alarmed. "Why would you punish Éndira for something that was my fault?"

"Because..." Elizabeth put the decanter down and replaced the stopper. She leaned inward. "Éndira should not have engaged with you."

"But?"

Elizabeth put her finger up to stop further questioning. When Anne nodded that she would listen, Elizabeth continued her speech. "I don't think you are helpless Anne. This is not what I think, nor does Éndira. But I will not allow harm to come to either of you. Éndira is on this ship to help protect you from your Aunt Miranda but she is also a member of my crew at the moment." Elizabeth quickly took a sip of port. "You are not my crew, therefore a passenger for the time being. Éndira is to be held to a higher standard than you at all times."

Anne rubbed her hand nervously on the linen tablecloth. She looked at her older friend, eyes confused. "But how will I get her to forgive me?"

"Have you told her why you did it?"

Anne looked away for a moment, ashamed. *How can I be expected to reveal the real reason?*

"She'd think me a fool," Anne said, troubled.

"Well. Unless you talk to her, you will never know, now will you?"

"No miss," Anne agreed.

Anne picked up her spoon and dug it into the stew. She forced herself to eat, sure she would have knots in her stomach all night.

How can I possibly tell Éndira— I fancy her?

Anne knocked on the aft cabin door for the fourth time.

Still, no answer.

"I know you are in there," Anne finally spoke up. "I really want to talk to you."

Again, nothing.

"Are you all right?" A familiar voice said from behind.

Anne turned around and shook her head.

"I'm fine Finlay," she lied.

Only then did Anne notice he was carrying a tray of food. He looked down at what he held and shrugged.

"I'm playing steward," Finlay snickered.

"I see," Anne said with a smile.

"Is Éndira not answering?"

"No."

"Maybe she isn't in there."

Anne raised an eyebrow. "Why wouldn't she be?"

"Maybe she jumped ship?" Finlay grinned.

His humor made her smile. Anne stepped backwards and let him knock on the door.

Again, there was no response.

"Maybe she did jump ship," Anne said loudly, trying to at least get some type of response.

"Oh well…" Finlay bent over and placed the tray down. "I will just leave this out here Éndira."

Anne crossed her arms. As he stood up, Anne felt a sudden wave of sadness hit her hard. She turned away from his gaze, afraid he might see her eyes. Quickly, she began to walk away.

Finlay jumped forward and touched her arm gently.

"I'm fine." Anne turned her head away, trying to hide her emotions.

"No you are not," he said kindly.

When he touched her chin, Anne let out a small sob.

"Please don't cry Anne," Finlay said. "I hate to see you sad."

Anne wanted to push him away. She wanted to run to her cabin and collapse on her bed.

Instead, Anne listened to his kind words.

What happened next, she had not anticipated.

Before she could react, his lips were on hers!

Anne opened her eyes wide. The sudden action had shocked her still. Quickly, she stepped back and swallowed hard.

Finlay's expression of love was not objectionable, just— undesired.

Anne touched her lips and looked at him.

"I'm sorry," Finlay stammered, shaking his head. "I should not have done that."

Before Anne could react, she felt another presence near. She turned and saw Éndira in the doorway, arms crossed, staring at them with a look of discontent and humor.

Anne felt her heart in her throat.

Finlay quickly exited, leaving the two girls alone.

"Éndira?" Anne sputtered, unable to find her words.

Éndira bent down, picked up her tray and roughly shut the door.

FINLAY WAS QUIET TONIGHT. Usually, he was chatty and telling Anne about what had been going on with the crew or telling her various stories about his time at sea.

Tonight... *not so much.*

He laid another card on the table. Anne scooped up the queen and placed it in her stack.

She quietly sighed. *Another lousy hand.*

"I fold," Anne placed her cards on the table.

"Already?" Finlay asked, disappointed. "That is five for you tonight."

"I'm lousy at this game."

"You are not," Finlay shook his head. "I've seen you whip the bosun and the captain."

"I'm just tired," Anne confessed.

She had been up all night thinking about what had happened between them and the sour look on Éndira's face.

The next morning, Anne found Finlay right away.

Anne explained to him that there was no room for a relationship. Finlay seemed to react with kindness but the disappointment etched on his face was transparent. He accepted her words, even reiterating he should have never kissed her without permission. Anne explained to him she was not angry, just taken by surprise at the action.

Even worse, Finlay was worried what Éndira might say to Captain Spencer.

Anne was more concerned about already losing Éndira as a friend, now there was no chance at more if— *I don't tell her my true feelings?*

"If you don't want to play," Finlay said crossly putting down his winning hand. "Just tell me."

"Tell you what?" Anne snapped, annoyed.

If he was now going to become petulant, she would have to nip that right now. When Finlay just glared at her, Anne huffed loudly.

"You're just upset with me!" she barked.

"And why would that be?" his voice asked in a sarcastic tone.

"I'm sorry Finlay," Anne reiterated once again. "I did not mean to lead you on."

How often must I keep saying this?

Finlay shuffled the deck and began to deal a new hand.

"It is fine Anne," Finlay said as he tossed the cards. "You don't fancy me. I understand."

Anne leaned forward and touched his hand. "It's not you— "

Finlay roughly pulled it away. "Oh please do not give me that speech! Just admit I am not handsome enough for you— or not well connected— or..." He whipped his head in anger and glared at her. "I am going to be a captain of a ship one day Anne. I am going to hunt down pirates and make lots of prize money like your father. I will be able to support you— buy you a big house!"

"Finlay! Stop it!" Anne said forcefully. "It is not about money, or how you look, or... whatever else you might tell me."

"Then what is it Anne? Tell me why I am not good enough for you?"

"Because I am not in love with you!"

"Not in love with me," he mocked himself as he dealt out the cards once again. "Of course not. Mr. Travers? His hair is always a mess! He is scraggly, will never grow tall. Who would FANCY him?"

"I have my reasons!"

"Well, what is it then?" Finlay pressed hard.

Anne needed to contain her anger. She was afraid of an energy she could not control. She unconsciously touched her necklace, feeling a twinge of heat.

I should leave before I hurt him by accident.

"Well?" he pressed even further.

Anne closed her eyes for a moment. *Should I just tell him? Will he understand or just laugh in my face?*

She looked at him and calmly asked, "If I tell you something, will you promise not to say anything to anyone? Especially Captain Spencer or Éndira?"

Finlay stopped dealing once again. He must have realized Anne was being very serious. "Yes... yes, of course. I would never betray your trust."

"Promise?"

"I give you my word as an officer."

Anne watched the door, afraid someone might be listening.

"No one is there Anne." Finlay could sense her unease. He reached out his hand and took hers in his. "You can tell me anything."

"I do not fancy boys," Anne blurted out.

She gasped and realized she had finally told someone— *and it feels good!*

Finlay just stared at her.

Anne realized he did not fully understand.

"Boys?" Finlay roared with laughter. "Of course boys are stupid. Even I know that. Thank God we are considered men when we became midshipmen and not— "

"— No Finlay, you are not grasping what I am saying. I do not fancy boys or men."

"Then what is left?" he asked perplexed, then his eyes suddenly lit up, finally aware of what she was getting at. "Do you mean?"

"Girls," Anne whispered. "Yes, I fancy girls."

"A game of flats!" he suddenly exclaimed.

"What?" Anne had no idea what he was saying.

"A game of flats!" Finlay took two queen cards and put them together as if they were laying on top of each other.

She quickly slapped the cards out of his hands.

"What in the hell Finlay?" Anne squealed, mortified.

"What? That's what it is called!"

"I don't even know what it means!"

When Anne tried to get up, he grabbed her by the hand. When she snapped her head and glared at him, he released.

"Please... sit back down," Finlay begged. "I did not mean to offend you."

Anne stared at him for a long moment then decided to return to her seat. "No, I overreacted... I'm... new to this."

"Don't worry... I am also new to this." Finlay lowered his head and blushed.

Anne could not be angry with him. He had always been sincere and honest. The truth was, she had overreacted. She knew little about being with another girl, and the sudden revelation took her by surprise. Anne always thought that kissing was the only expression of love you could have with another female. Now that she found out there might be more, her interest piqued.

She would have to research this further.

Anne leaned in and whispered in a low voice, "So... what else do you know about this, 'game of flats'?"

Finlay smiled.

Before he could open his mouth, the door abruptly swung open. Finlay dropped his cards. Anne widened her eyes, shocked.

The youngest midshipman stood in the doorjamb, eyes wide and panting severely.

"What is this Mr. Bishop?" Finlay chastised. He was still, after all, the senior midshipman on the HMS Defiant.

"Come quick sir," Bishop said through labored breaths. "Ship on fire... in the distance!"

Anne snapped her head towards Finlay. "The Fire Witch?"

"Don't know miss," Bishop answered for him. "But it's a Queen's ship. Second rate."

Anne suddenly felt her heart drop.

Her father's ship was a second rate, one of the finest in the fleet.

ANNE DID NOT EVEN NOTICE Éndira appear by her side. Anne only cared about what lay ahead. They could see fire in the distance, at least a half mile away.

"Mr. Hicks!" Elizabeth spoke loudly. "Have the sails doused with water."

"Yes, ma'am," Lieutenant Hicks replied then ran down the steps and began to bark the orders to his subordinate.

Elizabeth nervously rubbed her palms together. Éndira watched her carefully. The older woman touched Anne's shoulder and leaned inward.

"You should go below deck Anne," Elizabeth said softly.

Anne touched her necklace and felt for the ring. The gemstones were giving off a strange sensation. Anne had never felt this before.

It was as if they were speaking to her.

"That's my father's ship," Anne shook her head, tears already forming.

"We do not know that."

Anne turned, looking the woman dead in the eyes. "I know..."

Elizabeth blinked then glanced at Éndira. Anne did not wait for either reply. She ran down the steps and disappeared.

35

———

nne paced the hallway in front of her cabin. She ignored the sounds coming from the above decks. She did not care to listen to their cries, nor gasps of horror.

She already knew what had happened.

Anne could feel the residual energy of the Fire Witch. She had never met the bruja but had already once been affected by her presence. Anne did not realize that energy could remain.

Like the small granules of sand on the island the woman recently attacked— somehow, those crystals had recorded what had happened there.

Anne closed her eyes and remembered the sensation.

She felt anger— pain— vengeance!

Anne opened her eyes quickly.

The Bruja del Fuego was on a rampage that seemed bent on revenge. Anne could feel the woman's anger. The bruja left a trace wherever she went.

Anne leaned against the stairwell. She let her legs give way as she slid down. Carefully, Anne took her necklace off and held it in front of her eyes. The lone lantern gave off a small amount of light. Anne watched its reflection within the gemstones of the ring.

"Where is my father?" Anne said to the jewelry.

Nothing happened.

Anne was not going to repeat the question. It was stupid to speak to an inanimate object. She closed her eyes. This time, she took the item off the chain and finally put it on her finger.

Like the sting from a bee, Anne felt a sharp pain where the ring touched her skin. She winced but refused to take it off.

Now that the ring was finally on her finger, Anne knew instantly she was destined to wear it.

Again, another sharp pain stabbed at her skin. She touched the planks beneath her palms. She searched beneath the wood to deep within the ship. She followed a path to the saltwater then felt a sudden push through. Quickly, her perception changed to another hull.

Footsteps on that ship still ran around. Screams and yells were ones of terror, not battle. The canons were going off but the men who manned them were already dead. The wood planks were beginning to burn clear through. Anne felt herself suddenly on deck. She looked up. The sails had dripped molten metal instead of cloth. A deep laugh from behind alerted her. Anne turned quickly, hoping for a glimpse of her father.

Instead, a woman with coal dark hair smiled back. Her hands dripped with fire. The woman's skin had a coppery sheen. With red eyes, she threw her hands down and began to laugh.

All around, the ship was burning.

Instantly, the cannons started to explode, one by one.

Anne heard a cry in the distance. She immediately recognized the voice.

She turned, eyes wide.

Her father was engulfed in flames!

Anne opened her mouth to cry out but suddenly, everything around her became a bright red blur.

～

ELIZABETH HAD to be strong for Anne. If she showed any hint of how devastated she really was, she would break down in front of the girl. The worst thing that could possibly happen, had. Anne's father was most likely dead but Elizabeth could not bring herself to say those words.

"Anne?" Elizabeth knelt in front of the girl and held her hands. "You cannot think the worst... we do not know for a fact—"

"She burns her victims alive!" Anne snapped. "How can anybody survive?" When she put her hands up to her face and started to cry uncontrollably, Elizabeth leaned in and held her tight.

Éndira stood silently by the both of them. She looked lost, unable to say anything. Her own eyes began to tear as she quickly glanced away.

Elizabeth could feel Anne tremble under her embrace. As much as she wanted to take the pain away with a simple hug, there would be a long period of grief for both of them.

"Anne?" Elizabeth pulled back and tried to get the girl to look up. "Look at me."

Anne tilted her head upwards, tears flowing hard.

The sight of the young woman in pain made Elizabeth's own tears well up. "I have to attend to the ship right now. I want you to go in your cabin and lie down."

Anne nodded in compliance and let Elizabeth help her up.

"I will watch her." Éndira put her arms around Anne and slowly walked her away.

Elizabeth stood up and had to catch her breath. Suddenly, she felt dizzy. Elizabeth touched the passageway wall and tried to steady herself. She could not get the image of the smoldering wreckage out of her mind. She leaned forward and closed her eyes. Her stomach felt upside down, pain hitting her abdomen.

"Captain?" Lieutenant Hicks walked up next to her. He put out his hand and reached forward. "Are you all right?"

"No." Elizabeth turned and frowned at him. "I have to..." she closed her eyes, dipping her head low. "I have to go into my cabin for a bit."

Lieutenant Hicks nodded. "Please take as long as you need. I can take care of things on deck for the time being."

Elizabeth looked at him. She was extremely grateful for his kindness. "Thank you."

He watched as his captain shuffled along the passageway then disappeared into her cabin.

Elizabeth quickly turned then clicked the lock. She darted to the windows behind her desk and started to pace. Her hands rubbed together performing their nervous tick.

Agitated, she ran them through her hair and pulled downward. Her knees gave out as she collapsed against the wall, her back slowly sliding down the wood paneling. Tears that had been held back, suddenly came to the surface. She tried to scream; nothing came out but sobs.

She was completely devastated. All her life she had loved that man and now he was gone.

36

———

Anne said nothing to Éndira, she just lay in her arms and listened to the waves hit the bottom of the ship. Anne cared little anymore if the crystals in the sea wanted to 'talk' to her.

What was the point?

My father is dead.

My mother is dead.

Anne didn't even know if her brother was alive.

She thought back to that night in the parlor, when she was so happy to show her crystal art piece. Everyone had seen something that evening. Her mother was entranced by a vision then fell to her death days later trying to relive whatever she had seen. Anne had observed a blue wash of light. She'd realized later this might have meant her travel by ocean.

But Michael?

"Fire," Michael had said. "I saw reds dancing in the form of fire."

Anne didn't really understand how powerful that visual energy was until last night.

There were no survivors.

The Fire Witch had killed over 800 men, including dozens of officers, and— *my father!*

Anne closed her eyes, not wanting to relive the terrible vision she had been forced to watch. Had she also invited that vision with her ring?

She'd already blamed herself for her mother's death.

Anne did not know if she could even entertain the thought of causing her father's.

The one thing Anne did know, is that she would no longer run. From her aunt, from society, from— *whatever I am!*

Anne walked to the captain's cabin, knocked on the door and waited. She did not want to force the issue but there was no longer any room for simple hope. Anne wanted to plead her case. She only hoped Elizabeth would listen.

"Come in," a gentle voice responded.

Slowly, Anne opened the door. "May I close the door?"

Elizabeth looked up from her desk. She had been busy writing with quill and ink. "Yes, of course Anne."

As Anne closed the door, Elizabeth got up and walked over to give her a long hug. Anne received the gesture gratefully. It took all her strength not to start crying all over again.

She had done enough of that last night and this morning.

"I am sorry I have not been able to spend time with you." Elizabeth released her grip. "I have been overwhelmed with— "

"You have been busy with the ship," The younger woman understood. Elizabeth had not been trying to avoid her.

"Yes."

"I understand."

Anne could see the pain in Elizabeth's eyes. Her friend had not cried in front of her. She had shown little emotion. But that did not mean Elizabeth did not have feelings or did not care.

Elizabeth had loved her father and the loss must have been devastating for her.

For the both of them.

"Have you eaten anything this morning?" Elizabeth asked.

"Just a little soup."

"You need to eat something substantial." Elizabeth left the cabin to find some rations.

Anne stared at the seven windows opposite her. Seven had always been a lucky number. She watched the light penetrate the cabin. The dust was dancing as it usually was. It was midday and the color outside was a soft blue with little clouds in the sky. Only a few weeks before, Anne had been cowering for her life behind the overturned desk with just a cutlass by her side and a flintlock she had a hard time loading under pressure.

Anne had decided she would no longer allow her lack of competence to define her.

I will define myself.

Elizabeth came back into the cabin holding a small dish. She placed the item in front of Anne.

"Thank you," Anne said, then picked up the small piece of bread and ate. Her fingers then found a piece of cheese. Now that she had begun to eat, she realized she was more hungry than she thought. Satisfied, she brushed the crumbs off her hands and sat back in the chair.

Elizabeth had watched her every move. "How are you feeling today?"

"Like someone has ripped out my heart."

Elizabeth nodded then looked at the side cabinet. Anne knew that her friend was thinking about taking a drink. She seemed to use alcohol to help when her emotions or nerves ran high. "I too feel like someone has ripped out my heart."

They both sat in silence for a bit. Anne kept her eyes focused on the windows ahead, Elizabeth looking down at her desk and following the grooves in the wood.

"Has Éndira been helpful?" Elizabeth broke the silence.

"Yes," Anne answered. "She is extraordinarily kind hearted when she isn't being annoying."

They both let out a pained laugh. Anne quickly rubbed a tear out of her eye, unsure if it was pain creeping up again or if it was actual joy.

Elizabeth walked over to the front of the desk. She leaned on the edge and let one of her legs dangle, the other one firmly on the floor. She crossed her arms and dipped her head low for a moment, deep in thought.

"You are thinking about what to do with me?"

Elizabeth looked up, her eyes unhappy and nodded her head.

"Let me stay here," Anne pleaded with her own.

"I can't."

"Why not? You are mistress of this ship."

"I am not mistress of the Royal Navy Anne, I cannot justify you being on board this ship any longer."

"Then make me a midshipman!" Anne bit harsh. "There is no reason I cannot take the same path as you!"

Elizabeth sighed then rubbed the bridge of her nose with her fingertips. She looked exhausted. There was no room for debate on such an unusual subject.

"I want to fight the Fire Witch," Anne continued. She needed Elizabeth to understand this. "I want to help take her down! I need to do this!— I want... to do this..."

When Elizabeth did not raise her head, Anne pleaded.

"Please?"

"No." Elizabeth looked at her and tried to direct the conversation elsewhere. "I need to find someplace for you to live permanently. Someplace safe and away from your aunt."

Elizabeth got up and walked over to her cabinet.

Anne watched as her older friend was no longer able to deny herself a drink. She watched as Elizabeth poured a small portion of rum into a crystal glass and drank quickly. She then exhaled and leaned against the table as if she were pushing the object into the wall.

"I wanted to leave you with my friends. They helped me through my darkest times." Elizabeth turned and looked at her. "But now that Mama has interfered, I know not what to do with you in the West Indies."

Anne felt her stomach tighten. She had a terrible feeling what the woman was about to say. "You want me to go back to London?" Anne spat, the words like acid dripping off her tongue.

"Maybe in the country. Away from your aunt's reach. Have you stay with someone until at least we can contact your brother. I know a— "

"— What does HE have to do with my well being?"

"He is now the head of your family."

"So what? He does not own me!" Anne protested. "Why? Because he is a man? You of all people should loathe such an idea!"

"Of course I do!" Elizabeth confessed loudly, seemingly livid with herself. "But what else can I do Anne?"

"Let me stay on this ship!" Anne got up. She took off her ring and slammed it on the table. "I can fight!"

Elizabeth looked oddly at the item. Eyebrows bent in confusion, she glanced at Anne. "What does your ring have to do with fighting?"

"Because I have magical powers."

Elizabeth blinked for a moment then picked up the ring and rolled it around in her fingers. She put it closer to her eyes. The light in the room bounced off the various gemstones.

"You told my father that night... that the *affliction* may have skipped my generation," Anne said. "But my *affliction* is not loving girls—"

Elizabeth perked her eyebrows up. That news was not one she had obviously heard before.

"It is whatever has been passed down."

"How are you so sure?"

"Because the night my uncle attacked me... I willed him off of me and there was a sudden, electrical charge that shot from my ring."

Elizabeth tilted her head, listening closely.

"And..." Anne continued. "My Aunt Miranda said that we have a special relationship with crystals. That we can harness the energy from them. That is why she wants me."

"A Crystal Astrid?"

Anne did not recognize the term. "What is a Crystal Astrid?"

"What you just described. Someone who can harness the energy of a crystal and use it in any way they need." Elizabeth played with the ring some more. "A Crystal Astrid can also feel into natural objects and understand what is happening in their surroundings."

"Like the ship's wood?"

"Well not exactly. I do not know if wood contains crystals but the ship is certainly soaked in salt water. Why wood?"

"Because during the battle with the Spanish brig, I felt the fight, the ship," Anne said. "I knew something happened to you... I could almost feel your pain." Anne did not want to confess she had also seen her own father's death. Anne swallowed hard. "When you collapsed in your cabin yesterday. When you were grieving."

Elizabeth stared at her. Anne did not know if the other woman was amazed or just slightly scared. Elizabeth took the ring and handed the jewelry back to Anne.

"So what now?" Anne asked.

"Well... I think we need to test out your powers, do we not?"

Anne smiled.

She believes me?

Now, if only I knew how to bring this power out on command!

Elizabeth put her hand on Anne's shoulder as they walked to the door. "So you love girls, huh?"

Anne timidly glanced up. "Yes miss."

Her older friend shook her head for a moment then let out a small chuckle. "Good for you."

"You're okay with it?" Had Elizabeth accepted her secret that easily? *My father must have never told Miss Elizabeth about that night he caught me kissing my best friend Sarah.*

"Love is a hard thing to find and when you do," Elizabeth smiled. "Hold on to it tightly."

Anne made it halfway up the steps when she suddenly stopped. She had not been on deck since discovering the fiery wreckage of her father's ship. Anne took a deep breath and continued on. Another set of steps led to the quarterdeck.

A few moments later, Elizabeth stepped up with a few swords. She directed the quartermaster where to put the small table he was carrying. Next she began to lay out the weapons.

"Are we drilling?" Éndira asked as she walked over.

"Not us." Elizabeth handed Anne a dull, practice cutlass. The old, worn metal had many scratches and the hilt's design was practically rubbed away. "Anne and I."

"What am I supposed to do with this?" Anne took the weapon in her hands and held it tight.

"I will show you." Elizabeth grabbed her by the waist and showed her how to position herself. "You need a defensive block to start out with."

"Why?"

"Because I am going to attack you."

Anne's eyes widened. "What?"

They spent the next ten minutes going over standard, defensive sword tactics. Anne knew she was a quick study but this was ridiculous. She did not know if she would be able to remember all this in such a short lesson.

Watching Anne's panic, Éndira crossed her arms. "If I may... this is not how you showed me when I was trained."

"No, you're right." Elizabeth took another practice cutlass off the table and stepped forward. She slashed close to Anne, who dropped her own weapon and quickly jumped back.

"I need more practice!" Anne squealed. "What are you doing?"

"Don't question and do what I say." Elizabeth paced for a moment. "Pick up the sword."

Anne did as she was told. As soon as the weapon was firmly in her hand, her older friend attacked again. Anne managed to deflect with one move but stepped back too quickly and tripped. She fell on her backside.

Elizabeth swooped in and helped her up.

"Again," she ordered.

They drilled over and over again, each time Anne unsure of what was happening. Elizabeth's movements were so quick, Anne could not keep up. Anne pleaded for her older friend to slow down but Elizabeth just shook her head no.

"Did you ask your uncle to slow down?" Elizabeth bit.

"No!" Anne did not know why Elizabeth just said that. "He was attacking me! I had no idea what to do!"

"I am attacking you right now."

Another swish from Elizabeth's cutlass caused Anne to move to the side.

"Lizzy? What the hell?" Éndira barked, unsure what was going on. "Why are you doing this?"

"Quiet you!" Elizabeth began her offensive attack once again. She was focused only on Anne. "Were you scared when he had his hands on you?"

"Yes!"

"Were you scared when he grabbed you in your lower half?"

"Yes!" Anne swiped down hard, no longer committed only to defense.

"Are you scared of me right now?" Elizabeth pushed forward hard.

"Yes!"

"Make me stop."

"I can't"

"Concentrate harder!"

Anne danced around, desperately trying to keep Elizabeth from knocking her to the floor once again. Anne felt for the crystals in her ring. The piece of jewelry was on her right hand. The same hand that she was using to hold and maintain the cutlass. Anne closed her eyes for a moment and found a path, just like the crystals in the water that she boiled quickly, or the light show she was able to manipulate in her family's parlor. Anne knew that she could force them to do what she wanted.

And right now?

I want Miss Elizabeth to stop attacking me!

Elizabeth swung her cutlass down hard, hitting the metal of Anne's own as the girl held the weapon slightly above her head. When metal scraped against metal, an electrical jolt shot out and engulfed both swords. A thunderous boom threw Elizabeth off of her feet and shot her backwards. She slid for a good seven feet before hitting the side of the ship.

Anne was frozen in fear.

She stared at her own hand in awe.

Did I really just do that?

"Miss Elizabeth!" Anne threw down her cutlass and ran to help her friend.

Elizabeth was in a daze. She was being helped up by Éndira, who just looked at Anne in horror.

"Are you hurt?" Anne cried. "I did not mean to hurt you!" She thought about what had happened to her Uncle Randal. She could have easily killed Elizabeth like she did to him. Why would the woman push her to the brink, only to allow herself to be hurt?

"I am fine." Elizabeth shook her head and put her hand out to maintain her balance.

"Why did you force me to do that?"

"I needed you to push yourself. Whatever magics you have, they've lain dormant within you."

"But why attack me like that?"

Elizabeth cracked her own neck side to side, trying to loosen her body. "Because... that is often the only way to get magic to self start within a younger person coming into their own."

"How would you know that?"

"I've been around people like you before."

"My aunt?"

Elizabeth nodded in affirmation.

"You've always known what she is?" Anne asked.

"Yes."

"But how did you know that I might posses the same... skills?"

Elizabeth touched the back of her own neck, still trying to loosen her muscles. "I didn't really. I suspected something when I saw the ring hanging on your necklace. It was the same... " she sighed, finally confessing the truth to Anne. "It is the same ring your father gave me when we were engaged."

"You... you were 'engaged' to my father?" Anne blinked, processing this news. All of these sudden revelations were not only confusing, but somewhat disturbing.

"Yes."

"And he gave you the same ring first?" Anne asked, exasperated.

"Yes. It was a family heirloom. It was meant to be passed down to his future wife," Elizabeth admitted. "And with that, any female child we had. I understood what that meant."

Anne stared at her with a hint of anger. *Was Miss Elizabeth afraid to bear a child with powers like Miranda? Did the thought of having a child like her make Miss Elizabeth run?*

"Is that why you didn't marry him?" Anne said harshly.

Elizabeth shook her head. "No Anne. I loved him very much. I still..." she closed her eyes for only a second, remembering the recent loss which still stung. "I would have been happy to have a child like you Anne. I released him because I thought I was going to die from my injuries. I should have died."

"But why not go back to him?"

"Because I didn't return to the service for nearly two years. I stayed on the island of Nassau," Elizabeth said softly. "By that time, he had married your mother. He thought me dead."

"He must have been surprised to see you alive then?" Anne snarled.

Elizabeth nodded, but said nothing.

Anne crossed her arms. She snapped her head towards Éndira, throwing the pirate girl off guard. "And what about you?" Anne growled. "Did you know what I was the whole time?"

Éndira shrugged. "I suspected you had some supernatural abilities. But my power only works when energy is discharged or leaves a residue. Your ring leaks power. I started to feel your magical presence lately."

Anne leaned back on her left leg. She didn't understand why nobody told her these things. *Why would they keep this knowledge from me?*

"You should have told me," Anne accused.

"You're right, I should have." Elizabeth said. "But you also hid this knowledge from the both of us, did you not?"

Anne looked at them both, dumbfounded. "Are you kidding me? You would never believe me!"

"Why not?" Éndira said kindly. "We at least knew your aunt has magical powers. Zara was able to move through mirrors. And don't get me started on Mama DgBaba."

They're right. There was no reason you could not tell either of them.

"I was embarrassed," Anne confessed. "I think I was afraid you might think me like my aunt… and that I might become evil like her."

"You are nothing like her Anne," Elizabeth assured. "You have a good heart. Miranda never had that. You are so much like… your father." Anne smiled. Her heart beat with pride at the thought. "But you do have great power Anne. One that even rivals your Aunt Miranda's."

Anne looked at her, confused. "How would you know that?"

"In your aunt's house. The paintings have a way of… talking."

"I thought I heard something in that room!"

"Yes. There was chatter that a great power from the family would come into their own. Your father had told me long ago only one daughter could inherit the true gift. He gave you the ring. You are the only girl child. He knew it would be you."

"Then why did you leave me with my Aunt Miranda? Surely you knew she was insane?"

"Honestly Anne… your aunt has always been a bitch but I did not think she had become psychotic. I had no idea that she was capable of using you for whatever this… Dge tree thing is."

Anne shook her head. "Then what am I supposed to do now?"

"Learn to fight back."

"Can you teach me how to control these powers?" Anne asked, hopeful.

"No. I know nothing of the ways of the Crystal Astrid, just that it exists in your family."

Anne huffed, disappointed.

"But I will show you how to defend yourself properly." Elizabeth bent down and picked up a cutlass. She handed the weapon to Anne. "It is still one of the greatest powers one has."

Anne nodded and took the sword.

37

Anne spent the next three hours working with both Elizabeth and Éndira on the 'art of the sword'. The extended workout helped Anne keep her mind occupied. Her father had just died and Anne was still deep in grief. The last thing she wanted to do was sit in her cabin and start crying all over again.

When the bell was rung calling all hands to lunch, the training finally stopped.

Anne was famished.

She turned over her cutlass to Éndira, who then handed it off to Elizabeth. Elizabeth took a small rag and began to clean the weapons.

Anne felt a sharp pain creep up her arm. She touched the sore spot.

"Your ring?" Éndira asked, concerned.

"No," Anne shook her head. "My arm is stiff."

Elizabeth turned around. "It will hurt for a while. Normally we would have stretched our muscles before we sparred but I did not know if that would interfere with what I needed to do."

"Oh," Anne said, confused.

Why would one need to stretch before a fight?

"Here." Éndira touched Anne's arm and pulled it close. "Let me."

Anne allowed the motion. Before she realized, Éndira had her own arms around Anne and pulled inward.

Anne inhaled at the touch.

"Is it tender?" Éndira asked.

Anne nodded her head gently. She could not confess that her sudden 'tenderness' was actually Éndira's embrace. Anne closed her eyes, reveling in the body that was so close to her.

It did not last long.

Éndira released then softly touched Anne on the back.

"Let's go eat something," Éndira said then looked at Elizabeth. "Unless I am still restricted to the aft cabin?"

Anne had completely forgotten about her friend's punishment. Ever since they came across the burning hull of the HMS Latitude, everything changed.

"No," Elizabeth said kindly. "I'll join you in the great cabin in a few minutes."

"Yes ma'am," Éndira said.

Anne perked up for a moment. It was the first time she had heard Éndira say those words without a twinge of sarcasm in her voice.

The two girls walked in silence down the steps. When they entered the great cabin, Jolly was filling a single goblet with port. He looked up and smiled.

"Are you joining the captain for lunch?" Jolly asked.

"Yes, sir." Anne nodded with a smile. "Myself and Éndira."

"No more restriction for you?" Jolly chuckled, looking at the other young woman.

"No," Éndira smirked. "I've been let off the hook."

"You're a spitfire," he snickered.

As he pulled back one of the chairs, Anne sat down and let him push her in. He did the same for Éndira then started to fill two more glasses.

"Is that what I am?" Éndira asked, intrigued.

"Yes. Just like Captain Spencer."

Anne had to smile. Jolly was right. Éndira had more in common with

Elizabeth than she would let on. Jolly left the room to attend to their lunches.

Now that they were alone, Anne finally wanted to speak up.

"Thank you for staying with me last night," she said gratefully.

"Of course." Éndira nodded. "You needed a friend."

"Am I?" Anne swallowed hard. "Still your friend?"

"Of course you are. I was just angry with you."

"I have to apologize to you," Anne said softly. "I am sorry for starting the race."

"Don't worry about it Anne. I don't care anymore."

"But?" Anne stammered, afraid to push the subject harder. "You got in trouble for my actions!"

"I did. But I accept your apology anyway." Éndira winked, making Anne's stomach fill with butterflies.

Anne couldn't stop thinking about this girl.

Just then, Jolly walked in carrying a tray. Anne waited for him to put three plates down, each containing a cucumber sandwich and boiled potatoes. Anne had grown accustomed to the lack of cuisine on a queen's ship. When he put another bowl down, this time with mangos, Anne smiled. He must have picked them up at their last stop a few days back.

The ship had spent two days at Kingstown in St. Vincent. Anne watched the crew load new supplies on deck.

Even more curious, several loads of casks and barrels filled with molasses and other spirits were brought on board. The men on deck spent hours putting the items below, including unmarked crates. Anne had caught the eye of Jackson, the creepy seaman who was whipped for touching her.

Once Jolly was gone, Anne began to eat the potatoes. Her stomach was hungry but her nerves dulled her appetite. Anne thought once again about her father. She closed her eyes, holding back tears. She felt a kind hand on her own.

"I'm so sorry for your loss," Éndira said kindly.

Anne looked at her. "Thank you."

They ate in silence for a long while. Once Anne finished her sandwich, she looked towards the door. Elizabeth had yet to join them for lunch. Anne suddenly chastised herself, realizing maybe they should have waited.

Éndira must have sensed her thoughts.

"She wouldn't have wanted us to wait Anne," Éndira said. "I am sure she is busy."

"I guess you are right." Anne nodded then shook her head. She wanted to change the subject to something she'd been wanting to ask for a while now. "You know, your name is really beautiful." Anne looked at her friend. "Does it mean anything in particular?"

Éndira put down her drink. "Well, my proper name is Eréndira. I am named after the Princess Eréndira of the Purépecha people."

"Was she real?"

"Maybe... maybe legend. Who knows?"

"Can you tell me her history?"

"Well... legend has it that she led her people in a war against the Spanish. Her people had never seen a horse before, since they were not native to the region. It is said she killed a Spanish soldier and stole the animal and brought it back to her people. Soon, she trained others to ride, attacking and gaining more horses for their forces," Éndira said proudly. "Of course, as with all legends, everything gets mixed up from there. Some claim she drowned herself to avoid capture. Others said that her own people finally hid her in a temple, fearful of being captured by the Spanish."

"Like an Egyptian Queen?" Anne gasped. "Not walled up in a tomb I hope!"

"That's why they are legends Anne. They make no sense," Éndira chuckled. "What about you? Who are you named after?"

"No one special."

"But isn't your current queen an Anne herself?"

"She is," Anne smirked. "But no one has ever told me about my name or its importance. I think it is, you know, just a name."

"Well I think it is pretty."

Anne held her breath for a moment, trying to keep her face from getting red. She enjoyed Éndira's company immensely. The fact that the girl had forgiven her made her heart swoon even more.

"Are there no legends in your England with the name Anne?"

"Besides the queen that got her head chopped off?" Anne giggled. "Not that I know of. No one has told me my name is special."

"Well, I think it is."

Again, she shows me such kindness, Anne thought happily.

Éndira raised her glass. "You have the perfect opportunity to create yourself as a legend, Anne Sutton of the West Indies."

Anne raised her own in response. When the two glasses touched, Anne could not help but smile.

I seriously love this girl.

FOR THE NEXT FEW DAYS, Anne threw herself into learning how to use a cutlass. She was fearful that her ring might interfere with her training. Anne had Elizabeth lock up her jewelry in the captain's cabin during the day.

At night, Anne was given back her ring. She would feel the item on her hand and knew all would be right eventually.

Anne's hands took to the sword as if she were always meant to hold one. Working herself into a sweat, Anne realized what her friends were trying to do.

Keep her mind off her grief.

Only at night, did Anne cry.

Often, Éndira would try to comfort her with quiet conversation. Anne wanted to surrender herself to Éndira's kind words but even those soft musings could not relieve her sorrow.

Tonight, Anne could no longer stand to be brokenhearted.

"What do you think I should do?" Anne asked with a lopsided smile. When Éndira returned the gesture with a haunting look peppered with a hint of intrigue, Anne felt her heart flutter. She'd grown to not only adore everything about Éndira, even the little annoyances she had once found impossible to deal with were now quaint.

Anne truly felt a connection with this pirate.

I think I have really fallen for her... hard.

"You could come back to my island," Éndira offered. "I am sure you might like it."

"I can?" Anne said almost too enthusiastically. She quickly cleared her throat and shifted on her cot. "I mean... what is your island like?"

"It's nothing like you have seen I am sure." Éndira leaned back on her own cot. "First off, we have grand mountains... almost as tall as Jamaica's."

"I've only been to Barbados and Jamaica," Anne confessed. "And wherever we've sailed so far. Zara took me riding in the hills once. I really enjoyed it. We saw a beautiful waterfall and birds I had only read about in books."

"On my island," Éndira said with wonderment in her own eyes. "There are many waterfalls and streams. So much fresh water flows, we have whole areas unexplored or unused. I spend many hours enjoying a brisk swim."

Anne's lip twisted with amusement. *I have to ask.*

"Do you really skinny dip?" Anne chuckled.

Éndira grinned. "How else would you swim?"

"Covered," Anne said, almost embarrassed. "Isn't it indecent to do such a thing? What if someone saw you?"

"I'm not ashamed to be naked," Éndira said dryly.

"I didn't say that," Anne sputtered, afraid to start a fight. "I just meant, what if the opposite sex saw you?"

"No one bothers me," Éndira assured. "Like I said. I swim where there are no other people. I'm not worried about such things." She waved a hand downward.

"Aren't you afraid of... being attacked?"

"No one would dare touch me."

For a moment, Anne could see a hint of apprehension behind those beautiful green eyes. Anne wondered if she had uncovered a sensitive subject in her friend. Éndira quickly brushed off her momentary lapse with another sly grin. "I do have my knife."

"That you do," Anne chuckled, remembering her first night sleeping in this cabin with the pirate girl she knew nothing about and a knife under the pillow.

A beautiful naked girl, Anne thought blissfully.

"I am sure you are still a virgin." Éndira did not say these words roughly, only off handed.

Still, Anne took offense. "Of course I am! Do you think me a trollop?"

"Were they preparing you for marriage back home?"

Anne could not snap at the other girl this time. She knew by Éndira's tone that the question was meant to feel pity. Anne instantly felt jealous of the other one.

Éndira was free.

Me not so much.

Unless I go to her island. Live there and hope to find a life, and maybe a love?

"Yes, my infernal governess and shrew of a neighbor were going to find me a match after my mother died," Anne confessed. "If not for Miss Elizabeth stepping in and suggesting that I come to this part of the world I would surely be married by now."

"Because your mother died?"

Anne realized she had not spoken to Éndira about this topic. Perhaps Elizabeth had told her some of the story?

"Yes." Anne began to tell her the tale of how her mother had fallen to her death. About being catatonic for so long and forgetting the family. Anne told her how her mother was once a vibrant woman, full of life and joy. The memories flooded Anne's mind. She stopped when the pain became too much.

"I'm sorry for that Anne." Éndira sat back and crossed her arms to her chest. "You were lucky to have had her for so long."

"I was." Anne nodded in agreement. Éndira might be brash, but she also seemed to understand feelings better than she let on. "Of course, now I am on the run from my insane aunt!"

"Don't worry about her." Éndira slapped her own legs. "Lizzy will not let her take you!"

Anne unconsciously pulled her own legs back and drew her arms around them. She had felt uncomfortable for only a moment, then intrigued.

Was she starting to see more from Éndira's point of view?

Untamed and free— to explore?

Éndira was a new adventure waiting to help Anne loosen up a little.

"Are you then?" Anne whispered, almost too shy to say the words. "You know... a virgin?"

"Me?" Éndira guffawed. "No dear."

"Oh." Anne glanced at the wall. She did not want to press the matter. Secretly she had many questions to ask but Anne was a lady and ladies did not talk of such things.

A sudden knock at the door made Anne jump. When she looked at Éndira, the other young woman just started to laugh.

"You're too jumpy for your own good." Éndira stood up. "You need to learn to relax."

"Oh, right," Anne snickered. "Until my crazy aunt can no longer possess sailors, I think I might just start to sleep with a knife under my pillow."

Anne silently chastised herself for not thinking of doing that earlier.

"I told you," Éndira winked at her, making Anne feel her heart race once again. "All women would do well to do that."

Anne shook her head, amused.

When the door opened, Elizabeth stood with a sword in her hands. "May I?" She nodded towards the small area.

"Of course," Éndira said, moving to the side to allow the woman to enter.

Elizabeth glanced around the cabin and smirked. "I'd forgotten how tiny these cabins are."

"Living it up in the captain's quarters has its advantages," Éndira teased.

Elizabeth rolled her eyes and looked at Anne, who was standing at the far wall. If not for the well placed movements the three women would not be able to fit.

Elizabeth held out the sword. "Anne. I would like to give you this."

Anne said nothing. Her mouth was frozen in delight and shock. She held out her hands. When her palm touched the single edged sword's grip, she felt a rush of energy shoot up her arm. Anne gasped then glanced at them both.

"The sword has a ruby gem." Elizabeth pointed to the pommel, shaped in the silhouette of a lion.

In its eye, a small, vibrant red gemstone.

Anne held the sword upright, a proper grip now that she had learned how to handle one. Tears of joy welled up in her eyes. She looked at Elizabeth.

"Miss, this is too much for me!"

"No it's not," Elizabeth assured. "You are turning eighteen tomorrow are you not?"

"I am."

"Consider it an early birthday present."

Anne did not know what to say. When she looked at Éndira, her friend had raised her brows in surprise.

"I did not know your birthday was tomorrow," Éndira said.

Anne shrugged. "I sort of forgot... with everything going on..."

Elizabeth rubbed Anne's back gently trying to console her young friend. "Remember what I told you about when I was engaged to your father?"

"Yes," Anne nodded.

"I had this sword made for myself and I presented another, just like it, to your father as an engagement gift."

"But... but why is it meant for me?" Anne stammered, her words happy and sad all at once.

"I was going to pass this down to my daughter if I had one," Elizabeth confessed. "Only one daughter will bear the gift."

"I was the only one so..." Anne looked up, grateful. "My powers were naturally bound to me."

"Yes."

Anne perked up. "Are there others in my family like my aunt and myself?"

"I am not sure about your family Anne. Your father knew little and your grandmother was extremely tight lipped. I think she only shared knowledge with Miranda. But your father did tell me once that your mother had some on her side. Unfortunately Lara would never talk about it and it was not my position to ask her later."

"Was my mother a Crystal Astrid?"

"No," Elizabeth said. "But she was able to pass on the gift... which you obviously got."

Anne searched the floor for a quick moment trying to process the news. There were others like her out there. Family members that might be able to help find her path. She looked up with eager eyes. "If I can find others, maybe they can teach me?"

"Or maybe they are just as nutty as your aunt," Éndira said with a raised eyebrow.

Anne crooked her own realizing her friend's point. "Yes... that might be a problem."

Elizabeth rubbed Anne's back. "That is not something to worry about now Anne. Eventually you will find out but for right now it is not something you should dwell on."

Anne looked lovingly at the sword. If she had been born to Elizabeth, this sword would have been hers by right of inheritance.

Instead, Elizabeth had given it to her out of love.

"Thank you," Anne reached over and hugged her tightly.

Éndira waited for them to release. Once they did, Éndira took the sword from Anne and inspected it herself.

"You've always kept this away in your locker," Éndira said looking at the older woman. "I never understood why you had a sword you never used, yet polished frequently."

"And now you do." Elizabeth touched Éndira's shoulder gently.

Anne noticed the way Éndira lit up. Anne had known that as much as Éndira claimed to not really care about what Elizabeth thought, deep down inside she did. It was nice to see Éndira happy in the woman's presence for once.

"We are going to arrive at Frigate Island soon," Elizabeth said. "You both should go ashore and stretch your legs."

"We can?" Anne squealed. She had not been allowed off the ship for fear of her aunt. "But what about my Aunt Miranda?"

"Éndira will be with you. She will protect you. And besides," she nodded towards the sword. "Now you also know how to defend yourself."

"Yes." Anne watched the light bounce off the blade. "But what about my ring?" Anne asked, concerned.

"Avoid channeling your energy," Elizabeth said, handing the ring over. "But wear it for protection just in case."

"Yes miss," Anne said, holding her lifeline in her hand. She quickly put on the jewelry, feeling the familiar rush of energy as it connected with her body.

All might be all right in the world tonight, Anne thought happily.

38

————————

Miranda sat with a glass of rum and stared into the distance. She'd still not visited the silk-cotton tree making her absence evident. A full week had gone by and still Miranda had heard nothing about her niece nor anything from Mama DgBaba.

Miranda was very close to giving up. She suddenly stood, screaming at the top of her lungs. She threw her glass into the chimenea. It eagerly inhaled the alcohol then spit out fire like an angry dragon. Miranda watched the flames die down, the reflections beating off her skin under the soft moonlight.

"Miranda?" Selina said from behind.

Miranda felt her blood begin to boil. She looked down at her hand and watched her palm pulsate.

"Leave me," she told her lover.

"No!" Selina bit harshly. "Do not command me away again!"

Miranda closed her fist tightly. She was so angry at everything that had happened since her blasted niece escaped. Now that Selina was demanding attention like a petulant child, Miranda did not know if she could control herself.

She tried to calm herself with deep breaths.

"I would advise you to leave right now Selina," Miranda warned. "Lest you feel my wrath."

"I have news," Selina said happily.

The words broke Miranda's anger. She turned and looked at her lover with eager eyes. "Anne?"

Selina shook her head. "No, your brother."

"My brother?" Miranda sputtered, confused. "Why would I give a shite about my brother?"

"Because he is dead!" Selina said with a wide smile.

Miranda blinked, trying to sort out the importance of this news. Her first reaction was... *indifference?*

Do I even care... if... if he is indeed dead?

Miranda gently touched her chest, trying to see if her body had reacted any differently. For a quick moment her breath caught in her throat.

Perhaps I do?

"How... how did he die?" Miranda finally asked, her voice low.

"His ship was destroyed," Selina snickered. "The Fire Witch burned it!"

Miranda closed her eyes.

The Fire Witch? The dreaded Bruja del Fuego has murdered my brother?

Miranda shook her head in frustration forgetting any semblance of humanity. She glared at Selina and snarled, "What does this have to do with getting back my blasted niece!"

"I thought..." Selina stammered, swallowing hard. "I... I thought this might make you happy. Anne is now your ward. You have claim to her— "

"— and HOW will I do that when she is hundreds of miles away?" Miranda screamed.

Selina crossed her arms tight in frustration. "I... I do not know. But if... if Mama Dgbaba will not help you maybe... maybe you— "

"— Get to the point!" Miranda snapped cutting her off.

Selina took a moment, fearful of another outburst. As her hand shook she calmly said, "If your brother is dead. If Anne were to die by the Fire Witch's hand. Shouldn't, you know, extend the lineage yourself?"

Miranda closed her eyes remembering what she had once told her lover about the family roots concerning Crystal Astrids all of whom were female.

While the family might produce basic female witches throughout the ages, an Astrid was also a witch but so much more than a simple conjurer. They were extremely rare and would not always be guaranteed to be born in every direct generation from parent to child.

While there were others in the family tree throughout the ages, Miranda had little use in finding any descendants afraid they might try to usurp her own power. She knew that power could be siphoned but never learned how to do that directly. She had only the skill to siphon off crystals. Deep down, no matter how strong she felt herself to be, she was to afraid to confront any physical beings, afraid she might fail in her task and lose her own power.

But not now.

Once I conquer this island and all its inhabitants I will seek out those others and destroy them.

Especially Lara's side of the family.

Miranda snarled remembering how Lara had been matched to Trevor in hopes of producing a powerful female child. Elizabeth had upended those plans for the time being but eventually the courtship ended once Trevor came to his senses. Miranda did not approve of the Astrid match but loathed the thought of Elizabeth and her brother being happy together.

Lara came from a long lineage, and despite not being one herself, Anne's mother was fearful of ever passing down what she thought of as a curse. Miranda knew little of Lara's brothers and sisters, their own children and the many relatives before them all. Miranda was especially concerned one might find Anne and teach her before she was able to whisk the young woman away to Barbados so that her essence could be consumed by Dge and he could walk among mortals again.

Miranda never had any children. She was unable but would never tell anyone, not even Selina. Miranda often wondered if her own mother had not spelled her womb to be barren.

She was always afraid of my power.

"Are you even able to have children?" Selina added.

Miranda lost her temper at the hardened words. She smacked Selina hard across the face, knocking the woman onto the warm, wet grass.

Selina stared up in shock. She wiped blood away from her nose and began to cry. Quickly, she stumbled up and ran away.

THE RAUCOUS MOOD inside the tavern was a little more than Anne had expected. Anne pulled her drink forward, barely keeping it from being knocked over by the drunken painted lady dancing with a burley, equally intoxicated man in ragged sailor's clothes. Anne was sure he was a pirate. She had seen a few at the only other island tavern she had been in. Anne thought fondly of her first encounter with the young woman at her side.

"Not what you expected?" Éndira turned quickly, pushing her chair back when the dancers lost their footing. The lady fell backwards and into Éndira, who put her hands up quickly and caught the woman.

"Thank you love," the woman said to her rescuer then hopped up quickly and continued her dance.

"Not really," Anne answered, her eyes still marveling at the sight. *If my father could see me now,* Anne chuckled inside. She turned and smiled at her companion. "But I am thoroughly entertained!" she squeaked happily.

A loud ruckus at the bar grabbed their attention. A fight had broken out between two men over a single bar stool. The larger of the two grabbed the piece of furniture, took it and swung hard.

It hit the side of the bar.

The portly, well endowed female owner of the establishment pulled two flintlocks from behind the counter and threatened to shoot them. Both men began to apologize then one quickly ran out the door. The woman got off one shot before he ducked out. She chased after him, screaming that he owed her money.

Anne and Éndira had hidden under their table and could not stop laughing. They were slightly intoxicated but not so much that they didn't know danger when they saw it.

Éndira peeked her head up.

The scuffle had ended.

She stood up then held out a hand. When Anne touched the other girl's palm, another shiver ran up her own spine. Anne did not know if Éndira could feel this.

Is it my ring or is it really Éndira who gives me the shivers?

When Éndira looked at her with an inquisitive, crooked smile, Anne quickly diverted her eyes.

She hasn't backed away from me, nor looked at me with apprehension. Anne wondered. *Perhaps she knows I am interested in her?*

Is she open to an invitation for more?

After a few more drinks they left the tavern and went walking on the beach. Anne wanted to put her hand in Éndira's and walk together as one. Instead, she chose to ignore her feelings, trying to concentrate on what Éndira was saying.

"If we have any problems," Éndira finished. "I am sure Lizzy can find a way to outmaneuver her."

"Who?"

Éndira stopped and raised an eyebrow. "Your aunt. Were you not listening to me?"

"No," Anne shrugged her shoulders, quickly trying to think of a way to recover. "I'm just overwhelmed by tonight," she sort of lied. Truth was, she did enjoy the evening. There was a little too much alcohol in her system. She was afraid of saying something silly. "I'm just glad we got to go out!"

"Me too," Éndira smiled then started to walk once again.

"Your eyes are really pretty... did you get them from your mother?" Anne asked, remembering that when she met Éndira's father she had noticed he had brown eyes.

"Yes. My birth mum had green eyes... at least my father told me so."

Anne stayed by her side. "Can you tell me about her?"

"She's dead," Éndira said bluntly. "I told you that."

"I know, I'm sorry." Anne cleared her throat. "I apologize for bringing that up. I know it's a hard subject," she knew from experience.

"That's okay. I really know nothing about her."

"That is a shame," Anne said softly.

Éndira looked out at the ocean waves for a moment. Anne caught a small glimmer in her friend's eye, a possible tear wanting to shed. Éndira quickly turned her head and sniffed. She finally glanced at Anne, eyes no longer doubtful.

"What about your stepmother?" Anne asked. "You said she is an Englishwoman?"

"Yes," Éndira answered happily. "I've known her all my life. As far as I am concerned, she is my real mum."

They walked for a while, enjoying the sights in silence. But still, Anne wanted to know more.

"Do you have any brothers or sisters then?"

"Yes. I have five other step siblings."

"Five?" Anne gasped.

"Yes. Five," Éndira chuckled.

"How did your father meet your stepmother?"

"Mum was accused of a crime and was being sent back to England. They could not try her in Grenada."

"Why not?"

"Hard to justify hanging a woman of the upper class without a true English trial."

Anne slightly gasped.

"My mum was accused of committing murder," Éndira continued, smirking.

"Murder?" Intrigued, Anne leaned in a little, wanting to know more.

"Her ship was captured by my father and his crew. She commanded him to take her away!" Éndira snickered.

"Commanded him? Who does that?"

"My mum apparently. He must have fallen in love with her at first sight because he whisked her away to the island, married her and well, the rest is history as they say!"

"That is so adventurous... to take a chance with a pirate instead of a chance at avoiding the gallows."

"Oh, my mum was guilty all right."

Anne's eyes widened.

The look must have humored Éndira, for the girl stopped walking and started to laugh. A sudden caw in the distance caught their attention. Éndira took Anne's hand as they walked over.

In the palm tree, two macaws were nuzzling each other and making cooing sounds.

Anne felt the warm touch of Éndira's hand in hers. The alcohol in Anne's system was making her slightly dizzy. She leaned inward, hoping her balance would be close enough to the other girl to allow some satisfaction to her feelings.

Anne felt her heart want more. She stood up on her toes while her other hand dug into Éndira's long, brown hair and pulled close. Anne quickly pressed her lips to Éndira's own.

39

———————

Anne did not have time to enjoy the kiss.

Quickly, Éndira pushed her off and stared at her, eyes wide.

"What are you doing?" Éndira asked, stunned.

"I... I thought..." Anne stammered, trying to find her words through her drunken haze. "I thought you enjoyed being with me?"

"I do." Éndira stared at her, confused. "But why did you kiss me?"

"Because..." Anne closed her eyes for a moment, feeling the tears ready to come on. This was just as it had been with her friend Sarah. So many emotions had rushed through her head those last few years. Anne had finally found the courage to tell her friend Sarah, only to have that beautiful kiss interrupted by her father. Was she destined to never have a true, intimate moment with another girl?

Perhaps my love is wrong? Is something trying to tell me my feelings for girls are... unnatural?

"Because I like you!" Anne cried out, unable to keep her feelings at bay anymore.

Éndira just stared at her with wide eyes, still shocked at what had just happened. When Éndira said nothing, Anne realized she had made a huge mistake.

Anne felt tears beginning to form. She shook her head, wanting to escape before she completely lost her composure. She dug her heels in the sand and quickly took off running.

～

Selina was irate. Miranda had always been temperamental but this time the woman had gone too far.

Never has she struck me so hard!

Selina had a rough time walking in the sand but she pressed on. She angrily kicked a coconut out of her way. It hit a loose board sticking up from a recent shipwreck.

Her mind was racing uncontrollably. She had never had clear thoughts to begin with but being with Miranda had helped her 'disorder'."

Ever since Selina was young, she had problems with her mind. She heard voices, had outbursts of anger that were uncontrollable. Imaginary friends were silly things that children conjured up for fun but Selina thought them real.

When she turned thirteen, Selina's mother threatened to have her committed to an institution for the insane.

Instead, Selina ran away.

Miranda had found her in a park huddled near a statue and crying. Selina had taken to her instantly. When Miranda touched her face, Selina remembered a rush of energy come from those soft fingertips.

"You're a witch," Miranda had said to her.

Beating back tears, Selina saw in those eyes a love she had never had. "A what?" Selina asked.

"A witch," Miranda repeated without the slightest note of accusation. She took Selina's hand in her own. "Can you feel the connection?"

Selina looked down at their entwined palms. A small rush of green energy surrounded their embrace. Fearful at first, Selina pulled back her hand and cowered.

"I'm sick," Selina cried. "Momma says I am sick in the head!"

"Do you know why witches are found out?" Miranda asked softly.

Selina shook her head no.

"Because they so often have to hide their powers; it eats them up inside."

Looking up with eager eyes, Selina wanted to know more. "But I'm sick in the head, that's what my mother said."

Miranda put up her hand. "Your mother is most likely not one of us," she said, stroking Selina's hair back gently. "Do you know of your father?"

"She never told me much about him. Only that he was Basque."

"He was probably a witch, at least in his blood. Basque witches are very powerful."

Selina perked up. "They are?"

"Yes. Many a strong lineage came from that region." Again, Miranda stroked back loose hair. "I can teach you to control your powers. If you would let me?"

Selina nodded. "Yes, I would like that."

Miranda embraced her. Selina melted into the desperately wanted comfort.

Soon, thereafter, Selina came to live with Miranda in her grand house. She became a servant and worked for a girl she had grown to love.

Eventually, the two became intimate.

Selina would do anything for the woman who saved her that night.

"I love you," Selina cried out loud, slapping her hand against her temples angrily tonight.

"Stop beating yourself up woman," Mama DgBaba snickered from behind. "You'll only give yourself a headache."

Selina whipped around, her arms swinging. Mama quickly disappeared. As Selina looked for her target, Mama appeared behind and flicked her finger. She knocked Selina down easily.

On the sand, Selina sat like a defeated child. She crossed her arms to her chest and began to pout.

"Lover's spat?" Mama mocked.

"Miranda's just upset, that's all," Selina lied. "It's not my fault."

"Of course not." Mama touched Selina's head. "We do so much for our loved ones and still they betray us."

"She didn't betray me!" Selina spat.

"She didn't?" Mama snapped her fingers. She disappeared then reappeared on a red curule chair. The bottom legs had finely carved feet in the shape of sea serpents. Mama leaned to her side. "Did she not try and cast you aside for another's love?"

Selina blinked for a second, confused. She didn't even know if Mama was actually here or if she was imagining people again.

"Miranda hated her husband."

"Not him stupid woman." Mama snapped her fingers. A sword appeared on her lap. It was a finely decorated single edged straight blade with a solid gold plated hilt. The pommel was in the shape of a brass lion, a ruby as its eye. Mama played with the tip, touching her finger on the point gently. Mama looked at her. "Do you know whose sword this is?"

"I have no bloody idea," Selina sneered.

"This is Trevor Sutton's."

"He's dead."

"I know. I picked it up off the ocean floor." Mama swished the blade around for a moment, staring at the reflection bouncing off the blade. "It is a beautiful piece of work." She slashed downward hard. "I've collected many a sword of the dead from the sea."

"Did you take him as one of your own?" Selina accused.

"What I do is my own business," Mama warned. "And not for the likes of a mortal to know." She smiled once again, a pair of teeth sharp as daggers. "This sword was presented to Miranda's brother, by the person I am talking about."

Selina gritted her teeth, angered once again. Just the thought of that woman set her brain on fire. Closing her eyes for a moment, Selina shook her head hard.

I must be imagining this conversation.

No, dear... you are not.

Selina opened her eyes and stared at the trickster. *You can read my thoughts?*

"Yes, I can. But I prefer to talk to you directly," Mama said stiffly. She threw the sword down, the blade sticking in the sand. The sword vibrated back and forth for a slight moment. "Your mind is too troubled even for me to have the patience to sift through."

Selina blinked, unsure if she should be offended by the comment.

"How deeply do you love Miranda Sutton?" Mama asked.

Selina did not need to sift through her own mind for that answer. This was one thing she had always been sure of.

"With everything I am."

Selina looked at the trickster. She should be wary of what Mama wanted, for even Selina was lucid enough to know what a potential deal with the trickster would mean.

"What are you willing to give me for that love?" Mama grinned.

"Anything," Selina said without question.

Mama stood up and snapped her fingers. The curule chair and sword sank deep into the sand, disappearing. Mama walked over to Selina and put her hand on her head. "Are you sure of Miranda's love?"

"Why would I not be?" Selina looked up, confused.

"You've tried to bring her back from her own flirtation with insanity before have you not?"

"Miranda's only angry because of what she needs! Without Anne, she will fail," Selina growled then opened her eyes wide. She quickly realized what the solution was and it was standing right in front of her. "Bring me to Anne! I shall bring her back and all will be well again!"

"Let's see if you are strong enough," Mama smiled, her purple irides gleaming with silver flecks that danced. She closed her eyes. In her palm, a small flow of purple energy passed between her skin and Selina's head.

Selina closed her eyes happily, letting the sensation penetrate her mind.

TRYING NOT to completely lose her composure, Anne moved briskly over the sandy path. People idly sauntered by her, unaware of anything but themselves and their tasks at hand. Head down, Anne kept up her pace and tried to ignore the world around her. As she turned the corner near a dilapidated trading shack, she saw a group of seedy men arguing with one another. Anne quickened her pace, not wanting to draw their unwanted attention.

The hell with them.

In fact, to hell with this whole damn world!

I am such a fool. That is what kept mulling around in her head. *Am I too young to understand love?*

She remembered her friend Sarah Winters once again. She remembered that kiss they had shared.

That wonderful kiss.

Would anything have transpired if I had stayed where I belonged? Should I have remained in London? Should I have let that infernal governess Miss Barton and Sarah's mom make me a match?

But another lingering question floated around in her mind.

Would I have remained loyal to a husband; would I have grown to love him and my life with children and parties to attend? My life would have been busy with grand things, a comfortable life without a care in the world.

Who was she kidding?

She would have been as miserable as she was right now!

Anne shook her head, now angry.

How she longed for her mother and father right now. How she longed for her mother's arms, ones that held her tight and told her all would be okay.

Mentally exhausted, Anne walked up the hill towards one of the many shacks that littered the island. She laughed at the irony. Back home in London she would be a polished lady of society, but here on Frigate Island, like these shacks, she was a dilapidated mess with a foundation ready to crack.

"I should have never kissed her," Anne's voice cracked as she argued with herself. "I should have... talked to her first..."

She looked at me in horror. Like I had the plague or something.

Why did I... why didn't I just wait?

What is wrong with me?

Anne snarled, anger surfacing hard. *I drank too much. I let my heart overtake my senses! I presumed just like Finlay did with me.*

Her feet were tired, her boots hot. She made her way to the back of the structure, turned her body, leaned against the crooked wood and let her legs collapse. Only then, in the privacy of her own world, did she allow her emotions to run free. She pushed loose hair away from her eyes as she cupped her face in her hands. Anne had told herself she would only cry for a few minutes. She would then gather herself and decide what to do next.

A call from the distance alarmed her.

Éndira was trying to find her.

Anne quickly got to her feet and feverishly rubbed her eyes. She did not want the other girl to see her like this. As the voice got closer, Anne darted over to a nearby warehouse and ducked into a row of ferns. The bright leaves were high enough to conceal her body and hide her from the green eyes that made her heart melt.

After a while, the soft voice seemed to give up. Anne knew that the way the voice cracked, Éndira must also be upset.

Anne did not know if she could only be friends with Éndira after this whole debacle. She had made a mistake and had her love trampled.

Never again would she allow herself to be so stupid.

With new vigor, Anne proudly got to her feet, rubbed her eyes and made her way out of the bushes. Anne realized in this moment, that she needed to make a hard decision. Sailing around with Elizabeth sounded fun initially but ever since the Fire Witch killed Anne's father, she knew in her heart only she could stop the bruja.

I must find a way to do this!

This is my only mission now!

Anne thought hard about what she might do. *Will I have to leave the woman I have come to love as a mentor and friend?*

Even Éndira?

God help me, I think I will miss her the most!

Anne was about to leave when she heard another familiar voice. It was coming from within the warehouse. Anne was standing close enough to the open window to hear but did not want to intrude on the conversation. Elizabeth was inside speaking with some of her men.

"Polu is on his way with the other load ma'am," a deep voice said.

Anne recognized the voice to be that of the coxswain of the ship. He was an older, sturdy fellow whom she occasionally talked to.

"Good," Elizabeth said. "And be careful not to confuse the crates when he gets here. I'm returning to the ship. Call on me when everything is finished.

"Yes, ma'am."

Anne started to make her way out of the ferns. Perhaps, Anne thought, she could ask Elizabeth for a moment of her time. They could talk in one of the local taverns and discuss her future or lack of one.

She felt she had much to discuss.

Anne stopped abruptly when she heard the sound of the warehouse door open hard then a rustle of bodies resisting each other. She froze as the door slammed roughly behind.

"Don't shove me you grand ape!" snapped a new voice as his feet shuffled across the wood floor.

The voice was gravelly. Anne seemed to remember it but could not bring up the face to whom it belonged.

Anne did not know if she should continue to eavesdrop. She only wanted to know if Elizabeth was leaving. She did not need to pry into the woman's business. Anne decided she would wait outside the main warehouse doors instead.

The sudden cocking of a flintlock made Anne freeze in place. She pushed herself against the side of the open window and slid her hand over the grip of her cutlass. She then pulled the steel slightly upwards, ready to fight.

Anne tried to peek in but she could not get a good view. If Elizabeth was in danger should she go in? What could Anne possibly do against a pistol? How many men were in there? How many were armed with flintlocks *and* swords?

And can I even do anything with my ring?

Now she wished Éndira was here.

Should I go and try and find her?

Anne touched her ring and wondered if she could control the powers that she had barely begun to understand.

"Piece of trash told me he needed to talk to you Captain Spencer." Anne recognized this other voice belonging to Lieutenant Hicks. "Says he knows something only you can help him with?"

"What could that possibly be Jackson?" Elizabeth's voice had a hint of sarcasm embedded in the tone.

Jackson?

Anne remembered him and how he stared at her with that smile that showed his crooked, yellow teeth. The horrid little man had grabbed her arm as a threat. Elizabeth had him whipped as punishment.

Jackson reminded Anne of her Uncle Randal and how he tried to ravish her the night she fled to Elizabeth's ship.

I stopped him, Anne thought, touching her ring and feeling heat coming from the stones. *I can stop this man from hurting my friends.*

Anne could hear more footsteps enter as the door opened and closed. She held her ring tight and concentrated. The only question now was, how to control herself enough to not hurt the innocent ones.

"I want a cut of this," Jackson snarled.

"Cut of what?" Elizabeth asked dryly.

"Of this," Jackson continued. "I know the lot going to the prize court is light. You're siphoning off the top for yourself. You and your great ape here."

A shuffle of feet suggested a one-sided fight, followed by Elizabeth yelling at Lieutenant Hicks to stop when a body hit the ground.

Elizabeth's first officer must have hit Jackson hard. He was a beast of a man, and Jackson was a scrawny toad.

Just thinking of the toad made Anne shiver.

"I think you are mistaken Jackson," Elizabeth said with a sniff. "And this business I am conducting here is no concern of yours. I suggest you leave quietly and let me forget that you just threatened me, which I might remind you, is an act punishable by the articles of war, ending with you hanging from my yardarm."

There was a small laugh from the man.

"Oh, you are not going to 'ang me for treason lass. I know too much. You think you are so smart skimming off the top, like the purser does..."

always two percent for 'im?" Jackson snorted. "Makes one a rich man it does!"

There was cold silence in the room as Anne held her cutlass close. She could not believe what she just heard. Elizabeth was smuggling goods away from the prize court? Could all that Jackson just accused her of be true?

Is Miss Elizabeth really a thief?

"But you're a woman," Jackson continued. "And women do not posses the same aptitude as men, as much as you would like to fool this crew into believing. 'ow you got this commission is beyond me, but I'm guessing it 'ad something to do with your skills between the sheets?"

Anne forgot her thoughts of theft for a second and focused in only on that insult. How dare that man accuse Elizabeth of sleeping her way into her position!

My father said Miss Elizabeth was skilled but never got the chance because of her sex and lack of patronage. She had to buy her commission, which many in the Royal Navy have to do to advance.

How dare this man accuse her of such a thing!

"What is it that you want?" Elizabeth said, her voice low and serious.

You are not going to give in to him? Anne thought, knowing such a thing would haunt this proud woman forever. *Surely something else can be done?*

"I want a 'eavy purse and a written release from your service and our blasted queen!"

"And if I give this to you?" Elizabeth warned, keeping her voice calm. "You will remain quiet?"

Another pause with nothing spoken. Anne wished she could see Jackson's face.

Is he smiling?

Acting like he has won?

"Per 'haps," Jackson finally answered, most likely with a grin etched on his pockmarked face.

Anne shook her head. Jackson would not give Elizabeth a straight answer.

"You are right Jackson," Elizabeth countered. "You will not be hanging from my yardarm."

Anne heard the man laugh then start to speak again before a loud blast of a flintlock silenced him. Anne's heart jumped as she stumbled back, listening to sounds of choking on blood and small whimpers.

Anne did not realize she had also let out a small squeal. The sound was loud enough for the other eyes in the room to look through the window opening straight at her.

Captain Elizabeth Spencer was the one who held the smoking flintlock.

Still yet, the biggest shock to Anne's heart, beautiful green eyes that made her heart melt.

Éndira.

"Oh shite," was all the girl could say, looking straight Anne's way.

PART IV

40

Anne didn't even have a chance to run. Her clumsy footing caught on the terrain, as she tripped and fell face first into the sand. She was quickly lifted up by the coxswain and forcefully brought into the warehouse. He pushed her in and slammed the door behind. He handed Lieutenant Hicks Anne's newly acquired sword.

Anne stared at the body on the sand covered wooden warehouse floor. A pool of blood started to soak into the wood and congeal with the granules, slowly covering the minuscule crystals within. Anne closed her eyes and started to play with her ring. She could feel the crystals begin to record Jackson's death.

As Éndira stepped forward, Anne could feel the girl's presence walking on the sand. Anne lifted her hand as a warning. She opened her eyes, watching the way Éndira backed up, frightened.

"Bloody pirate," Anne muttered, eyeing the girl she had grown to love.

Before Anne had a chance to try and summon the power within her ring, her arm was locked behind her back. "Take her ring off," Elizabeth ordered Éndira. When the girl hesitated, the tone got louder. "NOW!"

Hesitantly, Éndira took Anne's hand. She would not look into Anne's eyes. Slowly, she removed the ring.

"Hand it to me," Elizabeth instructed.

Éndira did as she was told. The ring was given over and secured in the older woman's pocket; only then did Éndira release Anne's arm.

Anne jumped back near a load of crates and kept her distance in the shadows.

"I am not stealing this from you," Elizabeth tried to reassure her. "I need you to remain calm so you will not do anything rash." She turned to her men and pointed to the dead body. "Get him out of here."

"Should we throw 'im in the 'arbor?" The coxswain asked.

Elizabeth's eyes bored into him. Anne was sure, by the look the older woman had just given, Elizabeth was concerned about how to handle this situation.

I've just seen her murder a man! Is she going to shoot me with her flintlock next?

Am I next to die?

"Be discrete," Elizabeth said softly.

"Yes ma'am," the coxswain said.

Lieutenant Hicks stepped forward with a load of canvas. As the coxswain lay out the sail, Lieutenant Hicks picked up Jackson's lifeless body and placed the load gently down. Next was an added piece of loose metal to be used as ballast. They both hurriedly wrapped the body in rope. Quickly, they exited the warehouse with their somber package.

All that were left in the room were Elizabeth, Éndira and a very distressed Anne.

Éndira tried to approach Anne once again. Anne shook her head no and braced herself with her fists; Éndira stopped and stood still.

Anne scanned her surroundings. She looked around to see if any other windows were open. The one she had witnessed the murder through had been shut.

Anne felt the crates with her hands, looking for anything to use as a weapon. She put her fingertips on a small crack and touched a broken piece of wood. Anne tried not to make noise but there was a small snap as the wood came off. She held the weapon in both hands and waited.

"Anne," Elizabeth said gently. "We need to talk."

"About what? Theft? Murder?" Anne was hostile, her voice loud. *Is Miss Elizabeth trying to trick me with fake compassion?*

"If you will calm yourself and come out of the shadows, I can explain myself."

"Anne— please?" Éndira was upset, her voice cracking under the strain. "Just hear her out!" she insisted.

Suddenly, Anne leapt out of the dark with the wood weapon held high above her head. She slashed down at Elizabeth who easily jumped back, pulled her cutlass and caught the next blow. When Anne swung again, Elizabeth deflected then stepped in with a lower sweep and knocked Anne off her feet.

Anne fell ungracefully on her rump.

"You need to settle down!" Elizabeth snapped, now angered.

Anne pulled herself up onto her elbows. In front of her was the pool of blood left by Jackson's body.

She looked up with tearful eyes.

"Are you going to kill me too?" Anne hesitantly asked.

"No," Éndira blurted out. When she did not hear a confirmation from the older woman, she snapped her head towards Elizabeth for an answer.

Elizabeth shook her head for a moment as if she had actually been contemplating the idea. "No Anne, I would never!" She tossed her cutlass down and started to pace. After awhile, she threw her hands up and yelled at Éndira. "I told you to keep her occupied!"

As Éndira tried to explain what happened, Anne looked again towards the door. She slowly got to her feet.

Elizabeth must have anticipated her steps, for she positioned herself in front of the door. She knelt down, picked up her thrown cutlass and sheathed the weapon. "I did not intend for you to discover my extra-curricular activities."

"That is why we are here?" Anne accused. "So you can sell excess cargo?"

"The cargo in this warehouse was already agreed upon by the Admiralty as payment for the help of certain privateers."

"Don't you mean pirates?"

"Being called a privateer or a pirate all depends on a letter of marque," Elizabeth calmly explained once again. "The men in this camp have allied themselves against the Spanish... and allies need incentives to stay allies."

"So you just skim some off the top?"

"The cost of delivery."

Anne eyed Éndira. "And what about you?"

"Éndira is here as a liaison for her father," Elizabeth interrupted.

"So you did not come along to help protect me then?" Anne accused.

Éndira didn't give an answer. She looked at Elizabeth instead.

Annoyed, Anne hardened her tone. "Are you unable to answer? Or do you always take your cues from her?"

"No!" Éndira snapped back. "I was supposed to come along regardless. But, yes— I also wanted to protect you."

"Why?"

"I..." Éndira stammered, then looked at Anne with affection. "I've grown fond of you."

"I will make sure I pay you for your services when I go back to London," Anne said scornfully, no longer interested in Éndira's place in her heart.

Those words peaked Elizabeth's attention. "You cannot go back to London by yourself Anne. Your aunt will find you and take you into her custody by force of the courts."

"I'm safer with my Aunt Miranda than with the two of you!"

Silence sat between them for a long moment, each one in the room staring at the other. Anne shook her head, trying not to panic. She rubbed her shoulder with her arm, wishing she had her ring to protect her. Anne had grown to love them both as family. Could she strike them down if given the chance?

Anne did not know if she had that in her.

"What do we do now?" Anne asked, deflated, afraid of her own question.

Quickly, Éndira put up her hand in the universal sign of silence to them all. She began to focus in on the wall behind Anne.

"What is it?" Elizabeth turned and whispered.

"Not sure," Éndira said, trying to look closer.

Elizabeth pulled her cutlass out half way as Éndira walked over to the corner. Éndira put her hands up and moved around, feeling with her sixth sense. As she touched the wooden slats, her eyes diverted quickly to her right.

Suddenly, a body mimicking that wood appeared, grabbing Éndira by the neck and tossing her clear across the room. The form shifted into the body of a naked woman, who dashed across the room and grabbed Anne. She placed a knife to the young woman's throat.

"Move and I will slit you from ear to ear," the intruder threatened.

Anne did not know what to do. She calmly relaxed her body as best she could. Something familiar about the voice stirred Anne's memories. She could not see who was holding her from behind, but Anne suspected she would soon find out.

"Drop your weapons!" The woman yelled at Elizabeth.

Elizabeth did as she was told, dropping the steel and spent flintlock to the floor. She then looked towards Éndira. The girl was dazed as she lifted herself up onto her arms and lay there, stunned.

"Are you all right?" Elizabeth asked, concerned.

Éndira nodded. "I'll be fine."

"Stay on the floor witch," the intruder warned.

Éndira nodded her head once again and remained where she was.

Anne finally recognized the voice.

"Miss Barton?" Anne hesitantly asked.

"Oh how I have missed you Anne," Selina Barton whispered in her ear.

"What do you want?" Anne screeched, trying to pull away.

"Miranda says you have been naughty. I've come to bring you back to her. I've been counting the days 'till we finally feed you to Dge."

Anne inhaled sharply. "How do you know my aunt?" Anne demanded. She had no idea what her infernal governess was talking about.

"All those days babysitting you, you little brat," Selina sneered. "I was put there... to watch you. To wait until the time came to force you to go to Barbados... one way or another!"

"Force me?" Anne finally understood what was happening. Miss Barton somehow caused her mother's death. "You killed my mother?"

Anne tried to squirm her way out of Selina's grip but the older woman was too strong.

"She just needed a push. Who knew that silly crystal piece you created would do the trick."

"Let me GO! You hag!" Anne screamed, her anger coming to the surface. "I'll kill you!"

While they verbally sparred with one another, Elizabeth had slowly circled them. Selina hissed, pulling Anne back tighter within her grip. "Don't even try Elizabeth."

"If you kill Anne," Elizabeth said calmly. "Miranda will never forgive you. What will you do then Selina?"

Selina? That is her first name?

And how does Miss Elizabeth know this woman? Surely she only met her at my mother's funeral?

"I'll bring her back," Selina cooed.

"You don't have that kind of power," Elizabeth taunted. "And there is no way I am going to let you out of here with Anne."

They slowly circled each other like animals stalking in the jungle. Selina pulled Anne backwards towards the wall.

"I'm not planning on exiting though the front door Elizabeth," Selina said confidently.

"Lizzy!" Éndira yelled loudly from behind. "There is a mirror right behind them!"

Before Elizabeth could react, Selina touched the wall. A full length mirror materialized.

"No!" Éndira yelled as she jumped to her feet and ran forward. "Anne, fight her!"

Anne did not know why, but she felt herself want to give in. She let her body go limp as Selina pulled them both into the mirror. Before they disappeared, Selina let out a blood curdling scream, sending a shock wave through the small island. Éndira and Elizabeth grabbed their ears as the mirror exploded and violently shattered the wood sending splinters everywhere.

When the shock subsided, Éndira touched Elizabeth's arm, frightened.

"She's gone," Éndira cried in disbelief. "Anne's gone!"

ANNE FELL through the mirror and landed on her knees. The jarring, upended travel made her retch. She touched her mouth and wiped away the bile. When she looked up, her aunt was staring down at her, surprised.

"Welcome home Anne," she greeted the young woman with a look of shock and pure joy mixed in her crooked smile. "You've finally decided to return?"

Anne glanced around at her surroundings. She had landed in the portrait room back at the plantation. She looked back at the mirror. There was another low rumble, followed by a peculiar sound like rushing water. The glass surface vibrated as Selina Barton's naked body stepped through and immediately stretched her arms as if she had been traveling for hours. She giggled to herself as she looked down at Anne.

"Not feeling well deary?" Selina mocked.

"Go to hell you murderess!" Anne snarled as she wiped her mouth once again. When she went to try and hit Selina, the woman kicked forward, knocking Anne down.

"Come now!" Selina rolled her eyes then pulled Anne up roughly to her feet by her collar. "We have much to do!"

"Let go of me you hag!" Anne pulled her arm away from the woman and stood up straight on her own. "I will KILL YOU!"

Selina grabbed Anne's arm tight. When Selina finally looked at her lover, Miranda was still smiling from ear to ear.

"You've brought her back to me?" Miranda said happily.

"I have my love," Selina said, her own smile wide with anticipation. Selina threw Anne roughly to the floor. She opened her arms as Miranda walked over.

Anne watched, confused, as the two women began to kiss each other passionately. *Not only does Miss Barton know my aunt... but are they also... lovers?*

Anne sat on the floor, dumbfounded. Her body was frozen in fear and uncertainty. When the two women released from their display of devotion to one another, Anne felt her anger surface once again.

"Thank you my love." Miranda stroked Selina's hair out of her eyes. The warm touch seemed to soothe the other woman. "I should have never doubted your love for me."

"I would do anything for you," Selina assured.

Miranda looked at her, eyes content. "I know."

Anne had enough. She glared at the two of them, wanting to throw up once again. "You two are together? It figures. You are both made for each other. Rotten hearts to the core!"

Selina's eyes hardened. She bent her arm back to slap Anne but Miranda stepped in and stopped her.

"Not now dear," Miranda chastised in a soft voice. "It would be unwise to damage our gift."

"Of course," Selina smiled then giggled. "Do you think he will be happy with what we give?"

"I think he will be most pleased."

No longer feeling sick, Anne steadied herself and glared at her aunt. "What are you going to do with me?" Anne was determined not to sound as scared as she was.

"So many questions!" Selina cooed as she bent down and tried to stroke Anne's hair.

Anne snapped her head away. She tightened her fist daring the other woman to touch her once again.

This only made Selina laugh harder. Her tone was wicked and slightly deranged. The way her former governess was acting, Anne realized she had put on quite the show back in London.

The woman was crazier than a loon.

"Leave her alone," Miranda ordered.

"Fine," Selina pouted as she crossed her hands across her chest like a toddler.

"Why don't you go find Zara and have her make you a cocktail?"

Selina perked up. Her naked body quickly darted out of the room, leaving Anne alone with her aunt.

There was silence as the two family members studied each other. Anne put her hand up and pointed at her aunt. Only when the older one laughed did Anne remember her ring was gone. The ring that Elizabeth wanted removed, and her traitorous friend Éndira delivered.

"Did you lose your ring?" Miranda said, her voice dripping with sarcasm.

"It was stolen," Anne confessed, ashamed.

"Pity. I would have liked to have kept the heirloom even if it wasn't tuned to my body," Miranda sighed. "It doesn't matter anyway Anne. Even if you had your ring, you would still be— powerless."

"I was able to deflect your husband," Anne growled.

"Yes, you were. And by the way, nice work on that piece of magic. You are 'somewhat' gifted. It takes a long time to learn how to put someone into a catatonic state," Miranda smirked. "But I decided to further his condition."

Anne knew by the sly tone exactly what that meant. Miranda had finally decided to do away with her husband. Not that Anne really cared, especially after what Uncle Randal tried to do.

"You never did allow me to finish teaching you about your lineage." Miranda turned to the portraits and admired them from afar. "They all had particular gifts. This one for instance... your great, great, great Cousin Madge."

Anne followed the finger to a portrait of a portly woman, aged around fifty with a dead smile. Her hair was a familiar golden color, her hands folded as if she were praying. The ring on her finger was similar to Anne's but held an amethyst crystal instead. Anne did not have time to wonder about the other women of her lineage nor who might be their descendants.

"Cousin Madge was able to make people's grief subside with just a touch of her hand."

"Why does it matter anymore?" Anne snarled.

"My dear..." Miranda cocked her head. "Everything matters." When Anne did not respond, her aunt continued her lecture. "You do not seem to grasp the importance of what we are my dear girl."

"Yes I do. We are Crystal Astrids."

Miranda blinked, surprised at the response. She shook her head for a moment and tried to understand the correct answer. "Who told you that?"

"Miss Elizabeth."

Miranda's lip twisted slightly. "That horrid woman. I'm happy you have been rid of her company."

"Why? So you can kill me instead of her?"

Miranda just glared at her, face hard. Anne realized that her aunt did not really care.

Anne wanted to scream that her friends would come for her and try to save her. But how would that even be possible? They were hundreds of miles away. Unless they could travel by mirror? But why would they bother? Anne had just seen one of them commit murder. *Miss Elizabeth is probably happy I have gone away and am no longer her problem.*

"The Dago would have probably killed you in your sleep anyway," Miranda said with a smirk. "Pirates are like that."

"Don't call her that!" Anne spat as she felt her muscles tense. She hated the derogatory term used for anyone with Spanish blood.

Miranda raised an eyebrow. "Did I hit a nerve? Zara told me you had a little... friend."

Anne crossed her arms and remained defensive. She was not going to allow her aunt to call her friend names.

"Really my dear," Miranda taunted. "You could do better than her."

Anne shifted uncomfortably. She did not know what her aunt meant by the comment.

"I know you are partial to girls Anne," Miranda added.

"I— I do not know what you heard," Anne protested. "She is nothing but a friend."

"Like your friend Sarah?"

Anne gasped.

Miranda looked at the mirror. Only then, did Anne realize her aunt had also travelled to London to— *spy on me?*

"You... you saw me... in... in London?"

"Yes. I must say, I really did enjoy that kiss. What a... delicious display of passion," Miranda commented, licking her lips. "Well, until your father burnt down your workroom. He always did have a temper that boy."

The mirror in my workroom? Has my aunt been spying on me this whole time?

"How long?" Anne sputtered, now ashamed. "How long have you been watching me?"

"Long enough," Miranda said proudly. "You were a precocious child. Adventurous. Like your father. Of course, nothing like your mother. If she would have had her way with you, you would have never come into your own."

What is she saying? Come into my own? That I would have never made my way to Barbados if my mother had her way?

But my mother was sick.

I didn't have her to guide me when she got—

Anne suddenly felt nauseous. She dropped to her knees and threw up once again.

My mother's sickness... my... my aunt caused it?

"How?... how could you?" Anne looked up at her aunt with tears freely flowing down her cheeks. "You made my mother sick on purpose?"

"She would have never let you go otherwise." Miranda watched her niece, alone and broken. "Some of us are destined for greater things in this life, and beyond. But to achieve that greatness, others must be sacrificed as canon fodder. All good soldiers know this."

"So, that is all I am to you?" Anne whispered, defeated. "Nothing more than cattle for the slaughter?"

"It is all you are good to me for my dear."

41

———

Elizabeth was out of breath. She had already searched three shacks but none held a mirror of any kind. She sprinted up to another dilapidated dwelling and tried to open the door.

No luck.

It was locked.

Angrily, she kicked at the wood three times until it gave way. The door slammed open as she bolted in.

Quickly scanning the room, Elizabeth saw a large mirror, broken. There were shards of glass on the floor. Her feet crunched over the broken pieces. Elizabeth realized this is what it would be like all over the island.

That cursed Selina broke all the mirrors with her magic before disappearing with Anne! Elizabeth thought angrily.

"Dammit!" She yelled loudly. She exited the building and put her palms to her face. What the hell was she going to do now? Her ship would never make the trip to Barbados in time. They were at least three days away, even if the winds were good.

She sat on the porch and lowered her head. Elizabeth could not understand why Miranda would want to hurt Anne. Miranda had always been eager for more than her station in life but to kill her own niece to achieve that goal?

Frantic footsteps charged over the hill. Éndira fell to her knees next to Elizabeth. She tried to catch her breath. "Every... everything... is broken... she broke— "

"— All of them," Elizabeth finished for her, solemnly aware that without a solid mirror there was no way they could save Anne.

Éndira sat down; her breath labored. She wiped sweat off her forehead and turned.

"Can you reform any of these mirrors from the broken glass?" Elizabeth asked as she gestured to the entry way behind them still hopeful.

Éndira shook her head. "I already tried. That witch must have spelled them all somehow."

Elizabeth sighed, unsure of the next step to take. She waited for Éndira to go into the shack and double check. After a moment, she stepped back out distressed. "What do we do now?"

I have no idea, Elizabeth thought, looking at the young woman.

While Éndira stated the obvious about the distance they were from the island, Elizabeth closed her eyes.

"What do we DO?" Éndira snapped.

"I'm thinking," Elizabeth answered in a calm voice.

Éndira pulled her legs up to her chest and wrapped her arms around them. She remained quiet as she waited.

Elizabeth knew of only one option. One she did not want to take. *What price will she ask?*

If I do this, there is no going back.

Elizabeth opened her eyes and looked at her young friend. Éndira's face was filled with worry.

What else can I do?

Éndira is so frightened.

Anne must be so frightened.

"I know what to do," Elizabeth said as she got to her feet. She reached out her hand, helping the other one up. "Let's go."

Éndira quickly followed as Elizabeth sprinted towards the beach.

~

ÉNDIRA WATCHED CAREFULLY as Elizabeth pulled a throwing knife from her boot. Elizabeth put the blade to her own palm then quickly cut her skin.

"What are you doing?" Éndira widened her eyes as the blood flowed.

"Shhh," Elizabeth cut her off. She turned and walked to the shore. Slowly she bent down and let blood drip into the water.

"I summon you Mama Dgbaba," Elizabeth said. "I am your humble servant. I ask for your help in my time of need."

"Mama?" Éndira whispered to herself.

"Well, well... well," a deep voice said from behind.

Éndira and Elizabeth quickly turned. The trickster sat in a grand chair with a plush velvet cushion. Intricate gold carvings of snakes and women dancing adorned the red wood. She was focused on the easel in front, as she painted the dress of a scantily clad woman being seduced by a creature, half man, half demon. His hand was on her waist, his other stroking her long black hair.

Éndira widened her eyes. The woman in the painting looked just like Elizabeth.

Mama dipped her brush on her paint palette. "I told you that you would need my help Elizabeth Spencer!" she turned and smiled.

When Mama smiled directly at Éndira, Elizabeth stepped in front of the girl as protection.

"We need to get to Barbados," Elizabeth said forcefully.

"Hmm..." Mama went back to her painting. "Do you like this? I've been working on it for days now. My brother Dge. I have not seen him in over a century."

"Why have you painted her in such a— lewd way?" Éndira asked, lifting a hand.

Mama turned and grinned. "You cannot expect me to paint a seventeen year old girl like this?"

Elizabeth leapt forward with fire in her eyes. "What do you know about Anne's involvement in this?"

"I know that she is very fond of you," Mama pointed to Elizabeth. "But she feels betrayed." Mama quickly changed her focus, pointing at Éndira this time. "Especially by... you."

"We need to get to Barbados quickly," Éndira pleaded as she moved forward. "I need to help her."

Elizabeth put her hand up and stopped the young woman. Pleading would fall on deaf ears unless done right. They both needed to know what was happening.

"Do you know exactly what they are planning to do with Anne?" Elizabeth asked once again, this time her voice thick with anger.

"With Anne?" Mama turned back to her painting. She put the tip of her brush on her lips and toyed with it for a moment. "My guess is something fun!" She giggled, looking at them with an amused expression.

"Help us, God dammit!" Éndira cried out.

Mama just laughed. She lifted herself out of her chair, put down her palette and snapped her fingers. Her painting, furniture and palette disappeared.

She slowly walked up to Éndira.

"What are you planning on giving me?" Mama hissed at the younger woman.

"Stay away from her!" Elizabeth instinctively stepped in front of Éndira once again. She needed to protect her. "This is my calling!"

"I don't want anything from you," Mama growled. "You've tired me in the past."

"I did what I had to do."

"You broke our deal!" Mama yelled, her purple irises glowing sharply.

"And you got your revenge." Elizabeth was unshaken. "This is between you and me."

"What about you... Eréndira de la Cruz?" The words dripped off Mama's tongue like a smooth song. "What are you willing to give me to help your friend?"

Éndira was pushed back by Elizabeth's hands before she could say a single word.

"No," Elizabeth bit hard, her hand in the trickster's face. "She will not partake in this deal."

"Then I have nothing to help you with my dear," Mama Dgbaba purred.

When Éndira tried to step forward again, Elizabeth held her back.

"No!" Éndira snapped at the older woman. "I will give her what she wants!"

Elizabeth hardened her eyes as she took Éndira by the shoulders. "You have no idea what powers this monster has Eréndira. You are too young to—"

"— Don't tell me what to do!" Éndira cut in firmly. "You are not my mother!" Éndira ignored the sudden laughter coming from Mama.

Mama pointed her finger at Elizabeth as she continued to cackle.

"I have been in the West Indies longer than you Lizzy," Éndira snarled. "I have seen things that would make your skin crawl!"

Elizabeth did not respond. She would not be able to talk Éndira down.

The young woman was angry, irrational— giving in to fear. She was past the point of reason.

Elizabeth had only one other card to play.

"I invoke my right to colloquy." Elizabeth turned to Mama and made the demand.

The request took Mama by surprise. She stood for a quiet moment and stared at Elizabeth, her eyebrow cocked in amusement. Slowly, an evil, nefarious smile appeared. "This is your petition Elizabeth Spencer?"

"That is my petition."

"Wait?... what?" Éndira shook her head, confused.

Mama pulled a seed out of thin air and threw it into the sand. The granules began to move, as a large piece of wood appeared out of the ground. A mirror then rippled into place. The form shaped into a proper full length mirror, intricately carved with the same type of snakes and women that were on Mama's chair.

"The place you seek is Barbados?" Mama said rhetorically. She gently touched the surface of the mirror. The image turned from reflection to a beach in another part of the world.

The island of Barbados.

"Hold onto my hand so we do not get separated," Elizabeth instructed Éndira.

The younger woman did as she was told.

Mama quickly put up her own to warn.

"Do not forget your petition Elizabeth Spencer," Mama threatened. "After you help your friend, you *will* be held accountable for your betrayal."

"Yes, I understand," Elizabeth said, holding Éndira's hand tight.

As they walked through the mirror together, Mama started to laugh once again.

"YOU BROKE A DEAL WITH MAMA DGBABA?" Éndira screeched as she kept pace next to Elizabeth while they sprinted on the beach. Their boots were heavy in the sand.

"I did," Elizabeth answered between breaths.

"Why would you do something like that?"

Elizabeth darted around a patch of sea grass and took a slight hop. She tried not to get her feet stuck and trip. Éndira was able to follow with ease. The young woman was more agile.

"What is... a... colloquy?" Éndira hesitantly asked.

Elizabeth took in deep breaths as she ran harder. "A conference between... a judge and defendant."

"A defendant? You?" Éndira looked at her, shocked. "Why? What did you do?"

"I did something when I was younger, something... foolish." Elizabeth maneuvered over a root sticking up high as they made their way up a hill and parallel to the beach. "When I broke our deal I was never... tried for it."

"Tried? Like in a court?" Éndira darted forward and tried to keep up both literally and figuratively. "Where does this happen?"

"In a spirits court I assume."

Éndira shook her head. "Mama is not a spirit, she is a deity."

"Spirit, deity..." Elizabeth was winded. She stopped to catch her breath. She bent over, hands on her legs and looked up at the younger one. "What is the difference?"

"There is a big difference." Éndira stopped and followed the same posture. "There are a vast number of spirits that live and play in the ocean and islands but there are deities that rule over them and those territories."

"Do you know where?"

"Yes," Éndira answered. "Mama rules the western part of the Greater Antilles. She shares that alliance with her sister Aloi who rules the eastern." Éndira looked worried. "You never cross a sea deity. What did you do? What did you break?"

"I promised her something that in the end I was unable to give her."

"What was so valuable that you would do such a thing?"

Elizabeth closed her eyes for a moment, remembering. She shook her head then quickly struck off again on their mission, unable to tell the young woman the real truth.

Both women ran over a hill, leaving behind the sand for a more rocky surface. Finally, they would be able to have a smoother run to the plantation.

"Who rules the Lesser Antilles?" Elizabeth asked as she skipped over another root. She already knew the answers but would never tell Éndira.

"Gang Gang Sara rules the Windward Islands but she has somewhat 'disappeared'. Her sister Galiba rules the Leeward Antilles. She is sort of a caretaker of both territories. It is rumored that Gang Gang Sara is sick, or that something has sapped her will to exist."

Elizabeth put out her hand quickly and stopped Éndira in her tracks. Their feet skidded hard.

"Do you feel it?" Elizabeth asked, concerned.

"Yes." Éndira walked forward and scanned the horizon. "I smell something— "

"— Rotten."

Elizabeth pointed to the side. They walked over and crouched down behind a small dune. Silently, they listened.

There were no sounds other than the background island noise. Behind them in the distance, the ocean waves crested, broke on the sand and then quickly retreated to continue the cycle. The crickets hummed their lullaby, the macaws belted loud calls to one another.

Suddenly, a group of creatures jumped up and surrounded them.

"Jumbees!" Éndira yelled. She turned and kicked one before he could jump her. Quickly, she pulled her cutlass from her side and swung hard, lopping the creature's head right off its body.

Behind her, Elizabeth had already pulled her weapons and slashed at her attacker. She stabbed it in the heart, but nothing happened.

"The head!" Éndira shouted. "It is the only way to kill them."

"Where the hell did these things come from?" Elizabeth yelped as she jumped away from a decayed hand. She took a quick glance at the creature trying to attack her.

Had it once been human?

The man, at least she thought he might have once been a man, had no skin on his face. The skull was all that could be seen. His empty sockets burned red. The creatures were focused on their targets.

Éndira yelled, swiftly thrusting her saber forward and lopping the head off another. She turned and tried to take a quick count of the attackers.

There were at least ten, and more coming.

"There are too many of them!" Éndira cried. "We have to run!"

"You run! I will hold them off!"

"No!" Éndira blinked, confused. "What are you, insane?"

"You have to help Anne!" Elizabeth kicked at another, turned and cut the head off an attacker that tried to lunge from behind. "You are the only one who can do anything to help fight Miranda." Elizabeth managed to pull Anne's ring out of her pocket before twisting downwards, slashing at another quickly. She tossed the ring to Éndira, who caught it easily.

"Make sure to give that to Anne," Elizabeth yelled through labored breaths.

Éndira stopped for a moment, dumbstruck. She held the ring in her palm and looked at the woman with terror in her eyes.

"But? I need your help!"

"You will do fine Éndira." Elizabeth ducked and cut the legs off another. "I have faith in you," she smiled. "I always have."

Éndira had sudden tears in her eyes. Was it because of the words that Elizabeth had just said, or the prospect of losing her forever?

"RUN!" Elizabeth commanded.

Éndira pushed down the rocky path. As she looked back, all she could see were the jumbees as they overwhelmed Elizabeth. The woman screamed as they jumped on top.

Éndira cried out.

The jumbees had caught their prey.

42

The mindless jumbees knew only one thing, that the master that summoned them wanted the body they now carried. The jumbees' decayed, bony fingers dug tightly into Elizabeth's skin. She struggled hard and tried to break free.

Eventually, her strength gave out.

Elizabeth's exhausted body marched along with the creatures until her pace turned into a slog. The jumbees carried her for the last quarter of a mile, dragging her legs and boots over the sharp, rocky terrain. Elizabeth could feel blood drip down her skin. Silently, she wondered if these creatures would turn vicious the more her blood dripped.

So far, they simply ignored her presence.

Elizabeth lifted her head and saw the smoke from the plantation boiling house. Her legs would be thankful the journey was over but her gut told her she would be in for far worse treatment.

The jumbees pulled her onto a wooden deck and in front of the woman whom she had grown to detest.

Miranda waved her hand.

The jumbees turned into smoke and drifted away.

Elizabeth fell hard onto the deck. She lifted herself up but only had the energy to kneel. She leaned back on her heels and waited.

Elizabeth felt her hands.

Her gloves were ripped to shreds, her hands cut and bruised. Her body hurt all over, her uniform a mess. Dirt was embedded in her wounds. She brushed the sand off her jacket as best she could, pride taking over.

Elizabeth knew that Miranda would take sick pleasure in her degradation.

"Miranda. Please don't hurt Anne," Elizabeth softly pleaded. "Take me instead. Whatever you are planning— let me take her place."

Miranda stared downwards, like a parent to a child. "It is not that easy Elizabeth. Anne is the key."

Elizabeth could feel her eyes begin to tear. She closed them only for a second, trying to understand how Miranda had become so unequivocally evil. Miranda had always been vile, but never homicidal.

But to kill her own family?

Elizabeth felt a lump in her throat. She looked up and forced herself to try and reason with a woman gone mad.

"How can you want to hurt your own blood?" Elizabeth implored. "What about your brother? Did he mean nothing to you?" She stopped, wondering if Miranda knew her brother was dead. She waited to see if the other woman would react, if eyes filled with hate would change focus?

Miranda sniffed angrily. "You have no business talking to me about hurting my brother. He hurt me when he decided he wanted to marry you!"

Those words are not from one who mourns, Elizabeth thought sadly. *Miranda will keep the conversation focused only on her self centered goal.*

Elizabeth could feel her anger begin to rise. Miranda had always thought only of herself. The death of her brother would mean nothing to a woman who was trying to kill her own niece.

"We never married," Elizabeth implored. "Isn't that enough?"

"Only after he came to his senses!" Miranda snapped.

Elizabeth took a breath. She needed to remain calm for Anne's sake. "I let him go," she finally confessed.

Elizabeth did not know if Trevor ever told his sister this. Had Miranda simply assumed her brother had realized the marriage to be unwise? That her brother could never marry a woman of Elizabeth's status?

Miranda inhaled sharply, looking down her nose at her victim. "You... you are a liar," Miranda accused, shaking her head. She crooked a finger.

Elizabeth's suspicions were right.

Your mother was always against us, as were you Miranda.

"You would never be so stupid as to let him go," Miranda continued. "I know you all too well."

Elizabeth turned her head and stared at the ground. *Miranda does indeed know me all too well.*

But I never told her.

I never had the courage to tell her why I released him.

"I did," Elizabeth confessed, her hands held out like a sinner kneeling for redemption. "I'm the one who released him. I was burned severely, so gravely I was supposed to die." Elizabeth rocked back on her heels, her eyes now wet with sorrow. "I let him go Miranda. I did not want him to be burdened with me, so I... let him go."

Miranda leaned in and grabbed her by the chin. She forced their eyes to meet. "Yet... here you are."

"I am stronger than I thought."

"And yet you kneel before me like a whipped slave, begging for mercy?"

"I only beg for Anne."

"I like you like this Elizabeth. The subservient wretch you always were," Miranda snickered while she straightened herself up.

Elizabeth lowered her head, defeated. She did not know what else to do. Her hand touched her chest and felt for her chain. Her pendant always brought her comfort in times of trouble.

I will not survive this.

Anne may not... survive this.

Miranda roughly grabbed Elizabeth by the hair, pulling her backwards. Elizabeth's neck was now exposed. She feared Miranda would slit her throat this very moment.

"Is that how you stopped me?" Miranda sneered as she ripped the chain off of her victim's neck.

"Don't!" Elizabeth yelled to deaf ears. "It's all I have left of her!"

"Your dead mother?" Miranda shook her head and laughed, releasing Elizabeth. "You cling to this jewelry like a feeble, old woman!"

She watched Miranda examine the pendant while clicking her tongue. Elizabeth suspected the woman must have been thinking how her spell failed.

Miranda threw the piece of jewelry to the deck. She smirked, watching Elizabeth stumble forward to collect her meager belonging. "How you came to control it is beyond my understanding."

Elizabeth fumbled with the chain.

It was broken.

She pulled the pendant off, threw the broken link onto the deck and let out a small sob. Elizabeth did not want to cry in front of Miranda but she could not contain her emotions any longer. She had tried to keep herself strong for the sake of both her young charges.

I can't anymore. I'm tired of fighting.

Éndira may be Anne's only hope now.

Carefully, Elizabeth put the pendant in her jacket pocket.

"You are pathetic," Miranda sneered.

Eyes wet, she could no longer find her courage. "Just kill me now. I can't— "

"Now why would I do that?"

Elizabeth looked at her.

What can she possibly want but my death?

"I am going to turn you into my servant once again," Miranda smirked. "That is all you were ever good for."

Elizabeth's heart dropped.

Anything but that.

Please... anything but that!

Miranda turned and signaled to her men. Two walked over and roughly pulled Elizabeth to her feet.

"Why do you hate me so?" Elizabeth asked solemnly.

Miranda whipped around and slapped Elizabeth hard across the face.

"Because you betrayed me!" Miranda yelled loudly.

Elizabeth felt her cheek. The act was brutal, violent from a woman who never could accept the truth. Elizabeth looked up at Miranda with pity in her voice. "We were never meant to be together."

Elizabeth turned her head slightly, waiting for another hit.

None came.

She looked back at Miranda and waited.

Miranda flushed, face hard with tears. "You... you loved my brother," Miranda stuttered, having a hard time forming the words. "Instead of... me."

"I loved you like a sister Miranda," Elizabeth said sadly. "I just wanted to be your sister."

"And yet you left," Miranda snarled. "You left me, just like my brother did. Let me be shipped out here to this godforsaken island to be married to that man like I was a piece of cattle to be auctioned off."

Elizabeth did not know what to say. The hatred Miranda held in her heart was because of rejection. Elizabeth was never in love with Miranda. Still to this day, Miranda could not handle the refusal and abandonment.

"I'm sorry," Elizabeth said with genuine sincerity in her voice. "I'm sorry you felt so much pain from what you think I did to you."

"You have no idea what pain is!"

Miranda reached out her hand and placed her palm on Elizabeth's forehead. A short burst of blue energy shot out from Miranda's fingertips. Elizabeth screamed in horrifying pain, her body suddenly rigid as she fell to the deck and remained still.

Miranda smiled, happy with what she had just done. She signaled to the men to pick the woman up again as they dragged the limp body away.

43

———

Anne looked up and watched the sun begin to creep over the horizon. Today was her eighteenth birthday. Even with her wild imagination Anne never thought she would celebrate her coming into adulthood waiting to be fed to a tree.

Anne sighed.

She sat on the broken, wooden crate and contemplated all that had been revealed so far. Her father had been murdered by the Fire Witch. Her captain and her other so-called friend had deserted her.

And my aunt along with my former governess want to murder me.

Anne closed her eyes and sifted through her thoughts.

She was alone and no one would be able to help her now.

All I have is myself.

Anne refused to feel sorry for herself. She would find a way to defeat her aunt and make her pay. If she simply tried to escape, the older one would continue to find a way to harass her. Aunt Miranda was hell bent on using her to appease her so-called deity. Anne knew the only way to be rid of her aunt for good was to outsmart the woman.

If only I knew how to do this.

Inside this makeshift pen, Anne was a prisoner. The bars were made of strong reeds of sugarcane tied together and reenforced with iron bars. The walls were made of coral rock that had been formed into an L shaped wall. Rows and rows of palmetto reeds, tightly woven together, formed a waterproof roof.

Anne was thankful to at least be able to stay dry.

A quick movement in the corner caught her eye. Anne knelt down and lay out her hand as a small lizard tried to make an escape. She took her other hand and gently eased the creature into her palm. Delicately, she held the lizard in place by pressing her finger down softly enough for only a slight bit of pressure. The reptile opened its mouth in response and braced two front arms. As he wiggled, she kept a firm grip.

"You want out, I know," Anne spoke softly to the creature. She held the lizard near her eye. The lizard opened his mouth wider. "You're angry; so am I!"

She chuckled to herself as the lizard did not change expression. The reptile was not happy about being caught.

"I'll let you go. No need for the two of us to be trapped in here tonight." Anne got up and placed the lizard on one of the sugarcane rods. The creature ran to the top then stopped and stared a her.

"You wouldn't know a way out of here?" Anne whispered to her little friend. "Would you?"

"Never trust a lizard," Zara suddenly said from the side. "They will always lead you astray."

Anne jumped back slightly. The grass had softened the other's footsteps.

"Talk to many lizards do you?" Anne taunted.

"More than my share," Zara answered then turned and snapped her fingers. "In the back."

Anne reluctantly followed the instructions. She backed up until her feet hit the wooden crate. Zara pulled a key from her pocket and began to open the lock. She stopped for a moment and waited. Two men walked up. They carried the weight of a person who was unconscious. Anne felt dread hit her stomach. She had a feeling this was someone she knew.

Zara opened the gate as the men shoved the victim inside. Anne reached forward and grabbed the dead weight before it could hit the dirty, wet ground.

When Anne saw the face, she gasped.

"What did you do to her?" Anne cried as she pushed back loose hair from Elizabeth's face. Elizabeth was unconscious, her pale skin showing distress.

Anne felt a sudden wave of emotions hit her all at once.

Betrayal, sadness— anger!

She needed to settle on one.

"I want to see my aunt!" Anne demanded angrily. "NOW!"

"You will be seeing her soon enough," Zara said. She turned and put a small vial on the bar before leaving.

Anne had not seen the action. She was desperately trying to balance Elizabeth's body.

"Miss?" Anne was gentle as she moved her friend's weight off her leg and onto the floor. She did not know how badly Elizabeth had been injured. "Miss?" she asked once again.

There was a slight stir, followed by sudden panic. Eyes wide, Elizabeth threw her hands up to defend herself. Anne pleaded with her to remain still. Sudden, labored breaths exited the older one.

"Don't," Elizabeth pleaded, her eyes wet. "Don't touch me."

Anne released her grip and froze. She did not know what to do. Instead, she waited.

Elizabeth's labored breathing slowly calmed but the pain was still there. Her eyes were sunken in as she looked at Anne.

"My back," Elizabeth whispered through clenched teeth.

"Did they hit you?"

"No... I wish it were that... simple."

"Can I do anything?"

"No." Elizabeth bit her lower lip and sighed. "Your Aunt Miranda certainly has a way with her gifts."

"Why would she hurt you like this?"

"Because she can."

Anne did not know what to do. She waited a few minutes before insisting she might help in some way. "Well, you cannot lay on the wet floor miss. You will catch your death."

Elizabeth chuckled slightly.

Anne got up and retrieved the wooden crate. She slammed her foot on the surface and broke two loose pieces off. Her hands pulled on the other side. The rest of the wood came apart. She lay the pieces near Elizabeth and placed the only blanket in the pen on top.

"I am going to move you," Anne insisted.

Elizabeth did not protest. She closed her eyes as Anne lifted her up as best she could. Elizabeth could not help but let out a pained cry.

"I'm sorry," Anne said as she crossed her legs and sat.

"No... don't apologize," Elizabeth struggled through the pain. "You did not do this."

Anne looked up and finally noticed the small vial. What had Zara left? She got up and retrieved the item. There was no label. She sat down next to Elizabeth and inspected the reddish-brown liquid.

"What is it?" Elizabeth asked.

"I do not know."

"Take the stopper off."

"Are you sure? It could be poison."

Elizabeth waited for Anne to open the bottle. She put the stopper under her friend's nose.

"Opium," Elizabeth said, relieved.

"Are you sure?"

"Yes." Elizabeth leaned forward and drank the small dose. The effects took hold quickly. She started to breath more evenly, her face less pained.

"Why would she leave this?" Anne wondered.

"Maybe because you were kind to her?"

Anne remembered when Zara had been given truth serum. When they had all been desperate to find out what Miranda wanted. Anne had given Zara an alternative to the pain, a sleep potion that would knock her out for a week and avoid Miranda's wrath.

"I am sorry for what you witnessed Anne," Elizabeth said through saddened eyes.

Anne inhaled deeply. If she was going to die tonight, she needed to know why. "You murdered Jackson."

"I did," Elizabeth nodded, unashamed.

"Why? Surely you could have done something else?"

"Men like him... have no control. He would have wanted more than what he was initially offered. He thought he had leverage over me. Soon, he would get it in his mind he deserved more due to that simple fact." Elizabeth shook her head. "No... I would... never put my crew at risk over someone like him."

"How is it not a risk, to risk hanging for stealing from the Crown?"

"That is the risk I and my selected men are willing to take."

Anne leaned back slightly and sighed. "I don't understand why you would steal?"

Elizabeth stared at the floor for a long moment. Anne wondered if the woman was looking for an excuse.

Finally, Elizabeth frowned.

"I have little money Anne," Elizabeth confessed. "My only prospects are finding prizes for the Crown. Even then, the amount we are given is paltry compared with the Admiralty's share," she sighed. "I'm not trying to justify my actions, just... trying to explain."

"Then why do it?" Anne asked, unconvinced.

"Do you know what it is like to be a woman without funds?" Elizabeth asked. "Surely, even at your young age, you understand?"

Anne blinked, confused by the sudden change in direction. "What does your sex have to do with any of this? You've become what many men would love to be."

"Yes," Elizabeth nodded. "And, I also have few prospects."

"What do you mean by that?"

"I'm one cannon shot away from a missing leg or arm. Cripples do not fare well on the streets of London nor the West Indies, women especially."

Anne lowered her eyes. She was beginning to understand what her older friend was talking about. Anne had seen beggars with missing appendages before.

And the women?

They were often prostitutes.

"Surely the Admiralty would take care of you if you were hurt in the line of duty?"

"You would think..." Elizabeth shook her head. "But no. We are simply released from service."

"That is awful!" Anne cried.

"The only people who take care of their own if injured or maimed are pirates."

"Really?"

"Yes. They receive a share of money."

Anne could not help but smile, imagining Elizabeth in the service of pirates and not the Crown. Before she could speak up, Elizabeth started to laugh.

"And yes," Elizabeth chuckled. "I have considered that option."

"I would hate to see you hang for stealing miss." Anne crossed her arms to her chest.

"You are very young but very wise," Elizabeth exhaled, her eyes sad. "One thing you will learn as you get older Anne, is that we adults do not have all the answers, as much as we like to fool ourselves into so believing. I am a very flawed individual."

The sounds of macaws chattering stole their attention. Both women sat in silence for a long while, listening to the hum of the island.

"Have you really eaten a rat?" Anne suddenly asked.

"Anne? What kind of question is that?" Elizabeth chuckled.

"That night at dinner, on my father's ship. You started talking about eating a biller? "

"Millers?"

"Yes... millers, you said they were rats."

"They are."

"Have you eaten one?"

"Yes, many." Elizabeth tried not to laugh when she saw Anne have a sudden look on her face.

"Disgusting! Why?"

"Well... because you never get quite enough food when you are a midshipman. Now, I did not need as much food as the boys, but I still hungered often," Elizabeth explained. "The captain of the hold often caught them and... well, he made them 'presentable' so that we had nothing to do on our end but cook the miller."

"It is still disgusting."

"It is worse when you think we had to pay for them."

"Why didn't you just call them rats?"

"Because they are RATS!" Elizabeth laughed. "And you really do not want to remind yourself you are eating them."

Anne shook her head and laughed at her friend's response. Anne did not know if she could ever eat a miller. The thought alone that her father and friend ate such an appalling thing made her stomach turn slightly sour.

"How do you know Miss Barton?" Anne asked, curious, trying to direct the conversation once again.

"She was a servant in your grandmother's household when I worked there."

"Worked there? Doing what?"

"I was also a servant."

Anne gasped. She never imagined this proud woman working for another like that. "But how? Why?"

Elizabeth began to explain how she had come to lose her status in life, and how she and her mother came to work for the Suttons. Anne listened to the story, finally understanding the connection between herself and the family.

"Then why does my aunt hate you so much?" Anne hesitantly asked.

Elizabeth inhaled for a moment then let out a long breath as she looked towards the bars. She glanced at Anne then turned away once again. "In the end, I rejected her."

Anne stared at her with a blank look on her face. She did not exactly understand what Elizabeth meant by those words. She waited patiently for further explanation.

"She was in love with me," Elizabeth confessed.

"Oh," Anne said, intrigued and upset at the revelation. *Does my aunt live a life like the one I wanted with Sarah back home? Private, and away from society's norms with Miss Barton in secret?* "I saw Miss Barton and my aunt kissing," Anne confessed.

"They are lovers," Elizabeth said. "I caught them once... in bed together. Miranda threatened to have me removed from the household," Elizabeth said, ashamed. "But it did not matter. My mother took ill soon after and was consigned to Bedlam where I took care of her. After she died, I joined the Royal Navy."

Anne could see how much this memory pained her older friend. Anne wanted to reach out and hug her but knew that the physical pain Elizabeth had would be too much, despite the opium Zara had supplied.

"She blames me for the life she lives now," Elizabeth sighed. "Being sent out here to marry Randal," she straightened herself up slightly, despite her pain and shrugged. "I think she imagined we would run off somewhere and live a life together."

"But you loved my father."

"I did," Elizabeth said fondly. "I loved him so much."

Anne felt her sadness rise, not only for her friend but for herself, now without a family anymore to comfort her.

"I've always felt different around girls," Anne confessed. "But I know nothing of being with them... intimately," she looked at her. "Do you know how? I mean, well?"

"How two women make love?" Elizabeth said.

Anne swallowed hard. She really wanted to know, but was afraid of the answer.

"I do," Elizabeth nodded with a smile.

When Anne realized Elizabeth did not turn red nor blush at the idea, the possibility of knowing was real. Anne felt her worries disappear for a brief moment.

Still, she was to afraid to ask.

A blast of tom tom drums heated up in the distance. Anne stopped her questions and widened her eyes.

Elizabeth pulled Anne inward and hugged her tightly. "You will make it out of this... I promise. I am not the only one here."

"Éndira?" Anne blinked back tears.

"You did not expect her to leave you to die, did you?"

"I... I do not know what to expect anymore," Anne said, confused. She was afraid to confess she'd kissed Éndira, only to be rejected. *Why then is Éndira coming to help save me?*

"She has your ring," Elizabeth smiled when Anne lit up. "She loves you."

Anne opened her eyes wide, shocked at the comment.

"She just hasn't figured it out yet Anne." Elizabeth squeezed tighter. "You have to give her time."

Éndira is coming to save me?

Maybe everything will be all right.

THE AIR WAS thick with humidity. Éndira wiped her face once again with her sleeve, trying to ignore the heat that was starting to make her terribly thirsty. She licked her lips, wishing she had brought a bladder of water along.

Éndira watched the sugar cane cage carefully. She had been here for hours, patiently waiting for any break in the guard's routine. So far, Éndira had no luck. The men guarding the rickety prison never left their posts. Éndira watched the way they stared straight ahead, a blank look in their eyes. Everyone on this plantation seemed to be bewitched.

It was close to dusk.

If she didn't do something quick Éndira was afraid it might be too late. She could hear commotion in the distance near the silk-cotton tree.

They are prepping a ceremony that involves Anne, Éndira sighed, thinking of the girl whom she had grown fond of. When thoughts of the sudden kiss entered her head, Éndira shook her own. She did not want to dwell on what happened. She still had no idea— *why had it happened?*

But how can I not think about it?

A kiss that Anne had suddenly surprised me with! Éndira tightened her arms around her chest. She had not known how to respond to the gesture of— *love?*

The truth is... I enjoyed it.

I knew she was smitten with me, but still how could I be so blind?

Éndira bit her lower lip, suddenly afraid and very confused.

What if I lose Anne forever?

Her mind drifted to the two bodies silently sitting next to each other. Éndira had been relieved to see that Elizabeth survived the jumbee attack. Éndira did not know how she might handle the woman's death. She had never really gotten along with the older woman but she felt a deep connection with her in some way. Éndira could not explain why she admired Elizabeth so much.

She's always been tough with me but never cruel.

Éndira sighed, upset with herself that she could not figure out how to free her friends. If she attacked these men, they would overpower her easily.

When she spotted Zara walking in the distance, Éndira decided to try another tactic. She quickly ran through the bushes, low to the ground with stealth in mind.

Éndira watched as Zara walked into the side door.

The plantation house appeared to be quiet. Éndira waited outside in the bushes and watched some of the servants leave. She counted three.

Where are they going?

The sun is almost spent. Are they heading to the ceremony?

Éndira crept forward. Sometimes she was able to blend into a background, much like Anne's kidnapper had recently done. Éndira's powers were not strong enough to become completely invisible but in a dark atmosphere, she could easily blend into the shadows.

She focused her energy inward and willed herself to cloak her visibility.

Concentration was key.

Éndira walked through the side door of the dining room and looked around. Just a little light shown in. There were no candles lit. If the whole house was like this, Éndira would have no problem creeping around.

Éndira heard a noise coming from inside the kitchen. She peeked her head inside and saw Zara working at the center table. The girl's hands were busy chopping various herbs. Next to her, two blue crab claws and a feather lay in a bowl. A string of garlic and onion sat in another. Éndira watched her combine the ingredients. Zara then blew out a candle and let the wax drip onto the contents.

Zara quickly glanced up, making Éndira freeze.

Has she sensed me?

Zara turned her attention back to her concoction and placed the bowl behind her on another table.

Éndira slowly walked over. She picked up an empty bowl and crept behind Zara. As she went to strike, her intended victim suddenly swung around with a roller in her hand and struck hard.

Éndira fell to the floor. As her concentration wavered, so did her shield. She was now completely visible.

"Did you think I would not be able to see you?" Zara taunted. She dropped the roller and reached for a knife instead. She positioned herself above her victim. "You are not skilled enough to fool me!"

"And you are not especially smart to stand right above me." Éndira swept her leg forward and knocked the other one to the ground. Éndira leapt to her feet and kicked the knife out of Zara's hand.

Irate, Zara lunged for the knife. Éndira jumped on top of the girl and desperately tried to get to the weapon first. Éndira succeeded in grabbing the handle. She quickly turned, cutting Zara in the shoulder.

Zara sneered, angered. She pulled back and touched her wound.

"Barely a scratch," Zara snickered.

Éndira leaned back to try and get a better position. Zara found the rolling pin at her side. She swung the wood hard, catching Éndira's hand midair. The knife flew out.

Éndira howled in pain, afraid her wrist might be broken The trauma hit her lower half hard. Suddenly, she felt like she might vomit. Éndira struggled to remain conscious.

As she pushed herself back against the counter, Zara crept forward.

"You are a fool for coming here," the girl taunted.

Éndira could do nothing. The pain was overwhelming.

Zara picked up the knife. She examined the blade and smiled.

"And you..." Éndira bit her lower lip, forcing herself to keep from passing out. "Are a fool for serving that woman!"

"I have no choice."

"We all have a choice."

"You... you wouldn't understand," Zara said. The expression on her face changed, showing a girl caught between anger and sorrow.

"You serve a woman who treats you like a slave." Éndira put pressure on her wounded hand. Slowly, she pushed herself up more, her feet straight forward. Éndira was basically defenseless. "You are nothing in her eyes."

Zara knelt down and crept close. She stroked the tip of the knife near Éndira's face.

"You're trying to provoke me?" Zara asked, intrigued. "To make me lose control so you might overpower me somehow?"

"Something like that."

"I have learned to keep my senses under control," Zara said. "Isn't it ironic how I now have you in my grasp?" she played with the knife closer this time, pricking Éndira's skin. "What was it you bragged about? Wanting to 'thrash' me good?"

Éndira was starting to regret ever saying those words.

"I would say I am sorry," Éndira's eyes bored into hers. "But I am sure you wouldn't care."

"I would not."

Éndira pulled back and tried to get away. Zara leaned in and grabbed her by the collar and held her tightly. "Maybe I will just cut you, so that you will remember how you threatened me!"

Éndira said nothing. She took her breaths in a slow, deliberate rhythm. She needed to concentrate. Éndira turned her head away, thinking only of Anne.

"You are in a lot of pain, are you not?" Zara asked.

"And you're giving me a headache!" Éndira snapped. "Strike or just shut the hell up already!"

Zara crept near and sniffed close to Éndira's cheek. Éndira widened her eyes, staring at her with confusion.

"What *are* you doing?" Éndira asked, befuddled.

Zara cocked an eyebrow. "What are you?"

Again, Éndira had no idea what was going on. "What do you mean — what am I?"

"You smell... powerful."

"Sorry to disappoint," Éndira huffed, lifting her broken wrist.

"No, you are," Zara shook her head, getting to her feet. She tossed the knife into the dry sink. When she bent down slightly and offered her hand, Éndira stared at her, stupefied.

"No tricks," Zara assured. "I promise. I have no reason to hurt you."

"Are you sure?" Éndira said with a sniff. "You wanted to 'thrash' me good just a second ago." Éndira could not help but repeat her own words.

Eventually, Éndira realized she should at least hear the girl out. If she was offering a parlay, the best thing to do was to take the offer. Éndira put out her good hand and was gently helped up. The pain was still intense. Éndira leaned against the dry sink, trying to catch her breath. She watched as Zara reached in the side cabinet and pulled out a small bottle.

"Here." Zara poured some blue liquid in a small glass.

"What is it?"

"Drink it, it will help with the pain." When Zara saw Éndira staring at her with apprehension the servant sighed. "Or you can just suffer?"

"You are not trying to poison me, are you?" Éndira said, echoing the same words Zara had used a while back. Éndira lifted the glass up and sniffed it.

"If I wanted you dead," Zara repeated Éndira's own from that day. "You would be dead already."

Éndira quickly downed the potion. The effects were immediate. She could feel her hand start to become numb. When Zara touched it, Éndira automatically pulled back out of self preservation.

"I will bandage it," Zara said, pulling out a chair.

Éndira sat down. She watched as Zara carefully began to wrap cloth around the wrist.

"It's not broken." Zara continued her work.

"Why are you helping me?" Éndira asked.

"Because, Anne does not deserve to die. She is a kind person."

"She is," Éndira agreed solemnly. She shifted in her seat uncomfortably. "Why do you follow Miranda?"

"I don't follow her out of choice," Zara said, looking her dead in the eyes.

"Can you be freed of her influence?"

"I can," Zara said, finishing up the bandage. "If you defeat Miranda, I can be freed."

Éndira pulled back slightly surprised by the comment. Was this girl now pinning her hope— *on me?*

"Miranda is very powerful," Zara continued. "But she is blinded by ambition. She is unable to see what is right in front of her face."

"What do you mean by that?"

Zara reached behind her own neck and grasped her amulet. She motioned for Éndira to lean forward. "With this."

Éndira did as she was told. She let the other girl put the item around her neck. Éndira felt the clay bead in her fingertips.

"What does this do?" Éndira asked, curious.

"Watch and learn." Zara leaned forward, then breathed into Éndira's mouth.

Suddenly, Éndira felt a weird sensation. Her body began to ache slightly.

"What did you do?" she asked, concerned.

"You are consuming a breath of my essence," Zara said. She reached for the small mirror in her spelling kit. She showed Éndira her reflection.

The process took only a few moments. Éndira inhaled deeply once again, letting the essence consume her, find her... mold into her. Her facial features changed first, then her body. Even her clothes matched.

Éndira was now Zara.

If she could only convince the right people, she might have a chance to save Anne.

"You are sure Miranda cannot sense this?" Éndira asked. "I mean, is it her magic?"

"No." Zara shook her head then gave a sly grin. "My great-grandmother was a witch doctor in Africa. She created that amulet."

"Thank you," Éndira said as she stood up. "When this is over, I promise to give it back to you."

44

A nne and Elizabeth had been trapped in this cage for hours waiting to see what horrible deeds Miranda had in store for them tonight.

Her eighteenth birthday will soon be spent, Elizabeth sighed as she watched the sun begin to set. She had talked to Anne in positive tones, hoping to calm her young terrified heart.

Elizabeth felt in her own heart that this might be futile.

She understood Miranda all too well.

When the woman wanted something, there was nothing, nor anyone, that could change her mind.

Elizabeth pulled her pendant out of her pocket. She played with the surface, fondly remembering her mother. It was the only thing Elizabeth had left of her. The small, turquoise gemstone would always calm Elizabeth's mind. She wondered if, after all these years, there was an effect that she had not known about before?

Miranda had accused her of using it to— *block her?*

But how?

Is this stone actually more than it appears to be?

Elizabeth's fingers felt the surface. The hard indentations were a map for her fingertips to search. The stone always felt warm with each stroke. Elizabeth had always thought this to be something that was only in her imagination.

Gemstones did not heat up unless another source was there to act as a catalyst.

But myself?

Has it always been me?

Elizabeth closed her eyes, wondering if she could also be a Crystal Astrid.

She tried to stay awake but the combination of pain and the effects of the opium were strong. She had promised herself to close her eyes for what she thought would only be a moment.

Soon, she was fast asleep.

A sharp voice penetrated her ears. Elizabeth opened her eyes quickly and looked to her side, hoping that Anne was okay. When she saw no one, she lifted herself up and began to panic.

Looking around her surroundings, Elizabeth realized she was in a small room. The walls were simple, a familiar wallpaper covered with blue lilacs.

Suddenly, a smell hit her.

Elizabeth turned and saw her mother sitting next to the bed, pruning a bouquet of hyacinths. Her mother stopped and smiled.

"Look who decided to finally rise," her mother said.

"Mom?" Elizabeth heard herself say in a younger voice. She touched her own face, wondering how old she was right now.

"Miranda will be needing you soon dear," her mother said with another smile. "Make sure you attend to her quickly."

Elizabeth did not have time to respond. Her body seemed to jolt forward then stop abruptly. This time she was dressed in her simple house dress, holding a stack of linens. She looked around quickly, trying to figure out what had happened. The room was immediately recognizable as the one belonging to Miranda.

Elizabeth took in the large space, expertly decorated in red and purple hues. In the corner were toys no longer played with. Three dress mannequins adorned the side wall, each wearing long ball gowns. Elizabeth turned and looked at herself in the long full length mirror.

Her hair was much longer and her face much younger. She recognized herself as a girl at least fifteen years of age.

"Why am I here?" Elizabeth whispered to herself, not recognizing this as a dream she had ever had before.

No— this is from my past.

"I don't want to be here," Elizabeth said softly, closing her eyes and trying to will herself to wake up.

"Elizabeth!" Miranda's voice called from behind the dressing screen. "Come here!"

Elizabeth shook her head knowing she needed to get out of this room. A knot formed in her stomach.

"Elizabeth!!" Miranda called once again, annoyed.

"Yes miss," Elizabeth heard herself saying. Her feet began to move, despite not wanting to go towards the voice.

Inside, she could feel her body have no control. These were actions that had been played out in the past.

They were doomed to repeat, despite her protests.

When Elizabeth walked to the side of the dressing screen, she diverted her eyes. Miranda was naked from the waist up. She was much younger here, a seventeen year old girl with long auburn hair flowing down over her ample bosom.

Elizabeth had recently begun to blossom.

"Take these," Miranda said stiffly, handing Elizabeth a few loose items. Elizabeth quickly stuffed them in her arms. "Put them back in the chest. I have no need of them. Mother can have them replaced."

Elizabeth nodded, turning on her heels then kneeled at the chest. She hated to listen to the girl's spoiled attitude. At one time, Elizabeth remembered having her own room like this, filled with everything a girl could want.

That was before her father and his ships were lost at sea.

Now I am just a servant, Elizabeth sighed, remembering how much it hurt her to live in this house. The only thing that made it bearable was—

Trevor.

But he would be at sea at this time, if she remembered correctly. A sixteen year old midshipman living out his dream.

Elizabeth took her time to return. She stood by the outside of the screen listening to Miranda fuss and complain, many times throwing another garment to be removed. After a while, Elizabeth sat down in an adjoining seat.

Why am I having to relive something I can't even remember?

The matriarch of the family burst into the room holding a large broach. Mrs. Sutton glared at Elizabeth for a moment then pointed to the side.

"Step over there young lady," Mrs. Sutton commanded.

Elizabeth nodded her head then walked to the wall and stood with her head down, trembling. The young girl inside did not know what was going on but the older woman that possessed this body knew something was seriously wrong.

Why don't I remember this?

"Miranda!" Mrs. Sutton snapped. "Come out from behind that screen immediately."

"I'm busy mother," Miranda snarled, her voice low and full of frustration. "If I don't find a proper dress for tonight, I will refuse to come!"

"You might never leave this room again young woman!"

"What?" Miranda squealed, popping her head out. "What are you going on about?"

"Step out now!"

Miranda rolled her eyes. "Fine."

Elizabeth's eyes remained fixed on the floor. She waited for the rustle of feet to stop. The family matriarch's hand grabbed her roughly by the arm and pulled her over. Elizabeth felt her body pulled forward. A broach was pushed close to her face by crooked fingers.

"Did you and my daughter take this broach from Mr. Fields shop this afternoon?" Mrs. Sutton accused.

Elizabeth could feel fear creep up her neck.

She was finally beginning to remember!

I know exactly what we did that afternoon. Miranda forced me to distract the shopkeeper while she took it!

Elizabeth glanced at Miranda for a moment. Quickly, the matriarch's bony fingers grasped onto Elizabeth's cheek and forced her to look foreward. She immediately recognized the ring Mrs. Sutton wore as belonging to Anne now.

"Do not lie to me girl," Mrs. Sutton said sternly. "You and your mother will be sacked and out on the street!"

Elizabeth's eyes welled up with tears, remembering her own thoughts that day. She could not be the cause of her and her mother going homeless.

But Miranda was her friend, at least— she thought she was her friend now.

What kind of friend would do what Miranda had done?

I've never stolen before in my life, Elizabeth wanted to scream. *Even helping another steal is a crime.*

Will I go to the gallows?

They hang children for theft. Will Mrs. Sutton be that cruel? What will Trevor think if he finds out his mother had me arrested?

Could he even love a thief like me?

"Mother?" Miranda calmly stepped forward, placing her hands firmly on Elizabeth's shoulders. The girl was slightly taller and always in forceful command. "I do not know what Mr. Fields told you, or where you got that broach."

"He brought it here."

Miranda rolled her eyes once again. "Then how on earth could Elizabeth and I have stolen it?"

Elizabeth watched the way Mrs. Sutton's eyes narrowed, insulted that her daughter was questioning her. She roughly put the broach in Miranda's hand, then took her finger and firmly pushed onto the aquamarine stone.

"Whatever this crystal had is almost void. You may not have stolen the jewel, but siphoned off its energy," Miss Sutton accused.

"Mother?" Miranda calmly said. "Should we be speaking of such things in front of the help?"

Elizabeth did not care that her friend used that term. Miranda always referred to the 'help' as lower class citizens. But for some reason Miranda had taken a fancy to her. Elizabeth was not one to complain, until lately.

Odd things were happening between them.

Miranda was showing her much more attention than seemed appropriate between servant and master.

What stirred Elizabeth's thoughts the most were the accusations about the crystal itself. She looked at Miranda and questioned with her eyes. What was Mrs. Sutton talking about?

"Go outside girl," Mrs. Sutton commanded.

Elizabeth did as she was told. Once outside the closed door, she could hear a muffled argument. Elizabeth put her ear close to the wood, hoping to understand at least what they were fighting about.

Unfortunately, she could not understand through the thick mahogany.

Elizabeth pulled herself up then leaned her back against the door. The young girl inside herself remembered she could never distinctly make out the words.

Unexpectedly, the words slowly began to unravel.

Elizabeth was confused, wondering why she could suddenly understand them.

Why now, of all times?

"You cannot go around siphoning power off of crystals you have no understanding of," Mrs. Sutton accused her daughter.

"I'm almost an adult mother," Miranda snapped. "You treat me like a child when you should treat me like the goddess I will become!"

"Our powers are not to be flaunted. We have kept them hidden for a reason. Do you not remember the history I taught you? How we were almost hunted to extinction?"

"Perhaps it would make more sense to make these mortals cower in front of us, instead of hiding in the shadows like peasants?"

"Miranda!" Mrs. Sutton bit. "You are too early in your studies to be playing with powers you do not unserstand!"

"Then when mother? When will my teacher come to me? You keep telling me that we all are to begin training when we turn seventeen but I am almost eighteen and yet my master has not come," Miranda cried, exasperated. "Why am I not to be trained?"

"I do not know," Mrs. Sutton confessed, then waited for a moment. "I do not know why she has not come Miranda."

"Perhaps she has also been hunted to extinction?" Miranda snarled. "I am not going to wait to become a victim!"

"No one is trying to kill us Miranda. Our family has learned to stay—"

"— In the shadows," Miranda interrupted angrily. "I'm the one who was given the gift, your only daughter. So, if I do not train myself, who will? You?" Miranda snarled. "You are the weakest woman I know."

A sudden slap of skin against skin startled Elizabeth. She put her own hands to her face, scared that Miranda had hit her own mother. No more words were spoken, only the opening and slamming of the door. Elizabeth turned and watched Mrs. Sutton storm down the hallway and out of sight.

Elizabeth did not know what to do. She waited by the door and heard soft sobs.

"You can come back in," Miranda softly said.

Elizabeth inhaled, then gently opened the door. She saw that her friend had been crying.

When Miranda looked up, her eyes and skin were red.

"She's never hit me before," Miranda said, defeated.

Elizabeth walked over and hugged her friend. They embraced for a long time. After they released, Elizabeth wiped the tears away with a linen.

"Thank you for not saying anything," Miranda said with a shy smile. "I did not know I dropped the silly thing. I thought I put it back on the counter."

"Why would you want to take the broach when you can afford dozens of them easily?" Elizabeth asked innocently.

"You wouldn't understand."

"Why not?"

"Because," Miranda looked at her, her face flushed in embarrassment. "Because, I am not like you Elizabeth."

"I was once like you."

"Not wealth," Miranda confessed, brushing her hands against her shift. "My family is not..." she paused, then shrugged. "It's hard to explain."

Elizabeth sat down, eyes wanting more. "Then tell me?"

Miranda turned to her dresser and picked up a small aquamarine stone. It glowed slightly. She kneeled next to Elizabeth, the first time the girl had ever shown subservience. "May I see your necklace?"

Elizabeth automatically touched her jewelry, afraid to part with the only thing of value she had left. Her fingers found the pendant that lay at the end. With encouragement, Elizabeth decided to take the necklace off and hand it to the other girl.

Miranda put the two aquamarine gemstones together. Elizabeth watched in awe as a small flow of energy began to happen between them. Miranda gently put her hand on Elizabeth's.

"What is happening?" Elizabeth asked, curious.

"I have the ability to manipulate energy from crystals," Miranda confessed, squeezing hard. "It is something that few in our family can do."

"That is why you wanted that broach?"

"Yes," Miranda said, her eyes filled with happiness once again. "I wanted to see if I could filch the energy of another's heirloom. That broach glowed when I saw it."

"I didn't see anything."

"You wouldn't Elizabeth. Not without me. You don't have the gift."

"Oh. But did you find what you wanted?"

"No." Miranda shook her head. "I am not powerful enough... not yet." She continued to hold the two crystals together. "I've been trying to train myself."

Elizabeth still did not understand. She wanted to ask more questions, but the light from the energy flow entranced her. She could not look away from the show.

"I'm not supposed to tell anyone about what I am," Miranda said.

Elizabeth blinked, now focused only on her friend. "Then why tell me?"

"Because you're... special to me," Miranda confessed.

Before Elizabeth could speak, she felt Miranda's lips on her own. They were wet and full. Elizabeth closed her eyes. She had never been kissed before. Miranda's lips had a small amount of power seeping into Elizabeth's own.

Elizabeth enjoyed the taste and sensation.

Miranda finally pulled back. She watched the younger girl touch her own fingers to her lips.

"Why did you kiss me?" Elizabeth asked, intrigued.

"Because I wanted to."

Elizabeth smiled.

"Did you like it?" Miranda asked.

Elizabeth nodded her head. "Yes."

"Would you like me to do it again?"

Another nod and their lips were together once more.

Elizabeth easily dismissed what had happened in the store. She closed her eyes and enjoyed the closeness that was now between them. Miranda had always been authoritative but never cruel.

Was this what it was like between sisters she had wondered at the time?

Miranda released herself and turned to the crystals. She picked up Elizabeth's pendant and necklace. Elizabeth held her neck forward as Miranda clasped the chain. Elizabeth touched the stone and felt warmth.

"What did you do to it?" Elizabeth asked, curious.

"I charged it for you," Miranda smiled happily. "But you won't remember why it is so special."

"Why not?"

"Because that is the way it has to be," Miranda sighed. She picked up the uncharged one and grasped it in her palm.

Elizabeth sat still. She wanted to understand what was now to happen between them. She had no idea what love was at the time between those other than family. Was it possible to love a brother and a sister in the same way?

Suddenly, Elizabeth gasped as the scene disappeared. She pulled herself up and tried to find her balance. The air smelled different, with too much salt in the air. Elizabeth turned and saw Anne kneeling next to her.

"Are you okay miss?" Anne asked, concerned. She held out her hand, trying to steady her friend.

"I'm fine," Elizabeth said. She felt stiffness in her back and neck, familiar signs that she was back in her older body. "I had a bad dream, that's all."

Did I? Or was it a vision from this pendant? Elizabeth looked down and touched the aquamarine gemstone. The crystal felt cold. *Why do I finally remember why it feels the way it does?*

Elizabeth looked at Anne then realized what had happened. She had her hand in Anne's when they both fell asleep. Anne must have pulled out the vision from the crystal with her powers.

Elizabeth lifted her hand and stared at her pendant.

"Where is your chain?" Anne asked innocently.

Elizabeth sighed. "Miranda tore it off of my neck."

Anne reached behind her own and unlatched the chain Éndira had given her. She took Elizabeth's pendant in her own hand, then snaked the jewelry on. Anne motioned for her friend to lower her head. Anne clasped the chain, then let it dangle in place.

Elizabeth smiled, slight tears in her eyes. The pendant was back where it belonged.

"Are you a Crystal Astrid?" Anne asked innocently.

Elizabeth blinked, looking at the girl with uncertainty. "I don't think so," she confessed honestly. "I have no powers like you."

"But that gemstone," Anne nodded towards the jewelry. "It protected you from my Aunt Miranda's attack?"

Elizabeth thought about the vision she just had. Miranda had charged this crystal at one time.

Anne touched the surface, her fingertip firmly grasping the aquamarine. Anne nodded, then let the pendant drop down.

"It has almost no energy left," Anne sighed, wishing the words false. "I wish I could have used it against my aunt, to try and protect us at least. If I do not get my ring back soon, I don't know how we will survive."

"You are so much more powerful than you think Anne," Elizabeth said, empowered with hope once again. "I have faith in you."

You're a strong one Anne Sutton, stronger than Miranda. I only hope you have this faith in yourself.

45

———

É ndira walked towards the silk cotton tree with a calabash in her hands. She was careful not to spill the fake potion. Zara had given her sugar water laced with a hint of coffee, making the mixture appear light brown. Hopefully, with the added flavor of lemons and orange, Miranda would be tricked if she smelled the concoction.

When Éndira got over the hill, she could see a line of torches circling the massive tree. In front, a long table with two women standing near each other. As she got closer, Éndira recognized Miranda and the woman called Selina Barton.

Anne and Elizabeth were nowhere in sight.

Éndira walked up to the table and put down the bowl.

"What's wrong with your hand?" Miranda asked, eyebrow cocked.

"I cut it," Éndira lied, trying not to look at Selina. The woman was staring at her, eyes narrowed.

Can she sense me? Éndira wondered, panicked.

Éndira was worried about Selina discovering the deception. Because Selina appeared to not be in her 'right' mind, her inner vision might be attuned to see things that most would not normally see.

Éndira waited patiently next to them both.

Selina had turned back to Miranda and linked arms. Selina seemed to only be consumed with the other woman.

Please let it stay that way.

Éndira opened one of the wine bottles sitting on the table. She quickly dropped in another potion while the women were distracted.

Selina softly whispered in Miranda's ear, making the other woman giggle. Éndira realized by the curve of Miranda's smile, that the two must be lovers. She did not have time to think about the observation. She watched as two men led Elizabeth over the hill.

Éndira tried not to gasp in shock.

Elizabeth had her arms tied behind her back, her back arched with a sugar cane stalk in between. Her face was bloodied, her uniform dirty and ripped.

Next up the hill was Anne.

Éndira softly held back tears.

Anne was being led to the slaughter by two other men. Her hands were bound in front. Unlike Elizabeth, she had not been mistreated.

Éndira was thankful at least for that bit of comfort.

"Bring them forward," Miranda commanded.

The two prisoners were brought in front of her. She reached out her hand and motioned for the men to force Elizabeth to her knees.

They did as she requested.

"Don't torment her anymore you witch!" Anne snapped.

Miranda glared at her niece. She raised her hand and slapped Anne hard across the face. Elizabeth tried to lunge at the aggressor, but fell to the wet ground and onto her stomach and face. Selina cackled from a distance at the show.

Anne licked her bottom lip and tasted the blood.

"Do not presume to tell me what to do young lady!" Miranda signaled for her men to pull Elizabeth up once again.

Miranda grabbed Elizabeth's chin and forced her to look straight at her. "I will do you the courtesy of putting you out of your misery first so you do not have to watch."

"Please Miranda," Elizabeth started to plead her case once again. "I beg you. Don't do this to Anne! Take me instead!"

"I like when you beg Elizabeth. It will be just like old times," Miranda said evenly. "You disgust me. Of all people in this world you should understand why."

"I understand you have always been a lunatic!"

Miranda smirked unoffended by the comment. "Maybe it takes a lunatic to see the true path. A path where finally I will no longer be treated as less then human. I am just as smart as any man! This is my plantation! I have always run it... but do you think anyone gives me proper credit? Women like us will never be treated as the goddesses we are until we reach out and take it by force."

Elizabeth narrowed her eyes. "By killing your own niece? Why would you want to hurt her? She has done nothing to you!"

"The WORLD has done nothing for me!" Miranda spat, her eyes filled with rage. "She is lucky to leave this mortal plane before she truly learns the harsh reality of what being a woman is like in this world. You think my husband is the only one who will try and take her body in her lifetime? Do you think just because she wants to lay with girls means she would have been safe? Anne has yet to learn the cruelty of men. I have saved her."

"You are trying to turn this into something noble?" Elizabeth cried. "You are taking away her life! Her choices!"

"She would have been married off and bred like cattle if not for me!"

"Just because your mother sent you out here to marry Randal doesn't give you permission to destroy other people's lives!"

"It doesn't matter what you think Elizabeth." Miranda stood up, quickly snapping her fingers. "You will no longer remember any of this. When you wake back up," she curled her lips and smiled. "Your existence will be to serve me. You will no longer have to worry about anything else."

Miranda snapped her fingers again.

Éndira took a second to realize the crazed woman was signaling to her. She forgot for a moment she was in Zara's form. She ran forward with the bowl the other girl had prepped. Éndira handed the calabash to Miranda then pretended to trip. Éndira's good hand dropped a small knife near Elizabeth's own hands in the process.

"What is wrong with you?" Miranda snapped.

Éndira crawled up carefully, feigning illness.

"I'm not feeling well," Éndira lied.

"Go back to the table you fool, before you ruin everything!"

"Yes ma'am." Éndira nodded then did as she was told.

Miranda cracked her neck side to side, annoyed. She exhaled deeply before turning her attention back onto her captive.

"You will drink this Elizabeth." Miranda held the calabash up. "And all your troubles will be gone."

Elizabeth hardened her eyes as her neck pulsed with fury. "I will spit that in your face!"

"I like your anger. It will serve me well."

Elizabeth lifted her head proudly. Her eyes teared with rage and sadness. "You know nothing of love!" Elizabeth finally snapped, her anger screaming to come out. "You are a heartless old shrew who is going to die alone, weak and powerless! No matter what that creature in the silk-cotton promised you!"

Miranda ignored the taunt. She signaled to her men. They grabbed Elizabeth by the collar and seized her up. The victim struggled and bit the finger of one of the men.

For a quick moment, Elizabeth was able to loosen her tongue.

"Anne!" Elizabeth yelled as a hand grabbed her forehead and pulled her back. "You can defeat her! You have— " Another arm put her in a choke hold. "—STRENGTH," Elizabeth managed to say before the bowl was shoved in her face.

They held Elizabeth tightly. Hands forced her mouth to open. When the potion was pushed closer, green smoke sizzled off her lips. A finger pulled her mouth open wider, enough to shove the liquid down her throat. Elizabeth gasped and started to choke. She fell to the wet grass and tried to catch her breath.

Éndira looked on in horror. She quickly realized the reason why Elizabeth's arms were constrained like they were. It was to keep the woman from forcing herself to vomit.

ANNE PUT her bound hands to her face as she watched her older friend convulse on the ground.

"Miss Elizabeth!" Anne screamed, trying to help. She was pushed backwards by a pair of rough hands. Anne crawled onto her knees. She was helpless.

They both were.

Where is Éndira?

Why hasn't she come to help!

Anne looked at her older friend, broken and wounded as she lay on the wet ground. Elizabeth's eyes were open for only a brief moment. When they closed, Anne prayed that this would not be the last time. Slow, labored breaths came in rhythms.

Elizabeth was alive... for now?

"What did you do to her?" Anne asked in a soft tone. The fight had almost drained out of her.

"She will be one of my tribe." Miranda waved her hands around like she was showing off her plantation to a new subject. "My island will require more subjects than I have now."

"Subjects!" Anne sneered, no longer willing to sit by and listen to this madwoman boast. "You think you are going to become queen of this island? You are delusional."

"And you are a spoiled rotten snit who deserves everything coming to you," Selina growled.

"Why? Because I wouldn't eat your disgusting puddings?"

Selina tried to lunge at Anne but Miranda held her back.

"She is just trying to goad you dear." Miranda placed her hand on Selina's face and tried to calm her down.

"I hate her! I hate HER!" Selina screamed.

"The feeling is mutual," Anne bit.

It took Miranda a few seconds to calm Selina down. In that time, Anne leaned forward and listened to Elizabeth's breathing. She knelt down and whispered. "I will make sure I stop her miss. I will help you, I promise."

Anne was suddenly pulled to her feet. She snapped her head at the aggressor. She glared at Zara, not realizing that the girl was really Éndira in disguise.

"Stop being a cry baby," Éndira spat. "You are going to be a great gift to the spirit of Dge. You should be grateful for that."

Anne wanted to spit in her face but she was a lady, and a lady would never do such a thing!

Instead, Anne kicked her leg out and caught Éndira hard in the shin.

~

Éndira grabbed her leg and yelped loudly. Selina cackled from the side enjoying the unintended dance. Éndira did not know how she should react. *Should I just slap Anne to keep up appearances?*

Zara certainly would!

In fact... Zara would probably do much worse!

Éndira hauled off and hit Anne right in the face.

Anne fell to the ground unconscious.

~

"Wake up!" The harsh voice said as a hand slapped Anne, followed by a rush of water.

Anne shook her head. She was drenched. Anne glared at the sight in front of her. Her hands were in iron chains, bound to a cement block on the ground. She pulled herself up.

Before Anne could push out her hands to strike, Éndira grabbed them. "Don't fight me. You will only hurt yourself."

"Why do you care?"

"I care," Éndira said as she looked deep into Anne's eyes.

Anne was about to speak but stopped. Something about those eyes made her feel safe.

She studied them.

They look... familiar.

Brown eyes that should really be green? Anne began to feel like she could see another girl behind them.

"Éndira?" Anne whispered, confused.

"Yes," Éndira touched Anne's hand gently.

"How?"

"Zara has helped us." Éndira unconsciously touched the amulet beneath her own blouse. "She's given me her amulet to cloak my appearance."

"They all see you as Zara right now?" Anne asked, bewildered.

"Yes."

"Brilliant!"

"Listen Anne..." Éndira contained her smile as she looked around. Anne followed her eyes, noticing Miranda and Selina were distracted with each other. The men were stiff as the dead, looking at nothing. "We have to be smart about this. I am supposed to be checking if you are okay."

"For the slaughter?"

"Something like that."

Anne glanced at her surroundings. She looked towards Elizabeth who was still unconscious on the ground. "What did you give her?" Anne asked.

"Sugar water."

"She's playing dead?" Anne said as she grinned.

"She also has a knife to cut her ropes, and your cuffs are not locked." Éndira reached into her pocket and pulled out the ring. She gently placed it on Anne's finger. "I am going to knock Miranda out with her wine. Zara told me she drinks too much when it is this hot outside. She is the strongest. Hopefully I will also get Selina. Elizabeth should be able to take care of the men, but we need you to hit them with your ring if you can."

Anne looked at her, hopeful once more.

"What?" Éndira asked.

"I wish I could kiss you right now," Anne said happily.

"We can worry about that after we save your arse," Éndira chuckled as her cheeks blushed.

"ZARA!" Miranda yelled from the distance, interrupting the tender moment. "What is taking you so long?"

As Éndira stood up, Anne pushed her away to add to the illusion.

"Get away from me!" Anne yelled at her.

Miranda stood impatiently by the table and tapped her toes.

"She's a pain ma'am," Éndira lied as she walked back. "Begging for her life and all that. I was playing with her. Making her think I would help her. Pathetic."

Selina giggled. "Oh, good idea."

Miranda spun on her heels and clapped her hands together. She was about to put her hands up when Éndira knocked into the table and grabbed the wine bottle.

"What are you doing now?" Miranda raised an eyebrow, displeased.

"Sorry ma'am." Éndira pulled the bottle closer. "I was going to suggest a toast."

"What a splendid idea!" Selina cooed. She reached forward and grabbed a glass. "I shall toast to you Miranda, for your genius and inspiration."

Éndira wanted to vomit. She bit her lower lip and poured port into the glass. She followed with the other one. As Miranda lifted her own glass, she boasted like royalty once again.

"I shall toast to you Anne," Miranda gestured to the young prisoner. "Without you, none of this would be possible."

Anne said nothing. She put her head down, trying to act the part.

Selina drank her port in a large gulp. Miranda put her own glass to her lips when a sudden voice echoed in the distance.

"Good God Miranda!" Mama DgBaba snickered. "How are you ever going to be a ruler if you are this stupid?"

46

Miranda stopped cold and looked for the voice.

They all did.

"I would advise against drinking that," Mama continued. "Lest you sleep the whole night?"

Panic hit Anne's gut hard.

She looked on in horror as Mama Dgbaba slowly walked towards them. She wore a lustrous green dress suitable for the most magnificent of balls. The bodice was tight around her ample bosom, the bell skirt wide and plentiful. As the sea deity got closer, Anne realized that the dress was not made of a shiny cloth, but of seaweed.

Miranda glanced down at her glass then looked at Selina in shock. She watched as her lover fell to the ground and passed out.

"What did you DO?" Miranda screamed at Éndira still thinking she was actually Zara. She reached forward and grabbed her victim by the collar. The amulet fell into view. Miranda snapped the cord breaking the spell.

Anne watched helplessly as her aunt realized that Éndira was not her beloved Zara.

Éndira quickly took the glass bottle and hit Miranda hard in the head.

The horrid woman screamed and fell into the table, knocking everything over. Miranda fell down on her rump and sat there, dazed.

"Anne!" Éndira yelled as she ran towards her.

Through the corner of her eye, Anne could see Elizabeth on her feet. The sugarcane pole that had secured her had now become a weapon. Elizabeth knocked out one man with a swift lunge then pulled the pole up into another's groin. Quickly, she hit him in the face, rendering him unconscious.

Éndira flew onto her knees and kicked another in the kneecap, shattering it. Anne ran to her side and helped her up. Éndira turned and saw the last guard running after them. Anne put out her hand quickly to try and use her energy, but her hand was pushed down by Elizabeth. The older woman shifted her body and knocked the guard out with a spinning kick.

"Keep running!" Elizabeth yelled as an ear piercing scream could be heard behind them. "Miranda is not down!"

Anne turned and stopped. She swung her ringed finger up and willed herself to find the power in the crystals. She ignored the cries to keep running. She wanted to end her aunt for good.

For my mother!

Anne searched for the crystals in her mind. She felt her anger connect to one of the stones and flow through her hand.

Anne screamed in pure rage.

A burst of blue light poured out across the distance to find its target. Miranda had barely gotten to her feet when she was thrown backwards by the shot.

Anne stared in disbelief. She had finally found her strength and channeled it properly.

And it felt— *amazing!*

"Let's go!" Éndira yelled at her, pulling her arm.

"No!" Anne pushed her off. "I need to finish this!"

"Why?"

"Because!" Anne glared at her, eyes burning with hate. "I want her DEAD!"

As Anne began to walk towards her victim, Elizabeth jumped in front of her. "We have to go Anne."

"I want to end this!"

"Please don't," Elizabeth begged.

"Why not?" Anne cried, her voice starting to crack.

"She's not worth it."

Anne closed her eyes for a brief moment, trying to find the courage to accept what Elizabeth was saying. As she nodded, Elizabeth led her away.

"We have to find cover. Mama wants her brother free," Elizabeth said.

Anne swallowed hard, realizing the hard truth. *Aunt Miranda is indeed in league with Mama Dgbaba.*

"Oh for deity's sake," Mama scowled. She held her hands out and closed her fist. "Must I do everything?"

The three women barely got over the other hill when they suddenly felt like they were running in place.

The winds were as strong as a hurricane. Elizabeth held onto a tree trunk. Her hands reached out to Éndira to save her. Anne flew by and grabbed onto Elizabeth's pant leg. Éndira began to pull Anne up. The vortex was trying unmercifully to suck them all in. As the wind got stronger, the weaker Elizabeth's arm got.

"I can't hold on!" Elizabeth yelled through the heavy gusts.

Elizabeth lost her grip. They tumbled over the grass and dirt. As the winds died down, Anne was thrown right at the feet of Mama Dgbaba. Mama's lips parted and revealed her sinister smile.

~

MAMA DGBABA STOOD ABOVE ANNE, rubbing her hands together with a sly grin. Anne shivered, looking at those sharp white teeth. The dress dripped salt water down the long strands of seaweed onto Anne's boots.

"My dear," Mama sung in her soft, island lilt.

Anne crawled back onto her arms. She desperately wanted to get away. Her hands dug into the ground. She clung to bits of grass and weeds to help guide her.

Anne looked around, uncertain.

Where are Éndira and Miss Elizabeth?

"Where could you possibly go young one that I would not find you?" Mama watched as Anne crab walked backwards. Mama suddenly stopped and looked up. A loud yell, followed by approaching running footsteps caught her attention. The trickster laughed then shot a bolt of red energy out of her hand.

Anne saw Éndira fall down next to her. Another bolt brought down Elizabeth by her side. Anne watched roots from the silk-cotton tree grow out of the ground and coil around their bodies.

"Really Elizabeth?" Mama taunted, looking down at the woman. "You would have done better to have left and saved yourselves."

"Don't do this Mama!" Elizabeth fought desperately to get loose. "You can't release Dge. The Tarits imprisoned him for a reason!"

"Yes, I know." Mama cocked her head to the side. "But they were primitive, insatiable little natives who never understood or respected our dominion, which is why we had to rule them with a firm hand."

"The inhabitants of these islands will never stand for being subjected to supernatural rule like his."

"And why not? You English have been ruled by Celtic and Pagan spirits and such for centuries."

"And they were relegated to only minimal intrusion over time. They no longer—"

"— Only king's and queens now for your kind?" Mama mocked, waving a hand downward. "No Elizabeth. It is time for the real kings and queens to come back and rule." Mama pulled Anne up roughly by the collar and pushed her forward. "And this little one will bring my brother back to this realm!"

Anne struggled to no avail.

She could not escape Mama's vice-like grip.

Mama only laughed as she pulled Anne along harder. Mama stopped at the coral rock stock that Anne had only minutes ago escaped from. The trickster released her grip.

Anne raised her hands, trying to find her energy once again.

"That will not work against me," Mama snickered.

The heat on Anne's ring grew ice cold. She looked down. Her ring was encased in ice. She could no longer find a path to the crystal.

I'm completely defenseless?

Mama raised her hands and created chains out of nothing. The metal crept along the bottom of Anne's legs. They twisted up her torso, rounded her breasts and circled her heart. Chains crept along her hands and imprisoned her wrists.

Anne could do nothing.

She was trapped.

Mama grinned once again and touched Anne's face.

"I am so glad you came to the West Indies my dear," Mama whispered softly. "I was starting to get bored." When Mama caressed Anne's cheek, the girl snapped her face away angrily.

"You have a beautiful gift," Mama continued. She touched Anne's chest. Anne could feel a solid object placed between her heart and the chains. "Let's hope you know how to use it."

Mama turned around before Anne could ask her what she had done. The trickster spun around wildly, showing off the brilliance of her living dress to her audience. Gold and green colors shimmered in the moon and firelight.

Mama skipped over to Miranda and paused. "Do you think he will like it?"

"I think he will love it Mama," Miranda answered happily.

"Then what are you waiting for!" Mama slapped her hands together in quick successions. "Fetch me my brother!"

Miranda stepped forward, her legs swiftly walking over the sandy ground. She stopped in front of Anne and looked at her with little pity. As she tried to touch her niece's face, Anne pulled back roughly.

"Don't touch me," Anne snapped.

"I only wish you would understand," Miranda tried to sooth.

"What I understand is you are a selfish, maniacal sorry excuse for a woman. How dare you call yourself a Sutton!"

"No dear, not Sutton." Miranda leaned in and whispered. "I will be called… queen."

Anne watched as her aunt sauntered over to the silk-cotton tree and held up her hands.

"Great Dge, I call on you as your humble servant," Miranda said loudly for all to hear. "As you have commanded me to do in your service, I present my niece," she waved towards Anne. "This girl is of my own blood. I give her to you as my offering. She will surrender herself to you— "

"—I damn well will not!" Anne yelled.

Mama laughed as she fussed with a fingernail. "It is only a figure of speech girl. Whether you want to or not is of no consequence."

Anne was so consumed with anger towards them both, she did not hear the end of Miranda's speech. Suddenly, it became very quiet. The birds no longer chirped, the crickets no longer sang a song to one another. Winds, that usually whipped through the palm trees, came to a standstill.

A powerful boom was heard, followed by a flash of lightning. Anne closed her eyes to protect them. An immediate chorus of wails started all around her. Her ears hurt from the noise. She wished she could pull her hands up and block out the sounds. The more she tried to ignore them, the louder the weeping got.

Anne finally opened her eyes. All around her were ghostly images of people dressed in native garb.

Where these the spirits of the Tarits?

Were they warning everyone to keep Dge away from freedom? Or were these apparitions that were bound to him in his prison?

Anne tried to look away. She wanted to will herself free. She wanted to run to Éndira and Elizabeth an escape from this place of horrors.

Miranda grabbed Anne's chin and forced her to face the tree. "You will look at your destiny!"

The silk-cotton tree began to shake. Bark ripped open along the ridges of growth and peeled back like a piece of fruit. Large roots popped up and began to feel around like an octopus looking for food. Anne watched in sheer terror as the native spirits were sucked into the tree.

One by one they were lost.

Anne realized what was happening. They were lost souls who were being fed on.

The thing inside ate souls.

Anne felt her heart drop.

Dge is going to eat my soul?

Anne snaked her hand sideways and felt for the chain. She stepped back and pulled as hard as she could. If she tried hard enough, maybe the coral rock would give? Anne used her weight and leaned backwards.

Mama began to laugh.

Anne screamed in anger. She was not going to die like this! She was not going to give up!

A burning sensation near her heart started. She felt a force begin to pull her towards the tree. Anne turned, eyes wide.

The tree was engulfed in flames!

Anne watched the way the fire danced. In it, a shape of a man began to appear. It began to walk towards her.

The fire form stopped, slowly forming into a human male. Anne could not believe what she was seeing.

Was Mama playing a trick on her?

He... he looks just like my father!

"Anne?" The apparition asked. "Have you come to save me Anne?"

"Father?" Anne said, not knowing how to react. He looked so much like him. He had the same voice, the same blond hair and deep set blue eyes. They were so much like herself, so much like his sister Miranda.

"I need your help," his hand touched her face.

Anne recognized that touch. It was warm and tender. This could not possibly be a trick conjured up. Had her father come back from the dead to save her?

Yes that had to be it.

"Have you come to rescue me father?" Anne asked, hopeful.

"I have," the apparition said. "But I need your help first."

Anne nodded. "What do you need?"

"To release me." Her father's voice turned into a gravely, low pitched resonance, a lullaby that entranced Anne's ears. "So we may be together forever?"

"What must I do?"

"Give yourself over to me."

"Of course," Anne agreed, her eyes wet with tears.

"Good girl." The apparition reached out and placed its hand near Anne's heart.

Anne felt nothing.

She did not feel anything as her soul was violently ripped out. She did not feel anything when she hit the ground and remained still.

Even stranger, she did not understand why she was now looking down at her own dead body.

47

———————

nne looked down at her body. Her form was lifeless, her eyes—wide open.

Am I dead?

But I can still feel my legs.

My hands.

Anne quickly put her palms in front of her eyes and studied them. They were transparent, like a ghost. Anne could see the blood in her veins moving while her heart pumped.

Am I a ghost now?

Anne looked up. She heard her name being called. Voices of those who had loved her. No longer held by physical bonds, they ran over to her and sat by her side as tears began to flow.

Miss Elizabeth and Éndira?

They sat by her side and mourned her.

They had both loved her.

Anne wanted to speak to them, wanted them to know she was all right. She was ready to go on, but where?

Shouldn't my mother and father be here to greet me? Anne looked around. *Where is everyone?*

There was no one to claim her.

Anne sat next to those who loved her and watched them mourn over her dead body. She watched as Elizabeth closed the eyes on her dead body then tilted her own head down and lost herself to grief.

Éndira...

She was the stronger of the two. She hugged Elizabeth tightly and told her everything would be all right in time.

Anne leaned inward near Éndira's ear. *Do not cry for me. I am at peace. I love you Éndira.*

Éndira suddenly stood up, eyes wide. *Anne?*

Anne jumped up near her.

Yes! I am here! You can hear me in your thoughts?

Yes. You are outside your body! How are you doing this?

I have no idea. Anne paused for a brief moment. *Am I dead?*

I do not know.

Can you see me?

No.

Anne looked down at the older woman weeping over her body.

Miss Elizabeth?

She can't hear you.

Why not?

Her grief has blocked her.

Why can you hear me?

Because I see when no one else can.

I forgot.

You are forgiven.

What do I do?

I think you are supposed to go on.

There is no one here, besides you.

Maybe you are not ready.

I'm dead! I should be ready!

I do not think you are dead Anne.

But my soul? Didn't he eat my soul?

You are your soul.

What does that mean?

Your soul still exists. I can feel it.

Then what did Dge consume?

Éndira knelt down next to Anne's body and picked up a clear crystal with blue tint hidden in her blouse. **Do you recognize this?**

Yes! But I threw that in the ocean months ago!

Mama must have put this on you.

Why?

"What are you doing?" Elizabeth asked as she stood up. She wiped her face and looked down at the pyramid. "Where did you find that?" The older woman's eyes suddenly became very focused.

She knows something.

What?

She helped me dispose of that, she knows something!

Elizabeth took the crystal from Éndira's hand and inspected the object. Her eyes became hard with anger. Quickly, Elizabeth started down the path towards Mama.

What is she doing?

I think she is trying to save you Anne.

DGE WAS a foot taller than his sister. His human shoulders were broad, his eyes wide set with dark pupils that flicked green when he talked. The clothes he wore were simple, canvas pants tied around his waist, no shoes or shirt. His chest was well defined and muscular. As he laughed, his body moved with him. The moonlight glistened off of his mocha skin.

"How long I have waited for this Baba!" Dge grabbed Mama by the shoulders and kissed her, calling her by her given name. She accepted the gesture with caution. When he released her, Mama leaned back on her leg and crossed her arms. "You are not still mad with me, are you girl?" Dge asked, his voice a deep resonance low like a drum.

Mama just glared at him.

"Come now girl! I have heard of a woman scorned but you are no woman Baba!" Dge laughed loudly.

"I did not release you so I may hear how superior you are," Mama said evenly. "Time has changed since you last traversed these islands."

"I may not have walked but I could still hear. You and your sisters have mucked up our existence, allowing these..." Dge pointed towards Miranda and gave her a hardened look, "foreigners to invade and not pay tribute?"

"They follow their own deities brother," Mama said. "It is not that easy to make these cattle change their beliefs."

"Then you change them by force!" Dge walked up to Miranda and watched her closely. As he put out his hand, Miranda fell to her knees and lifted her hands. He turned to his sister. "See how easy it is to make them beg?"

"You were stuck in a tree dear brother," Mama pointed out. "If she hadn't given you the girl, you never would have been released."

"Yes." Dge licked his lips. "It has been a long time, but... she tasted... old."

"Old?" Miranda looked up, suddenly afraid.

"Did you try to trick me woman?" Dge accused. His eyes glowed a deeper green.

"No! I swear! Anne is only seventeen."

"Eighteen," Mama corrected. She fussed with a fingertip as if she were bored. "As of today."

"See?" Miranda whimpered. "Eighteen and pure."

"Hmm," Dge growled, unconvinced.

Miranda crawled forward on her knees and touched his hand. Dge smiled. A look of pleasure slowly crept around his eyes as he smiled.

"I have not felt the touch of a subject for so long. I have... missed this," Dge said, looking down at her. "You have done well Miranda."

"Tha... thank you," Miranda stuttered.

"If you were younger," Dge taunted. "I would have made you a wife."

Miranda tried to hide the sudden hurt she must have felt. She unconsciously patted her hair back, looking around, uncertain.

Mama suddenly raised her head. Something had caught her attention.

"MAMA! You need to explain yourself!" Elizabeth yelled as she got close, anger dripping off her tongue like acid. "NOW!"

The trickster rolled her eyes. "Not now woman! Do you not see I am busy?"

"Are you?" Elizabeth snapped. She stopped and put the crystal in front of Mama's eyes. Light from the moon reflected off the surface. "Busy enough now?

"What is that?" Mama lied.

"You know damn well what this is! You took this from Anne. That night on her father's ship, when she thought she saw a woman hiding in the shadows. It was you! Why were you there? Planning on killing her all along?"

Elizabeth braced herself as Dge moved towards her. When he tried to snatch the crystal, Elizabeth quickly moved to the side. She fell on her back leg and tried to sweep his with her other one. He only laughed as he caught her ankle and twisted it, forcing her body to flip onto her stomach. Elizabeth could not stop him from taking the crystal from her hands.

"These mortals still humor me," Dge admitted. He looked down at Elizabeth, helpless on the ground. "Perhaps I will take this one as a paramour." Dge licked his lips. "I like— passionate."

Elizabeth started to crawl away. Eyes wide, her anger had now transformed into fear.

Dge started to laugh. He turned and held the crystal up to the light. His eyes were entranced by the reflections and refractions of moonlight dancing off the blue surface.

"Baba?" Dge turned to his sister, eyebrows suddenly bent in concern. Something in the crystal's inner being must have alarmed him in some way. "What is this?"

Mama walked over to him and touched his hands. She forced them to fully engulf the crystal. Mama pushed them into his chest and near his heart. His eyes pulsed with a shade of lime green that glowed.

"What are you doing?" Dge asked her, frightened,

"You know what brother?" Mama said with the sinister smile she was famous for. "I really haven't forgiven you."

Dge screamed as the crystal penetrated his chest. He could not stop the force from devouring him from within. The crystal was pulling him into it, tearing him away from this mortal plane. Little by little, his body disappeared.

When it was over, the crystal fell to the ground.

Mama bent down and picked up the object. She tossed it in the air and grabbed it once again. "You will be a happy addition to the collection on my wall brother."

Mama turned to the disbelieving audience and bowed. She quickly snapped her fingers, disappearing in a flash of light.

48

Miranda stared in disbelief at the empty spot. Mama Dgbaba had just disappeared with her brother trapped in a crystal.

Of all things a crystal?

Miranda was in complete shock. How had she not sensed the crystal? How could she have been so stupid as to not know Mama might betray her?

Mama Dgbaba was a trickster!

Miranda screamed loudly. She was beyond angry. Frustration and hate surged through to the crystal in her pendant. She had done everything that her deity had asked! Why had she been forsaken?

Betrayal!

Deception!

Disgust!

These words kept repeating over and over in her head.

Miranda could hear the paintings taunting her— laughing at her!

Her failure would be the stuff of legend in the family!

Disgrace!

Embarrassment!

"Shut up!" Miranda screamed. She held her hands to her ears desperately trying to shut the voices out.

You failed because of your ambition!

She screamed once again. Why wouldn't the paintings just leave her alone?

"This isn't my fault!" Miranda cried, focusing in on her niece. Elizabeth was near Anne helping her sit up. The young woman seemed to be in a daze, most likely trying to understand how she was not dead.

Miranda crooked a finger at her target and growled, "No... it's yours."

Overcome by her rage, Miranda let her emotion surge through her body and connect with her pendant. The inner molecules vibrated and pulsated as if they were alive; the force within screaming to be released.

A burst of dark purple energy poured out of the tips of her fingers. She willed the electric charge to find the target she so desperately wanted to destroy.

Anne felt an instant change in the air. She turned and saw a beam of light coming at her. Anne put her ringed hand up as a defense but the movement could not save her. She was overwhelmed by a bright flash and knocked to the ground. Instantly, pain overtook her body. She crept onto her hands and knees, trying to escape the vortex of light swirling around her body.

For a moment, the brightness shied away from her, moving back and forth like a wave crashing into the sand. Anne put her arm up and tried to block the light blinding her eyes. She did not know what was happening.

Only when her Aunt Miranda stepped through did she understand.

"You've destroyed everything!" Miranda yelled as she walked forward. A swirl of energy circled her hands. "Everything!"

Anne said nothing, she could do— nothing.

Her body refused to move. It was frozen in complete fear.

"You will join your mother and father!" Miranda yelled. She lifted her hand and targeted Anne with all her hate.

ELIZABETH CLOSED HER EYES, blinded by the light. She had been thrown backwards violently by a surge of energy. She forced herself to her knees just as Miranda screamed a second time. The blood curdling howl reverberated in Elizabeth's ears. She covered them quickly and tried to drown them out.

The sound was not normal.

This was the sound coming from a person who had tapped into a frequency so hateful, the vibrations resonated through the vocal cords like the piercing howl of the most violent of storms.

Elizabeth looked up.

She watched in horror as Miranda attacked Anne. The energy released was beginning to devour Anne's life essence.

Elizabeth crawled on the floor and desperately searched for any kind of weapon. Anything to destroy that woman before she killed Anne!

Again, Miranda hit Anne hard. The sound of the young woman's screams turned Elizabeth's stomach. She had to figure something out fast. Anne's soul had never left her body, only remained dormant during Mama's trick.

But Anne's life essence was her core.

Elizabeth stood up and decided to take her chances. She ran full speed into Miranda and knocked her over. The other woman fell onto her rump. Elizabeth spun her heel around, kicking Miranda hard in the face. Miranda fell into the mud and lay there, stunned.

Elizabeth ran over to Anne and slid on one leg.

"Anne?" Elizabeth cried as she grabbed the young woman by the shoulders and pulled her up.

Anne had no response.

Elizabeth gently slapped Anne in the face. Slowly, Anne began to stir.

"Oh thank God," Elizabeth said through tears. She hugged Anne tightly, afraid she had lost her for good a second time.

Elizabeth heard another cry. She turned quickly, only to see Éndira charge at Miranda with the sugarcane rod. The woman looked up and for a brief second appeared to be ready to fight before Éndira hit Miranda hard in the face.

For a second time, Miranda's face wound up in the mud.

Éndira swung the rod hard again, hitting Miranda harder. The mistress of the plantation covered her head and screamed in pain.

"Stop it!" Elizabeth ordered.

Éndira ignored the command. As she went to strike another blow, her motion was forcefully stopped by Elizabeth's hand.

"Don't do it," Elizabeth said softly.

"She deserves to die!" Éndira yelled back with tears streaming down her face.

"No."

"Why are you protecting her?" Éndira asked, not understanding. "She tried to kill Anne! She is evil!"

"If you murder her," Elizabeth said. "Then what will you become?"

Éndira looked at the defeated woman on the floor. Miranda's head was bloody. She tried to get up but lost her balance. Her legs wobbled as she fell back into the mud.

Éndira dropped the rod. She turned and ran over to Anne.

Elizabeth looked down at the broken woman.

"It's over Miranda," Elizabeth said as she pulled her own pendant out from beneath her blouse. She took off the chain and held the jewelry for the other to see. "I finally remembered why I survived your attack. You charged this out of love for me. To protect me from harm."

Miranda looked at her, for a second confused. Slowly, her lip twisted in denial. "I did no such thing."

"You did. That night we first kissed."

"If I meant to protect you!" Miranda sneered. "You wouldn't have gotten burned in the first place!"

"You're right to think that," Elizabeth sighed. "But it was not meant as protection against an injury like that."

"Then what was it meant to protect against?" Miranda snarled.

"It was meant to protect against you... deep down you must have realized that one day you might turn on me.

Elizabeth did not wait for an answer. She turned on her heels, replacing the jewelry. She joined Éndira, who was busy tending to Anne. She watched as the girl was gentle and caring, touching her friend's head for any sign of injury.

Elizabeth thought about how they might one day care for each other as more than friends. She hoped that Anne would get her wish some day.

"Are you okay?" Elizabeth asked Anne.

"My head hurts," Anne said, touching her temples.

"How many fingers am I holding up?" Elizabeth asked with her hand showing three, her other hand on Anne's arm.

"Three?"

"That is good," Elizabeth said, holding Anne's hands in her own. "You may be stunned for a while. But I am sure you will be fine."

Elizabeth felt her palms warm up drastically. Quickly, she looked down at them. Anne's ring was glowing with a deep blue energy coming from the aquamarine stone.

"Do you see that?" Elizabeth asked the young woman.

"See what?" Anne said.

"Your ring?"

Anne looked down then shrugged. "What am I supposed to be looking at?"

Elizabeth realized that Anne was not summoning the crystal.

Am I?

"ELIZABETH!" A sudden voice screamed from behind.

They all turned and watched as Miranda began to stagger toward them. She limped and barely could keep her balance. Her head was bleeding, blood dripping down her face. She looked like a woman gone mad.

Elizabeth closed her eyes for a split second. She realized what she needed to do.

"Go," Elizabeth told them both. "I will end this."

"She will kill you!" Anne said with fear etched in her voice.

"I will be fine," Elizabeth lied. She touched Anne's hand, feeling the ring on her finger. "May I borrow this?"

Anne hesitated for a moment then nodded yes. Elizabeth pulled off Anne's ring and placed it on her own finger. Her third finger on her left hand, the same one Trevor had put it on so many years ago.

"You will always have a place in my heart." Elizabeth pulled Anne inward and gave her a kiss on the forehead. When they released, Elizabeth looked deep into her eyes. "I love you."

Elizabeth turned and looked at Éndira next. The young woman had tears in her eyes. Elizabeth bent down, put her hands on the young woman's shoulders and began to speak softly. "You've become a wonderful woman Eréndira. I've only been hard on you because I love you. Keep your heart open and pure. You will need this in the end."

After a long hug and a kiss, Elizabeth stood up and waited for them to leave. She watched as Éndira had to force Anne to walk away towards the far hill. She waited for them to be safe before turning to confront the aggressor.

Elizabeth knew what would happen between her and Miranda tonight. *One of us has to die.*

49

"I am so sick of you!" The crazed woman spit blood out of her mouth. "You've always thought you were better than me!"

"Miranda, I never thought that. I wanted to be your sister." Elizabeth held her hands to her side as they pleaded for calm. "Why could you never accept that? Why wasn't that enough?"

Miranda stopped. She stood there broken and defeated. She looked at her hands and stared at the blood stains on her skin. The red fluid seeped over her fingertips. Everything she had fought for had been erased in one night.

For a brief moment, Elizabeth thought the other woman might just— walk away.

Miranda shook her head violently. Enraged, she grabbed her pendant with one hand and raised her other. Elizabeth raised her own hand, Anne's ring now on her finger.

Miranda looked at her oddly then started to laugh. It was a mad cackle from a woman who had completely lost everything.

"You think that will stop me?" Miranda snarled. "Suddenly you have a way with crystals?"

Elizabeth said nothing, only stood in a defensive position and waited.

"You are NOT a Crystal Astrid!" Miranda's eyes hardened, her smile wild. "You are nothing but a pathetic mortal like your mother! So easy to manipulate, so easy to... tamper with?"

Elizabeth looked, confused. *What is she going on about?*

"Minds are so weak," Miranda added. "Play with them long enough, and they— break."

Elizabeth swallowed hard.

Is Miranda confessing to destroying my mother's mind?

Anger slowly began to creep up Elizabeth's arm as rage began to build within. Elizabeth shook her head, trying to push out these horrible thoughts.

"You..." Elizabeth barely got the word out, her body was shaking so hard. She looked at Miranda with wet eyes. "You did that to my mother?"

"Life is so short," Miranda taunted.

"WHY?" Elizabeth yelled, fury ripping from within her throat. "WHY would you do that? Why would you hurt HER!?"

"Because you hurt me."

Elizabeth could no longer feel her legs. She wanted to collapse, to fall down and lose herself completely to grief. All these years she had blamed herself for her mother's sickness. Why would a woman so healthy suddenly succumb to an illness with no name? *Mother promised me she would never leave me alone.* Elizabeth closed her eyes as she felt the tears drip from beneath her eyelids. She often wondered if her mother had worried herself to death.

Elizabeth opened her eyes and stared at her old friend. *All these years Miranda still blames me for her life, yet she already got her revenge.*

Elizabeth wanted to allow the anger to overtake her senses. It would be so easy to reach inward and let the rage out. She could find the energy in this ring and burn the woman alive.

Instead, Elizabeth remembered her mother and all the good times they had together. She remembered her father and how proud he was of her.

Elizabeth chose to remember the best times in her life.

"I HATE YOU!" Miranda yelled at the top of her lungs, breaking Elizabeth's concentration.

Elizabeth's lips twisted in a genuine smile. "I forgive you."

The words danced around the other woman's head as she stopped and stared, dumbfounded. Miranda had most likely not expected that reaction.

Resolute and stubborn to the end, Miranda swiftly shot her hand up and let her final energy scream out. This time, the dark purple light twisted within a sickly color red. The beam of radiance cracked loudly, the vibration seeking out its target.

Elizabeth raised her ringed finger and deflected the beam. She willed her emotion to find the vibrations of what she held in her heart. She thought about the love she had with Trevor, the man she had loved all her life. She thought about the last few months with Anne, and how she finally got to know a young woman with tremendous strength and courage.

She thought of Éndira, her headstrong attitude and potential to be a great woman and force to be reckoned with, even though she had yet to come into her full power.

Elizabeth silently wondered— *should I have told Éndira the truth?*

Should I have told Anne?

She pushed back with all her strength as her own bolt of energy released from her ringed hand. The bright, blue light hit Miranda's new attack. Their energy met head-on, caught in a standstill as both bolts fought for dominance.

Miranda stepped forward as if she were caught in a hurricane, wind blowing sideways.

Elizabeth followed the same motion, fighting as hard as she could as she too stepped forward. Each movement was a fight to stay upright, the muscles in Elizabeth's legs seizing up. She ignored their pleas, pushing as hard as she could.

Miranda screamed. She focused her rage with all she had left. Her concentration wavered.

How dare Elizabeth stand in my way!

Miranda was furious. Why could she not will her energy to destroy someone she had grown to hate with every fiber of her being?

Miranda could not understand how this was happening.

Then, slowly, she realized why.

Elizabeth had Anne's ring, the ring Trevor gave when they were engaged.

My own mother's ring.

Miranda held back tears.

My own mother who refused to give the ring to her own daughter! She said I was not deserving of that kind of power. That I had tarnished the memory of our family. A family that could trace its origins back to the time of the Celtic warriors. The females that had ruled over our clan.

The paintings always reminded her of this.

Elizabeth had never lost her attenuation with the crystals in the ring. They were hers to command, hers to focus and direct.

Both women were at a standstill. Both pushed forward inch by inch, trying to get the upper hand on one another. The closer they got, the hotter the beams of energy sparked, the more the light combined and turned into a mix of physical fluid that spit and sizzled, falling to the ground and burning the grass.

Elizabeth took her last bit of strength and pushed as hard as she could. She was feet from Miranda. Sparks hit their faces and burned their skin.

"I'm sorry Miranda," Elizabeth yelled over the loud noise. "This is the only way."

Miranda looked on in sheer terror. She knew what Elizabeth was going to do. She had only heard about this once from her own mother. No one else could have told Elizabeth.

Unless?

Did my mother's painting whisper to Elizabeth how to stop me?

Elizabeth pulled forward and grabbed Miranda's pendant. The crystals united and a sudden wave of energy exploded between them.

The huge blast engulfed their bodies, vaporizing them both.

50

The morning had slowly turned into afternoon. Anne was exhausted. She stepped out onto the porch and scanned the horizon. The plantation was quieter now that her aunt's prisoners had been freed. Anne immediately released the men and women who had been enslaved. They would most likely not be able to return to the lands they had been stolen from, most growing up on the island as children, but Éndira had offered them life on the island she lived on. Many former slaves lived a free life there.

Once Miranda had disappeared, the spells she had cast on them simply vanished. Those who had been bewitched were no longer stuck in a perpetual nightmare with no control over their own actions.

Most everyone was relieved to hear that Miranda Sutton-Langdon was gone and never coming back.

At least, Anne *hoped* she was never coming back.

Anne told them all that those who would like to stay could partake in the plantation's profits. She could never truly make amends for her aunt's sins against them but she would try. She even offered a small parcel of land to build a house. Most of the former indentures chose to leave and seek their own fortunes elsewhere; all of the slaves took up Éndira's offer. Anne offered them all barrels of sugar to take, so that they might sell them and take the profits for their new lives.

She had no idea how to run a sugar plantation, now that she had essentially inherited. In fact, once Éndira found Miranda's will, the whole plantation was Anne's legal right. Anne wondered how long ago it took for her aunt to decide which was better, a niece inheriting a business or feeding said niece to a tree.

The couple who was whipped by her aunt chose to stay. The girl who he loved was now pregnant and wanted to remain by his side. The man had even offered to help run the plantation. He was good with numbers and had once been a secretary to a lawyer before being caught up in a scandal. When he was sent here to Barbados, Miranda had used him to help manage her warehouse.

Anne quickly took him up on his offer.

Now that Anne was free of her responsibility this morning, she sighed, wanting to crawl into bed and cry.

Anne leaned against the porch railing and closed her eyes, remembering her friend fondly. She and Éndira had both watched Elizabeth and Miranda fight to the death. Both women had suddenly been vaporized by a large blast of energy. Anne and Éndira had hoped that this was only a momentary effect. Surely Elizabeth was protected by the ring's energy?

Surely the woman was not really dead?

Anne dipped her head low. *Miss Elizabeth stepped in and took my place? How? She said she was not a Crystal Astrid, but how could she control my ring like that?*

Unless?

"What are you thinking?" Éndira asked as she joined her.

Anne smiled as she wrapped her arm in Éndira's. Her friend did not object. Anne would give the other girl time. She would not press. This was enough for now.

Elizabeth would have wanted that.

"Was Miss Elizabeth my real mother?" Anne turned abruptly and asked.

Éndira looked at her oddly. "Why would you think that?"

"How else could she control my ring like that?"

"I can't answer that Anne." Éndira shook her head. "I do not know enough of her story, nor yours."

"And the only people who can tell me are dead." Anne closed her eyes.

"Well," Éndira asked. "What if she wasn't your birth mother?"

Anne opened her eyes and tilted her head to listen.

"Think about it," Éndira shrugged. "She was in contact with that ring before your father gave it to your mother. You said he did love her."

"And she loved him with all her heart."

"Maybe she never lost her connection to your ring. She might not have been a Crystal Astrid but somehow she could still pull out enough power to save you."

"To save us," Anne said with love in her eyes for both of her friends.

"She sacrificed herself."

"I know... and I will never be able to thank her." Anne grasped the pommel of the sword that the older woman had given her. Anne was happy to have it back in her possession.

Éndira rubbed Anne's back. The gesture was small but meant so much to one who was hurting.

Anne remembered when Elizabeth took her on the ship, when she was afraid and needed protection. She leaned her head on Éndira's shoulder. Anne lost herself in this small bit of affection. She silently spoke a prayer in Elizabeth's name.

Anne would never forget Elizabeth and the sacrifice she had made for the both of them.

Éndira reached in her pocket and pulled out a small sash. She smiled at Anne.

"What is that?" Anne asked with a raised eyebrow.

"I missed your birthday yesterday."

"I think you will be excused for that," Anne snickered. She gently took the sash and opened it. Inside was a leather bracelet with three cords. It was adorned with beads and a top plate with a stamp of a conch. "Thank you," Anne said to her friend.

"I know it cannot replace your ring." Éndira rubbed the back of her own neck nervously. "But I thought you might like it."

"I do," Anne nodded.

Éndira leaned in and hugged Anne tight. "I am glad you are all right."

Anne inhaled her scent. She was happy to be close to the one who had risked her life to save me. *She did not have to do that. She could have just walked away.*

When they released, Éndira nervously touched the back of her own neck again.

Anne realized her friend was not uncomfortable with the touch, just... *unsure at the moment.*

Soft steps behind drew their attention. They both turned, quick to strike defensive poses, Anne with her hand extended, Éndira with hers gripped on a cutlass.

"Shall we defer hostilities for a moment so we may speak?" Zara asked.

Anne nodded then put her hand down. She'd forgotten for a moment her ring was lost forever.

"Where have you been hiding?" Éndira folded her arms, careful not to hurt her bandaged wrist.

Anne realized Zara looked well. Her face had a new-found sparkle, her eyes more hopeful.

"Thank you for your help," Anne said with a nod.

"And thank you both," Zara said. "For freeing me."

"You are no longer bound?" Éndira asked.

"No," Zara smiled, looking up towards the clear sky. "When Miranda disappeared, so did her hold."

They stood in silence for a long moment.

"Where is Selina Barton?" Anne asked, concerned that she had not seen the last of her former Governess.

"I do not know. I have not seen her since last night."

"She probably skulked back to a mirror and escaped," Éndira said. "Did she forget to bring you?"

"I was never going to go anywhere with her. I was only bound to Miranda."

Anne folded her arms inward and studied the girl once again. Zara would need food and shelter. Did she want to stay, or leave to find her own way? "Would you like to stay here? I can offer you room and board if you would like?"

"No," Zara shook her head. "I have no reason to remain on this land."

"Can I at least give you some money?"

"I have no need of currency."

"But how will you buy clothes, food?" Anne looked at her oddly. "Surely you cannot survive without it?"

"I have my own means Anne," Zara smiled. "But I thank you for your offer."

Anne turned and glanced at Éndira. Her friend looked equally confused. Anne had never really gotten to know Zara. Her aunt had kept them apart on purpose.

"I came to thank you once again Anne and Éndira. You both kept your word." Zara nodded then bowed her head. She turned to Éndira and did the same. "And I offer something in return."

Anne cocked an eyebrow. Surely Zara did not mean to bind herself to her?

"What is it you offer?" Éndira asked, apprehensive.

"Information," Zara said. "There is a chance that your friend is still alive."

Anne blinked for a quick second.

"Miss Elizabeth?" she happily asked. "But how?"

"The crystals." Zara lifted her hands and put them together. "When they hit each other, they created a vortex."

Éndira and Anne patiently listened with eager ears.

"Vortexes are how the spirits and deities travel," Zara continued. "It may seem that they simply disappear but they have to enter a path that has a beginning and an end."

Anne played with her bare finger, silently hoping what the girl was saying was true. "How sure are you of this?"

"Very sure. I feel a presence still in the vortex. Only one."

"How can you know whose that is?"

"Because I am attuned to my former mistress. That is Miranda stuck in the vortex."

"Is my aunt lost?"

Zara shrugged. "In a manner of speaking— I suppose Mama DgBaba could pull her out but I do not see that happening any time soon."

Anne waited for a moment. She did not know if all Zara was speaking of was true. If Elizabeth was still alive in some form, would they be able to save her? Could they even traverse where deities travel?

"What do you want for this information?" Éndira broke the silence.

"I need nothing," Zara said.

"Zara? Please," Anne asked. "Let me give you something?"

"I will need nothing," Zara protested, then immediately softened her tone. "But I thank you for your offer."

Éndira looked at Anne with a pained expression. Anne wondered if Éndira believed the girl, or simply thought the idea ridiculous?

A swift breeze caught them by surprise. Anne felt a sudden change in the air. When she saw Zara's eyes harden, Anne quickly turned around.

Mama DgBaba stood right behind them.

Éndira stepped in front of Anne and drew her cutlass.

"Oh please." Mama rolled her eyes. "You are just as foolish as Elizabeth."

Mama laughed when Éndira angrily slashed downward. Mama leaned back on her leg and folded her arms. She grinned, amused at the motion.

Anne watched the blade slice through the trickster. Mama quickly snapped her hand forward and grabbed the blade. It immediately turned to dust.

"Damn you!" Éndira threw the hilt onto the floor. "My father gave me that sword!"

"Then you shouldn't go poking it where it does not belong," Mama chastised like a parent.

Anne raised an eyebrow. *Again, Éndira acts familiar with this woman? What is their story?*

"What do you want Mama?" Anne asked as she found a small bit of courage.

"You've released Miranda's subjects," Mama sneered. "They belong to me, not you."

"How?" Anne asked, concerned.

"I made a deal."

"Not with me."

"No…" Mama leaned inward, making Anne step back a few. "With Miranda… obviously."

"My aunt is lost, unless you are going to pull her out?"

"Not likely," Mama grinned. "She is a nuisance and not really worth my time."

"Where is Elizabeth Spencer?" Éndira demanded. She put her hand in Anne's. The sudden touch made Anne smile. Was Éndira holding her hand to find her own strength. "Is she alive?"

"Perhaps."

"Tell us then."

Mama's eyes bore into hers. "Give me my souls, and I might consider telling you."

"No…" Anne shook her head firmly. She would not even entertain the idea. "The indentures contracts and slaves lives became mine once my aunt was lost. I am mistress of this plantation and I make the decisions now. They will remain unbound and free."

Mama skipped forward fast and grabbed Anne's chin. "Stupid child. You know nothing of the ways of these islands. I would advise you to reconsider your decision."

Éndira grabbed Mama's arm and tried to force it off. A small plume of green smoke burned between the grip. Mama pulled back and hissed, her arm smoking.

Eyes wide, Éndira stared at what she had done in disbelief.

"Leave," Anne warned. Even if she were shaking inside, she would defend the people on this plantation.

"We shall meet again Anne Sutton," Mama said, twisting her lips into her sinister smile. "You can be assured of this." Mama turned and eyed Éndira. "Especially you."

Mama snapped her fingers and disappeared into the wind.

As the breeze died down, Anne began to shake.

"Are you okay?" Éndira asked, holding her by the shoulders.

Anne smiled, then touched her friend's hands. "Just a little shaky. That woman scares the bloody hell out of me!"

"Me too."

"How did you do that?" Anne asked, intrigued.

Éndira shrugged. "No idea."

They both turned, looking for the girl who they had been talking to before being rudely interrupted. Both were surprised that Zara had not fled.

In fact, Zara looked very calm.

"Does Mama not scare you?" Anne asked.

"I have seen worse than Mama," Zara said knowingly. "But do not take her threats lightly. She is a force to be reckoned with."

Anne shook her head in agreement. She unconsciously folded her arms inward. "Why would Mama come to me after I released them?"

"Because Mama never actually agreed to the deal. She never gave Miranda a definite answer. I was there."

"Perhaps she thought you were dimwitted?" Éndira chuckled, looking at Anne.

Anne rolled her eyes in return.

Éndira turned to Zara. "Thank you again for your help Zara." Éndira reached into her blouse and retrieved the amulet that had changed her appearance last night. She took it off and held it out. "I believe this is yours."

Zara held her palm out, rejecting the offer. "Keep that for now. It may come in handy when you search for your friend."

When Éndira turned, Anne simply shrugged. "If she is confident Miss Elizabeth is alive then I believe her."

"So do I," Éndira smiled, replacing the amulet on her neck. "Thank you again for your help."

"You are very welcome," Zara said as she nodded.

Anne looked at her fondly. She really liked Zara as a person. Anne had wanted to become friends with Zara the moment she came to the plantation.

But the other girl had been so reserved, so distant.

Anne had not understood at the time why this was. She did not know if Zara had been mistreated or abused? *What terrible things did my aunt do to this poor girl?*

"I just wanted to be your friend," Anne finally confessed.

"I know." Zara was suddenly quiet. She looked as if she were thinking about the last few months. "I was... I was not allowed to become familiar with you... lest I become attached."

"You're not a pet," Éndira smirked.

"Leave her be." Anne was not forceful but she did not want the former servant girl to feel unwelcome if she ever felt the need to come back. She was young and barely fourteen. How would she make it in the world alone?

"I will be leaving now," Zara smiled happily as she looked towards the sky once again.

When Zara began to walk away, Anne stepped forward.

"Wait!" Anne reached out her hand, wanting to shake. Zara eyed the gesture, then reached out her own. They both shook hands as equals.

"Where will you go?" Anne asked as they released.

"Wherever the winds may take me."

"How cryptic," Éndira chuckled, looking at the other girl with a lopsided smile. "Why were you bound to Miranda in the first place?"

Anne glanced at Éndira, intrigued by the question. She silently chastised herself for not thinking of that earlier. Anne really wanted to know. She looked at Zara, eyebrow cocked in curiosity.

"I was bound to Miranda because of my mother," Zara admitted. "As long as Miranda needed my services— I had to serve."

"What was your exact connection to her?" Éndira crossed her arms, leaning back on her leg.

"I was her familiar."

"Oh..." Anne blinked, suddenly realizing why they could never have been friends. A familiar was bound to only one witch. One witch at one time. Anyone else that could be deemed a threat had to remain at a distance.

"Yes," Zara said, nodding. "Now that I am free I will be on my way."

"Wait a minute," Éndira protested. "How were you her familiar? You're human."

Zara smiled, her eyes looking straight at them. Quickly, her brown eyes changed into a shade of rich cerulean blue that began to glow.

"Who said I was a human?" Zara said with a deep grin.

Zara quickly raised her hands and flapped them down. Her feet lifted off the ground as her body morphed into the body of an Anhinga. A beautiful display of light brown feathers covered in a green gloss wrapped around her body. Her beak was long and pointed like a dagger, the color many vibrant yellow hues. With webbed feet tucked in, Zara hurled a series of loud, vibrant croaks before taking flight.

The two girls stared in disbelief as they watched the bird fly away.

"She's a water turkey?" Éndira snorted. "Really?"

Anne's eyes were wide and her cheeks red. She could not contain her laughter. They both started to giggle. After so many hurtful hours, they both needed this.

Éndira took Anne's hand in her own.

"Ready to go find your cap— ee— tan?" Éndira chuckled, repeating the words she had used the first time they met.

Anne smiled once again. She leaned her head back on Éndira's shoulder and softly exhaled.

They would find Elizabeth, they would rescue her... and maybe?

Maybe our friendship will turn into something more.

51

Her head felt like it was filled with lead. Slowly, she opened her mouth and felt nothing but a dry texture as if she had been parched for days on end. She swallowed hard but felt no relief. Carefully, she leaned over, got onto her knees and pushed forward with her hands. Her legs had no strength in them. Defeated, she rolled over onto her bottom and placed her hands behind, balancing herself slightly.

She had no idea where she was. Light from a sea of candles bounced off the rock walls. When she looked up, she saw nothing more than stalactites.

There was no sky.

She had to be in a cave.

— *His cave.*

"That little witch knocked you out good Selina," a low voice cackled.

Selina glared at him.

"How did I get here?" she demanded of her host.

"You should be thanking me woman," Baka walked forward. "I saved you from the gallows."

"Never," Selina slowly got to her feet. "Who would hang me Baka? The whole town is—"

"— Rejoicing!" Baka snapped, cutting her off harshly. "All because you and that infernal mistress of yours could not keep an eighteen year old girl in line? They will hang you the first chance they can."

Selina curled her lip. Rage crept up into the lines of her face as she scowled. She leapt forward and snatched a knife from the weapons he kept on the wall.

"I will cut her throat ear to ear!" Selina proudly showed on her own neck.

"Don't be a fool woman!" Baka walked over to her and gently took the weapon away, replacing it where it belonged. "There are other ways to get revenge."

"What could be better than snuffing the life out of that little brat?" Selina asked impatiently.

"This girl Anne?" Baka threw a few twigs into the fire. He sat down on his small stool and looked at her. The flames reflected off his glistening skin. "Miranda spoke of her independence. How the girl was hard to... tame."

Selina listened to him as he continued, trying not to think of the lover she might have lost for ever.

"Take away her freedom," he said.

"How do we do that?" Selina crossed her arms. She sat down on another stool, watching him carefully across the fire.

Baka leaned into the fire and felt the heat on his palm. He pushed his hand in quickly and pulled out a piece of flame that magically danced on his skin. Selina was entranced as the fire turned into the silhouette of a woman.

"Who is that?" Selina asked, curious.

"The Bruja del Fuego," Baka answered, smiling at her.

Selina furrowed her eyebrows, confused. "Why on earth would the Fire Witch be interested in Anne?"

"Because the girl is powerful, according to Miranda." Baka looked at her. "But she is without training and guidance. The Bruja is preparing for a great war," Baka continued. He played with his hand, making the figure rotate with his motions. "She will need an army and Anne can be an essential tool for her, with proper grooming of course."

Selina rolled her eyes, not believing completely in this plan.

"I would rather kill her," Selina snarled.

"Impatience can be the death of the strongest of rulers. Miranda could not control her impulses. She was doomed from the start."

"You knew Miranda would fail?" Selina accused, her voice thick with anger.

"I did," Baka confessed. "I warned her not to allow ambition to cloud her judgement. She refused to listen to me."

Selina looked around, uncertain. She was angry at all that had happened. Selina had done everything Miranda had wanted, even bringing back her impetuous niece.

Still, Miranda had failed.

"Anne is headstrong and full of righteous ideas," Selina argued. "She will never work willingly with a woman like that."

"Then the Bruja will break her, just like she has done to all her enemies." Baka flipped his hand and extinguished the flame. "Selina Barton? Will you help me deliver this girl to the future ruler of the the West Indies?"

Selina did not need to think over this offer. She wanted revenge for what Anne had done to her lover.

"Nothing would give me greater pleasure," Selina purred.

COMING SOON

Stay tuned for the continuation of the six part
Crystal Astrid Series

- COMING SOON -

Crystal Revelations
Crystal Deception
Crystal Endurance
Crystal Redemption
Crystal Odyssey

Check my social media for updates!

ABOUT THE AUTHOR
R.E. SCHICCHI

About R. E. Schicchi: R.E. Schicchi has worked in major markets of local television news, including WPLG and WSVN in Miami/Fort Lauderdale and WKMG in Orlando. She holds a Bachelor of Arts in Broadcast Communications from Barry University, and a Master of Fine Arts from Florida Atlantic University.

R.E. is also an accomplished artist who is always learning new techniques and skills. She is proud to have digitally painted her own cover with instruction from a slew of professional artists.

She currently resides in Central Florida with her beloved Shih-tzu.

FOLLOW THE AUTHOR

THREADS at @re_schicchi

INSTAGRAM at @re_schicchi

PINTEREST at @reschicchi

ETSY at @grumpyfrogstudio.etsy.com